About the Authors

Brenda Harlen is a multi-award-winning author for Mills & Boon who has written over twenty-five books for the company.

With a background of working in medical laboratories and a love of the romance genre it's no surprise that Sue MacKay writes medical romance stories. She wrote her first story at age eight and hasn't stopped since. She lives in New Zealand's Marlborough Sounds where she indulges her passions for cycling, walking and kayaking. When she isn't writing she also loves cooking and entertaining guests with sumptuous meals that include locally caught fish.

Louisa Heaton is a married mother of four (including a set of twins) and she lives on an island in Hampshire. When not wrangling her children, husband or countless animals, she can often be found walking her dogs along the beach, muttering to herself as she works out plot points. In her spare time, Louisa reads a lot, or crochets. Usually when she ought to be doing something else!

A&E Docs

December 2020
His Baby Surprise

January 2021
Taming the Brooding Doc

February 2021
Her Knight in Shining Armour

March 2021
Emergency Medicine

April 2021
The Maverick Doc

May 2021
His Emergency Secret

A&E Docs: His Baby Surprise

BRENDA HARLEN

SUE MacKAY

LOUISA HEATON

MILLS & BOON

First Published in Great Britain 2020
By Mills & Boon, an imprint of HarperCollins*Publishers*
1 London Bridge Street, London, SE1 9GF

A&E DOCS: HIS BABY SURPRISE © 2020 Harlequin Books S.A.

Two Doctors & a Baby © 2016 Brenda Harlen
Dr. White's Baby Wish © 2016 Sue MacKay
Their Double Baby Gift © 2017 Louisa Heaton

ISBN: 978-0-263-28172-9

MIX
Paper from
responsible sources
FSC™ C007454

This book is produced from independently certified FSC™ paper to ensure responsible forest management.

For more information visit: www.harpercollins.co.uk/green

Printed and bound in Spain
by CPI, Barcelona

TWO DOCTORS & A BABY

BRENDA HARLEN

This book is dedicated to all the real-life doctors, nurses, EMTs and others who work in the medical field—because you make a difference, every single day. Thank you!

Chapter One

After six years at Mercy Hospital, Dr. Justin Garrett knew that Friday nights in the ER were inevitably frenzied and chaotic.

New Year's Eve was worse.

And when New Year's Eve happened to fall on a Friday—well, it wasn't yet midnight and he'd already seen more than twice the usual number of patients pass through the emergency department, most of the incidents and injuries directly related to alcohol consumption.

A drunken college student who had put his fist through a wall—and his basketball scholarship in jeopardy—with fractures of the fourth and fifth metacarpal bones. A sixty-three-year-old man who had doubled up on Viagra to celebrate the occasion with his thirty-six-year-old wife and ended up in cardiac arrest instead. A seventeen-year-old female who had fallen off her balcony because the Ecstasy slipped into her drink by her boyfriend had made her want to pick the pretty flowers on her neighbor's terrace—thankfully, she lived on the second floor, although she did sustain a broken clavicle and had required thirty-eight stitches to close the gash on her arm, courtesy of the glass vodka cooler bottle she had been holding when she fell.

And those were only the ones he'd seen in the past hour. Then there was Nancy Anderson—a woman who claimed she tripped and fell into a door but whom he recognized from her frequent visits to the ER with various and numerous contusions and lacerations. Tonight it was a black eye, swollen jaw and broken wrist. Nancy wasn't drunk, but Justin would bet that her husband was—not because it was New Year's Eve but because Ray Anderson always hit the bottle as soon as he got home from work.

More than once, Justin had tried to help her see that there were other options. She refused to listen to him. Because he understood that a woman who had been abused by her husband might be reluctant to confide in another man, he'd called in a female physician to talk to her, with the same unsatisfactory result. After Thanksgiving, when she'd suffered a miscarriage caused by a "fall down the stairs," Dr. Wallace had suggested that she talk to a counselor. Nancy Anderson continued to insist that she was just clumsy, that her husband loved her and would never hurt her.

"What did she say happened this time?" asked Callie Levine, one of his favorite nurses who had drawn the short straw and got stuck working the New Year's Eve shift beside him.

"Walked into a door."

Callie shook her head. "He's going to kill her one of these days."

"Probably," Justin admitted grimly. "But it doesn't matter that you and I see it when she refuses to acknowledge what's happening."

"When she lost the baby, I honestly thought *that* would do it. That her grief would override her fear and she would finally tell the truth."

"She fell down the stairs," Justin said, reminding her of the explanation Nancy Anderson had given when she was admitted on that previous occasion.

Then, because talking about the woman's situation made him feel both frustrated and ineffectual, he opened another chart. "Did you call up to the psych department for a consult?"

"Victoria Danes said she would be down shortly," Callie told him. "Did you want her to see Mrs. Anderson?"

"No point," he said. "I just need her to talk to Tanner Northrop so we can figure out what to do there."

"Is that the little boy in Exam Two with Dr. Wallace?"

"Dr. Wallace is still here?" He'd crossed paths with Avery Wallace earlier in the evening when he'd sneaked into the doctor's lounge for a much-needed hit of caffeine and she'd strolled in, wearing a formfitting black dress and mile-high heels, and his eyes had almost popped right out of his head.

She'd barely glanced in his direction as she'd made her way to the women's locker room, emerging a few minutes later in faded scrubs and running shoes. It didn't matter that the more familiar attire disguised her delectable feminine curves—his body was always on full alert whenever she was near.

She'd moved to Charisma three and a half years earlier and started working at Mercy Hospital. Since then, he'd gotten to know her pretty well—professionally, at least. Personally, she wouldn't give him the time of day, despite the definite sizzle in the air whenever they were around each other.

Although she wasn't on the schedule tonight, she'd assisted him with a procedure earlier in the evening because they were short staffed and she was there. He'd expected that she would have gone home after that—making her escape as soon as possible. Apparently, he was wrong.

Callie nodded in response to his question. "She's teaching the kid how to play Go Fish."

He smiled at that, grateful Tanner had some kind of distraction. The eight-year-old had dialed 9-1-1 after his mother shot up a little too much of her favorite heroin cocktail and wouldn't wake up. She still hadn't woken up, and Tanner didn't seem to know if he had any other family.

"Send Victoria in to see Tanner when she comes down," he said. "I'm going to see how Mrs. Anderson is doing."

"Good luck with that."

Of course, it was his bad luck that he'd just opened the door to Exam Four when the psychologist appeared.

"What's *she* doing here?" Nancy Anderson demanded.

"She's not here to see you," Justin assured her. Then, to Victoria, "Exam Two."

"Thanks." The psychologist moved on; the patient reapplied the ice pack to her jaw.

"Are you planning to go home tonight?" Justin asked her.

"Of course."

"Do you need someone to call a cab for you?" he asked.

Nancy shook her head. "Ray's waiting for me outside."

He scribbled a prescription and handed her the slip. "Pain meds—for the wrist."

She had to set down the ice to take it in her uninjured hand. "Thanks."

There was so much more he could have said, so much more he wanted to say, but he simply nodded and left the room.

"Dare I hope that things are finally starting to slow down?" a pretty brunette asked when he returned to the nurses' station. She'd only been working at Mercy a couple of months and he had to glance at the whiteboard to remind himself of her name: Heather.

"I wouldn't," Justin advised. "It's early yet—still lots of champagne to be drunk and much idiocy to be demonstrated."

She laughed. "How did you get stuck working New Year's Eve?"

"Everyone has to take a turn."

"Callie said it was Dr. Roberts's turn."

He shrugged. It was true that Greg Roberts had been on the schedule for tonight. It was also true that the other doctor was a newlywed while Justin had no plans for the evening. He'd received a couple of invitations to parties—and a few offers for more personal celebrations—but he'd declined them all without really knowing why. He usually enjoyed going out with friends, but lately he'd found himself tiring of the familiar scene.

"What's going on with the guy in Exam Three?" Heather asked. "Are we going to be able to open up that room pretty soon?"

He shook his head. "Suspected alcohol poisoning. I'm waiting for the results from his blood alcohol and tox screens to confirm the diagnosis." In the interim, the patient was on a saline drip for hydration.

"Speaking of alcohol," Heather said. "I've got a bottle of champagne chilling at home to celebrate the New Year whenever I finally get out of here."

"You plan on drinking a whole bottle of champagne by yourself?"

Her lips curved in a slow, seductive smile. "Unless you want to share it with me."

What he'd intended as an innocent question had probably sounded to her as if he was angling for an invitation. But honestly, his thoughts had been divided between Nancy Anderson and Tanner Northrop, and Heather's overture was as unexpected as it was unwanted.

"I've got the rest of the weekend off and my roommate is in Florida for the holidays," Heather continued.

"Lucky you," he noted.

She touched a hand to his arm. "We could be lucky together."

He stepped back from the counter, so that her hand fell away, and finished making notes in the chart before he passed it to her. "Sorry," he said, without really meaning it. "I've got other plans this weekend."

"What about tonight?" she pressed. "Surely you're not expected to be anywhere when we get off shift at two a.m.?"

"No," he acknowledged. "But it's been a really long night and I just want to go home to my bed. Alone."

The hopeful light in her eyes faded. "Callie told me that you always go for the blondes."

He wasn't really surprised to hear that he'd been the subject of some conversation. He knew that the nurses often talked about the doctors. He also knew that some of them weren't as interested in patient care as they were in adding the letters *M-R-S* to their names. But the fact that Callie had been drawn in to the discussion did surprise him, and he made a mental note to talk to her. If he couldn't stop the gossip, he hoped to at least encourage discretion.

"My response has nothing to do with the color of your hair," he assured Heather. "I'm just not interested in partying with anyone tonight."

She pouted but turned her attention back to her work.

As he was walking away from the nurses' station, a call came in from paramedics at an MVA seeking permission to transport multiple victims to the ER. Justin forgot about the gossip and refocused his mind on real priorities.

Avery Wallace rolled her shoulders, attempting to loosen the tight muscles that ached and burned. She was an obstetrician, not an ER doctor—and not scheduled to work tonight in any event. But she'd been on her way to a party with friends when she got the call from her answering service about a patient who was in labor and on her way to Mercy. She knew the doctor on call could handle the birth, but the expectant mother—a military wife whose family lived on the West Coast and whose husband was currently out of the country—was on her own and incredibly nervous about the birth of her first child.

Avery hadn't hesitated to make the detour to the hospital. After texting a quick apology to Amy Seabrook—the friend and colleague who had invited her to the party—she'd exchanged her dress and heels for well-worn scrubs and running shoes.

After Michelle was settled with her new baby, Avery headed back to the locker room with the vague thought of salvaging her plans for the evening. She didn't make it far before she was nabbed to assist Dr. Romeo—aka Justin Garrett—with a resuscitative thoracotomy in the ER.

While she might disapprove of his blatant flirtations with members of the female staff, she couldn't deny that he was an exceptional doctor—or that her own heart always beat just a little bit faster whenever he was around. He stood about six feet two inches with a lean but strong build, short dark blond hair and deep green eyes. But it was more than his physical appearance that drew women to him. He was charming and confident, and not just a doctor but also a Garrett—a name with a certain inherent status in Charisma, North Carolina, where Garrett Furniture had been one of the town's major employers for more than fifty years.

After more than three years of working beside him at the hospital, she would have expected to become inured to his presence. The truth was exactly the opposite—the more time she spent with him, the more appealing she found him. She respected his ability to take control in a crisis situation as much as she admired the compassion he showed to his patients and, as a result, she'd developed a pretty major crush on him—not that she had any intention of letting Dr. Romeo know it.

When the patient had been resuscitated and moved to surgery, he'd simply and sincerely thanked Avery for her help. That was another thing she liked about him—he might be in command of the ER, but he never overlooked the contributions of the rest of the staff.

She'd barely discarded her gown and gloves from that procedure when she was steered to the surgical wing to help Dr. Bristow with a femoral shaft fracture. She passed through the ER again on her way out, and that was when she saw Dr. Garrett hunkered down in conversation with a little boy. The child's face was streaked with dirt and tears, but it was the abject grief in his eyes that tugged at her heart and had her slipping into the room after the ER physician had gone. She chatted with him and played Go Fish until Victoria Danes arrived. Once she was confident that he was comfortable in the psychologist's company, she headed back toward the locker room. And ran straight into the one person she always tried to avoid.

"Good—you're still here."

Her heart bumped against her ribs as she looked up at Justin, but she kept her tone cool, casual. "Actually, I'm just on my way home."

"We've got two ambulances coming in from an MVA—one carrying an expectant mother."

"Dr. Terrence can handle it."

"He can, but Callie asked me to find you."

"Why?" she wondered.

"The pregnant woman is her sister."

According to the report from the paramedics, the taxi in which Callie's sister and her husband were riding had been broadsided by a pickup truck that had sped through a red light.

Avery watched the clock as she scrubbed, conscious that each one of the five minutes she was required to spend on the procedure was another minute the expectant mother was waiting. Dr. Garrett was already working on the pregnant woman's husband, who had various contusions and lacerations and a possible concussion.

When Avery finally entered the OR, she was given an immediate update on the patient's condition.

"Camryn Ritter, thirty-one years old, thirty-eight weeks pregnant. Presenting with moderate bleeding and uterine tenderness, BP one-ten over seventy, pulse rate one-thirty, baby's rhythm is steady at ninety BPM."

The numbers, combined with her own observations, supported the diagnosis of placental abruption with evidence of fetal bradycardia, which meant that delivering the baby now was necessary for the welfare of both mother and child. Thankfully, Dr. Terrence had already requested that the anesthesiologist give the patient a spinal block, so she could start surgery almost right away.

She'd lost count of the number of C-sections that she'd performed, but she'd never considered a caesarean to be a routine surgery. Every pregnancy was different and every baby was different, so she was always hypervigilant, never taking anything for granted. But at thirty-eight weeks, both mother and baby had a really good chance as long as she could get in before anything else went wrong.

"Where's Brad?" the patient asked worriedly.

Avery glanced at Callie, who was holding her sister's hand. Ordinarily she would have banned the nurse from the operating room because of the personal connection, but in the absence of the woman's husband, she was counting on Callie to help keep the expectant mother calm.

"Brad's her husband, my brother-in-law," Callie explained. Then, to her sister, she said, "He was a little bumped up in the taxi, but Dr. Garrett's checking him over now and running some tests."

"He was bleeding," Camryn said. "There was so much blood."

"Head injuries bleed a lot," Callie acknowledged. "Remember when you got hit with a baseball bat in third grade—while you were wearing my pink jean jacket? It took mom three washes to get the blood out."

Her sister managed a weak smile. "So he's okay?"

"He's going to be fine," Callie promised, more likely to soothe the expectant mother's worries than from any certainty of the fact. "Dr. Garrett's one of the best doctors on staff here. Dr. Wallace is another."

"Brad really wanted to be here when the baby was born."

"I'm sure neither of you expected that your baby would be born tonight, under these circumstances."

The anesthesiologist was near the head of the bed, monitoring the mother's vital signs and intravenous levels. He nodded to Avery and, after confirming that her patient could feel nothing, she drew the scalpel across her swollen abdomen.

A planned caesarean usually took between five and ten minutes from first cut until the baby was lifted out. In an emergency situation like this one, an experienced doctor could perform the procedure in about two minutes.

Dr. Terrence—who had scrubbed in to assist—worked to keep the surgical field clean, swabbing with gauze and holding the incision open while she worked. They were approaching the two-minute mark when she reached into the uterus. Clear fluid gushed around her gloved hand as she cradled the small skull in her palm and carefully guided the head, then the shoulders, out of the opening.

Her hands didn't shake as she lifted the baby out of the mother's womb. Her hands never shook when she was under the hot lights of an operating or delivery room. She didn't let herself feel any pressure or emotion while she was focused on a task. Her unflappable demeanor was, she knew, only one reason some of the staff referred to her as "Wall-ice."

The baby's color was good, and when Avery wiped his

mouth with gauze and gently squeezed his nostrils, she was immediately rewarded with a soft cry.

"Is that—" Camryn's voice hitched. "Is that my baby?"

"That's your baby," Avery confirmed.

"He's a boy," Callie told her sister, watching with misty eyes as the cord was clamped and cut. "You have a beautiful, perfect baby boy."

"I want to see him," the new mother said.

"You will—in just a moment."

"Seven pounds, five ounces, nineteen inches," another nurse announced from the corner of the operating room, after the newborn had been wiped, weighed and swaddled.

Camryn wiped at a tear that spilled onto her cheek as the baby was placed in her arms. "Where's Brad? I want to see him. I want him to see our baby."

"He'll be here as soon as he can," Callie soothed.

While the nurse and her sister talked quietly, Avery continued to work, suturing up each layer of abdominal tissue. But even as she focused on her task, she was thinking of the awe and wonder on Camryn's face when she saw her baby for the first time—and immediately fell in love with him. Avery had seen it happen countless times, but it never failed to tug at her own heart.

Half an hour later, when she finally left the new mom with her baby, she again crossed paths with Dr. Garrett in the hall.

"How's dad?" she asked, referring to the baby's father whom he'd been working on in the adjacent room.

"Aside from two broken ribs, a punctured lung, mild concussion and a head laceration that required twenty-two stitches to close, he's doing just fine."

"Twenty-two stitches? I just put in more than twice that number *and* delivered a baby."

"Competitive, aren't you?" Though his tone was teasing, his smile was weak.

"Maybe a little," she acknowledged.

"Boy or girl?"

"Boy."

He slung a companionable arm across her shoulders as they headed down the hall. "Good work, Wallace."

"You, too, Garrett."

They walked together in silence for a few minutes, until Avery caught him stifling a yawn. "I imagine it's been a very long night for you," she said.

"It's New Year's Eve," he reminded her.

"Was," she corrected.

He scrubbed a hand over his jaw. "What?"

"It's after midnight now." Afterward, she would wonder what caused her to throw caution and common sense to the wind. But in the moment, it seemed perfectly natural to lift herself onto her toes and touch her lips to his cheek. "Happy New Year."

She could tell he was as startled by the impulsive gesture as she was, but when he looked at her, she saw something more than surprise in his eyes. Something that made her heart pound harder and faster, that made her weary body ache and yearn. Something that warned her she'd taken the first step down an intriguing—and potentially dangerous—path.

He took the next step, pulling open the nearest door—to a housekeeping supply closet—and tugging her inside. She didn't balk or protest. For more than three years, they'd danced around the attraction between them. They weren't dancing anymore.

"Happy New Year," he echoed, then crushed his mouth down on hers.

Chapter Two

His kiss was hot and hungry and demanding. She kissed him back, just as hotly and hungrily, responding to his every demand and meeting them with her own. If she'd been able to think clearly—if she'd been able to think *at all*—she might have drawn back. But the moment his lips touched hers, all rational thought slipped from her mind. In fact, her brain seemed to have shut down completely, letting the hormones that flooded through her veins lead the way.

And they were leading her to a very happy place. A place where his hands were all over her, touching and teasing, giving her so much pleasure and still making her want so much more.

He eased his lips away from hers. "I like the sparkly things in your hair, Wallace—they really dress up your scrubs."

"What?" She frowned as she reached up, startled to realize that her hair was in a fancy twist instead of her usual ponytail. So much had happened since she'd left home, she'd almost forgotten about the party and the decorative pins she'd impulsively added to her updo for the occasion. "Oh."

"You were out celebrating the New Year," Justin guessed.

"I never actually made it that far," she told him.

"I'm sure your date was disappointed."

"It wasn't a date," she said. "Not really."

"Good." He slid his hands up her back, drawing her

closer, and lowered his head to nip playfully at her bottom lip.

This was dangerous. He was hardly touching her and her resistance was melting. He wasn't her type. Not at all. He was a player and a doctor and everything she didn't want in a man.

But right now, she didn't care about any of that. Right now, she *did* want him. Or at least her body wanted to feel the way she knew he could make her feel, the way he *was* making her feel.

"But I am sorry your plans were ruined," he said.

"They were actually Amy's plans—and I was kind of relieved to escape another blind date."

"Then you weren't planning to ring in the New Year with wild, sweaty sex?"

"The thought never crossed my mind." His hands grazed her breasts as they skimmed up her sides, making her breath hitch. "Until now."

"Really?" He smiled against her lips. "You're thinking about it now?"

She slid her hands beneath his scrub top, over the smooth, taut skin of his abdomen. "Yeah, I'm thinking about it now."

"If you want to hold that thought, I'm off shift in a couple of hours."

She scraped her teeth lightly over his jaw. "I'll change my mind in a couple of hours."

"I definitely don't want you to change your mind." He whisked her scrub top up over her head, unveiling her pink lace bra, and his brows lifted. "You sure you didn't put this on for your date?"

"Forget about my date," she suggested. "And focus on me."

"I'm focused," he promised, his thumbs stroking over her rigid nipples through the delicate fabric. "Very focused."

Her head fell back against the door as arrows of sensation shot straight to her core. Her body was on fire. She was burning with want, with need. Desperate, aching need. She was so tightly wound up she was practically vibrating.

Then he dipped his head and found her breast with his mouth, suckling her through the lace. She slid her fingers into his hair, holding him against her as waves of exquisite sensation washed over her.

His mouth moved to her other breast as his hand slid down the front of her pants, his fingertips brushing over the aching nub at her center. The light touch made her gasp and shudder. He parted the soft folds of skin, groaning his appreciation when he found that she was already wet.

"You do something to me, Wallace," he admitted gruffly.

"Do something to me," she suggested, reaching a hand into his pants to wrap around the hard length of him, making him groan again. "Do me."

"I will," he promised.

But for now, he continued to touch and tease her. She bit hard on her lip to keep from crying out, her palms flat against the door to hold herself upright as her knees quivered and her body shuddered.

She was gasping and panting and on the verge of melting into a puddle at his feet when he pushed her panties down to her ankles with her pants, then shoved his own pants and boxers out of the way. Finally he covered her mouth with his and thrust into her, kissing her hard and deep as he took her body the same way.

She was ready for him. More than ready. But it had been a long time, and she'd almost forgotten how good it could feel. How exquisitely and blissfully good.

It was pretty much a consensus among the female contingent of the hospital nursing staff that Dr. Garrett could satisfy a woman's every want and need, and he lived up to that reputation now. He used his hands and his lips and his body to drive her to the ultimate pinnacle of pleasure and far beyond, soaring into the abyss with her.

When she finally floated back to earth, her body was still pinned against the door, still intimately joined with his. She took a minute to catch her breath as he did the same.

"I think I might need the paddles to restart my heart, Wallace."

She forced herself to match his casual tone. "Then it's a good thing you're a doctor."

But even while her body continued to hum with the aftereffects of pleasure, her mind was beginning to remember the hundred and one reasons that giving in to the attraction she felt for Justin was a bad idea. The number one reason was the *MD* that followed his name; the hundred other reasons were the hundred names of other women he'd undoubtedly pleasured in a similar manner.

He brushed his lips against hers—the kiss surprisingly tender and sweet on the heels of their passionate and almost desperate coupling.

"Do you ever wonder how we didn't end up here before now?" he asked her.

Her brows lifted. "Mostly naked in a housekeeping supply closet?"

"I was focused on the mostly naked part," he said. "And thinking that I'd like to take you back to my place and progress from mostly to completely naked."

She shook her head and pushed him away so she could pull up her pants and gather the rest of her discarded clothing. "Not a good idea."

"Why would you say that?"

"Because we have to work together."

"We've always worked well together," he noted. "And now we know that we play well together, too, and—"

She touched a hand to his lips, silencing his words as she shook her head. "No."

He frowned. "You don't even know what I was going to say."

"It doesn't matter," she insisted, refastening her bra.

"You're just going to walk away?"

She tugged her shirt over her head. "Well, someone is eventually going to need something from this closet, so it's probably not a good idea to stay here."

"You know I'm not referring to the closet but what happened between us," he chided.

"It was an impulse, Garrett. Nothing more than that."

"An impulse," he echoed.

He sounded oddly hurt by her characterization of their actions—but she was probably just imagining it. After all, Justin Garrett didn't do emotions or involvement. He moved in and then moved on, and she thought he would appreciate that she didn't want anything more than that.

"It was an intense situation in the ER tonight and we both worked hard to ensure a young couple had reason to celebrate rather than mourn the start of the New Year."

"You think that what just happened between us only happened because of *adrenaline*?" he asked incredulously.

"And proximity," she allowed.

"So this is normal postoperative procedure for you?"

"No!"

"Then it was out-of-character behavior?" he pressed.

"Very," she admitted.

"And probably an inevitable result of the fact that you've been denying the attraction between us for more than three years."

Probably. Although she had no intention of admitting it. To Avery's mind, it was bad enough that she'd succumbed to the attraction she'd tried so hard to ignore without giving him the additional satisfaction of knowing that she'd harbored those feelings for so long.

But he was right—she'd been attracted to him from the

beginning. The day she interviewed with the chief of staff at Mercy Hospital, the first time she'd met Justin, he'd smiled at her and her pulse had skyrocketed.

She wasn't unfamiliar with attraction, but she couldn't remember ever having it hit her so immediately and intensely. On her first day of work, he'd flirted with her a little, and she'd flirted back.

And then, later that same day, she'd seen him flirting with someone else. The day after that, it was someone different again. It had only taken three more days—three more shifts at the hospital—for her to realize that Justin Garrett, aka Dr. Romeo, was not her type. He'd continued to flirt with her—or try to—when their paths crossed, but she'd given him no encouragement.

Not until she'd kissed him.

"I have to go."

He slapped his hand against the door to prevent her from opening it. "And you're still denying it," he noted.

"Let me go, Garrett."

"I'm not holding you hostage. I'm just trying to have a conversation."

"There's nothing to talk about. You got another notch to add to your bedpost—isn't that enough for you?"

"I don't have bedposts," he said. "Which I'd be happy to prove to you if you come home with me when I get off shift."

"No," she said firmly.

He brushed a loose hair off her cheek and tucked it behind her ear, the light touch of his fingertips on her skin making her shiver and want him all over again. *Damn him.*

"What did I do wrong?" he asked her. "Aside from taking you against the closet door with all the finesse of a horny teenager, I mean."

She wished she could blame him for that, but she'd initiated everything. She wished she could dismiss the experience as unsatisfactory, but the truth was, despite the setting and the pace of the event, her body had been very thoroughly satisfied.

"You didn't do anything wrong," she said.

"Then why are you pulling away?" Justin asked, sincerely baffled by her reaction.

Before she could respond, his pager started beeping.

Mentally cursing the untimely interruption, he scooped it up from the floor, where it had fallen when he'd dropped his pants. He glanced at the display and sighed. "Two ambulances are on their way from another MVA."

But there was no response.

Avery was already gone.

With a sigh, Justin tucked the pager back in his pocket and headed to the ER.

He wouldn't be a good doctor if he couldn't set aside personal distractions and do his job. But after he'd finished stitching up another head wound, helped cast the broken arm of a screaming, squirming four-year-old, checked on the college student with alcohol poisoning and confirmed that Tanner Northrop was in the temporary custody of Family Services, it was almost two hours past the end of his shift.

He went to the locker room, physically and mentally exhausted, and let the water of the shower pound down on him. When he finally came out of the shower, he wanted nothing more than his bed.

Then he thought about Avery in that bed, warm and willing and naked, and his body miraculously stirred to life again.

The pretty baby doctor could believe whatever she wanted and make whatever excuses she wanted, but he knew that what was between them wasn't even close to being done.

Avery's apartment was dark and empty when she got home from the hospital, the quiet space echoing the hollow feeling inside her. The physical pleasure she'd experienced in those stolen moments with Justin Garrett had already faded away, leaving her aching and ashamed.

She should never have kissed him. She certainly should never have let him drag her into the closet. And she most definitely should never have succumbed to the lustful desires that stirred deep inside whenever she was near him.

Dropping onto the edge of the sofa, she buried her face in her hands, thoroughly mortified by her own behavior. She had a reputation for being cool and untouchable, but she'd been so hot and desperate for Justin that she'd let him screw her in a housekeeping supply closet.

What if someone found out?

Her cheeks burned with humiliation at the possibility. No doubt the hospital grapevine would love to know that the charismatic Dr. Romeo had succeeded in melting the frosty Dr. Wall-ice.

Of course, the more than two years that had passed since she'd last had sex might have been a factor, too. She missed physical intimacy. She missed the sharing of close personal contact with another person, the rising tension, the exhilarating release. But she'd never been good at sex outside of a relationship, which explained why it had been such a long time since she'd had sex.

Prior to the scheduled setup with Nolan tonight, she couldn't even remember the name of the last guy she'd dated. Was it Simon? Or Mike? Simon was the real estate agent who lived on the ninth floor of her building. Dark hair, darker eyes, sexy smile—but a sloppy kisser. Mike was one of the cameramen on *Ryder to the Rescue*, her brother's TV show. Shaggy blond hair, hazel eyes, great laugh and—she was informed by her brother after she'd agreed to meet Mike for coffee—engaged to one of the show's producers.

Or maybe it had been Kevin. She'd almost forgotten

about him. They'd met on the Fourth of July, having struck up a conversation while they were both in line at the Fireman's Picnic—a charity barbecue for the children's wing of the hospital. He'd asked for her number and he'd even called a few times after that, trying to set up a date, but they'd never actually made it to that next step.

Her life really was pathetic.

Spending time with Amy and Ben, she sometimes found herself wondering if she would ever find that once-in-a-lifetime kind of love that her friend shared with her husband. The kind of love that she'd once believed she shared with the man she'd planned to marry.

Avery had met Wyatt Travers at med school, when she was in her first year and he was in his third. Even then, she'd had reasons for not wanting to get involved with a doctor, but he'd swept her off her feet. Two years after they met, he put an engagement ring on her finger, and six months later, they moved in together.

Their lives were undeniably busy and they were often going in opposite directions, but whenever they had time just to be together, they would talk about their plans for the future, where they would set up a medical practice together, when they would start a family and how many children they would have.

Then he'd decided to go to Haiti as part of an emergency medical response team. Avery had wanted to go with him, but she was just finishing up her residency, so Wyatt went alone. He was gone for six months and when he finally came back, it was to tell her that he'd fallen in love with someone else. When Avery reminded him that he was supposed to be in love with her and that their wedding was scheduled for the following summer, he admitted that he hadn't just fallen in love with Stasia—he'd married her.

Avery had immediately packed up and moved out of their apartment, because it seemed a little awkward to con-

tinue to live with her former fiancé and his new wife. She'd
crashed with a friend for a few weeks until she figured out
what she wanted to do with her life now.

It had taken her a long time to get over Wyatt's betrayal.
He'd argued that she couldn't blame him for falling in love
with someone else, but she could and she did. If he'd really
loved her, he wouldn't have fallen in love with Stasia—
and since he'd fallen in love with Stasia, it proved that he'd
never really loved *her*.

Either way, what it meant for Avery was that there wasn't
going to be a joint medical practice or a wedding in August
or a baby born two and a half years after that. Not for her,
anyway. Wyatt, on the other hand, had accelerated the time-
line he and Avery had mapped out for their life together,
becoming a father five months after his return from Haiti.

That was when Avery realized she needed to make some
changes, and when her brother, Ryder, was offered a contract to do a cable television show, she decided to go with
him to Charisma. She was immediately charmed by the
small town and grateful that it was far enough from Boston
that she wouldn't worry about running into Wyatt or Stasia
at the grocery store. Because as unlikely as that might seem
in the city, it was a risk she didn't want to take.

She threw herself into her career and focused on proving herself to the staff at Mercy Hospital. She'd succeeded
in building an impeccable reputation, and she'd also made
some really good friends, including Amy Seabrook. She
even went out on the occasional date, but she hadn't fallen
in love again.

And when she went home at the end of the day, it was
always to an empty apartment. She tried to convince herself that she liked it that way—that she was glad she didn't
have to worry about anyone leaving wet towels in the bathroom or dirty socks on the floor; that she appreciated the

freedom of choosing whether she wanted to listen to music or watch TV or simply enjoy the quiet solitude.

But deep in her heart, she couldn't deny the truth: she was alone and she was lonely. She wanted a partner with whom to share her life and build a family, but she was growing increasingly skeptical about either of those things ever happening for her.

In the past six months, she'd attended three bridal showers, four baby showers and two first-birthday parties. All of her friends and contemporaries were at the point in their lives where they were getting married and having babies, and she was sincerely happy for them. But she was a little envious, too.

She was thirty-two years old and her life was so far off track she couldn't see the track anymore. She was so desperate for physical contact with a man that she'd turned to Justin Garrett.

Not that he ever bragged about his conquests—he didn't need to. The women he bedded were only too happy to add their names to the extensive and ever-growing list of those who had experienced nirvana between his sheets.

Now Avery was one of them—one of the nameless, faceless masses who could say that she'd slept with Dr. Romeo. Except that she hadn't actually slept with him; she hadn't even been horizontal with him. No, she'd been so willing and eager, she'd gotten naked with him in a supply closet. Or mostly naked, anyway.

She'd just wanted to feel as if she wasn't completely alone for a few minutes. And while it was true that he'd helped her feel not just connected and desired but incredibly good, now that she was home again she had to face the truth: those stolen moments in the closet didn't change anything.

She was still alone.

But at least there was no one around to see the tears that slid down her cheeks.

Chapter Three

Wellbrook Medical Center was a privately funded clinic that provided medical services primarily to unwed mothers and their children. One of Avery's jobs at the clinic was to talk to young women about the importance of safe sex— reminding them to protect themselves not just against unwanted pregnancies but sexually transmitted diseases. For those who missed coming in for that talk, the clinic also offered the morning-after pill, testing for pregnancy and STDs, and prenatal care.

Avery was making notes in a patient's file when Amy set a mug of coffee on her desk. She glanced up. "Did you say something?"

"I said you seem a little preoccupied today."

"Sorry—I was just wondering how Callie's sister and her baby are doing. I think I'll stop by the hospital to check on them when I'm finished here."

"*If* we ever finish here," Amy noted.

"Brenna and Tess are coming in at two," she reminded her friend.

Amy lifted a hand to cover a yawn. "Why does two seem so far away?"

"Maybe because you had such a good time last night," Avery teased.

Her friend smiled. "What time did you escape from the hospital?"

"It wasn't long after midnight."

"It didn't take you that long to deliver a baby."

Avery shook her head. "No, but the ER was crazy, so I stuck around for a while to help out, which is how I ended up delivering Callie's sister's baby, too."

"You missed a great party," Amy told her.

"I'm sure I did," she acknowledged.

Her friend sighed. "You could at least sound a little disappointed—I really think you would have liked Nolan."

"You say that about every one of Ben's friends that you try to set me up with."

"And I remain optimistic that, one of these days, you'll actually go out with one of them."

"I'm focusing on my career right now."

"I get that, but your focus shouldn't be to the exclusion of all else."

"It's not."

"When was the last time you were on a date?" Amy asked, then she shook her head. "No—forget that question. When was the last time you had sex?"

Last night.

Not that she was going to admit as much to her friend. Of course, even if she did tell Amy the truth, it was unlikely her friend would believe it. Because Avery Wallace didn't have casual sex, and she definitely didn't succumb to the obvious charms of sexy doctors like Justin Garrett.

"Why is it that everyone wants to talk about sex today?" she countered, in an effort to divert her friend's attention.

"Because a lot of people got a little crazy and a little careless last night," Amy admitted. "I don't understand it—we give out condoms for free at the front desk. Why aren't people using them?"

"Don't you remember what it was like to be a teenager? All of the emotions and the hormones?"

"I remember the heady thrill of first love and the exciting rush of sexual desire," Amy acknowledged. "But I was never so overcome by lust—or so intoxicated—that I would have had sex without a condom."

"If everyone was as smart as you, we wouldn't have patients in the waiting room," Avery countered.

"And since we do, I guess we'd better get back to work."

So they did, and a steady stream of patients kept them both busy until Brenna and Tess arrived shortly before two. Avery was almost disappointed when their colleagues showed up, because now she would have time to think about the hard truths her earlier conversation with Amy had forced her to acknowledge.

Most notably that it wasn't only teenagers who made impulsive and stupid decisions about sex—otherwise responsible and intelligent adults could sometimes be just as impulsive and stupid. As she and Justin had proved last night.

Justin often felt as if he spent more time at the hospital than he did in his own apartment, which made him question the amount of rent he paid every month for his apartment overlooking Memorial Park. For the past few years, his parents had been urging him to buy a house—"an investment in real estate"—but Justin didn't see the point in paying more money for more rooms he wasn't going to use.

Besides, his apartment was conveniently located near the hospital—which he particularly appreciated when he had the early-morning shift. And the late-evening shift. And especially after a double shift.

When he was home, he felt comfortable in his space. It was his sanctuary from the craziness of the world. Four days into the New Year, he was enjoying that sanctuary—until his phone rang, indicating a visitor downstairs. He scowled when he glanced at the monitor and recognized the young woman in the lobby, curiously looking around the foyer as she waited for him to respond to the buzzer.

"Yeah?" he said, his tone deliberately unwelcoming.

"Girl Scout cookie delivery," she responded cheerfully.

"If you expect someone to buy that story, you should wear the uniform," he told her.

"Is that what it takes to get an invite to your apartment—a short skirt and a sash?"

"Jeez, no. I'm not a perv."

"You're also not opening the door," his unexpected visitor pointed out.

With a barely suppressed sigh, he punched in the code to release the lock so that she could enter. A few minutes later, there was a knock on his door.

"What are you doing here, Nora?"

His half sister moved past him into the apartment. "You're not a believer in traditional Southern hospitality, are you?"

"Please, come in," he said, his sarcasm contradicting the invitation of his words. "Let me take your coat and offer you some sweet tea."

Ignoring his tone, she took off her coat and handed it to him. "Sweet tea would be nice."

He hung her coat on one of the hooks behind the door. "Sorry, I'm all out."

"A glass of wine?"

"Are you old enough to drink?"

"You know I'm only eleven years younger than you."

He snapped his fingers. "That's right—I was playing Little League when my father was screwing your mother."

"Which isn't my fault any more than it's yours," she pointed out.

He sighed, because she was right. And because he knew his mother would be appalled if she ever found out that Nora had come to visit and he'd been less than welcoming.

His mother was another innocent devastated by her husband's infidelity, although she had forgiven John Garrett a long time ago—before anyone knew that the affair had resulted in a child. And even after learning about the existence of her husband's illegitimate daughter, Ellen had gone out of her way to make Nora feel she was a part of their family—efforts that the woman in question had mostly resisted.

"Red or white?" Justin asked her now.

"Red, please."

She followed him into the kitchen, settling herself on a stool at the island while he uncorked a bottle of Napa Valley merlot. He slid a glass across the counter to her and decided—*what the hell?*—he wasn't on call, and poured a second glass for himself.

"Thank you." She took a tentative sip, then set the glass down. "I'm looking for a job."

"And you want to cash in your DNA results for a cushy office at Garrett Furniture," he guessed.

She shook her head. "I have no interest in your father's company."

"Isn't he your father, too?"

"Well, yes, but that was more by accident than design."

He nodded in acknowledgment as she sipped her wine again.

"Besides, an office job would bore me to tears," she told him. "I like to work with people—that's why I became a registered physical therapist."

Which he already knew but had no intention of revealing to her, because she'd then want to know how and why he knew it, and he didn't intend to share that information. Yet.

"Where'd you go to school?" he asked, pretending he didn't know the answer to that question, either, as he lifted his own glass to his lips.

"The University of Texas at San Antonio. Graduated

with honors." She opened her purse and took out an envelope, offering it to him. "My résumé."

"What do you want me to do with this?"

"Look at it and, if you think it's warranted, consider writing a letter of recommendation for me."

"Why me?"

"Because there's an opening at Mercy Hospital and the Garrett name carries a considerable amount of weight there."

"I'm surprised you didn't go straight to my mother," he commented. "If you've done your homework, you're aware that she's on the hiring committee."

"I'm aware," she admitted.

"So why didn't you knock on her door?" he challenged.

She traced the base of her glass with her finger. "Because a part of me was afraid she'd refuse to give a recommendation...and another part was afraid she *would* give it."

He shook his head. "Every time I think I have you figured out, you say or do something that surprises me."

"I don't need you to understand me—I just need a letter."

"I can't give you that without some understanding of who you are and whether or not you'll fit in with the rest of the staff."

She slid off her seat. "Then I guess I should be going."

He stepped in front of her, blocking her path to the door. "Why Charisma? Why Mercy?"

"Why not?"

"You didn't come here just for a job."

She met his gaze evenly. "I have family here."

"Speaking of family, what do Patrick and Connor think of your decision to move to North Carolina?"

Her eyes narrowed at the mention of her brothers. "What do you know about Patrick and Connor?"

"Quite a lot, actually," he told her. "Patrick is twenty-seven, single and a deputy in the Echo Ridge sheriff's department. Connor is twenty-eight, a graduate of the Thurgood Marshall School of Law currently employed as a prosecuting attorney, which is probably why he's trying to keep his relationship with a certain young woman who works as a public defender under wraps."

"You had my family investigated?" she demanded, her question filled with icy fury.

"Does that bother you?" he challenged. "Does it seem wrong that some stranger could come along and meddle in the lives of the people who matter the most to you?"

"Touché, Dr. Garrett." She reached past him to pick up her glass and tossed back the rest of her wine. "I guess that means I'm not going to get a recommendation."

"I'm not saying no," he told her. Because he was a firm believer in the old adage about keeping friends close and enemies closer, and he wasn't yet sure which category his half sister fit into. "I just want some more information."

"My life's an open book—and one that you've apparently already read."

He ignored her sarcasm. "Can you meet me at the hospital tomorrow?"

"What time?"

"Two o'clock. By the fountain in the courtyard."

She nodded. "I'll be there."

He followed her back to the foyer and plucked her coat off the hook just as another knock sounded. Since no one had buzzed from the lobby, he assumed that it was probably Lianne from across the hall. For a woman who was always baking something—muffins or cookies or banana bread—it baffled him that his neighbor never had all of the ingredients she needed. His brother, Ryan, liked to tease that Lianne asking to borrow sugar was code for her wanting to give him some sugar, but her flirtations were mostly harmless.

But when he opened up the door, it wasn't Lianne on the other side. It was Avery Wallace.

"You're on your way out," she said, noting the coat in his hand.

He shook his head. "It's not mine."

Her eyes flickered past him to Nora, then to the island with the bottle of wine and two glasses. Her color went frosty and her tone, when she spoke again, had chilled by several degrees. "I'm sorry—I obviously should have called first."

He turned to hand the coat to Nora, whose gaze was openly curious as it shifted from him to his new guest and back again. Clearly she was hoping for an introduction, but he wasn't inclined to make it.

"I'll talk to you later," Avery said, already turning away.

He caught her arm. "You can stay. Nora's on her way out."

Thankfully, Nora didn't have to be told twice. She slipped past him. "I'll see you at two o'clock tomorrow."

He nodded, pulling Avery through the door before closing it.

She tugged her arm out of his grasp, looking uncertain and slightly disapproving. "She's a little young for you, isn't she?"

"I don't know," he said mildly. "How young is too young to be my sister?"

"Your—" she looked back at the door through which Nora had departed "—sister?"

He nodded.

She frowned. "I didn't know you had a sister."

"Neither did I until seven months ago."

"Sounds like there's a story there," she mused.

"I'd tell you about it sometime, but you barely stick around long enough to finish a consult never mind an actual conversation."

She flushed but did not respond.

"So why are you here?" he asked. And then, because he couldn't resist ruffling her feathers a bit, he said "Did you come to count the notches on my bedposts?"

She sent him a scathing look. "You said you don't have bedposts."

"Because I don't," he confirmed. "Which I'd be happy to prove to you if you come down the hall with me and—"

She cut him off by shoving an envelope against his chest. "This is why I'm here."

He held her gaze for a long minute before he opened the flap and pulled out a single page. He immediately recognized the logo of Charisma Medical Laboratories at the top, then saw her name in the "patient name" box. "What is this?"

"You did get that MD behind your name from medical school, didn't you?"

"Okay, I guess what I should have asked is '*why* is this?'"

"New Year's Eve."

His brows lifted.

She huffed out a breath. "I should have figured you'd make me spell it out. We didn't just have sex, Garrett. We had unprotected sex."

Justin nodded soberly. While he had no objections to casual sex, he was never careless about protection. Not since that one time when he was a teenager. That one time— one forgotten condom and one terrifying pregnancy false alarm— had been enough to scare the bejesus out of him and make him swear that he would never be caught unprepared again.

And he never had—until he'd found himself in a hospital supply closet with Avery. Then everything had happened so fast, and his desperate need for her had overridden everything else.

"I'm sorry," he said, because although the words were grossly inadequate they were also true.

"Obviously neither of us was thinking clearly that night or what happened between us never would have happened," she said.

He wondered how it was that—despite all the other thoughts screaming in his head—he could be amused by such a prim remark delivered in her characteristically cool tone. Wanting to shake some of that cool, he stepped closer to her.

"We had sex, Avery. Incredible…mind-blowing… ground-shaking sex."

"I was there," she acknowledged, her gaze remaining fixed on the ceramic tile floor. "I know what happened."

He tipped her chin up. "So why can't you say it?"

She jerked her head away. "Because I'm embarrassed."

"Why?"

"Because I used to take pride in the fact that I was one of probably only a handful of women on staff at the hospital who had *not* slept with Dr. Romeo—and I can't say that anymore."

He'd grown accustomed to the nickname so that it didn't bother him anymore. Not that he would acknowledge, anyway. "Honey, I haven't slept with *that* many women who work there."

"I don't care," she insisted. "Or I wouldn't care, except that now I'm one of them."

"It's not as if I've been walking around wearing a sign— I Melted Dr. Wall-ice."

She glared at him. "This isn't funny."

"I agree," he said. "Nor is it anything to be ashamed of. We're two unattached, consenting adults who gave in to a mutual and compelling attraction."

"We had unprotected sex."

He nodded. "My bad. I'm not in the habit of carrying

condoms in my scrub shirt," he said, attempting a casualness he did not feel. "But that still doesn't explain—" he held up the lab report "—this."

"I wanted to reassure you that there's no reason for you to worry—" she bit down on her lower lip "—on my side, I mean."

"But you're worried about mine," he realized.

He couldn't blame her for being concerned. He was well aware of his reputation around the hospital—and well aware that it had been greatly exaggerated. That knowledge had never bothered him before, but now, seeing Avery's misery and distress, he wished he'd clarified a few things. Or a lot of things.

Of course, it was too late now. She'd obviously made up her mind about him and nothing he said was going to change it. He put the lab report back into the envelope and returned it to her. "Most of the other women I've been with just want to cuddle after sex."

"Most of the other women are why I'd like some quid pro quo."

He nodded. "I'll take care of it tomorrow."

Chapter Four

In retrospect, Avery probably could have handled the situation better, but the whole experience with Justin was way outside her comfort zone. She wasn't great with personal relationships in general, and men like Justin—not that there were many men like Justin—flustered her beyond belief.

He was so totally confident and unapologetically sexy, and completely aware of the effect he had on people. Especially women. It was why, for most of the three and a half years she'd worked at Mercy Hospital, she'd put as much distance between them as possible.

Of course, distance wasn't always possible. There were times that they needed to consult and collaborate with respect to the care of patients, and at those times, she did what had to be done, careful to maintain a calm facade and professional demeanor. But when she had a choice, she chose to stay far away from his orbit, because she didn't trust herself to resist the magnetic pull that he seemed to exert on women without even trying. She hadn't been able to resist it on New Year's Eve. She hadn't *wanted* to resist him.

When she'd realized that they'd had sex without a condom, she'd panicked a little. Or maybe a lot. And then she'd started to think about all the possible repercussions of having unprotected sex with a man who'd had numerous other sexual partners. As a doctor, she would have been irresponsible to ignore his history, especially after she'd already been irresponsible in having unprotected sex with him.

She didn't see much of Justin over the next few days after her visit to his apartment, which wasn't unusual. Depending on their schedules, she might cross paths with him numerous times in a day or not at all for several shifts. What was unusual was that she found herself looking for him, wondering when she might see him and even the wondering filled her stomach with an uncomfortable fluttery feeling.

When she did see him, his demeanor toward her was nothing but professional, and she strove to treat him with the same courtesy. But her awareness of him was heightened now, and whenever he was near, her body stirred with not just memories but longing.

Friday afternoon, she'd just finished a consult regarding the course of action for a multiple pregnancy when he caught her in the conference room.

"I've got those test results you wanted," he told her.

She'd been so focused on her work that it took Avery a moment to realize what he was talking about. But when she did, the knots that had been in her belly since New Year's Day tightened.

She looked at him expectantly. His statement suggested that he intended to share the results with her, but his hands were empty. "Are you actually going to let me see them?"

"Of course," he agreed. "At dinner tonight."

She sighed. "Dr. Garrett—"

"Dr. Wallace," he countered, his tone amused.

"I'm *not* going to have dinner with you."

"Yes, you are," he said confidently. "Because you want to hold the lab report in your hands and meticulously scrutinize every letter and digit."

She did, of course. Because she needed to be sure. But she didn't believe he, as a medical professional, would really hold back the results. Certainly not if there was any reason for her to be concerned.

"You're clean," she decided, feigning a nonchalance she didn't feel. "You wouldn't be playing games otherwise."

"And if I'd told you I was clean, that our romantic—" she snorted derisively at that, while he narrowed his gaze and continued "—liaison was the first time I've forgotten a condom since I was a horny, fumbling seventeen-year-old, would you have believed me?"

"Probably not," she admitted.

"Which is why there has to be a tiny niggling of doubt in your mind," he said. "Barely a seed right now, but if you don't hold those results in your hand, that seed will grow…and grow."

She glared at him, because *dammit*, he was right. "What time did you want to eat?"

His smile was smug. "Seven o'clock. Valentino's."

She shook her head. "Seven o'clock works, but I'll cook."

"I'd be flattered by your offer to cook for me if I didn't suspect your true motivation is that being seen in public with me might damage your reputation."

"I suspect you're just as worried about your own, considering that I'm not your usual type."

"And what is my usual type?" he asked curiously.

"Ready, willing and able."

"You've got me there," he acknowledged. "But then it's not really true to say you're not my type, because you were all of those things when we were in SC together."

She frowned. "SC?"

Despite the fact that they were alone in the room, he lowered his voice to a conspiratorial whisper. "I decided that should be our code for the supply closet. That way, if anyone overhears us talking, they'll think we stole away to South Carolina together rather than a six-by-eight utility room."

"No worries," she told him. "We're not going to be talking about it. Not after tonight."

"Seven o'clock at your place?" he prompted.

She nodded and gave him her address.

"You're not worried that being alone with me will tempt you to jump my bones again?"

"I didn't 'jump your bones' the first time," she denied hotly.

"You made the first move."

"It was a kiss. Simple, casual, friendly."

"It was a spark," he countered. "And considering how skillfully you've dodged me for more than three years because of the red-hot attraction between us, you had to know that one little spark would ignite a firestorm."

Thankfully, he didn't stick around for a response, because she didn't know what to say to that. He was right—for more than three years, she had dodged him and the uncomfortable feelings he stirred inside of her. And as soon as she got through this dinner tonight, she would go back to dodging him again.

It was the only way to ensure that the red-hot attraction didn't lead to her getting burned.

Justin immediately recognized the address that Avery had given him because it was on the opposite side of Memorial Park from his own place. He knew their dinner wasn't technically a date, but he picked up flowers for her, anyway, and had the bouquet in hand when he buzzed her apartment at precisely seven o'clock—just as she rushed in through the front door.

"I'm sorry," she said. "I got caught up at the clinic so I'm running a little bit behind schedule."

"That's okay," he said.

She fumbled with her keys. "Why don't you come back

in half an hour?" she suggested. "By that time, I should have everything well under way for dinner."

"Because I'm here now and I can help," he told her.

"I invited you to eat dinner not make dinner," she pointed out, clearly unhappy that he wasn't going away and letting her control the timetable.

"I don't mind." He followed her into the elevator, where she stabbed a finger at the button for the fifth floor.

It was a corner unit of the U-shaped building, with a view of the tennis courts and pool. The interior was exquisitely—and he suspected professionally—decorated, with comfortable furniture in neutral colors, framed generic prints on the walls and a bookcase filled with medical texts. They were no personal touches in the room. No magazines or candles or decorative vases or bowls.

She went directly into the kitchen and, when he followed, he saw that the galley-style cooking area was equally pristine—the cupboards were white with simple steel handles. The white quartz countertops were bare of clutter except for a single-serve coffeemaker. The deep stainless steel sink was literally spotless, without even a spoon or a cloth in sight.

"Can I get you something to drink?" she asked.

"What are you having?"

"Water." She opened a cupboard to take out a glass and filled it with ice then water from the dispenser in the door of the refrigerator.

"That works for me," he said.

She turned to hand him the first glass—and nearly dumped the contents all over him when she discovered that he was directly behind her.

Thankfully, he caught it before it tipped too far. "Relax, Avery."

She managed a strangled laugh as she filled a second for herself, drinking down half of it before setting it aside.

"We can go out if you're not comfortable with me being here."

"It's not you—or not specifically you," she amended. "It's just that I'm not used to other people being in my space."

"Apparently," he noted, offering her the bouquet.

"Oh." She looked at the bright blooms as if she wasn't quite sure what to do with them.

"They probably want some water, too," he told her.

"Of course," she agreed, moving to the cupboard above the fridge to pull down a clear glass vase.

She seemed more comfortable when she was doing something, and she kept her attention focused resolutely on the task while she filled the container with water, trimmed the stems of the flowers, then arranged them in the vase.

"These are really beautiful," she said. "Thank you."

"You're welcome."

She carried the vase to the dining room and set it in the middle of the table. When she returned to the kitchen, she pulled a plastic container—neatly labeled and dated—out of the fridge, then dumped the contents into a glass bowl. He glanced over her shoulder at the thick red sauce with chunks of sausage and peppers, onions, mushrooms and tomatoes.

"That looks really good," he said.

"I don't always feel like cooking when I get home from work, so a couple of times a month I go on a cooking binge where I make all kinds of things that I can throw into containers in the freezer for quick meals later on."

"What do you make besides pasta sauce?" he asked.

She bent to retrieve a large pot from the cupboard beside the stove, then filled it from the tap and set it on the back burner. "Enchiladas, jambalaya, chicken and broccoli—"

He must have instinctively cringed at that, because she

laughed, the unexpected outburst of humor surprising both of them and easing some of the tension.

"You don't like broccoli?" she guessed.

"Much to my mother's everlasting chagrin," he admitted.

"That's too bad, because my chicken and broccoli casserole is delicious."

"Well, it's been my experience that the right company makes any meal taste better, so it's possible I could change my mind if you wanted to make it for me sometime."

She smiled at that. "Let's see if we get through this meal before making any other plans."

He sipped his water as she went back to the fridge and retrieved various items for a salad. She washed the head of lettuce under the tap, then spread the leaves out on a towel to dry. It was apparent that she had a system and she lined up her ingredients and utensils on the counter as if they were surgical instruments.

"I know how to chop and dice," he told her.

She glanced up. "What?"

"I'm offering to help make the salad."

"Oh. Thanks, but it's not really a two-person job."

And he could tell that the idea of letting someone else help—and mess with her system—made her twitchy.

"You're right," he agreed. "So why don't you let me handle it while you go do whatever you usually do when you get home from work and don't have someone waiting in your lobby?"

She hesitated a minute before admitting, "I was hoping for a quick shower."

"So go take a shower," he suggested.

"I will," she decided. "After I get this finished—"

He took her by the shoulders and turned her away from the counter. "Go take your shower—I'll take care of this."

She still looked skeptical. "Are you sure you don't mind?"

"Of course, I don't mind. But if you'd rather I forget about the lettuce and come wash your back—"

"I can wash my back," she interjected. "You handle the salad."

As he tore up the leaves, he tried not to think about Avery down the hall in the bathroom, stripping out of her clothes. As he chopped up celery and peppers, he ordered himself not to envision the spray from the shower pouring over her sexy, naked body. As he sliced cucumber and tomato, he didn't let himself imagine any soapy lather sliding over her breasts, her hips, her thighs.

But damn, all the not thinking, envisioning and imagining made him hot and achy. He shoved the finished salad back into the refrigerator and put the cutting board and utensils in the dishwasher. He could still hear the water running in the bathroom, and the mental images he refused to allow continued to tease at his mind.

Desperate for a distraction from his prurient fantasies, he decided to give himself a quick tour of her apartment. There was the spacious and stark living room, which he'd glimpsed upon entry into her apartment, then the kitchen and the dining room that was connected to the kitchen. The first door in the hall was a second bathroom. Like the kitchen, white was the color scheme in here, dominating the floor tile, the fixtures, even the towels and the liquid soap in the dispenser on the pedestal sink.

Beside the bathroom was a spare bedroom that she'd set up as a home office. Two walls were covered in bookshelves made of pale wood and neatly filled with yet more medical texts and journals. Her desk, also in pale wood, was just as ruthlessly organized—with pens, pencils and highlighters neatly lined up in distinctly separate containers.

The Twilight Zone theme started to play quietly in his head. There were no real personal touches anywhere. No indication of her interests or hobbies or insights into her personality, and if he didn't know better, he'd think her career was the sum total of who she was.

But he did know better. He'd kissed her and touched her, and she'd responded with a passion that had taken his breath away. She'd wrapped herself around him as he'd thrust into her body, shuddering and sighing and completely coming undone. Yeah, there was a lot more to Avery than the impersonal and sterile environment of her home indicated.

A spot of green caught the corner of his eye, and he smiled when he noted the stubby plant on the windowsill, recognizing it as some kind of cactus. Even her plant carried the same hands-off vibe that she did. Except that beneath her prickly exterior, she was warm and soft and shockingly uninhibited.

The challenge, of course, was getting past that exterior, and Justin suspected that scaling her walls once would only make a subsequent breach that much more difficult. He also realized he didn't want to breach her defenses—he wanted to tear them down completely.

He turned away from the cactus in the window to return to the kitchen. That was when he saw it. Another bookcase tucked into an alcove beside the door. He moved in for a closer inspection. The books here were mostly classical literature and popular fiction, with some surprisingly racy titles in the mix, all of them arranged alphabetically by author.

On top of the bookshelf was a framed photograph—the only one he'd seen in the whole apartment—of a little boy and a little girl. The picture had been snapped from behind as the two children walked, hand in hand, away from whoever was in possession of the camera and toward the iconic castle at Disney World. He instinctively knew the children were Avery and her brother, Ryder, even before he looked closely enough to see their names embroidered on the matching Mickey Mouse ears they wore.

It was a snapshot of her childhood, a brief glimpse of a happy moment somehow made more poignant by the realization that she couldn't have been more than eight years old in the photo and there were no other, later pictures to be found anywhere else in her apartment—or at least in any of the rooms he'd visited so far.

"What are you doing in here?" Avery demanded.

He glanced over, his heart doing a slow roll inside his chest when he saw her standing in the doorway, looking so naturally beautiful and sexy. Her face was scrubbed free of makeup, her hair had been released from its habitual ponytail and skimmed her shoulders. She'd dressed in a pair of black yoga pants and a long, fuzzy V-neck sweater in a pretty shade of blue that almost exactly matched her eyes. Her feet were bare, her toenails painted a bold crimson color that seemed out of character for her but which he knew was not.

"I was looking for you," he finally answered her question.

She arched a brow. "You didn't trust I'd find my way back to the kitchen?"

"No, I meant I was looking for a glimpse of you somewhere—anywhere—in this sterile apartment."

She didn't blink at his criticism. Nor had he expected her to. It wouldn't be nearly as much fun to ruffle her feathers if they ruffled easily.

"Remind me not to give you the name of my decorator," she responded lightly.

"I didn't think the white was your choice."

"Did you find what you were looking for?" she asked, in a deliberate change of topic.

"I think I did." He held up the photo.

She took the frame from his hand and carefully set it back into place on the bookshelf. "Dinner will be ready in—" she glanced at the watch on her wrist "—six and a half minutes."

He smiled. "Precisely six and a half? Not six or seven but six and a half?"

"The pasta takes twelve minutes to cook and I dropped it into the pot approximately five and a half minutes ago."

"What would happen if you forgot to put the timer on and cooked it for—" he gasped dramatically "—thirteen minutes?"

"Then we'd have to eat overcooked spaghetti," she said matter-of-factly, but she frowned at the prospect.

He shook his head. "Where did you go to medical school?"

She seemed startled by the abrupt change of topic but, after a brief hesitation, she responded, "Harvard."

"Figures."

"I actually wanted to go to Stanford, but my parents thought Harvard was more prestigious."

"I bet you graduated summa cum laude, too, didn't you?"

"So? I worked hard and studied hard."

"I'm sure you did," he agreed. "And I have no doubt you're a better doctor because of it. But sometimes, instead of blasting a tunnel through a mountain, you should climb to the top and enjoy the view."

"If you have a point, I'm not seeing it," she told him.

"My point is that you're obviously dedicated, focused and driven, and those are great attributes in the practice of medicine. But when they carry over into your personal life, it suggests that something happened that compels you to rigidly and ruthlessly control every aspect of your life."

"You're reading an awful lot into the fact that I use a kitchen timer when I cook my pasta."

"It's not just the pasta," he told her. "You have your high-lighters aligned in the spectrum of the rainbow."

"I didn't realize being organized was a character flaw."

"I'm the same way when it comes to every examination and procedure I perform in the ER," he admitted. "But when I walk out of the hospital at the end of my shift, I let that go and relax."

"Good for you."

"You should let go a little, too," he suggested. "You're wound up like a torsion spring and one of these days, all of the energy trapped inside of you is going to let loose. Or maybe that *is* what happened in the supply closet."

"That's a better explanation than anything I could come up with," she acknowledged. "And maybe, after more than two years, it was time to let loose a little."

His brows lifted. "Are you telling me that it was more than two *years* since you'd had sex?"

"I'm sure it's not some kind of celibacy record."

"Sorry, it's just that—wow. Two years." He shook his head. "I can't imagine."

She rolled her eyes. "We both know you can't imagine—that's why I wanted the test."

Chapter Five

"Right. The test."

For a few minutes, Justin had forgotten the reason he was here—the only reason Avery was making dinner for him.

As if on cue, a buzzer sounded from the kitchen.

"That's the pasta," she said, automatically turning away.

He caught her hand, halting her before she reached the door. She glanced over her shoulder, a quizzical expression on her face.

"I just wanted to say thanks—for offering to cook for me tonight."

"You're welcome," she said cautiously.

"I know that you don't really approve of me—"

"And I know you aren't really concerned about my approval."

He lifted a shoulder. "But you should know that only about half of the rumors that circulate around the hospital are true."

"I'll keep that in mind," she said.

"And while I can't control what other people say, I don't kiss and tell. Ever."

"I know," she admitted.

The timer in the kitchen buzzed again.

"I really need to get that pasta off the stove."

But he still didn't release her hand and there was a mischievous glint in his eyes that made her uneasy.

"The noodles are going to be overcooked," she said again, and that was when she realized what he was doing. "You're stalling me on purpose."

"Why would I do that?" he asked innocently.

"To wind up my torsion spring."

"People don't actually have torsion springs—I only said you were *like* a torsion spring."

"If you don't let me get back to the kitchen right now, I'm going to let loose all of my tension in your direction."

He grinned. "Promises, promises."

But this time when she turned away, he let her go.

She had a colander in the sink and a distinctly unhappy look on her face when he returned to the kitchen. She dumped the noodles into the bowl and carried them to the table she must have set when she got out of the shower.

"If dinner is ruined, it's your fault," she told him.

"Dinner is not ruined," he promised, retrieving the salad from the fridge.

But she still looked skeptical as she scooped penne out of the serving bowl and into her pasta bowl. She ladled sauce on the top and waited until he had done the same before she picked up her fork.

"Did your mother teach you how to cook?" he asked, after he'd sampled his first mouthful.

She shook her head. "My mother is a senior research supervisor at the Centers for Disease Control in Atlanta—she can isolate a pathogen but I doubt she knows how to pound or purée."

"So who taught you how to cook?"

"I took a few recreational cooking classes at a small culinary institute in Boston while I was doing my residency."

"Did you graduate with top honors from there, too?"

She shook her head. "It wasn't for grades, it was for fun."

"For fun?" he asked skeptically.

Her lips curved, just a little. "It was more fun than starving."

"Well, your pasta gets top marks from me," he told her.

"The sauce was good," she allowed. "The noodles were overcooked."

"Maybe by about thirty seconds," he acknowledged, smiling at her.

She smiled back, a wordless acceptance of the truce he'd offered. "Okay, maybe I could learn to relax a little bit."

"I'd be happy to teach you."

She shook her head. "I don't want to be *that* relaxed."

He chuckled, unoffended.

"I didn't make anything for dessert, but I do have ice cream," she told him.

"I don't think I have room for dessert—even ice cream," he told her.

"It's cookies 'n' cream," she said, in a tone that suggested no one could refuse her favorite flavor.

But he shook his head. "No, thanks."

When she started to stack the dishes, he pulled the lab report out of his pocket and slid it across the table to her.

Avery's heart pounded as she unfolded the page.

Her eyes skimmed the document quickly the first time, then again, more slowly. She'd been right. Just as she'd suspected, his results were all clear.

She exhaled a grateful sigh. There was nothing to worry about. But she'd needed to be sure—just in case there were other repercussions from that night.

"That's it, then," she said, almost giddy with relief as she pushed away from the table to help clear it. "There's no need for either of us to ever again mention what happened on New Year's Eve."

He leaned back against the counter, holding her gaze for a long moment before he finally asked, "Are you sure about that?"

She hugged the salad dressing bottles she carried closer to her chest and eyed him warily.

"There are other potential consequences of unprotected sex," he reminded her.

She nibbled on her lower lip, as if she didn't know where he was going with the conversation. Because she hadn't expected him to go there, she hadn't expected the possibility to cross his mind. And maybe it hadn't. "What do you mean?"

He continued to hold her gaze, his own unwavering. "I mean a baby," he told her. "Is it possible you could be pregnant?"

She shook her head as she turned away from him to put the dressings back in the fridge. "I don't think so."

"That's not very reassuring."

She couldn't see him, but she could hear the scowl in his voice. "Well, that's the best I can do right now," she admitted, shifting around some items in the door of the refrigerator to avoid facing him.

"You're not on the pill or the patch?" he pressed.

"No."

"You didn't take the morning-after pill?"

She shook her head.

He nudged her away from the fridge and firmly closed the door. "Why not?"

"I—I didn't think about it."

His hands settled on the counter behind him, his fingers curled over the edge. "You're a doctor, Avery. You know how babies are made—and you know there are steps that can be taken to prevent a baby from being made, even after the fact."

She felt her cheeks burn, but she nodded. "You're right. And I did get a package of morning-after pills from the clinic—the morning after."

"So why didn't you take them?"

"Because when I stopped at the hospital after I left the clinic, to check on Callie's sister and her baby, something inside of me...yearned."

She'd hoped for some kind of understanding, but the darkness of his scowl warned her otherwise.

"I know it sounds stupid," she continued to explain, "but that's how I felt. Then I got home and I sat at the table with the package in front of me, and I stared at it for a really long time. Because the possibility of an unplanned pregnancy completely freaked me out, but the possibility of a baby...somehow the possibility of a baby didn't freak me out at all."

She looked at him, silently begging for his forgiveness—or at least acceptance. "I mean, I'm not a teenager, and I do want to have a baby someday, so I decided that if I did get pregnant, having a baby might not be the worst thing that could happen to me at this point in my life."

"Not the worst thing that could happen to *you*," he echoed, pinning her with his hard and unyielding gaze. "Did you give any consideration to what it might mean to *me*? Did you think, *for even one minute*, about how a baby would affect *my* life?"

"No." She whispered the admission, ashamed that it was true. She hadn't thought about him at all. She hadn't thought about anything but how the possibility—minuscule as it might be—of having a baby filled her heart and soul with joy. "All I could think about, all that mattered, was that I might finally have the baby I've always wanted."

"You were *trying* to get pregnant?"

"No! I didn't plan any of what happened between us that night," she promised him. "But when I realized it was possible that we might have conceived a child, I just didn't do anything to stop it."

"A decision I'm still struggling to understand," he told her.

She nodded, acknowledging that she owed him a more thorough explanation of her actions. "When I graduated from medical school, I had a fiancé and a five-year plan."

His brows lifted at that, but he remained silent, allowing her to continue.

"The plan included a wedding and, a few years after that, a baby. Then my fiancé decided to go ahead with that plan with someone else, and I moved on with my life without him."

"And moved to Charisma," he guessed.

She nodded again. "I've helped a lot of women deliver a lot of babies, and I always believed that someday it would be my turn. But I'm thirty-two years old and maybe my biological clock isn't actually ticking just yet, but that someday doesn't seem to be getting any closer."

"You still had no right to make a decision that could affect both of our futures without talking to me," he told her.

"I know," she admitted. "But I promise you, if it turns out that I am pregnant, I will take full and complete responsibility for the baby."

"You don't want anything from me?" he challenged. "Not child support? Not even my name on the birth certificate?"

She shook her head, eager to give him the reassurance he seemed to be seeking. "Nothing," she confirmed. "No one will even need to know that you're the baby's father."

"Which only proves you don't know me nearly as well as you think you do."

"What are you saying?"

"I'm saying that if all you wanted was a sperm donor, you should have gone to a clinic."

"Hey, I didn't plan for this, either," she reminded him hotly. "I didn't seduce you or sabotage birth control. We both acted impulsively and *if* it turns out that I am pregnant—and that's still a pretty big *if* at this point—it will be the culmination of various factors that neither of us could have predicted."

"When will you know?"

Her cheeks burned. Somehow, talking about her monthly cycle with him seemed even more intimate than what they'd done in the supply closet. "Sometime in the next seven to ten days."

"Okay," he said. "So between now and then, we're going to spend as much time together as possible."

She frowned. "I don't think that's necessary."

"It's absolutely necessary," he told her. "Partly so that the people around us—friends, family, coworkers—start to see us as a couple. But mostly, and much more importantly, if you are pregnant, we need to know one another a lot better in order to coparent our child."

She stared at him, horrified. "Coparent?"

"I might not have had any say in the choices you've made up to this point, honey, but I promise you, I'll be involved in any decision making that takes place going forward."

He kept his eyes on hers, implacable and unyielding. "If you are pregnant—you don't just get a baby. You get me, too."

His words had sounded more like a threat than a promise, but Avery decided not to worry too much about what Justin had said in the heat of the moment. She understood that he was angry—and that he had reason to be. They'd both forgotten about birth control on New Year's Eve, but she'd unilaterally decided to accept the possible risk of pregnancy.

And maybe it was foolish to want a child under the current circumstances, but she couldn't deny that she did. Even if this wasn't the way she'd envisioned it might someday happen, she refused to have any regrets. She had no illusions that being a single mother would be easy, but she was fortunate to have a job she enjoyed along with a steady income that would pay her bills. She had a lot of patients who lived under much more difficult circumstances on a daily basis.

She'd seen Justin frequently in the week that had passed since the night they'd had dinner at her apartment—and he'd made a point of being seen with her as often as possible—but she'd managed to keep their conversations mostly short and impersonal.

The prospect of coparenting with him made her more than a little uneasy, but there was no point in worrying about that unless and until her pregnancy was confirmed. And even then, nine months was a lot of time. She was confident his determination to be involved would wane long before their baby was born. Maybe that was an unfair assumption to make considering how attentive and solicitous he'd been, but he had a notoriously short attention span when it came to his relationships with women.

She could have taken a test already. The presence of hCG, the hormone that indicated pregnancy, could be found in very low levels within seven days after conception. But she wasn't ready to confirm her pregnancy just yet. Because as soon as she knew for certain that she was going to have a baby, she'd feel obligated to tell Justin, and she wanted to hold the excited anticipation close to her own heart for a while before he trampled all over it.

Three more days.

The words echoed in her head as she waited for sleep to come.

She awoke a few hours later with a crampy feeling low in her belly. Uneasy, she got up to go to the bathroom. That was when she realized her instincts and intuition were wrong.

She wasn't pregnant, after all.

She crawled back under the covers of her empty bed, in her quiet apartment, and cried softly.

* * *

When Justin finally got a break and went in search of a much-needed caffeine fix, he found Avery sitting alone in the cafeteria with a single-serving tub of cookies 'n' cream ice cream in front of her. He took his extralarge cup of coffee over to her table, wondering if the ice cream was evidence of some kind of pregnancy craving or just strange eating habits.

"Do you mind if I join you?"

She glanced up when he stopped by the chair across the table from her. "Of course not."

He lowered himself into the empty seat. "Breakfast?" he asked, nodding toward the ice cream container.

She dropped her spoon into the melting dessert and shook her head. "I was hoping to see you today."

He was surprised and pleased to think that she wanted to see him rather than avoid him, which was her usual modus operandi. "You were?"

"I figured you'd want to know as soon as possible that you're off the hook."

"Off the hook?" he echoed, the implication of her words taking a moment to sink into his brain. "Oh."

She nodded. "I got my period last night."

"Oh," he said again.

"We successfully dodged that bullet."

But her clichéd phrases and the forced cheerfulness warned him that her feelings weren't as simple or straightforward as she wanted him to believe. "How are you doing?" he asked.

"I'm relieved, of course."

"You are?"

She shrugged. "Sure, I'm a little disappointed, too," she admitted. "But considering the circumstances, it's probably for the best."

"You're probably right," he agreed.

He was certainly relieved to have "dodged the bullet," and grateful that their impulsive actions wouldn't have long-term consequences. He liked his life just the way it was and hadn't been thrilled to think of the adjustments he would need to make to accommodate a child. Of course he would have, if it had turned out that she was pregnant, but he was undeniably relieved that wouldn't be necessary just yet.

"Now our lives can go back to normal," she said, her words echoing his own thoughts.

"By normal, you mean that you intend to go back to ignoring me as much as possible," he guessed.

"I mean that you can go back to dating a different woman every weekend," she countered lightly.

He started to protest her erroneous assumption of his habits, but what was the point? She'd made up her mind about him a long time ago and obviously nothing he'd said or done in the past couple of weeks had changed her opinion.

Instead, he nodded his agreement. "There is that."

"Who was that?"

Justin glanced up as Nora slid into the seat Avery had recently vacated. "What are you doing here?"

"Thanks to the introductions you made, I've got an interview with Jovan Crncevic," she explained, naming the supervisor of the hospital's physiotherapy department. "Of course, I came way too early so I decided to stop in here and grab a cup of coffee and I saw you having a deep tête-à-tête with…your girlfriend?"

He shook his head. "No."

"Ex-girlfriend?"

"No," he said again, lifting his own cup to his lips to finish his coffee.

"Really?" she challenged. "Because I'm pretty sure that was the same woman who stopped by your condo when I was there, and there were some serious vibes between the two of you just now."

"We work together," he explained.

Nora laughed. "It was definitely *not* a work vibe."

He scowled. "How long were you watching?"

"Long enough to know it was *not* a work vibe," she assured him.

"We had a thing," he admitted.

"A thing?"

"A shared moment of insanity."

"Ah." She nodded. "A thing." She sipped her coffee. "You still hung up on her?"

"No."

"I think I understand why it didn't work out—she's probably intimidated by your conversational prowess."

"You're a real smart-ass, you know that?"

"I always figured it was better than being a dumb ass."

His lips twitched a little in response to that, but all he said was, "Shouldn't you be preparing for your interview?"

She shook her head. "Even thinking about it makes me nervous—your love life is a great distraction."

"Glad to be of service."

"Do you want my advice?"

"No," he said bluntly.

She frowned. "Just because I'm young doesn't mean I don't have any wisdom to offer. I've got some experience in matters of the heart."

"Good for you."

"I'm only telling you because I recognize the symptoms of a serious infatuation."

"Dr. Wallace is not infatuated with me," he assured her.

Nora laughed. "I wasn't talking about Dr. Wallace."

Chapter Six

Life did go back to normal—eventually.

Although Avery had lived with the possibility of a baby for only a couple of weeks, she'd wanted to be pregnant so much that she'd let her imagination run with it, and it took a few days to shake off her melancholy.

The depth of her disappointment forced her to reevaluate her life and her choices. It was time, she decided, to stop being passive and go after what she wanted. Which meant that she needed to start dating again—and actually make an effort to meet the man who might want to father her future children.

Maybe she'd even ask Amy to set her up again—as soon as she shook the exhaustion that had recently taken hold of her body and which she suspected was a result of some lingering disappointment.

"Are you up for grabbing a drink?" Amy asked, when the last patient of the day had finally exited the clinic.

"I thought you'd be anxious to get home to Henry," Avery said, referring to her friend's fifteen-month-old son.

"He's spending the night with Ben's parents."

"So that you and your hubby can have a romantic evening together?" she guessed.

"That was the original plan," her friend admitted. "Until

his brother snagged a couple of tickets to a Canes game and asked Ben to go with him."

"In that case, a drink sounds good."

"And nachos?" Amy prompted hopefully.

She laughed. "Marg & Rita's?"

"I'll meet you there."

Avery left her white coat on the hook behind the door in her office, untied the fastener around her ponytail, brushed out her hair and added some lip gloss. A quick glance in the bathroom mirror confirmed that she looked better—but she still felt like crap.

She arrived at the restaurant first and didn't wait for her friend. It was Friday night, which meant that if there was a table available, it wouldn't be for long. Shortly after she was seated, the waiter brought two menus. Knowing her friend's preferences, she ordered a Top Shelf margarita for Amy and a virgin classic for herself along with a platter of deluxe nachos.

"Sorry I'm late," Amy said, sliding into the empty seat across the table. "Ben called as I was on my way out to remind me to watch the game so I can see him on TV."

"Maybe we should have gone to the Bar Down," Avery said. "No doubt the game will be on one of the screens there."

Her friend shook her head, then smiled at the waiter who set her frosty drink in front of her. "I have less than zero interest in hockey and I'll see Ben when he gets home." Then she picked up her drink and tapped the rim of her glass against Avery's. "I didn't think this week was ever going to end."

"It's not over for me yet," she said. "I've got morning rounds at the hospital tomorrow."

Her friend made a face. "I'm planning to sleep in late and then have leisurely morning sex with the man of my dreams."

"I'd be happy enough just to sleep in," Avery told her. "I've been exhausted and nauseated for the past several days."

"Maybe tequila isn't the best medicine for that," her friend said worriedly.

"I didn't think so, either," she agreed. "That's why mine is a virgin."

The waiter delivered their heaping platter of nachos and they both dug in.

"Exhausted and nauseated you said?" Amy queried a short while later.

"Trying not to think about that right now," Avery told her.

"Well, I was just thinking that's how I felt when I was pregnant with Henry."

"I'm not pregnant," Avery said quickly.

"I wasn't suggesting that you were," Amy agreed. "Unless you somehow managed to orchestrate an immaculate conception."

When she didn't respond to her friend's teasing comment, Amy's gaze narrowed. "Or is there something you're not telling me?"

"There are a lot of things I don't tell you," she said.

"Such as?" Amy prompted, brushing a jalapeño off her nacho chip.

Avery glanced around to ensure there was no one they knew within hearing range, but still dropped her voice to a near whisper before confiding, "Such as the fact that I had sex with Justin Garrett."

Amy choked on her margarita.

"When did this happen?" she asked, when she finally managed to stop coughing.

"New Year's Eve—actually, in the early hours of the morning on New Year's Day."

"Oh. My. God."

Avery nodded.

"So…" A smile teased at the corners of her friend's mouth. "How was he?"

She took her time selecting another chip. "A colossal disappointment."

Amy's eyes widened. "Really?"

"No. Not really." She sighed. "In fact, it was the single most incredible sexual experience of my life, which probably tells you more than you ever wanted to know about my sexual experience."

"I always wondered if his reputation was exaggerated," her friend confessed.

"It's not," she admitted unhappily. "And now I belong to the not-so-exclusive club that includes almost every other woman who works at the hospital."

Her friend smiled. "Sweetie, if Dr. Romeo slept with even half the women who claim to have slept with him, he'd hardly have time to get out of bed.

"I've known Justin a long time," Amy continued. "There's a lot more to him than most people realize—and he's not nearly as indiscriminate as his reputation would imply."

"So you don't believe he'd get naked with someone in a supply closet in the middle of his shift at the hospital?"

"No way," her friend said. Then her eyes went wide. "Are you telling me that's what happened?"

She nodded.

"Oh. My. God," Amy said again. "You and Justin. In a supply closet. Wow."

"It was wow," she agreed.

"So…are you guys together now?" her friend asked hopefully.

She shook her head. "No."

"Why not?"

"Because he's Dr. Romeo and I don't want to get involved with a man described in either of those terms."

Amy sighed. "Your parents really did a number on you, didn't they?"

"They taught me an important life lesson," she countered. "Which is that two career-focused medical professionals cannot make a marriage work and definitely should not be parents."

"I don't believe that."

"Says the woman married to a newspaper editor."

"I was in love with Ben long before he was a newspaper editor or I was a doctor," Amy pointed out.

"Since I didn't know you in high school, I'll have to take your word for it."

"Now—getting back to the exhausted and nauseated part of our conversation, I have to ask…were you careful?"

She felt her cheeks burn. "You'd think, being a doctor, I wouldn't be anything else."

Amy nodded, accurately interpreting her response as an acknowledgment that she hadn't been. "Then is it possible that you're pregnant?"

Avery shook her head. "I got my period last week."

"Did you take a pregnancy test?" her friend pressed.

"I was going to," she admitted. "And then, there didn't seem to be any point."

"You know as well as I do that it's not unusual for a woman to experience some bleeding in the early months of a pregnancy."

"It was more than that."

"Maybe it was," Amy acknowledged. "But I think you'll feel better if you take a test."

Avery nodded, though she didn't really believe it was true.

Taking a test and confirming that she wasn't pregnant wasn't going to make her feel any better. It would just be one more reminder of how completely her life had gone off track.

* * *

Justin had enough experience with women to know when one was attracted to him, and it frustrated him beyond belief that Avery was continuing to deny the attraction. But that was "back to normal" as far as their relationship was concerned.

He'd wanted her when he first met her and he wanted her now, but he didn't chase women. Not even a woman who stirred his blood and haunted his dreams.

He thought they'd made some real progress over the past couple of weeks. During dinner at her house, they'd talked and laughed and connected on a whole other level. Maybe it was his own fault—maybe he hadn't handled the possibility of a baby very well, but he'd felt angry and betrayed and helpless.

Yeah, there had been two of them in that supply closet, and yeah, the thought of protection had never crossed his mind because he'd been thinking about Avery and being inside Avery and that was all that had mattered. And then, to learn that she'd consciously decided not to take the morning-after pill—a decision that had potential consequences for both of them—without even talking to him, had made him furious.

He didn't have an issue with her choice, just with her complete and total disregard of his thoughts and feelings. She'd deliberately cut him out of the process—as if he wouldn't care. As if he'd walk away from his own child. *That* was what had pissed him off.

But now the possibility and the panic were past. Avery wasn't pregnant. There was no baby and no future for them together. And eight days after their conversation in the cafeteria, he decided it was time to stop obsessing about the woman who didn't want him and enjoy the company of one who did.

He decided to take Heather up on her offer of dinner followed by drinks at a popular club. While they were out, she flirted with him outrageously and rubbed up against him on the dance floor, and Justin found himself wondering why he wasn't tempted. She was offering him a good time without any strings, and he could really use the distraction of a simple fling to help him forget about the impossible woman who was stuck in his mind.

But when he'd walked Heather to her door, she'd put her arms around him and pressed her mouth to his, and he'd felt disgusted. Not with the young nurse but with himself, that he'd considered—for even half a minute—using her to help him forget about Avery. That was one thing he'd never done. He enjoyed women—their company and companionship—but he didn't use them.

So he'd quickly extricated himself from Heather's embrace, thanked her for an enjoyable evening and walked away.

The next day, wanting to ensure there was no repetition of the same scene, he decided to seek out some male camaraderie instead. With his younger brother in Florida and his older brother dealing with his own issues, he headed over to the headquarters of Garrett Furniture to see if anyone was around. He found Nathan in the CFO's office.

"Where's Allison?" he asked, having noted that the desk outside his cousin's office—usually occupied by Nate's wife, who was also his administrative assistant—was vacant.

"Dylan had a dentist appointment so she took off early."

"You dock her pay for the missed time?"

"Nah—she makes it up with sexual favors."

Justin winced. "I don't need to know things like that."

Nathan laughed. "Maybe you do. Maybe you need to realize that being with one woman—the right woman—night after night is far more satisfying than being with a different woman every night."

"I'm not with a different woman every night," he denied.

"That's true—some nights you're working."

"And to think that I came to you for advice."

Nathan leaned back in his chair and crossed his feet on the edge of his desk. "You did? This oughta be interesting."

"I had a date last night," Justin admitted.

"See point above," his cousin noted drily.

"Her name's Heather," he continued, ignoring Nate's sarcasm. "She's a nurse. Young, attractive and apparently willing to get naked with me."

"So far I'm not seeing why you need my advice."

"Because at the end of the evening, I said goodbye at her door and walked away."

His cousin's brows lifted. "Now that *is* a surprise."

"Do you think there's something wrong with me?"

To his credit, Nate didn't offer a flippant reply but took a minute to consider the question. "I think," he eventually said, "that you're finally growing up and realizing that you want something more substantial than a short-term fling, which you're never going to find if you keep dating women who worship the ground you walk on."

"Avery would more likely spit on the ground I walk on," he admitted glumly.

"Avery?" Nate prompted, sounding intrigued.

"Avery Wallace." Justin shook his head. "I need to get her out of my mind."

"This conversation just got a lot more interesting."

"Except that Avery's made it clear she's *not* interested."

"And you, of course, look at that as a challenge."

"Maybe. Partly," he acknowledged. "But it's more than that."

"Is it?"

"I think I could really fall for her—and she won't even go out with me."

Nate chuckled. "I'm sorry," he said. "I know this isn't funny to you. But after having seen so many women fall at your feet for so many years, it's refreshing to learn that there are still some females who are immune to your considerable charms."

"I'm glad you find this amusing," Justin grumbled.

"I can laugh now, because I've been in your shoes," his cousin admitted. "Allison had all kinds of reasons for not wanting to get involved with me—even before I was her boss."

"Really?"

"Really," Nate confirmed.

"What changed her mind?"

"I think it was the chicken soup."

"Huh?"

His cousin grinned. "Long story. Let's just say that some women need to be convinced that a man has staying power—that he'll stick around through good times and bad, in sickness and in health."

"And you managed to do all of that with chicken soup?" he asked skeptically.

"I think it was what the soup symbolized more than the bowl of broth and noodles itself," Nate told him.

"How am I supposed to show Avery that I want to stick around when she keeps pushing me away?"

"That's a dilemma," his cousin acknowledged. "And before you commit to any course of action, you need to decide if she's worth it."

Justin didn't need to think about it. "She's definitely worth it."

The Sixth Annual Storybook Ball—named to reflect both its fantasy theme and the fact that the proceeds benefitted the children's wing of Mercy Hospital—was held annually on the last Saturday in January. It was their biggest fund-raiser of the year and all doctors were invited and encouraged to attend, to mingle with patrons, talk to them about the work that was being done at the hospital and how past donations had been used to benefit their young patients, and explain why their support was needed now.

A handful of staff were always on hand to greet the guests as they arrived, and Avery had planned to be one of them this year—her support of the cause overrode her usual inclination to avoid formal events. Unfortunately, a complicated delivery put her behind schedule so that by the time she got home, showered and dressed for the event, she'd missed dinner. In fact, she was just sliding into her assigned seat as dessert was being eaten and coffee was being served.

No one asked any questions about her tardiness—they all understood that a career in medicine often caused scheduling conflicts with other events. Dr. Terrence, seated beside her, nudged his untouched strawberry shortcake toward her, offering a second dessert to compensate for the other four courses she'd missed. She gave him a grateful smile. The table of ten was rounded out by an accountant and her husband, a software designer and his wife, and a couple of prominent local business owners and their respective spouses.

As a result of her late arrival, it wasn't until after the coffee service was over that Avery realized Justin was in attendance. When she finally did see him, when his eyes skimmed over her even from the other side of the room, her body tingled as if he'd actually touched her.

The man was spectacular in scrubs. Dressed in a shirt and tie, he was mouthwatering. And in black tie, he was breathtaking. Literally. Because when he started across the room, his gaze locked on hers, she could not draw any air into her lungs.

"Dr. Wallace," he said, inclining his head in greeting.

"Dr. Garrett," she returned, grateful that her cool tone

gave no hint of the heat that flooded her system. "I didn't expect to see you tonight."

"I usually prefer to write a check in lieu of attending these kinds of events," he admitted.

"But not this year?"

He lifted a shoulder "I heard that you were going to be here."

"You didn't pay $1500 for a ticket because I was going to be here," she chided.

"You're right—I didn't," he admitted. "I convinced my cousin Nate—the CFO of Garrett Furniture—to pay $1500 for a table in support of a good cause and for the charitable tax receipt. But I only sat at that table because I wanted to see you."

"I should thank your cousin, on behalf of the Mercy Hospital Foundation, for his generous contribution toward the purchase of an EOS imaging machine for the orthopedics department."

He raised his eyebrows. "That's a pricey piece of equipment."

She nodded. "And it will provide clear and detailed images of children's entire limbs–the spine, arms or legs— with a single scan and a lot less radiation exposure."

"I know what it does," he told her.

She flushed. "Of course, you do."

"Are you nervous, Dr. Wallace?"

"A little," she admitted. "These gala events aren't really my thing."

"So it's the event that has you feeling…edgy?"

"What else could it be?"

He just smiled—the slow, sexy curve of his lips making her heart pound even harder.

"You've got those sparkly things in your hair again," he noted.

Again. He was referring, of course, to New Year's Eve.

And though he said nothing more explicit in reference to that night, she could tell by the heat in his eyes that he was remembering what had happened between them.

She hadn't forgotten, either. Not for one minute. But she wasn't prepared to go down that road again. Instead, she shifted her gaze away, scanning the crowd. "Is your cousin here?"

Justin nodded. "That's him on the dance floor—the one in the black tie."

She smiled at that because all of the guests were in black tie—but no other man that she'd seen wore it quite as well as the one standing beside her right now. "Could you be a little bit more specific?"

He moved closer. "His wife is the gorgeous brunette in the fire engine–red dress."

That description helped her narrow in on the couple. His cousin's wife *was* gorgeous, and she and her husband made a striking couple.

"My parents were here earlier," he told her. "But they left right after dinner to attend a showing at the art gallery for a friend's daughter's boyfriend's sister—or something like that."

She smiled. "Well, I hope they enjoyed their meal."

"It was good, but the lobster ravioli was a little overcooked."

"I can't argue with that—I missed the pasta. And the spinach salad. And the beef tenderloin with mushroom risotto. I got caught up at the hospital and arrived late," she explained.

He frowned. "What did you eat?"

"Strawberry shortcake."

"If you're hungry, I can ask someone to heat you up a plate."

She was touched that he would think of it, and tempted to accept his offer. But she wasn't really here for the food.

She was supposed to work the crowd and squeeze every last dime that she could out of their fat wallets.

"Do you want the beef and risotto?" he asked, ready to invade the kitchen.

She laid a hand on his arm. "I'll probably stop for something on my way home, but for now, I'm fine."

He looked at her hand on his arm, then up into her eyes.

She felt it then—the hum that started beneath her palm and spread through her whole body. She snatched her hand away, but it was too late. Awareness crackled and sizzled between them.

He opened his mouth to speak, but before he could say anything, the couple he'd pointed out to her left the dance floor and came over to join them. He made introductions instead.

"So this is Avery," Nate said, sliding a meaningful look toward his cousin as he shook her hand. "Now I understand."

"Understand what?" she asked, glancing from Justin to his cousin and back again.

When Justin didn't respond, Nate decided that he would. "Now I understand the reason my cousin—"

Chapter Seven

"Wants to dance with you," Justin hastily interjected, grabbing for Avery's hand. "Come on—this is a great song."

"I don't want to dance right now," she told him. "I want to chat with Nathan and Allison."

"I'll dance with you, Dr. Romeo," Allison offered, sending a conspiratorial wink in Avery's direction.

Nathan chuckled as his wife dragged Justin away.

"Are you going to finish what you were saying now?"

"Of course not," he said. "That would break the guy code."

"Then why did you let him think you'd tell me?"

"Because it's so rare to see Justin squirm about anything, I couldn't resist needling him a little." He glanced at her. "That was doctor humor, in case you missed it."

"How could I miss an obvious jab like that?"

He grinned at her response. "In any event, all you need to know is that Justin mentioned your name."

"Is that significant?"

"Much more than you might think," he told her. "My cousin's problem—or one of them—is that everything has always come easily to him. He's smart, talented, good-looking and rich. And on top of all of that, he's a doctor. He saves lives on a daily basis, and he does it without breaking a sweat.

"The combination makes him pretty much irresistible to most females, and he has dated a lot of women, but none of them has warranted mention to his family or held his attention for very long."

"Your wife seems to be doing a pretty good job," she noted, watching Justin and Allison dance and laugh together.

"That's because my wife is the most amazing woman in the world." He grinned again. "Not that I'm biased at all."

"Of course not," she agreed.

His gaze shifted back to the dance floor, and she wondered how it would feel to have someone look at her the way Nate looked at Allison—as if she was the center of not just his whole world but the entire universe.

The Rolling Stones gave way to Whitesnake asking "Is This Love?" and several people left the dance floor, including Allison and Justin.

Nate shook his head. "Does this DJ own anything from the last decade?"

"Probably not," Avery said. "He was likely given a specific playlist to appeal to the demographic with the most money."

Allison sidled up to her husband. "Now it's *your* turn to dance with me."

"You know I hate eighties hair bands," he grumbled.

"But you love me," she reminded him.

"With my whole heart," he agreed, letting her lead him to the dance floor.

"Come on," Justin said to Avery. "It's time for you to get out there, too."

"Oh, um, I don't think I should," she hedged.

"Why not?"

"I'm supposed to mingle," she reminded him.

"One dance," he cajoled.

She wanted to refuse, because dancing with Justin—

even one dance—was a bad idea. But if she continued to protest, he would suspect the true reason for her reluctance: she was afraid of the feelings that churned inside her whenever she was near him.

Instead, she let him take her hand and lead her to the dance floor, her heart pounding every step of the way. And then she was in his arms, so close to him that she could feel the heat emanating from his body. So close that every nerve ending in her body actually ached with wanting to be closer.

She forced herself to concentrate on the music and follow his lead, but the muscles in her legs were trembling and her head was spinning—

"Breathe."

She tilted her head to look up at him. "What?"

"You're not breathing," he told her.

"Oh." She managed to drag air into her lungs, which alleviated some of the dizziness. But at the same time, she inhaled the clean masculine scent that was uniquely Justin. Now her head was spinning for a different reason.

Yep, agreeing to dance with him hadn't just been a bad idea, it had been a monumentally bad idea. Like the Taj Mahal, Great Wall and Giza pyramid of bad ideas. And the song was barely half over.

She wanted him. It was pointless to deny it. No other man had ever affected her the way he did, made her want the way he did. And being with him here, somehow so close and not nearly close enough, was wreaking havoc with her system.

But even more dangerous than the attraction between them was her growing realization that she'd misjudged Dr. Romeo. Yes, he was the undisputed playboy of Mercy Hospital, but there was a lot more to him than the title implied, and the more time she spent with him, the more she genuinely liked him.

"This was worth the price of the ticket," he said, the

words whispered close to her ear, making her shiver. "Just being able to hold you like this."

"Don't let Tilly hear you say that," she responded lightly. "The fund-raising chair might decide to add 'dances with the doctors' to the list of auction items for next year."

"It will be our secret," he promised her.

"And speaking of fund-raising, I really do need to talk to some people."

He nodded. "I know."

She stepped away from him as the song faded away.

"Can I see you tomorrow?" he asked.

The Taj Mahal, Great Wall and Giza pyramid loomed over her again. She shook her head. "I'm making no plans for tomorrow—it's my lazy day."

"We could be lazy together," he suggested.

"Why are you doing this, Justin?"

"Because I tried the 'back to normal' thing you suggested and realized it wasn't what I wanted. I want to be with you. I want a real relationship with you."

"You don't do real relationships," she reminded him.

He linked their fingers together. "I think we faked it pretty well—imagine what we could do if we actually tried."

But she shook her head. "I don't want to try."

"Why not?"

She sighed. "Didn't we have a similar discussion a couple of weeks ago and agree that I'm not your type?"

"Apparently we remember that conversation differently," he told her. "As well as what happened on New Year's Eve."

"I'm not going to sleep with you again, Justin. Although what happened between us a few weeks ago might suggest otherwise, I have too much self-respect to let myself become the latest name in a long list of your sexual conquests."

"There isn't a list," he told her. "And maybe I haven't

had a long-term relationship in a lot of years, because I hear enough 'Yes, Dr. Garrett' at the hospital, I don't want that in my personal life.

"I want to be with someone who has her own thoughts and opinions, and who is willing to argue when she disagrees with mine. I want to be with someone who challenges me to think and entices me to try different things, someone who makes me a better person. I think you could be that someone."

She shook her head. "I'm not that someone."

"How do you know?" he challenged.

"I like you," she admitted. "You're smart and funny and charming, and I admire your professional skills and abilities, but I have no interest in dating a doctor."

He looked at her as if she was speaking a foreign language. "Let me see if I've got this right—it's okay that you're a doctor...but you won't go out with someone who's a doctor?"

"It's not personal."

He laughed, but it was without humor. "I don't think it could get much more personal than that."

"There's Dr. Bristow," she said. "I promised to introduce the Langdons to him if I had a chance."

Justin just nodded.

Avery went after the chief of orthopedic surgery and steered him toward the couple that had been seated at her table for dinner.

When she looked around again, Justin was gone.

Avery put a smile on her face and made her way through the crowd, talking to as many guests as possible to ensure they understood how important the coveted equipment would be to the hospital. Many of them wrote checks to the foundation before they left, making her feel good about the success of the event.

Unfortunately, she didn't feel good about the way she'd left things with Justin. But there was no way she could continue to spend time with him without falling for him, and that was a road she refused to go down.

By the time she left the gala, she was exhausted and her stomach felt unsettled. Probably because the strawberry shortcake that had been her dinner had disappeared a long time ago. She stopped to grab a banana-nut muffin and a bottle of juice on her way home.

The food didn't make her feel any better and as soon as she opened her apartment door, she raced to the bathroom and threw up her late-night snack. After her stomach had finished heaving, she scrubbed her face with a cool cloth, brushed her teeth and fell into bed—and dreamed about Justin.

She spent all of Sunday morning in bed, nibbling on saltines and sipping ginger ale to appease her still-queasy stomach. By midafternoon, she was feeling a little better. She went for a walk to the market, bought some chicken and broccoli to make her favorite casserole—and thought about Justin.

Monday morning she was at Wellbrook early to meet with Amy before their patients started to arrive. She grabbed a cherry Danish from the box of pastries that their nurse habitually brought in and filled her favorite mug with coffee. When Amy came in, she filled a second mug and offered it to her friend.

"So tell me," she said, when they were both seated at the table. "How did the interview go?"

Amy grinned. "So much better even than I expected. Olivia is only a third-year resident, but I think she'll be a great addition to our staff. She has a wonderful demeanor— warm and reassuring—and she's not afraid to ask questions when she doesn't know what to do."

"When can she start?"

"Well, I want all of you to meet her before I officially offer her the job. But if you agree, I'd love to get her on the schedule for the middle of February."

"Sounds perfect," Avery agreed. "So why do you have that little furrow between your brows that you always get when you're worried about something?"

Her friend tore off a piece of doughnut. "It has nothing to do with Olivia."

"Okay," she said cautiously.

"It's about... Justin."

"Okay," she said again.

Amy swallowed another mouthful of coffee. "You know what I think about hospital gossip," she began.

"Just tell me what you heard," Avery suggested. Then she shook her head. "On second thought—don't. It doesn't matter."

"Normally I would agree," her friend said cautiously, "but I don't want you to hear it from anyone else."

She sighed. "Okay—hear what?"

"That he spent the weekend with Heather Delgado."

It took Avery a minute to match the name to a face. Heather had only started working at the hospital in the fall—probably not long after she'd graduated from nursing school—but she seemed competent enough. She was also a very attractive woman with dark curly hair and a bubbly personality.

"Oh." She'd have to be blind not to have seen the way Heather looked at Justin—the open admiration and blatant speculation that gleamed in the nurse's dark eyes. She'd watched her flirt boldly with the sexy doctor—and witnessed him flirting right back.

Of course, she hadn't thought anything of it at the time, because Justin flirted with everyone. But the idea of him *with* the young nurse bothered her more than she wanted to admit, as the Danish and coffee churning in her stomach attested.

"It might not be true," her friend said now.

"It doesn't matter," Avery said again.

Amy squeezed her hand. "I'm sorry."

"There's no reason to be sorry. I told you—it was just a one-time thing. He can see whoever he wants to see, sleep with whoever he wants."

"But...weren't you with him at the Storybook Ball on Saturday?"

"Where did you hear that?"

Amy shrugged. "Lucinda Singh told Gabbie Holtby who told Tess that you were dancing with him at the ball."

"It was one dance," she said. "Yes, we were both there, but we weren't together."

"But that proves he wasn't with Heather all weekend."

"No, it only proves that he wasn't with her for the few hours that he was at the ball," she pointed out.

Monica tapped on the door before poking her head into the small kitchenette/staff room. "You've got a five-month prenatal in room one, a physical in two, 'I'm not talking to anyone but the doctor' in three and suspected chicken pox in six."

Amy nodded. "Thanks for keeping that one far away from the expectant mom."

"That's why you pay me the big bucks," Monica joked.

"I guess we'd better get started," Avery said, pushing away from the table.

Amy caught her arm as she started to move past. "Give him a chance to explain."

"There's nothing to explain. We talked last week, agreed that we were lucky to have dodged a bullet and happy to go our separate ways."

"That might have been what you said," her friend acknowledged. "But how do you *feel*?"

"Right now—I'm incredibly grateful that I'm not pregnant with his child."

But she also knew that if she wasn't feeling better by the weekend, she would pick up a pregnancy test—just to be sure.

Justin didn't see Avery again until Wednesday.

He was still a little annoyed and frustrated with her prohibition against dating doctors, but he didn't think she had any reason to be mad at him. But when he passed her in the ER corridor, she immediately dropped her gaze to the chart in her hand, and when she realized that he was in line ahead of her at the sandwich counter, she moved to the salad bar instead.

He made sure he caught up with her as she was leaving the cafeteria and fell into step beside her.

"What did I do?" he asked.

She sent him a sideways glance, but her quick steps didn't slow. "I don't know what you're talking about."

"Well, I know we're not the best of friends, but I thought we'd progressed to the point where we could actually have a civil conversation."

"Isn't this civil?" she asked.

"Sure," he agreed. "Except that I might get frostbite if I move any closer to you."

She pushed open the doors to the ER department. "So don't move any closer."

"Come on, Avery. You're pissed about something—just tell me what it is."

"I'm not pissed," she denied. "And your new girlfriend's trying to get your attention."

He scowled. "What?"

She nodded her head in the direction of the nurses' station and, when he glanced in that direction, he saw that Heather was gesturing for him to come over to the desk.

"She's not my girlfriend," he denied, even as he held up a finger, asking Heather to give him a minute.

"Really? Because that's been the hot topic of conversation at the coffee station for the past few days."

Despite the deliberately low pitch of her voice, the increasingly heated nature of their discussion was starting to draw some curious looks. Not wanting to generate yet more gossip, he took Avery's arm and steered her down the hall and into the doctors' lounge.

"I don't care what the latest gossip is," he said, when the door had closed behind them. "She's *not* my girlfriend—new or otherwise."

"So you didn't go out with her Saturday night?" she challenged.

"I was with *you* Saturday night," he reminded her.

"Only until I told you I wouldn't sleep with you again—then you disappeared pretty quickly."

"I went home," he told her. "But thanks for that confirmation of your lousy opinion of me."

"So when were you with her?" she asked. "Friday?"

"No." He shook his head. "I did go out with her Wednesday night last week, but I *didn't* sleep with her."

"Whether you did or not is none of my business."

"You're right," he agreed. "It's not any of your business. You made it clear that you weren't interested in going out with me, so you have no right to get all bent out of shape when I go out with someone else."

"I'm not bent out of shape," she denied, though the flush in her cheeks suggested otherwise.

"You seem pretty bent to me."

"Well, I'm not," she said again.

"And I wasn't with Heather," he said again. "Not on Saturday or any other night."

"Except Wednesday."

"I went out with her on Wednesday," he acknowledged.

"And then I said good-night to her at her door and went home to my own apartment."

"If that's true—"

"Dammit, Avery. Of course, it's true."

"—she's not going to want that information to get out. Especially when you slept with Madison, Emma and Brooke."

"I didn't sleep with Madison or Emma. I did sleep with Brooke," he admitted wearily. "Once. About four years ago."

"Apparently your legend lives on."

"And I only agreed to go out with Heather because you made it clear that you weren't interested in a relationship with me," he told her. "And even then, the whole time I was with her, I was thinking of you.

"I'm not proud of that fact, but there it is," he told her. "I'm not used to thinking about only one woman, wanting only one woman. But that's the way it's been since New Year's Eve." He shook his head. "No, the truth is, it's been like that since long before New Year's."

She backed away from him. "Why do you do that?"

"Do what?"

"Say things that make me want to believe I'm different from every other woman who ever got naked with you."

"Because you *are* different," he told her. "God knows you frustrate me a hell of a lot more than any other woman I've ever known."

He was furious with Heather for starting the rumors, but he was even more frustrated with Avery for believing them. And he was exasperated by her determination to ignore the attraction between them—especially after what had happened between them on New Year's. And no matter what he did to prove himself to her, she wasn't willing to give him or a relationship between them a chance because she had some ridiculous and arbitrary rule about not dating doctors.

"In that case, you shouldn't have any objections to me cutting this tête-à-tête short so I can get back to work," she said, moving toward the door.

He stepped in front of her. "What I object to is you walking away every time you don't like the direction of a conversation."

"I can't talk to you about this anymore."

"That's fine," he decided. "Because I'm done talking."

Instead, he pulled her into his arms and kissed her.

Chapter Eight

Avery should have seen it coming. It was just the kind of high-handed macho move she should have expected from him. But he'd looked so sincerely frustrated to hear about the latest rumors churning through the hospital gossip mill, and when he'd looked into her eyes—damn, but she was a sucker for those deep green eyes—she'd felt every last ounce of her resistance melt.

She heard a soft, needy moan and realized that it had come from her. She poured everything she was feeling into the kiss. Anger. Frustration. Hurt. Need. Any pretension that she didn't want this—want *him*—was decimated by that sound.

But still, there were so many reasons not to get involved with him. Even aside from the fact that he was a doctor, he was totally wrong for her. And completely out of her league. She believed he was telling the truth about Heather, so maybe he wasn't quite the Casanova that his reputation implied, but he was still a major-league player and she was just learning the rules of rookie ball.

With that thought in mind, she managed to draw away from him, pressing her lips together as if that might stop the exquisite tingling. But when she lifted her gaze to his, the heat and hunger in his eyes made her tremble inside.

"What are we doing here, Justin?"

"I don't know about you, but I'm trying to remember where the nearest supply closet is," he told her.

She shook her head. "I don't know how to do this—how to play these games."

"I'm not playing games with you, Avery."

"This doesn't make any sense to me," she admitted. "None of this. I know all of the reasons that this is a bad idea. And then you touch me—or even just look at me—and I don't seem to care."

"Despite your fondness to control everything, attraction doesn't work that way. You can try to ignore it, but you can't manipulate it."

"I guess I'll just have to ignore it, then," she decided.

He smiled. "You can try."

When his mother called to invite him for dinner and cake Saturday night, Justin was so frustrated and preoccupied by the situation with Avery, it never occurred to him that the simple invitation was anything more than that. Not until he turned onto the street and saw the long line of cars already in her driveway. Apparently "cake" was code for "party," and he was the guest of honor.

His cousin Lauryn met him in the foyer.

"Happy birthday," she said, brushing her lips against his cheek.

"Thanks." He rubbed her pregnant belly, where her second child currently resided, then asked about her firstborn. "Where's Kylie?"

"Off somewhere with Oliver, and I hope Harper's got her eye on them, because I can't keep up anymore."

"Harper and Ryan are here?"

"Of course," she said, as if it wasn't anything out of the ordinary for his brother and sister-in-law to make the trip from Miami, where Harper was the producer of a popular daytime television show. "If you're going to be surprised by anything, it should be the presence of your other brother."

"I thought I recognized Braden's car in the driveway."

She nodded. "Dana's here, too."

"They haven't both been to a family event since…I can't remember," he admitted.

"Well, they're here today," she said.

Then she hooked her arm through his and guided him to the family room where her middle sister, Jordyn, was snuggled up on the sofa with her new husband, Marco. Lauryn released his arm and squeezed onto the other end of the sofa. Her youngest and still-single sister, Tristyn, was across the room in conversation with their cousin Daniel. He didn't see Daniel's wife, Kenna, anywhere, so he suspected she was chasing around after their almost two-year-old son, Jacob. Andrew and Rachel's daughter, Maura, was teaching her cousin Dylan—Nathan and Allison's son—to play poker.

"Don't bet your college fund," Justin warned the boy. "She'll clean you right out."

Dylan looked up and grinned. "Nah, I'm winning."

"Really?" He looked at Maura, who was scowling at the cards in her hand.

"Beginner's luck," she insisted.

"Maybe *you* shouldn't bet your college fund," he told her.

"We're playing for Rayquaza," she told him.

"I don't know what that is, but it sounds dangerous."

Maura giggled. "You're so funny, Uncle Justin."

Of course, the uncle designation was more honorary than accurate, but he'd always enjoyed being "Uncle Justin" to his cousins' kids. There were quite a few of them now, and they were all underfoot today.

"The house seems so big most of the time," his father said, coming up to Justin and offering him a beer. "And then we invite the family over, and your mother starts to fret about where we're going to put everyone."

He accepted the bottle. "Thanks. There is a full house today."

"Your mother thought your thirty-fifth birthday warranted a party."

"I wish she'd told me."

"She obviously told you something to get you here," John noted.

"She said we were going to have a family dinner. And cake."

"It is family," his father assured him. "And there will be cake."

"Who's the woman with Tristyn and Daniel?" He nodded in the direction of a third person he hadn't noticed earlier.

"Emmaline Carpenter."

"Who?"

"Veronica Carpenter's granddaughter," John said, as if that should explain everything.

"She's not family," he noted.

"Well, no," his father admitted.

Justin sighed. "I guess that means Mom's matchmaking again."

"She thinks that thirty-five is time for you to get serious and settle down."

"Why doesn't she believe that I could get my own date if I wanted one?"

"Because you never bring home any of the women you date."

"Because bringing a woman home to meet the parents is the quickest way to give her the wrong idea," Justin pointed out.

"Just talk to the girl," John urged. "You might find you actually like her."

He was sure that she was a perfectly nice woman, and she was undoubtedly attractive—but she wasn't Avery.

"Right now, I'm going to talk to Mom," Justin said.

He found Ellen in the kitchen, where she was sprinkling mozzarella on top of a tray of cannelloni. She wiped her hands on her apron before she enveloped him in her arms. "There's my birthday boy."

He winced visibly, making his aunt Susan laugh.

"I'm thirty-five, Mom," he reminded her.

"As if I didn't know," she admonished. "I was there, you know. In fact, I'm the one who gave birth to you—after twenty-eight hours of labor."

"Ah, the 'twenty-eight hours of labor' story," Tristyn said, having followed him into the kitchen to grab a handful of juice boxes from the refrigerator, no doubt for the various kids spread around the house. "As much a birthday tradition as candles on the cake."

Susan shooed her daughter out of the kitchen.

"It was thirty-six hours with Braden," he reminded his mother.

She nodded. "But only six with Ryan."

"Are you implying that he was the easy one?"

She laughed. "None of you were easy. Not during labor or all of the years since. But you were worth every minute of every day." She opened the oven to check on the chicken drumsticks and roasted potatoes.

"I'm not sure thirty-five is really a milestone that warrants all of this," he said cautiously. "Not that I don't appreciate it."

"Maybe I just wanted an excuse to get the whole family together," she said. "It's been a long time since everyone's been able to coordinate their schedules."

He nodded. "Yeah, it's been a whole five weeks since Jordyn and Marco's wedding."

She swatted at him with a tea towel. "Andrew and Rachel weren't at the wedding," she reminded him. "They were in Florida visiting Rachel's parents."

"Well, you managed to get everyone here today—which hopefully means you also got a really big cake."

"I should have guessed that would be your biggest concern and not realize that we're still missing someone."

"I didn't actually do a head count, but I can't think of anyone who's missing—aside from Rob," he said, referring to Lauryn's husband, who always seemed to be at the Locker Room—the sporting goods store he owned. "But I figured he was working."

"That's what Lauryn said," she confirmed. "And I was referring to your sister."

"You invited Nora?"

"Of course I invited Nora."

He didn't think there was any "of course" about it considering that the woman she so easily referred to as his sister had been born as a result of his father's extramarital affair during a difficult period in his parents' marriage.

"Does Dad know that you invited her?"

"I wouldn't have done so without talking to him first," she chided. "There's been more than enough secrecy about his daughter."

"What did she say?" he asked.

His mother sighed. "She thanked me for the invitation but said that she had other plans."

"She came to see me a few weeks ago," Justin admitted.

"She did?" Ellen sounded surprised but not displeased by this revelation. "Why?"

"She's applied for a PT opening at Mercy and wanted a letter of recommendation."

"Did you give it to her?"

"I did one better—I introduced her to some of the staff in the physio department. She starts on Monday."

Ellen smiled. "You have a good heart, Justin."

He slid an arm across his mother's shoulders. "I wonder where I get that from."

"You need someone to share that heart of yours," she told him.

"Are you really going to start this again?"

"Nate told me that you're seeing someone—another doctor. Is this true?"

He should have known his cousin wouldn't be able to resist telling someone about Avery, but he'd hoped Nate had enough sense not to open his big mouth to Justin's mother. "I'm not sure our relationship is that clearly defined," he hedged.

"You should have invited her to come tonight."

"Then you would have had to uninvite Mrs. Carpenter's granddaughter."

His mother flushed. "All I did was ask a young woman who didn't have any other plans to join us for dinner."

"Would you have asked her if she was married?"

"If she was married, I would have told her to bring her husband, too."

Which, knowing his mother, was entirely possible.

"I invited Josh Slater, too," she pointed out, referring to Daniel's business partner in Garrett/Slater Racing.

"And I'll bet you've arranged the seating so that he's beside Tristyn."

She neither confirmed nor denied it, saying only, "Get out of here now so we can finish up and get dinner on the table."

Avery's stomach was being uncooperative again. Of course, staring at Justin's phone number might have had something to do with the nerves tangled into knots in her belly.

She had to call him—and she was going to. She just

wanted to be sure that she wasn't going to throw up in the middle of their conversation before she dialed.

She looked at the stick on the table—at the two parallel lines in the narrow window. She'd bought the test because she was still feeling fatigued and occasionally queasy, but she'd expected it to rule out a pregnancy. Seeing those two lines... She wasn't sure how she felt, but she knew that she wanted her baby.

Not just her baby, but hers and Justin's. And if her own emotions were in turmoil, she couldn't begin to imagine how he might react when he learned that he was going to be a father. He'd made it clear that he would be involved if there was a baby, but he'd also been obviously relieved when she told him that they'd dodged the bullet.

Now she had to tell him that she'd been wrong.

And she had to be prepared for the fact that those words would change everything for both of them.

She took a few more slow, steady breaths and punched in his number.

She could hear voices in the background when he connected the call. Voices and laughter.

"I'm calling at a bad time," she realized.

"No, it's okay," Justin said. "It's good to hear from you."

He sounded as if he meant it, which only made her feel guiltier about the reason for her call.

"What's up?"

"I was hoping we could get together, to talk about some things," she admitted. "But obviously you're busy so—"

"I'd say 'stuck' rather than busy," he told her. "But I should be able to get away in about an hour, two at the most."

"Where are you?"

"Family birthday party," he said. "Did you want to meet somewhere or do you want me to stop by your place?"

"Why don't you come here?" she suggested. "That way it doesn't matter if you're an hour—or two."

"I could probably get away sooner, if it's important," he offered.

It was more than important—it was terrifying and exhilarating and life changing. But all she said to Justin was, "I'll see you when you get here."

She disconnected and set the phone back in the cradle. Only then did she realize how much her hands were shaking. Now that she'd made the call, there was no going back.

But she had an hour—or maybe two—and no idea how to pass the time. Her apartment was clean, her laundry done, the dinner dishes washed up and put away. She tried to read, but she couldn't focus on the words on the page. She turned on the television, but nothing held her attention there, either.

She picked up the plastic stick again and stared at the two narrow lines in the window.

Yes, from this point forward, everything was going to change.

Avery immediately released the lock on the door when Justin buzzed, as if she'd been waiting for him. He'd been surprised by her call—even more so by the invitation to stop by her apartment, especially in light of the way their previous conversation had ended.

He wanted to believe that she'd reconsidered, that she'd realized it was pointless to continue to ignore the attraction between them and had decided to explore it instead. Yeah, it was probably wishful thinking on his part—or maybe it was his birthday wish come true.

"What's that?" she asked, when she opened the door and saw the plate in his hands.

"Birthday cake."

"You took the leftover cake?"

"It's my cake," he told her, stepping into the foyer.

"I didn't realize—" She dragged a hand through her hair. "The birthday party was for *you*?"

He nodded. "Apparently thirty-five is some kind of milestone in my mother's world, so she invited the whole clan—aunts, uncles, cousins, spouses and kids."

"Sounds...fun," she said, a little dubiously.

"It was fun. And chaotic. And lucky that there was any leftover cake, which I brought to share with you."

"I should refuse, but I have no willpower when it comes to chocolate cake."

"I thought your weakness was cookies 'n' cream ice cream," he said, following her into the kitchen.

"Okay, so I have more than one weakness," she admitted. "Do you want a glass of milk with your cake?"

"I'd rather have coffee—if it's not too much trouble."

"It's no trouble at all," she told him.

She took a mug out of the cupboard, popped a pod into her home brewing system and pressed the button. Her movements were usually smooth and effortless—indicative of a woman who was confident in herself and her abilities. But she seemed a little jumpy today, and unwilling to hold his gaze. It was as if she was anxious about something, and her nervousness was starting to make him nervous.

Justin found plates and forks in the cupboard, and divided the slab of cake into two pieces. Avery carried his mug of coffee and her glass of milk to the table.

"Cream? Sugar?"

He shook his head. "Black is fine."

They sat at the dining room table and ate their dessert. Actually, he ate his while Avery—despite her declared weakness for chocolate cake—picked gingerly at hers.

"So, why did you call?" he asked, swallowing his last bite.

Avery's fork slipped from her grasp and clattered against

her plate. She pushed her half-eaten dessert away and picked up a napkin, her attention focused on wiping each and every finger. "Maybe we should do this another time."

"Why?"

"Because it's your birthday and there's probably somewhere else you'd rather be."

"I want to be here, Avery," he said patiently. "I want to know what's on your mind."

She folded her napkin in half once, and then again. "I just wanted to follow up our earlier conversation…about what happened…on New Year's."

She wasn't the type to meander through a conversation rather than get straight to the point, but she was meandering now. "What—*exactly*—requires follow-up?"

"Well…it, um, turns out that we didn't, um…dodge the bullet."

It took him a minute to figure out what she was saying, probably because his brain didn't want to figure it out. They'd had a close call, she'd assured him he was "off the hook."

And he'd been grateful—so incredibly grateful—because he knew there was no way he was ready to be a father. Now, he felt that hook slice deep into him, lodging painfully in his gut.

"You're…pregnant?"

She nodded and pulled a narrow plastic stick out of her pocket to show him the two lines in the window.

"You're going to be a daddy."

Chapter Nine

Justin stared at the plastic stick for a long minute.

"Well," he finally said, "this is an even bigger surprise than my mother's party."

Avery nodded again. "I'm sure you need some time… to process."

Yeah, processing would probably be good, because right now, his mind was blank except for the *holy crap* going around and around inside his head.

When she'd told him that she got her period, he'd breathed a sigh of relief that they were in the clear and chalked up the birth-control faux pas to an "oops" that he promised himself would never happen again. And over the past couple of weeks, he'd mostly managed to put the whole pregnancy scare out of his mind.

Now…he wasn't sure what to think or how to feel. He'd already told her how he felt about the decisions she'd made without any communication or consultation, so there was no point in rehashing all of that again.

But—*holy crap*—he really hadn't been prepared for this.

And though he was certain he already knew the answer to the question, he had to ask, "You're going to have the baby?"

Avery tilted her chin and narrowed her gaze on him. Maybe it was a question he felt compelled to ask, but after their previous discussion on the topic, she couldn't help but feel angry and annoyed. "Yes, I'm going to have the baby."

He drew in a deep breath and nodded. "Do you want to get married?"

She stared at him, certain she hadn't heard him correctly.

"Did you just ask—" She shook her head.

"I asked if you wanted to get married," he repeated.

The question was so completely unexpected, even the second time, that she wasn't sure how to respond.

"I always thought I would get married someday," she finally told him. "But not because I'm pregnant and not to a man who doesn't understand the meaning of commitment or long-term."

"Just because I haven't had a long-term relationship in a while doesn't mean I'm incapable of making a commitment."

"Then what does it mean?" she challenged.

"Maybe I just haven't wanted to commit to any of the other women that I've dated."

"But I'm supposed to believe that you're willing to commit to a woman you haven't dated at all?"

"The only reason we haven't dated is that you have some nonsensical ban on dating doctors," he told her.

"It's not nonsensical," she denied.

"Then explain it to me," he suggested.

She shrugged, figuring she probably owed him that much. "Both of my parents were doctors—more committed to their careers than either their marriage or their children—and I decided a long time ago that that's not what I want for my life."

"Except that we are both doctors and we're having a baby together, so that pretty much decimates your logic, doesn't it?" he challenged.

"I don't expect you to make any decisions right now," she said, striving to remain calm and reasonable.

"When should I make them?"

"When you've had a chance to think about what this means for you."

"You said it yourself—it means I'm going to be a father," he acknowledged bluntly.

"That's true," she agreed. "But the last time we talked about this, I told you that it was my decision to accept the potential consequences of what happened between us and I'm not asking for anything from you."

"And I told you that if you were pregnant—and now we know that you are—you don't just get a baby. You get me, too."

She frowned at the grim determination in his tone. "I thought that was just...an emotional outburst."

"I'm not prone to emotional outbursts," he assured her. "I say what I mean and mean what I say. I want to be part of our baby's life, and that would be easier to do if we were married."

"And a lot harder on both of us and the baby when we decide it isn't working, we can't stand to live together anymore and can't figure out who's going to get stuck with the kids," she argued.

It was her use of the plural pronoun that made Justin realize she was projecting her own childhood experience onto the current situation and made him want to throttle both of her parents. But at the moment, the best he could do was proceed cautiously.

"You might want to consider the possibility that we *could* make a marriage succeed," he told her.

"If you're serious about coparenting, we need to be able to work together for the sake of the baby. Which means we need to keep our focus on the baby and not get distracted by other stuff."

"Other stuff?" he echoed, amused despite the guilt and

responsibility weighing on him now. "As in the attraction between us? The reason we're going to be parents?"

"Maybe we're not ready to talk about this," she decided, pointedly ignoring his questions.

"When do you think we will be ready to talk about it?"

"I've had about—" she glanced at her watch "—four hours to think about this. You've had twenty minutes."

"To think about the baby," he agreed. "I've been thinking about us for a lot longer."

"There is no 'us,'" she snapped.

But beneath the frustration, he heard the desperation in her voice. She obviously wanted to believe what she was saying, to establish some control over the situation— because he knew how important it was to Avery to be in control.

"Maybe we both need some time," he suggested.

"That's probably best," she agreed, relief evident in her tone.

"I'll give you a call in a couple of days."

She nodded, apparently willing to be agreeable and reasonable now that he was on his way out the door.

But if she expected him to back off, she was going to be disappointed. Because their future was too important—to both of them and their baby.

She told Amy about her pregnancy a few days later, in part because she continued to be plagued by fatigue and queasiness and it wouldn't take her friend long to put the pieces together, but also because she wanted Amy to know that she'd need to reduce her hours later in her pregnancy and after the baby was born.

Amy was unreservedly thrilled by the news. She knew how much her friend wanted a child and she was convinced that Avery and Justin would be fabulous parents. When Avery pointed out that she and Justin weren't together, Amy reaffirmed her belief that that would change before their baby was born. Avery didn't argue with her friend—preferring to save her energy to have that battle with her baby's father.

After sharing the news with Amy, she thought about telling her family. And when she thought about family, she thought about Ryder, her brother and—aside from Amy— her best friend. She sent him a text message inviting him to come over for dinner, because she'd never known Ryder to turn down a free meal.

She decided on pulled pork, because she could put it in the slow cooker before she went to work and also because she knew how much he liked it. When she got home, she made garlic mashed potatoes and corn—more of her brother's favorites.

He was appreciative of her efforts and was on his second helping when Avery said, "I haven't seen much of you over the past few weeks."

"Our filming schedule has been pretty chaotic," Ryder told her. "The director wants to wrap up the season before the beginning of April so that he can take an extended vacation, which means that all of the crews are working around the clock to finish projects before then."

"I've been busy, too," she said. "In addition to my usual shifts at the hospital, we've extended the hours at the clinic to accommodate our growing list of patients. It's amazing how many women are having babies and, coincidentally, I'm going to have one, too."

She'd hoped that sharing her news as a footnote might diffuse the impact of the words, at least a little. When Ryder paused with his fork halfway to his mouth to stare at her, she realized it had not.

"You're pregnant?"

She forced a smile. "Isn't that great?"

"I don't know." He continued to hold her gaze. "Is it?"

"It is," she assured him. "I'm ready for this, and I really want this baby."

"And the father?" he prompted.

"We're…figuring things out."

"I didn't know you were dating anyone."

"You've been busy," she reminded him.

"So you have been seeing someone?"

She nodded.

"For how long?" Ryder asked.

"Not very long," she admitted.

"Does he have a name?"

"Of course," she said, "but I'm not going to give it to you—not until I'm sure that you won't go all Neanderthal on me and beat him over the head with a club for messing with your sister."

"Then you better give me some more information," he suggested.

"Such as?" she asked warily.

"The date of the wedding."

She shook her head. "Jesus, Ryder—what century do you live in?"

"Hopefully a century in which my sister wouldn't screw around with a guy who doesn't believe in doing the right thing."

She sighed. "Then you'll be happy to know he did offer to marry me."

"And the date of the wedding?" he prompted again.

"I said no."

"Why?"

"He's a doctor."

Ryder sighed and shook his head. "You don't learn, do you?"

"Apparently not."

"But you obviously like the guy—at least well enough to get naked with him."

"Yeah, I like him," she admitted.

"So maybe you could make it work," he said, though not very convincingly.

"Liking someone is hardly a foundation for marriage."

"Maybe not," he allowed. "But you need to think about your baby, too."

"I *am* thinking about the baby. And we both know that putting the responsibility of kids on top of a shaky foundation is a blueprint for disaster."

Her brother reluctantly nodded. "I just want you to be happy, sis. After what happened with Wyatt—"

"I'm over Wyatt," she told him. "My broken heart is mended, fully and completely, and now I'm going to have a baby, and I'm happy about that. I wish you could be, too."

"I am happy for you," he said. "I just wish you were planning to marry the baby's father."

"Because a woman having a baby out of wedlock offends your sense of propriety?"

"I'm not worried about propriety—I'm worried that you've closed off your heart."

"My heart's not closed," she denied. "It's just not open to the baby's father."

The clinic was decorated for Valentine's Day with hearts and flowers and adorable little cupids. When Avery finished for the day, her only thoughts were of dinner and bed—and then she got home and found Justin standing outside of her apartment door with several bags at his feet and a bouquet of flowers in his hand, and her traitorous heart swelled up inside her chest.

"What are you doing here?"

"I brought dinner and flowers for Mr. Gunnerson across the hall, but he already had a date for Valentine's Day so he suggested that I bring everything over here to you."

"Mr. Gunnerson let you into the building," she guessed.

"And Mrs. Gunnerson said you were lucky to have such a handsome and thoughtful beau to share this special day with, because you're a lovely young woman who works too hard and needs someone to take care of *you* every once in a while."

Avery shook her head as she unlocked the door. "This was a really thoughtful gesture, but I had leftover chicken and broccoli in the freezer that I was planning to have tonight."

"Then you should be doubly grateful the Gunnersons sent me over here," he said solemnly, handing her the flowers so he could pick up the rest of the bags to carry into her apartment.

Her heart gave a little jolt inside her chest when she unwrapped the dozen long-stemmed red roses mixed with lush greens and starry gypsophila. "These are…gorgeous," she told him, tracing the edge of a velvety soft petal with the tip of her finger.

"I know you want to pretend this is all about the baby," he told her. "But it's not. There's something going on between us that has nothing to do with the child you're carrying—or maybe it would be more accurate to say it's the reason for the child you're carrying."

She sighed. "I really just want to focus on what's best for the baby right now."

"You don't think having two parents who are together would be the best thing for our baby?"

"I think a lot of things can happen in nine months and we should just take things one day at a time."

"Fair enough," he said, and began to unpack the food.

"How many people were you planning to feed?" she asked, when she saw the number of containers on the table.

"I wasn't sure what you liked, so I got manicotti, lasagna, fettuccine Alfredo, and penne with sausage and peppers. Plus salad, garlic bread and dessert, because you're eating for two now."

"That's a myth," she told him, as she snipped the stems of the flowers. "A pregnant woman only needs about three hundred additional calories a day. Too much weight gain during pregnancy can increase her risk of gestational diabetes, high blood pressure and caesarean delivery."

"I was teasing, Avery," he said patiently. "Believe it or not, I did learn some things during my obstetrics rotation in medical school." He found plates and cutlery and carried them to the table. "How are you feeling?"

"I'm okay. Tired, but that's common in the first trimester."

"Any morning sickness?"

She carried the vase to the table and placed it at the center. "Rarely, and not usually in the morning."

"Have you been to see a doctor?" He held her chair for her to be seated.

"I see doctors every day," she assured him.

"You know what I mean," he chided, settling into the chair beside hers.

She nodded. "Yes, I've seen Dr. Herschel."

"And she doesn't have any concerns about anything?"

"He," Avery told him, lifting a manicotti onto her plate. "Dr. Richard Herschel."

He frowned at that as he reached for the lasagna. "Why did you pick a male doctor?"

"Because he was highly recommended. In fact, he delivered Amy and Ben's son, Henry."

"Is Dr. Herschel at least old and bald?"

She tapped her chin with a finger as she considered the question. "I'd guess early forties, curly blond hair, blue eyes, great bedside manner."

His scowl deepened.

She laughed as she added a slice of garlic bread to her

plate. "Even if I did date doctors—which I don't," she reminded him, "Dr. Herschel is happily married with four kids."

"You could have mentioned that at the beginning."

"I could have," she agreed. Then she said, "I had a consult in the ER this morning, and I saw Heather's name on the schedule."

He nodded. "She was there."

"She didn't invite you to celebrate Valentine's Day with her tonight?"

"She did," he admitted. "And I told her I had other plans. I was tempted to tell her that I was going to be with you, but I wasn't sure how you'd feel about that."

"I'd rather not be the hot topic of conversation at the nurses' station tomorrow."

"You do know that people are eventually going to find out that you're pregnant—and that I'm the father."

"Eventually," she acknowledged. "But I don't want to tell anyone else about the baby until I'm past the first trimester."

He nodded. "Will you come to dinner with me at my parents' house next Saturday?"

"Were you listening to anything I just said?"

"I heard every word," he assured her. "I'm not suggesting that we tell my parents next weekend—I just want them to meet you, to get to know you before they know that you're going to be the mother of my child."

"You want to pretend we're in a relationship," she realized. "You don't want them to find out about the baby and then have to explain that we had a quickie in a closet."

"I don't want to pretend anything," he denied. "I want to give us the chance to actually build a relationship."

She stood up from the table and began clearing away the dishes. "We had this conversation already," she reminded him.

"Actually, we didn't, because you said we weren't ready to have the conversation."

"And I'm still not ready."

"I'm not asking for anything more than one day at a time," he told her. "And I don't think wanting you to meet my parents—our baby's grandparents—is unreasonable."

She nodded. "You're right, it's not."

"Then you'll come to dinner next Saturday?"

"Don't you think you should clear it with your parents first?"

He waved a hand dismissively. "I'll let them know, but it won't be a problem. My mother always cooks more than enough food."

"Okay," she relented. "I'll go to dinner next Saturday."

"Good." After they finished their dessert, he helped her tidy up the kitchen.

"Thank you for tonight," she said, as she walked him to the door. "I was planning on leftovers when I got home—this was better."

"I thought so, too." He settled his hands on her hips and drew her toward him.

She put her hands on his chest, determined to hold him at a distance. "What are you doing?"

"I'm going to kiss you goodbye."

"No, you're not," she said, a slight note of panic in her voice.

"It's just a kiss, Avery." He held her gaze as his hand slid up her back to the nape of her neck. "And hardly our first."

Then he lowered his head slowly, the focused intensity of those green eyes holding her captive as his mouth settled on hers. Warm and firm and deliciously intoxicating. Her own eyes drifted shut as a soft sigh whispered between her lips.

He kept the kiss gentle, patiently coaxing a response. She wanted to resist, but she had no defenses against the masterful seduction of his mouth. She arched against him, opened for him. And the first touch of his tongue to hers was like a lit match to a candlewick—suddenly she was on fire, burning with desire.

It was like New Year's Eve all over again, but this time she didn't even have the excuse of adrenaline pulsing through her system. This time, it was all about Justin.

Or maybe it was the pregnancy.

Yes, that made sense. Her system was flooded with hormones as a result of the pregnancy, a common side effect of which was increased arousal. It wasn't that she was pathetically weak or even that he was so temptingly irresistible. It wasn't about Justin at all—it was a basic chemical reaction that was overriding her common sense and self-respect. Because even though she knew that he was wrong for her in so many ways, being with him, being in his arms, felt so right.

She pulled him closer, so that her breasts were crushed against his chest, but still it wasn't close enough. She wanted to tear away her clothes and his, so that there was nothing between them. She wanted to feel his warm, naked skin against hers; she wanted to feel his hard, sexy body intimately joined with hers.

It was almost as if he could read her mind, because he slid a hard thigh between hers, the exquisite friction dragging a low, desperate moan from deep in her throat. Her fingers curled in the fabric of his shirt, holding on to him, as she rocked her hips against his, silently begging for more. He pressed into her, the hard evidence of his arousal sending happy little sparks dancing through her system.

"You make me crazy," he said, muttering the words against her lips.

"I'm feeling pretty crazy right now, too," she admitted.

"Which is precisely why I need to go."

"Go?" she echoed, confused—and more than a little hurt—by his sudden withdrawal.

He nodded.

"What was this?" She gestured between them. "Just a quick demonstration of how easily you can turn a woman on? How easily you can turn *me* on?"

He rubbed his thumb over her bottom lip, swollen from his kiss. "Do you think you're the only one turned on?" he asked her. "I want you so badly I ache."

"Then why did you stop?" she demanded.

"Not because I don't want to make love with you," he assured her. "Because I want you to realize and accept that I want more than a few stolen hours with you. I don't want you to wake up in the morning and justify your actions on the basis that it was Valentine's Day and you were feeling lonely, and then push me away again because you're angry with yourself for giving in to the attraction between us."

"I wouldn't do that," she denied. Then, in response to his skeptical look she added, "Probably not."

"This way we'll be sure," he said, and brushed his lips against hers again. "Good night, Avery."

Chapter Ten

Avery didn't like to call Amy at home because she never knew when Henry might be napping—or when Henry's parents might be taking advantage of the fact that their little guy was napping. Instead, she sent her friend a brief and concise text message.

Help.

Amy immediately called her. "What's wrong?"

"I'm sorry—I didn't mean to make it sound urgent, like I was trapped in the back of a closet with a knife-wielding maniac outside the door."

"There's no knife-wielding maniac?" Amy asked, sounding just a little disappointed.

"No," Avery assured her. "Although I do feel like I'm trapped by my closet."

"Why?"

"Justin's taking me to meet his parents and I have nothing to wear."

"You're going to meet his parents?" Amy sounded intrigued. "That's an interesting turn of events."

Avery continued to push hangers on her closet rod, shaking her head. "I don't know why I agreed to this. I don't know what I was thinking. And I have no idea what to wear. Are pants too casual? Is a skirt and jacket too businesslike?"

"How about a dress? Something informal but pretty."

"Informal but pretty?" Avery echoed, shaking her head. "I don't own anything like that."

"I'll be over in fifteen minutes."

"You don't have to come over—I just need you to talk me out of my insanity."

"More easily done in person," Amy said.

"But it's Saturday, and I'm sure you're busy with Ben and Henry."

"It's good for Ben to be busy with Henry sometimes," her friend said. "Besides, they'll both still be here when I get back."

True to her word, Amy was there in fifteen minutes— with a garment bag and several shoe boxes in hand.

"Because you knew there was nothing appropriate in my closet," Avery noted.

"I just wanted you to have a few more options," Amy said.

"I'm not sure anything from your closet will fit me— I've got bigger boobs than you do."

Amy dumped the shoe boxes on the sofa. "Stop bragging and I won't hold that fact against you."

"Merely stating the facts."

"You've got longer legs, too," Amy admitted, unzipping the bag. "You should show them off more."

"I don't—" Whatever Avery had intended to say was forgotten when Amy pulled out a deep blue dress. "Oh."

"This is my favorite," Amy told her. "And I think the color will look great on you."

"You must be my fairy godmother."

Her friend grinned. "Go try it on."

She did and was pleasantly surprised to find that the garment looked even better on her than it had on the hanger.

The dress had a round neckline, cap sleeves and twisted pleating at the waist that added a nice touch of detail.

Amy nodded approvingly. "It's feminine and flattering without being too much for a casual dinner—and you really do have bigger boobs."

"Can we talk about shoes instead of boobs?"

"Okay. What size do you wear?"

"An eight."

"Then we better look at what's in your closet because your feet are bigger than mine, too."

They found appropriate footwear to go with the dress, then Amy looked through Avery's admittedly limited selection of jewelry to help her accessorize. She found a pair of hammered silver hoop earrings and a couple of silver bangle bracelets.

"You have no idea how much I appreciate this," Avery said. "Not just letting me borrow your dress but being here to distract me so that I didn't go crazy watching the clock."

"Happy to help," Amy said. "Are you okay now?"

"Actually, I feel like I'm going to throw up."

"Morning sickness?" Amy asked, immediately concerned.

She shook her head. "It's the thought of meeting Justin's parents that's making me feel nauseated. Tell me again why I agreed to this."

"Because Justin's parents are your baby's grandparents," Amy reminded her gently. "And they're lovely people."

"You know them?"

Her friend nodded. "Ellen Garrett is on the hospital board so they attend a lot of functions. She's an absolutely wonderful lady, and her husband is incredibly charming—not unlike his son."

"So they're lovely people who will probably hate me when they find out I'm pregnant with Justin's baby."

"Are you telling them tonight?"

"No. Justin wanted them to meet me before we said anything about the baby."

Her friend glanced at her watch. "And I should get out of here before your boyfriend shows up."

She rolled her eyes. "You know he's not my boyfriend."

"That's right—you're not dating, you're just having a baby together."

"Thanks for the dress," Avery said, pointedly ignoring the teasing comment.

Amy kissed her cheek. "Be home by midnight or you'll turn into a pumpkin."

Dinner at his parents' house wasn't a big deal. Taking a woman to dinner at his parents' house, on the other hand, was.

A very big deal.

Justin had tried to downplay the significance of it to Avery, certain she would have refused his invitation if she suspected what it meant—or what his mother would interpret it to mean. But it was important to him that his parents meet her. He wanted them to know her before they found out about the baby. He wanted them to know not just the mother of their future grandchild but the woman who had captivated him from the day he first met her.

He knew his parents would like her because he did. He wasn't so sure what Avery would think about his family. It was hard to get a handle on what she was thinking or feeling. He thought he was starting to know her pretty well, but there were still parts of herself that she kept closed off, not just from him but from everybody.

He heard the door unlatch and opened his mouth to speak, then she stepped into view and his brain shut down.

He was accustomed to seeing her at the hospital, with a long white coat covering up whatever else she was wearing. Tonight she didn't look like a doctor but a woman.

The dress she was wearing gently hugged her tantalizing curves, the knee-length skirt showcasing shapely legs that were further enhanced by the slim heels. Her hair fell in loose waves over her shoulders and her lips shone with a hint of gloss. He'd always thought she was beautiful, but now she was absolutely breathtaking.

He managed to roll his tongue back into his mouth to speak. "I want to say something charming and clever about how great you look, but all I can think is 'wow.'"

"'Wow' works," she said, offering a shy smile. "So long as it's a 'wow, she looks perfect to take home to meet my parents' rather than 'wow, I'm making a huge mistake here.'"

"It's definitely a 'wow, you look perfect.'"

"I borrowed the dress from Amy," she admitted. "I didn't have anything in my closet that seemed appropriate. To meet your parents, I mean. I have clothes, of course, but it's been a long time since I've met anyone's parents and I didn't know what to wear. And now I'm babbling like an idiot."

He smiled at that. "You seem a little bit nervous."

"Of course I'm nervous."

"I didn't think anything ever fazed you," he admitted.

"I wouldn't be a very good doctor if I fell apart at the sight of blood," she pointed out. "But those two lines on the pregnancy test fazed me. Big-time."

"Well, you don't need to be nervous about meeting my parents," he promised her.

"What time are we supposed to be there?"

He glanced at his watch. "In about fifteen minutes."

"Do they live very far from here?"

"About a ten-minute drive," he told her.

"Then I guess we'd better get going." She opened the closet to get her coat. He was sorry that she was covering up the dress, but it was still February and although it had been a sunny day, the temperature tended to drop significantly after the sun went down.

"Ready?" he asked, when she picked up her purse.

"I think so." She took her keys out of her pocket. "Oh, wait—I almost forgot the pie."

"Why do you have pie?"

"Because when you're invited to someone's house, you don't show up empty-handed." She detoured into the kitchen to pick up the dessert.

"I do. At least once a month when I go over to beg a meal."

"That's different—they're your parents."

He looked at the covered glass dish in her hand. "You actually *made* a pie?"

"I told you that I took cooking classes," she reminded him.

"But you didn't tell me that you could make pie," he said, undeniably impressed. "So…" He put his hand on her back as they made their way to the elevator. "What kind of pie?"

When they arrived at his parents' house—a sprawling bungalow of stone and brick—Justin gave a perfunctory knock on the front door before he walked in.

"They're here," Avery heard a female voice call out. "Come on, John."

"I'm coming," a male voice, sounding eerily similar to Justin's, replied.

"They don't get much company," Justin said, his dry tone making her smile.

Then his parents were there and he made the introductions.

John Garrett shook her hand warmly; his wife, Ellen, pulled her into her arms for a quick hug.

"Avery brought pie," Justin said, holding out the plate he'd carried from the car.

"You didn't have to do that," Ellen said.

"That's what I told her," Justin pointed out.

"But it's very much appreciated," his mother said.

Her husband peered over her shoulder. "What kind of pie?"

The echo of his son's question made Avery smile. "Pecan."

John winked at her. "My favorite."

"What's for dinner?" Justin asked.

"Beef Wellington." Ellen looked apologetically at Avery. "I'm sorry—I didn't even think to ask Justin if you were a vegetarian or had any food allergies."

"I definitely eat meat and I don't have any allergies," she assured the other woman.

"I never worry about what I'm feeding Justin," his mother explained. "He'll eat almost anything that's put in front of him."

"Any food I don't have to cook is a favorite," he acknowledged.

"Except broccoli," Avery noted.

Ellen chuckled. "You know about that, do you?"

She realized that she'd inadvertently given the impression that she and Justin were closer than they really were. Aside from his abhorrence of broccoli and his affection for pasta, she really didn't know much about his likes and dislikes.

"Did you know that he can cook, too?" Ellen asked her. "I made sure that each of my boys knew enough of the basics to put a meal on the table, but he'll pretend that he can't if it means someone else will cook for him, so don't you let him fool you."

"No one fools Avery," Justin said.

"But I've cooked for you and not had my efforts reciprocated."

"It sounds like you owe Avery a home-cooked meal," his mother said.

"I brought her here tonight," he pointed out.

"That doesn't count."

"It should count for something," he insisted.

Ellen shook her head. "John, take your son into the den and turn on the television to see what's happening in Daytona—I want to know how Daniel's driver is doing."

"You want us to leave you alone with Avery so you can interrogate her?" Justin guessed.

"Of course," his mother agreed easily. "But don't worry—I'll save the waterboarding for after dinner."

"After dessert," he suggested. "I want to make sure I get a piece of that pecan pie."

Avery didn't panic when Justin left the room. To her surprise—and profound relief—her earlier nervousness had dissipated almost immediately upon entering John and Ellen's home. Justin's parents were simply the kind of people who knew how to make a guest feel comfortable and welcome, and even Ellen's teasing promise of an interrogation didn't worry her.

At least, not too much.

Ellen started mashing the potatoes. "Can you get the milk out of the fridge, please?"

As Avery did so, her attention was snagged by the numerous photographs on the refrigerator door, affixed by magnets advertising everything from pizza delivery to Pier 39. But it was one picture in particular that caught her eye—a couple with four children, including two boys who couldn't be anything but identical twins.

"My nephew's family," Ellen said, when she saw what Avery was looking at.

She swallowed, suddenly uneasy. "Do twins run in your family?"

The other woman shook her head, and Avery exhaled a quiet sigh of profound relief.

"Quinn and Shane are Georgia's boys from her first marriage," Ellen explained. "Pippa was born a few months after her husband died, then she married Matt and they added Aiden to the family."

"They must be very busy."

"I'm sure they are," she acknowledged. "Unfortunately,

I don't get to see them nearly as often as I like because they live in upstate New York. Both of Matt's brothers are there, too, along with their wives and families."

"They're all married?"

"All within twelve months of one another," she admitted. "Justin's cousin Nate almost didn't go to Lukas's wedding— he was afraid there was something in the water up there.

"Now that I think about it, I don't think he did drink any water that weekend. Of course, Nate's married now, too, and not too long after both of his brothers, so maybe he should have worried about the water here."

Avery smiled. "I actually met Nate and Allison at the Storybook Ball."

Ellen frowned. "John and I were there, too. I wonder why Justin didn't introduce you to us that night."

"I arrived late and he said you left early—something about a friend's cousin's boyfriend's show at the art gallery?"

"Oh, that's right," Ellen remembered. She shook her head. "We never should have wasted our time. We've always believed in supporting the arts, and young artists in particular, but I'm not sure that what we saw that night would fit even the broadest definition of art. However, I heard the ball was a tremendous success."

"It was," Avery confirmed. "And the orthopedics department is going to get its EOS imaging machine."

"That is wonderful news." Ellen opened the oven to check on the beef Wellington. "But I've got myself sidetracked again—I wanted to know more about you."

"Well, you know that I'm a doctor."

"Harvard Medical School followed by a residency at Massachusetts General."

"You're on the hiring committee," Avery suddenly recalled.

Justin's mother nodded. "I remember when your résumé came in—no one could understand why you'd leave a major hospital in a big city to come to Charisma, and many didn't believe, even if you did come, that you'd stay."

"I had some doubts myself," Avery confided. "Charisma is a different world from Boston, but Mercy is an excellent hospital, and within six months, I knew I didn't want to be anywhere else."

"How quickly did Justin hit on you?" his mother asked.

She felt her cheeks flush. "The day of my interview."

"And now, three-and-a-half years later, he finally got you to go out with him."

"I know I'm not his usual type," Avery began.

"I wouldn't know his usual type," Ellen admitted. "Justin doesn't typically bring home any of the women he dates."

"He doesn't?"

"Not since college. So when Justin told me that he was bringing a guest to dinner—I didn't know what to think. Now that I've met you…I'm so glad that you're here—that he found you."

The sincerity in the other woman's voice made Avery uneasy. "I'm afraid you're thinking this dinner means more than it does," she told her.

Ellen smiled. "I think it means more than you're willing to admit."

"Mrs. Garrett—"

"Call me Ellen."

"Ellen," she said, trying again. "Justin and I are friends and coworkers, but our relationship really isn't much more than that."

"Not much more means that it is something more."

Trapped by her own words, Avery reluctantly nodded. "I guess it does."

"That's good enough for now," Ellen said, handing her the bowl of mashed potatoes to carry. "Now let's get this food out before the men start banging their fists on the table."

Chapter Eleven

Justin slid his arm across Avery's shoulders as they made their way down the walk toward his car. He was disappointed but not really surprised when she immediately tensed in response to his touch. But she didn't shrug it off, which he took as a sign of progress.

He opened the passenger door for her and offered a hand to help her into her seat.

"Thanks for doing the dinner thing with me," he said, when he'd slid behind the wheel of the car.

"I enjoyed meeting your parents," she told him. "But you could have warned me that it's a big deal for you to take a woman home with you."

"It's not *that* big of a deal," he hedged.

She slid a look in his direction. "That's not what your mother said."

"I'm sorry you were disappointed to discover that I don't take a different woman home every week."

"I wasn't disappointed," she denied.

"But you were surprised."

She nodded.

"What else did my mother say to you?"

"Before or after she pulled out your baby pictures?"

He looked at her, horrified.

She laughed.

"I can't imagine your mother would ever embarrass you in such a way—if your baby pictures are even embarrassing, which I'm sure they're not."

"I was a pretty cute kid," he acknowledged.

"Whoever would have guessed?" she asked drily.

He grinned. "Are your parents the type to pull out baby pictures when I meet them?"

"I don't know that you'll have the opportunity to meet my parents. It's even more unlikely that they have any baby pictures."

"You're kidding."

She shook her head. "I told you that my mother works at CDC and my father's a cardiac surgeon at Emory. They married seven months before I was born and divorced seven years later."

"I'm sure it wasn't as simple and straightforward as you make it sound."

She shrugged, but Justin wasn't fooled by the gesture. "There really wasn't a lot of drama—they both had very busy lives, demanding careers. Truthfully, I'm not sure how they decided that they wanted to live separate and apart, because I don't really remember them ever being in the same place together." She shrugged. "For whatever reason, they decided to split and share custody of me and Ryder. We spent one week with Mom, the next with Dad, and alternated holidays. It was all very civil and reasonable."

And confusing, he imagined, for a child who might never feel sure where she belonged—or if there was anywhere she did.

"Did both of them being doctors have anything to do with your decision to go into medicine?"

"My brother thinks so. He claims it was a last and desperate attempt to get them to notice me—to finally do something that was worthy of their attention.

"I'm ashamed to admit that it might have been true, at

least in the beginning. But once I started med school, I knew I'd found what I was meant to do. And I didn't need their approval so much as I needed to succeed for myself, because I couldn't imagine any other career."

"It shows," he told her. "The way you are with your patients and coworkers—there's no doubt medicine is your calling."

She glanced away, as if uncertain how to respond, but finally murmured softly, "Thank you."

"So why obstetrics?" he asked.

"I guess that was partly a way of proving that I was different from both of them. I might have followed generally in their footsteps, but it was a specialty that was uniquely mine. And it's a lot of fun to deliver babies."

"Why do you think your brother chose to pursue a career outside of the medical field?"

"I would have said pure obstinacy," she said. "Ryder is brilliant. His marks in high school were far superior to mine. He could have done anything he wanted—he could have been a doctor or an engineer, a college professor or an astrophysicist. It took me a long time to accept that he didn't throw away his choices to spite our parents, that he's doing exactly what he wants."

"Now that wasn't so bad, was it?" he asked, when he pulled into a visitor's parking spot beside her building.

"What?"

"Making conversation, getting to know one another."

"No," she agreed. "It wasn't so bad at all."

"Then maybe we could do this again."

"Dinner with your parents?"

He smiled. "That, too."

It was almost one thirty by the time Avery stripped off her soiled gloves and gown, and she was on the schedule at Wellbrook for two o'clock. She'd been called in to the ER to deal with a suspected ectopic pregnancy that ended up rupturing while the patient was undergoing an ultrasound exam. The patient had lost a lot of blood and one of her fallopian tubes, but she was going to be fine. Avery was relieved—and exhausted.

She took a quick shower in the women's locker room in a desperate effort to revive her flagging energy. When she exited into the staff lounge, she found Justin waiting for her.

He held up a prepackaged sandwich and a carton of milk from the cafeteria. "I brought you lunch."

"I'm not hungry."

"I don't care if you're not hungry," he told her. "You have to eat."

"I don't have time to eat right now. I've got to be at Wellbrook—"

"You have to take care of yourself," he admonished, his tone gentle but firm as he nudged her toward a chair. "Sit."

"I have to go," she said again.

"Is there an emergency at the clinic?"

She huffed out a breath. "No, but—"

"Then sit."

She hated being pushed around. She hated men who thought they could push women around. But the fact was, she was so hungry she was feeling a little dizzy, and she was afraid if she didn't capitulate and sit down voluntarily, she might fall down. So she sat.

He peeled back the plastic wrapping and handed her half the sandwich.

She took a bite. "Where's the mustard?"

He took a handful of packets—both mustard and mayo—out of his pocket and tossed them onto the small table beside her.

She didn't really want mustard. She'd only asked for it because she was being difficult and ungrateful, but she opened a packet, peeled the bread away from the roast beef, and squirted the condiment onto the meat.

She ate the sandwich, dutifully drank the milk. "Can I go now?"

"That depends."

"On what?" she asked warily.

He took a huge chocolate chip cookie out of his other pocket. "On whether or not you want dessert."

Her gaze locked on the cookie and her mouth started to water. "I definitely want dessert."

He grinned and passed her the cookie. "Feeling better now?"

"I am," she admitted. "Thanks."

"You do know that the world's not going to stop turning if you slow down a little?"

She nodded. "I know. And I am taking care of the baby—I promise."

"Do you really think all I care about is the baby?"

She frowned as if she didn't understand the question.

Justin hunkered down beside her chair and laid his hands on her knees. He immediately felt the muscles in her thighs tighten—Avery withdrawing. He'd thought it was just him, but watching her over the past several weeks, he realized that she wasn't freezing only him out—she froze almost everyone out. Aside from her best friend and her brother, she didn't seem to let anyone get too close. The realization challenged rather than discouraged him.

"Has no one ever taken care of you?" he asked gently.

She was silent for a minute before she responded. "Hennie."

"Who?"

"Henrietta was the nanny we had when Ryder and I were little, but we called her Hennie."

"And if Hennie said to you, 'Avery Wallace—you need to eat,' what would you do?"

"I'd eat," she admitted.

"So eat," he suggested.

She unwrapped the cookie.

"I know you have a job to do," he said to her. "But it's also your job to take care of yourself and our baby."

Our baby.

He said the words so casually, so easily.

Then he touched his lips to hers, the kiss as casual and easy as his words.

And she thought—at least in the moment—that maybe they could do this.

Just because her hormones immediately went into overdrive every time he was near didn't mean that she had to do anything about it. They could be friends and coparents of their baby without muddying things up with unnecessary attraction or emotions.

Maybe.

Justin was generally pretty good at reading people, and he was confident that Avery would come to accept that he was going to be part of her life. Unfortunately, he wasn't confident that it would happen before their baby was born.

He deliberately stayed out of her way for a few days, to give her a chance to relax. He knew she was sensitive to hospital gossip, and even he was aware that there had been some talk about the two of them spending time together. There would be a lot more when word got out that she was going to have his baby so, for now, he backed off a little.

Until he got a call on the afternoon of February 29 that drew him to the maternity ward.

"You're a little far from the ER, aren't you, Dr. Garrett?"

"I had to come and take a peek at my cousin's baby," he said, gesturing to the bassinet with a tag that said 'Schulte' on it.

"Almost nine pounds and twenty-two inches, and Mom barely batted an eyelash," Avery told him.

"You delivered him?"

She shook her head. "I just caught him—Mom did all the work."

"Lauryn's second," he explained. "Although I seem to recall that Kylie didn't give her much trouble when she was born, either. Of course, those are the ones that my mother always says you need to worry about when they hit their teen years."

"Which of her sons did she need to worry about the most?" Avery asked.

"Probably me," he admitted.

"Why am I not surprised?"

He grinned and slid an arm across her shoulders. "Was Lauryn's husband there when the baby was born?"

She shook her head.

"Figures," he said. "It's the story of his life—expecting his wife to handle everything on her own."

"She wasn't alone," Avery told him. "Her sister—Tristyn—was with her."

He chuckled. "I would have paid to have seen that. Tristyn practically passes out if she gets a paper cut."

"Well, she held up very well in the delivery room. She did look a little green at first, but after I suggested that she stay at the head of the bed, away from all of the activity, she was fine."

"Is it different now?" he asked.

Despite the apparent disconnect from their previous topic, she understood what he was asking and nodded in response.

"Delivering babies has always been my favorite part of the job," she told him. "There's something incredibly satisfying about helping to bring a new life into the world—especially when the mothers do most of the work.

"It was only today that I realized it's not going to be so long until I'm the one actually pushing a baby out of my body. And suddenly, it wasn't just amazing—it was a little scary."

"I'll be there with you," he told her.

"You can't guarantee that. You could be—"

"I'll be there with you," he said again.

She was quiet for a minute before she said, "What if I don't want you there?"

"You don't know what you want."

Her brows lifted but she didn't deny it.

"So I'll be there," he said again. "Every day, every step of the way, until you realize it *is* what you want."

The original plan not to tell anyone about Avery's pregnancy until she was past the first trimester changed when she registered to attend the Spring Conference on Women's Sexual Health Issues in Atlanta the second weekend in March. Deciding that it would be the opportune time to share the news with her parents, they agreed to tell Justin's family about the baby the weekend prior.

Ellen cooked another delicious meal—baked lemon-and-herb chicken breasts served with a creamy risotto and green beans. Avery had again brought dessert, this time an apple crisp.

After everyone had consumed their fill, Justin reached for her hand and linked their fingers together. She might have thought his action was a show of togetherness for his parents' sake except that their hands were beneath the table where no one else could see. For some reason, that fact made the gesture all the more reassuring.

"We've got some news to share," he told his parents.

"You're getting married?" his mother guessed, her expression hopeful.

"No," Avery said quickly, sending a panicked look in Justin's direction.

He squeezed her fingers reassuringly. "We're going to have a baby."

Ellen drew in a quick breath. "A baby," she echoed, her whispered tone almost reverent. Then her attention shifted to Avery for confirmation. "Really?"

She nodded.

"Oh, that's even better than a wedding," Ellen decided, sounding sincerely thrilled by the news. "Although a wedding *and* a baby would be even better still."

This time Avery squeezed Justin's hand—a silent and desperate plea.

"Let's just focus on the baby right now," he suggested.

"Of course," his mother agreed. "This is definitely cause for celebration. John—is there any champagne downstairs? Wait—what am I thinking? We don't want champagne but sparkling grape juice. Do we have a bottle of that?"

"I can go check," her husband told her.

"Please do," Ellen urged. Then, when John got up from the table, she said, "Justin, go help your father. Half the time he can't find his nose on his face."

He looked at Avery. She knew he wasn't actually asking for permission so much as seeking confirmation that she didn't mind him abandoning her with his mother. She managed a weak—and probably not very convincing—smile.

"I'll be right back," he promised.

"Glasses," Ellen said, popping up from her seat. "We'll need glasses."

Avery got up from the table to start clearing away the dessert plates while Justin's mother opened the cabinet for the champagne glasses.

"No, no," Ellen admonished. "I'll take care of that later. Please sit and rest—and tell me how you're feeling. Are you experiencing any morning sickness?"

She shook her head. "Some occasional queasiness, but nothing too serious."

"I was sick as a dog through the first trimester with each of the boys," Justin's mother confided. "It started somewhere around week three and didn't let up until week twelve, but then I never had any further problems." She brought the crystal flutes to the table. "How far along are you? When is the baby due?"

"Almost ten weeks. The baby is due September twenty-fourth."

"September seems so far right now, but really, the months will fly by." Her eyes misted. "And we'll have a new grandbaby before Christmas."

"You're really not upset about this?" Avery asked cautiously.

"I'm not going to lie," Ellen said. "I would have preferred if there had been a wedding *before* a baby, but I understand that things don't always work out the way we plan.

"I've always worried about Justin," she continued. "Because despite his active social life, I could tell that he was lonely. Not that he would ever admit it, of course, but I was anxious for him to find the right woman, to finally realize how much he wanted to share his life with someone."

She reached across the table and took Avery's hands. "I'm so glad he found you, and I'm overjoyed that you're going to have a baby together."

While Ellen was talking to Avery, her husband was silent as he made his way down the stairs.

"You haven't said anything about the baby," Justin said, when they reached the climate-controlled wine cellar.

"I'm not quite sure what to say," his father admitted.

He nodded. "My initial reaction was pretty much the same."

"Then this wasn't planned?"

Justin shook his head.

"Have you talked about getting married?" John asked.

"Avery likes to take things one step at a time."

"Having a baby doesn't give you the luxury of leisure," his father warned as he scanned the labels. "Sparkling grape juice, apple grape, sparkling cider, cranberry-orange and fizzy peach-pomegranate juice."

"Why do you have so many choices?" Justin asked.

"Your mother insists on having it on hand for the kids."

"Avery likes cranberry juice, so let's go with that one."

John opened the door and pulled the bottle from the shelf. "How much else do you know about her?"

Something in his father's tone got his back up. "What are you asking?"

"Where's she from?"

"Atlanta originally, but she attended med school and did her training in Boston."

"How did she end up in Charisma?" John pressed.

"I don't know," he admitted.

"Did she chase after you?"

The question was so outrageous he couldn't help but laugh. "No, Dad. *I* chased *her*. For more than three years."

His father frowned at that. "Some women play hard to get on purpose—it's part of the game to snag a wealthy husband."

"Not Avery. If you want the truth, she'd probably prefer if I wasn't the father of her baby."

John didn't look convinced. "Does she know that you have an interest in Garrett Furniture?"

Justin sighed. "I promise you, she's not after my company shares."

"You should think about a prenup, anyway."

"A prenup assumes there are going to be nuptials," he pointed out, already not liking the direction of this conversation.

"You need to protect your assets," John warned. "And your parental rights."

"Whether or not Avery and I get married, I will be part of this baby's life from the beginning," he said, trying to keep his escalating anger in check. "My child won't need to come looking for me on Father's Day twenty-something years from now."

His father's face flushed. "You know damn well I would have been in Nora's life from the beginning if I'd known she was my daughter."

He nodded. "I guess I just wonder if you would still have been in mine. If your lover had told you that she was pregnant with your child, would you have left Mom to be with her?"

"How can you even ask that question?" John asked indignantly. "You know I love your mother."

"Did you love her even when you were screwing around on her?"

A muscle in his father's jaw ticked. "I'm not going to discuss this with you."

"That's fine," Justin agreed. "Because I really don't want the details—and I don't intend to take relationship advice from a man who couldn't honor his own wedding vows."

"I made a mistake," John said wearily.

"Locking your keys in the car is a mistake. Washing whites with colors is a mistake. A ten-month affair while your wife is raising your three kids and caring for her ailing mother?" He shook his head. "That's selfish and self-indulgent behavior."

He didn't wait for his father's response—he wasn't willing to listen to any more of his excuses. He turned and carried the bottle of juice upstairs.

Chapter Twelve

"Is everything okay?" Avery asked Justin as they were driving away from his parents' house.

"Sure," he said.

"There seemed to be some…tension," she said cautiously, "between you and your dad when you came back to the dining room."

"It wasn't about the baby," he promised. "My parents are both thrilled that they're going to be grandparents again."

"I have to admit, I wasn't expecting that."

"Because you haven't seen them when the whole family is together. My mother is never happier than when there are a bunch of little ones around. It nearly broke her heart when Ryan and Harper moved to Florida with Oliver last year."

"You're lucky to have such a close family," she told him.

He could tell that she was thinking ahead to the following weekend, when she would be in Georgia for a medical conference—and to share the news with her parents.

"Do you want me to go to Atlanta with you?"

She seemed surprised that he would offer and, after only the briefest hesitation, she shook her head. "You have to work Saturday night."

"I can get someone to cover for me," he offered.

"There's no need."

"Would you tell me if there was?" he asked her.

"I'm not going to pretend that my parents will be even half as excited or supportive as yours, but I can handle it."

Of course she could. Avery didn't need anyone to help her with anything. Not only could she handle everything on her own, she preferred it that way—a truth that continued to frustrate him. "I'd really like to be there with you when you share the news with your parents," he said.

She shook her head. "Having you there will only shift attention from the baby to our relationship."

"And that's a problem?"

"Yeah, because right now, I'm not prepared to face questions that I don't know how to answer."

"All the more reason for me to be there," he suggested.

"Not this time," she said.

"Okay," he finally agreed.

They rode in silence for another few minutes before she said, "If the tension between you and your dad wasn't about the baby—what was it about?"

He should have realized she wouldn't be distracted from her original inquiry. "Old wounds," he said simply.

"Anything to do with your sister?"

He frowned. "What hat did you pull *that* out of?"

"It makes sense," she said. "Your father had a child out of wedlock and now you are, too."

"It's hardly the same thing. For starters, I wasn't married— or even involved with someone else—when I was with you."

She nodded in acknowledgment of that fact.

"Because regardless of what you think of me and my reputation, I don't juggle women."

"I know," she said.

"But you still think I'm a bad bet," he guessed.

He was surprised by the shake of her head and even more so by the response that followed.

"I don't think you're a bad bet," she denied. "I think *I* am."

* * *

As Avery got ready to go out for dinner with Justin Wednesday night, she couldn't stop thinking about her last patient of the day. Karen Greer's fourth child had died in utero at twenty-eight weeks as a result of listeriosis and although an induction was scheduled for the following morning, Avery was still apprehensive.

She called the clinic to get Karen's home number so that she could check on her patient. It rang six times before the young mother answered, and she sounded harried and out of breath when she finally did. Of course, chasing after three young boys, she was often harried and out of breath.

"Your procedure is booked for eight a.m. tomorrow," Avery reminded her. "I just wanted to make sure that works for you."

"That's fine," Karen said. "I've made arrangements for my sister to come and watch the boys."

"I'll see you in the morning, then," she said.

But even after she hung up the phone, Avery couldn't shake the uneasy feeling in the pit of her stomach. She considered that there might be another cause for her preoccupation—maybe she was worried about her date with Justin and desperately trying not to think about it.

She saw him almost every day, and they occasionally had lunch or dinner together. But grabbing a bite after work was casual and easy, tonight was a DATE. Tonight he was taking her to a restaurant that required reservations, and for some reason that put their relationship on a completely different level—a level she wasn't entirely sure she was ready for or even wanted.

No, that wasn't entirely true. She did want to take the next step with Justin, and that scared her almost as much as her growing feelings for him. She wanted to believe that he could make a commitment to her and that they could raise their child together as a family, but personal experience warned her otherwise.

Amy kept urging her to give him a chance, but giving Justin a chance meant risking heartbreak, and that was a risk she wasn't willing to take. So she'd go out for dinner with him, and she'd work with him to figure out what was best for their baby, but she wasn't going to be foolish enough to hand him her heart.

She'd just fastened her earrings when her phone rang. She automatically checked the display, more curious than concerned until she saw R&K Greer. She dropped the lid on her jewelry box and connected the call.

Ten minutes later, she was on her way to the hospital.

Justin had made reservations at Casa Mercado, an upscale tapas bar and restaurant that had been highly recommended by his brother, Ryan. While he and Avery had made some slow and steady progress in getting to know each other, he'd deliberately kept their dates low-key: casual meals, movies at home, walks in the park. Tonight, he was determined to wow her.

And maybe tonight, when he kissed her good-night, he would turn up the heat a little. And then, if she invited him inside, he wouldn't walk away. The chemistry between them was one more reason he believed they could make a relationship work, and he was prepared to exploit it if necessary.

Except that when he arrived at Avery's building just after seven to pick her up for their seven-thirty reservation, there was no response when he buzzed her apartment. He called her cell phone next and sent a text message, but got no answer to either. It was then that he returned to the parking lot and saw her car was missing from its designated spot. He called the restaurant and canceled their reservation.

He wasn't upset or angry. Being a doctor meant that the best-laid plans often went awry—he understood that as much as anyone. A medical emergency required immediate response—he wouldn't expect her to take the time to call him and, in fact, he would have been surprised if it had occurred to her to do so. She would have been focused on caring for her patient and that was how it should be.

But when the emergency had been dealt with, when she had a minute to catch her breath and focus on other matters, he hoped that she would call to explain. His phone remained silent.

Avery sank down onto one of the overstuffed sofas in the doctors' lounge, drawing her knees up to her chest and wrapping her arms around them. Her chest felt tight and her eyes were burning, but she didn't cry.

She hadn't let herself shed many tears since she was nine years old and found out that her grandmother had died. Dr. Cristina Tobin—Avery's mother—had tolerated a few sniffles, then she'd told her daughter to dry her eyes, because if she ever wanted to have a career in medicine, she was going to have to accept that death was a fact of life and learn not to give in to her emotions.

Avery had broken down a few times since that day, but not ever again in front of her mother. The first time was when she'd broken up with Mason Turner, her first love and first lover; the next was when she'd lost a twenty-five-week-old baby during her obstetrics rotation in medical school.

She'd known the baby's chances of making it were slim, but the neonatal team had worked so hard to get the nearly two pound baby through the first and most critical twenty-four hours after birth and he'd seemed to be doing well when she went home at the end of her shift. But when she returned to the hospital the next day, he was gone. It wasn't the first patient she'd failed to save, but for some reason losing that baby—an infant that she'd helped deliver, that she'd held in her very hands—had really shaken her.

Tears were a sign of weakness, Cristina had told her. She was already fighting an uphill battle as a woman. She couldn't afford to be weak and she especially couldn't afford to show any sign of weakness.

She wasn't crying now, but the tears were there—burning her eyes and clogging her throat. She'd known that Karen's baby was gone, of course, but holding on to the tiny lifeless body, she'd been overwhelmed by a wave of grief and frustration and fear. Karen had carried and delivered three other children without any difficulty, but an undercooked burger had introduced dangerous bacteria to her system and ultimately cost the life of this one.

And suddenly Avery was in a panic about her own unborn child, overwhelmed by the knowledge of how many things could go wrong in a pregnancy and swamped by a feeling of complete helplessness. Because even if she did all of the right things—and she was trying—there were no guarantees that her pregnancy would go to term or that the baby would be born healthy.

She heard the door open and footsteps enter the room, but she didn't look up. The footsteps drew nearer, and then Justin lowered himself onto the battered coffee table, facing her.

"It's cookies 'n' cream," he said, offering her a single-serving tub of ice cream and a spoon.

She looked at him blankly.

"There's conflicting evidence about the safety of herbal teas during pregnancy and I know you hate decaf coffee," he explained. "I figured this was a more appealing option."

"Thanks." She accepted the frozen offering. "But what are you doing here?"

"Well, my plans for the night fell through so I thought I'd hang out at the hospital and try to pick up a hot doctor."

She tried—and failed—to muster a smile for him. "Good luck with that," she said, peeling the lid off the tub to dip the spoon into the ice cream.

He settled his hands on her thighs. "It seems to be working out so far."

"I should have called you," she said, before she shoved a spoonful of cookies 'n' cream into her mouth.

"I'm a doctor, too," he reminded her. "I know how it works."

She dipped the spoon into the container again and nodded. "How's your patient?"

"Stable," she answered around the mouthful of ice cream.

"How are you?"

Her eyes filled with tears again. She shook her head as she swallowed. "Apparently not so stable."

He moved to sit beside her on the sofa, putting his arm across her shoulders. She didn't know why, but it felt natural to tip her head back, so that she was leaning against him. He was so solid and warm and, for some inexplicable reason, just being close to him made her feel safe enough to finally let go of the grief that she'd been holding inside. Justin didn't say anything as the tears spilled onto her cheeks, only held her close while she cried.

"I knew the baby was gone," she told him when she'd gathered her composure enough to speak again. "We did an ultrasound earlier today and confirmed an intrauterine death. She was scheduled for induction tomorrow morning, and although she started to bleed around four o'clock, she thought she could hold off until the morning."

Avery closed her eyes and sighed wearily. "She didn't call me until after she'd made dinner for her other kids. I immediately called 9-1-1 but she was unconscious even before the paramedics arrived."

"But she's okay now," he reminded her gently.

She nodded. "Physically, anyway. The emotional scars will take longer to heal."

"They always do."

"I'm not sure if it's a blessing or a curse that she's got three other kids to take care of at home."

"Is there a dad in the picture?" he asked.

"A great dad—devoted to his wife and kids but busy working two jobs to keep a roof over their heads, so he doesn't get to spend much time with any of them."

"A common dilemma for a lot of parents," he noted.

She nodded again and scooped up some more ice cream.

"Are you going to share any of that?" Justin asked her.

"I thought you bought it for me."

"I did," he agreed. "But I missed dinner, too."

She offered the spoon to him.

There was something incredibly sensual about sharing an eating utensil, about watching his lips close around the spoon that had been inside her own mouth. And a slow growing awareness pushed through the bubble of grief that had enveloped her.

She tore her gaze away. "I am sorry about our date."

"We'll reschedule," he promised.

She wanted to, because she enjoyed being with him— so much more than she knew was smart. It was crazy how quickly and completely he'd infiltrated her life, how much she looked forward to seeing him every day, and how much she missed him when she didn't.

Being with him was exciting and scary, because her feelings for him were already so much stronger than she'd ever intended. He had this uncanny ability to know when she needed him—even if she wouldn't admit it. And the more time she spent with him, the more she was in danger of not just relying on him but falling in love with him. Despite her earlier promise to herself not to give him her heart, she was afraid that she'd already done so.

"What are we doing here?" she asked softly.

"Sharing ice cream."

She shook her head. "I didn't mean at this particular moment."

"What did you mean?"

"I'm just wondering why we're going through the motions."

He scooped up another spoonful of ice cream. "Is that what you think we're doing?"

"We had sex and I got pregnant and now we're trying to turn that into a relationship, and I'm not sure that's a good idea."

"I know you're accustomed to having a life plan," he acknowledged. "But not everything can be scheduled and organized according to your timetable. Sometimes you just have to let things happen and be willing to deal with the consequences."

"Isn't our baby proof that I'm doing that?"

He tightened his arm around her. "I think that's the first time you've said that."

"Said what?"

"*Our* baby."

She frowned. "I say it all the time."

He shook his head. "You say 'the baby'—you don't usually acknowledge that we're both responsible for the life growing inside of you."

"Maybe I was subconsciously trying to absolve you of responsibility."

"I don't think it was subconscious at all."

"Maybe not," she admitted. "When I first suspected that I might be pregnant, I was certain you wouldn't want to have anything to do with the baby—*our* baby."

"And now you know you were wrong?" he prompted.

"Now I'm starting to believe I was wrong," she acknowledged.

He kissed the top of her head and hugged her close. "Then we're making progress."

Chapter Thirteen

The next day, Avery was carrying her lunch tray into the atrium when she spotted Callie. She hadn't seen the nurse in several weeks and started automatically toward the long table where she was seated with several other nurses. As Avery drew nearer, their conversation faded away.

"I didn't mean to interrupt," she said. "I just wondered how Camryn and Brad are doing with their new baby."

"You're not interrupting," Callie said, speaking loudly enough to ensure that she could be heard by everyone at the table. "Nothing more than the usual hospital gossip, anyway."

Heather shot her a venomous look as she picked up her tray and left the table. A couple other nurses commented that they were due back at their stations and followed suit.

"I guess the talk was about me," Avery said, which didn't really surprise her.

Anyone who had seen her with Justin would be able to tell that the relationship between them had changed. And people were watching, because Dr. Romeo had always been the subject of much scrutiny and speculation around the hospital. People liked to talk about who he was dating and guess how long a relationship would last. Some of the nurses ran a pool—anything outside of two weeks was always considered a long shot—and bonus points were awarded to anyone who correctly identified the lucky woman chosen as his next companion.

No one would have guessed that he would pick Avery, and she could tell that they were as baffled as they were envious that he was with her now. Of course, only she and Justin knew the truth—that they were only together because she was pregnant with his child.

She hated that people assumed she was sleeping with him—which was both ridiculous and hypocritical, because while she wasn't actually sleeping with him now, she had been naked with him. She had no right or reason to be upset that they were judging her for the truth.

The worst part, though, was that her body had apparently not gotten the memo from her brain that what had happened between them that night was not going to happen again. Every time he touched her or kissed her, her hormones started clamoring for more.

"Heather's all bent out of shape because she saw you and Dr. Garrett in the lounge together last night," Callie explained, gesturing for her to sit down.

"And?" Avery prompted, setting her tray on the table.

The nurse shrugged. "She said he was—" she made quotation marks in the air with her fingers "—consoling you."

"I almost lost a patient last night," she explained. "Dr. Garrett could tell I was upset, and we sat and talked for a while."

"You don't have to explain," Callie assured her. "Everyone thinks the two of you would be great together. Well, almost everyone. Not that *everyone* is talking about you," she hastened to explain. "Because that would be completely unprofessional and inappropriate."

Avery managed a smile. "Well, thanks for the heads-up about the gossip that's not gossip."

The nurse smiled back. "Anytime."

"And your nephew?" she prompted.

"He's fabulous." Callie opened the camera app on her phone. "Let me show you some pictures."

Friday night, Avery was in Atlanta and Justin was alone at home, contemplating his dinner options. Because he didn't have neatly labeled containers in his freezer, those options were pizza and Chinese, both of which he could have delivered to his door.

He opted for a large pizza that would fulfill his requirements for dinner tonight and lunch the following day. He'd just hung up the phone after placing his order when the buzzer sounded from downstairs.

He knew it couldn't be his pizza delivery already, and a quick glance at the lobby display made him frown. He picked up the phone again, answering the summons.

"It's Ryder Wallace—Avery's brother."

Justin figured the man would show up somewhere, and he was grateful he hadn't tracked him down at the hospital. Of course, it was probably out of deference to his sister that he'd avoided a showdown in that arena. No doubt she'd told him that she didn't want anyone at work to know about her pregnancy yet—or the identity of her baby's father at all.

"Come on up," he said, releasing the lock on the downstairs door.

He'd never met Avery's brother, but he'd seen him on TV. The guy seemed taller in person—about Justin's own height, but broader. His shoulders seemed to fill the doorway, and the muscles in his arms confirmed that his job required him to wield tools much heavier than a scalpel or stethoscope. Not that he felt intimidated, exactly, but Ryder's grim expression was hardly reassuring.

"Are you going to invite me to come in?" he asked, when Justin continued to block the door.

"It depends," he said. "Are you planning to hit me?"

Ryder shrugged his broad shoulders. "I thought we'd try talking first."

"Talking works for me," Justin said, stepping back so Avery's brother could enter. "Do you want something to drink?"

"I wouldn't say no to a beer."

He pulled a couple of bottles of his favorite microbrew from the fridge, twisted off the caps and handed one to the other man.

Ryder glanced at the label, then lifted the bottle to his lips and sipped cautiously. "Not bad," he decided.

"Thanks, but I'm guessing you didn't come over here to critique my beer selection."

"I didn't," he confirmed. "I'm here because Avery told me about the baby."

"I suspected as much," Justin said.

"My sister's a smart woman," Ryder noted. "She likes to gather facts and evidence before she decides on a course of action. She's never careless or impulsive, so you can imagine how surprised I was when she told me that she was pregnant."

"Me, too," he admitted.

"I don't know what your relationship is, and Avery would say it's none of my business—"

"I disagree," he interjected. "She's your sister and the child she's carrying is your niece or nephew. It's understandable that you'd be concerned."

"I am concerned," Ryder said. "She thinks she's prepared to do this on her own—from everything she's said to me, she's determined to do this on her own—but a child should have two parents."

"Our child will have two parents," Justin assured him.

"I'd be more convinced of that if you were planning to marry her."

"I am."

Ryder frowned. "Well, that was a lot easier than I expected."

"Easy?" Justin laughed. "It doesn't matter that you and I are in agreement. Try convincing your sister—*that's* the hard part."

"You've talked to her about this?"

He nodded. "And she said she wants to get married someday—but not to me."

Ryder winced. "Sorry."

Justin shrugged. "I understand some of her reservations."

"If you met our parents, you'd understand a lot more."

"Maybe you could fill in some of the details for me," he suggested.

Ryder tipped the bottle to his lips again, considering what—or maybe how much—to say. "For starters, they got married in May and Avery was born in November the same year—and she wasn't a preemie."

"So they got married because your mother was pregnant," Justin acknowledged. "That's hardly an unusual situation."

"You're right. But the unplanned pregnancy forced them to detour from their plans. Whenever either of us would make the mistake of asking if they could attend a school activity or sporting event, Mom would remind us that she had to work to make up for the time she lost giving birth."

"And your dad?" Justin prompted.

"He always said he would try to be there," Ryder admitted. "Which made it even harder when he never showed up."

"It sounds like you had lousy parents," Justin said. "But there are plenty of couples who manage to have successful careers and happy families."

"Sure," the other man agreed. "But a doctor doesn't punch a clock—people's lives depend on them being available."

"But not every minute of every day," he countered. "And I think that both Avery and I have been doing this long enough that we've found some necessary balance."

"Until a baby throws the scale out of whack."

"I'm confident that we can figure it out together."

Ryder tipped his bottle to his lips again. "You're not at all what I expected when Avery told me about you."

"What did you expect?" he asked curiously.

"I expected to want to hit you," Ryder admitted. "But now, I actually think you could be good for her."

"If I can convince your sister to give me a chance."

"If you've got another beer, I might be persuaded to share some insights."

"I've got more beer *and* pizza coming."

Ryder grinned. "Now I'm really glad I stopped by."

Avery had decided to attend the Spring Conference in Atlanta because the trip would also give her the opportunity to see both of her parents. Not that she expected either of them to adjust their own schedules to accommodate hers—and her mother did not disappoint in that regard.

When Avery called to set up a time for Saturday, Cristina advised that she had a lunch meeting with a pharmaceutical rep at one o'clock, and then she was presenting a research paper on new vaccines that were in development for sexually transmitted diseases at four. She offered to squeeze out some time for Avery in between these commitments.

At two-thirty, Avery was seated at the hotel bar, waiting. Her stomach was tangled in knots and her hands were clammy because, despite the fact that she was thirty-two years old, apparently she was still reluctant to disappoint her mother.

The knots in her stomach tightened when her mother walked into the bar. Cristina air-kissed Avery's cheek before sliding onto the vacant stool beside her daughter.

"G&T, extra lime," Cristina told the bartender.

"I'll have the same," Avery said. "Hold the G."

Her mother frowned. "That's just tonic."

"With lime."

"You said you wanted to meet for a drink," she said, her tone disapproving of the fact that her expectations had not been met.

Avery was all too familiar with that tone. "No, *I* said I wanted to meet for dinner," she reminded her mother. "*You* said you didn't have time for dinner but we could do drinks."

"Tonic water isn't a drink."

"Well, gin isn't good for the baby," she said bluntly, unable to endure any more of her mother's nitpicking.

"The—" Cristina's mouth dropped open. "You're pregnant?"

Avery nodded. "Yes, I am."

"How far along?"

"Ten weeks."

Cristina immediately lifted the glass the bartender set down in front of her and took a healthy swig. "It's not too late, then."

"Too late for what?" she asked, a sinking feeling in the pit of her stomach. But she pushed the uneasiness away, because there was no way her mother was saying what she thought she was saying.

"To terminate the pregnancy."

The blunt statement felt like a physical blow, but Avery lifted her own glass and sipped. Her throat was tight and her eyes burned, but she refused to give in to her emotions—refused to give Cristina that ammunition to use against her.

"I don't want to terminate the pregnancy," she said, pleased that her voice was clear and calm.

"You can't honestly think that it's a good idea to have a baby at this point in your life."

"I didn't plan to get pregnant," she acknowledged. "But I want this baby."

"Because you have no idea how demanding a child can be—especially an infant," Cristina warned. "And you're not married, so you won't have any support system to help you through the long nights and other difficult times."

"I know there will be challenges, but Justin and I will figure it out," she said, with more conviction than she felt.

"He's the father?" her mother guessed.

"Yes, he's the father."

"So you have a…relationship?"

She nodded.

"Are you planning to get married?" Cristina asked. "Or live together?"

"We haven't worked out all of the details yet."

Her mother sipped her drink. "Is he pressuring you to do this?"

"What?"

"Is he pressuring you to have the baby?"

"No, Mom. This was *my* decision."

"Because I have a friend—she works at a private women's clinic in Forest Park. I can give her a call and get you in to see her this weekend. Then you can go back to Karma and tell him that you lost the baby. Ten to twenty percent of women miscarry in their first trimester."

She drew in a slow breath and mentally counted to ten. "It's Charisma," she reminded her mother. "And I'm well aware of the statistics about miscarriages—and I want to have this baby."

Cristina lifted her glass again, frowning when she saw it was empty.

"Can I get you a refill?" the bartender asked.

"No," Avery responded before Cristina could, because she didn't want to prolong this painful encounter a single minute longer than necessary. Then, to her mother, she said, "I appreciate you squeezing in some time to see me, but I know you're busy and anxious to get back to the conference."

"I do have to review my notes for the presentation," Cristina acknowledged, taking out her wallet to pay for their drinks.

Avery just nodded.

"Think about what I said," her mother advised, tucking the money under her glass. "I'm happy to make the call for you, if you change your mind."

"I won't change my mind," she promised. "But what is even more important, I won't ever let my child doubt that she was both wanted and loved from the minute I learned of her existence."

After meeting with her mother, Avery took off her conference badge, tucked it into her bag and headed up to her room on the eighth floor.

Her mother's reaction to the news didn't just bother her—it worried her. Cristina Tobin was the only example of a mother Avery had ever had. Anything she thought she knew about parenting had been learned from her own parents, and neither of them had been the warm, fuzzy type.

Justin's family was different. Even in her limited interactions with them, she could tell that much. She could tell even more by the way he talked about them—the easy but unmistakable affection in his voice. And it wasn't just his parents and his brothers that he was close to. When he talked about his family, he meant all of his aunts, uncles and cousins, too. Even his half sister.

There were still a lot of months before their baby would be born, but she realized that she no longer wanted him to lose interest. Instead, she was hoping his family could be an example that she and Justin might emulate for their child, because she had no intention of basing her parenting style on her own family.

Thinking about Justin now, she impulsively pulled her cell phone out of her purse and called his number. He answered on the second ring and the sound of his voice, so strong and familiar, brought tears to her eyes. And because no one was around to see, she didn't worry about holding them back.

"Avery? What's wrong?"

"Nothing's wrong," she lied. "I just…I wanted to hear your voice."

"Then I'm glad you called," he said. "How's the conference?"

She swiped at the tears that spilled onto her cheeks. "It's good."

"That doesn't sound very convincing," he said gently.

"I was just thinking…and wondering…do you…do you think we're doing the right thing?"

"About what?"

"The baby."

He was silent for a minute. "Well, I'd prefer if we got married—"

"No," she said. "I mean…do you wish I had taken the morning-after pill?"

"No," he said, his immediate and vehement response soothing some of her anxiety. "Maybe in the beginning, before we knew that you were pregnant, I might have thought that was the right choice. But now, I'm so glad that you didn't. I *want* this baby—*our* baby."

The tears were falling in earnest now.

"What's this about?" he asked.

"I saw my mother today and told her that I was pregnant," she admitted.

"And she didn't respond well to the news," he guessed.

"She told me…" She swallowed around the lump in her

throat. "She told me that it wasn't…too late…to terminate my pregnancy."

"Tell me you're joking."

She shook her head, though she knew he couldn't see her. It was all she could manage without sobbing.

"Avery?" he prompted.

"I'm not joking," she told him. "She said that I have no idea how—" she drew in a shuddering breath "—how difficult it will be to juggle the demands of a baby with my career."

"It won't be easy," he agreed. "But I know we can do it."

We can do it.

The words, combined with his unwavering conviction, helped steady her. She only wished he was there with her so she could feel the solid warmth of his arms around her and not feel so alone. But that, of course, was the danger she was fighting against—needing him, relying on him, loving him.

"Please tell me you're not considering what she suggested," he pleaded.

"I'm not," she told him. "Of course not."

"Good."

"You really do want this baby?"

"More than I ever thought I would," he admitted. "And more and more every day."

And me? She wanted to ask.

But, of course, she didn't. Because she had no idea what his answer might be, and she wasn't prepared to open herself up for yet another rejection.

They talked awhile longer and she felt a lot better about everything when she finally disconnected the call. Not good enough to want to go back downstairs and risk running into her mother again, but better.

Though it was only four o'clock, she took a shower, put on her pajamas, fell asleep on top of the covers and woke up three hours later to realize it was past dinnertime and she was hungry. She ordered room service, then booted up her computer to look at changing her return flight to Charisma. She'd originally planned to see her father for brunch the following day, but she wasn't sure she could deal with a second round of what she'd gone through with her mother.

Maybe that wasn't fair. Maybe her father would be more supportive of her choices. She honestly didn't know, and that alone said everything about their relationship.

And now that the insult wasn't quite so fresh, Avery found it interesting that Cristina didn't believe her daughter would be able to balance her career with the responsibilities of a child. Because, as far as Avery could tell, neither of her parents had ever really tried to do so, preferring to work longer hours to pay someone else to raise their children.

A knock sounded at the door, dragging her attention away from those unhappy memories. Her stomach growled in anticipation of her dinner, but when she opened the door it wasn't room service on the other side.

It was Justin.

Chapter Fourteen

It seemed like forever that she just stood there, staring at him. Certainly it was long enough for Justin to question the wisdom of rearranging his schedule and hopping on a plane just because she'd called and he thought she might need him.

"I was in the neighborhood," he began, and her lips curved, just a little.

It wasn't even really a smile, but it was all he needed to be glad that he'd made the trip.

"Are you going to let me come in?" he asked.

"I was waiting for the rest of the story—" she stepped away from the door, gesturing for him to enter "—about why you were in the neighborhood."

"Because I needed to see you," he admitted, setting his overnight bag inside the door. "To be sure that you were okay."

The warmth in her eyes dimmed a little. "You thought I was going to do it."

"Do what?" he asked, baffled by the accusatory tone.

She folded her arms over her chest. "Get rid of our baby."

"No, I didn't." He stroked his hands down her arms. "I promise you, Avery, the possibility never even crossed my mind."

"It didn't?" she asked uncertainly.

"Of course not," he told her. "There may be a lot I still don't know about you, but I know you want our baby as much as I do."

"Then why are you here?"

"Because you sounded like you needed a friend."

She unfolded her arms and splayed her palms on his chest. "You flew four hundred miles because I sounded like a needed a friend?"

"And because it would have taken too long to drive," he said logically.

She shook her head, but she was smiling again. "You constantly surprise me."

"Good, then I shouldn't have to worry about you getting bored with me," he said, and lowered his head to touch his lips to hers.

It was a fleeting kiss—friendly, casual—that might have led to something more if another knock hadn't sounded at the door.

"Room service."

She pulled away from him, drew in a breath. "That's my dinner."

He went to the door and slipped some bills from his pocket in exchange for the tray. He set it on the table and lifted the lid to uncover two slices of bread with thinly-sliced roast beef in between and a scoop of potato salad on the side. "*This* is your dinner?"

"I didn't know what I wanted," she admitted. "Then I remembered the day you showed up in the doctors' lounge with the roast beef sandwich, demanding that I take care of myself."

"A sandwich is fine for lunch when you're rushing from the hospital to the clinic, but you need something more substantial for dinner," he said, putting the lid back on the plate. "Let's go out and get some real food."

She glanced pointedly at her plaid pajama pants and rib-knit Henley. "I can't go out like this."

"Why not?"

"Because these are my pajamas."

"Then put some clothes on," he suggested.

"And I've cried off all of my makeup."

He cupped her face in his hands. "I hate to think of you here, by yourself, crying," he admitted.

"I think it's the pregnancy hormones," she said. "I feel like I don't have any control over my emotions anymore."

He thought it was probably as much the fault of her mother, but he wasn't going to go there now. "How about pregnancy cravings?" he asked instead. "What are you in the mood to eat?"

"A whole cow."

"Okay, I'll call the concierge and ask for a nearby cattle ranch recommendation while you get dressed."

She gathered up her clothes and moved toward the bathroom, pausing in the doorway. "Justin—"

He turned back.

"Thank you," she said quietly.

He smiled. "My pleasure."

He took her to a restaurant called the Chophouse. The decor was simple: sturdy tables covered with neatly pressed linen cloths, leather booth seating and muted lighting. But it was the mouthwatering scent of grilled meat that really appealed to Avery and made her stomach growl so loudly that Justin turned to look at her.

She started with a field greens salad with a tomato-parmesan vinaigrette, followed by a ten-ounce filet mignon with roasted fingerling potatoes and grilled asparagus. He had the same type of salad, then the New York Strip with sautéed sweet corn and mashed red-skinned potatoes.

"I can't believe I ate all of that," she said, after she'd cleared her plate.

"It was too good not to," Justin said, having polished off his own meal. "And you look better now that you've got some food in you."

She managed a wry smile. "I probably couldn't look much worse than I did when you showed up at the door of my hotel room."

"You're always beautiful," he told her. "But you looked a little tired and a lot sad."

"I was feeling a little tired and a lot sad," she admitted.

"And now?"

"I feel better." And maybe a little foolish that she'd let her mother's insensitive remarks get to her. Maybe she should have been stronger. Maybe she shouldn't have called Justin. But she couldn't deny that she was glad he was there with her now.

"Dessert?" he asked.

She managed a laugh. "You've got to be kidding."

He nudged the dessert menu that the waiter had left on the edge of the table toward her. "They have homemade ice cream."

"You are the devil."

He just grinned. "I'm going to try the raspberry mango cheesecake."

"Some women lose weight in the first trimester, but I've gained three pounds already," she told him.

"Gaining weight is necessary when you're growing a baby," he said matter-of-factly.

She looked at him across the table, his gaze steady even in the flickering light of the candle. He was so incredibly handsome—and so much more than his playboy personality had led her to believe.

"You know, a few weeks ago I was thinking that I'd completely screwed up, getting pregnant with your baby," she confided. "I've only recently started to realize that if I had to get pregnant, I'm so glad it was with *your* baby."

He reached across the table to take her hand. "Me, too."

"Does that mean you'll come with me to see my dad tomorrow?"

"I was just waiting for you to ask," he told her.

"And if I didn't ask?"

"I was going, anyway."

His answer didn't surprise her. What did surprise her was that she was grateful for his determination to stand by her side. Over the past few weeks, he'd proven that he was a man she could count on and trust—maybe even a man she could fall in love with—which was why she was trying very hard to keep her balance.

When the waiter came back to the table, Justin ordered the cheesecake and Avery opted for the ice cream.

By the time they left the restaurant, it was after ten o'clock. He took her hand again as they walked to the hotel. It was a cool night, but she didn't feel the chill in the air with Justin beside her.

"I need to stop at the desk," he said, when they entered the lobby and she started automatically toward the bank of elevators.

"Why?"

"I was in such a hurry to get here, I didn't book a room," he admitted.

Until that moment, she hadn't given a single thought to where he might be sleeping. Of course, he needed his own room—offering to share hers would be tempting fate. Despite his claim that he'd come to Atlanta because she'd sounded as if she needed a friend, there was more between them than friendship. And the more she grew to like Justin, the harder it was to ignore the attraction.

So she nodded and followed him to the desk. Unfortunately, the clerk informed him, there was a medical conference in the hotel and no rooms were available. He offered to contact the Sheraton across the street, but Avery shook her head.

"I have a room here," she reminded him, trying to sound casual. "It has two beds—and I'll only be sleeping in one of them."

Justin appreciated the offer, especially because he knew it couldn't have been an easy one for her to make. "Are you sure that won't be...awkward?" he asked cautiously.

She shrugged. "You said you plan to be there when I have the baby. In comparison, I don't think sharing a hotel room for one night even registers on the scale of awkward."

"In that case, I'll say thank-you."

When they got back to her room, Avery went directly to the bathroom with her pajamas. She came out again a few minutes later, wearing the same plaid pants and rib-knit Henley she'd had on when he arrived. And she didn't have anything on beneath the top, because he could see the outline of her nipples clearly—two hard points pushing against the fabric, making all the blood in his body head south.

Which reminded him of another problem: he hadn't worried about bringing something to sleep in because he hadn't considered the possibility that they might end up sharing a room. So he waited until she was under the covers, then he turned out the light and stripped down to his boxer briefs before slipping between the sheets of the other bed.

He'd gotten up early that morning to help his cousin Daniel put together the backyard climbing apparatus he'd bought for his almost two-year-old son, so he should have been exhausted. And he was. He was also conscious of Avery's every movement, every breath. About an hour after the lights had been turned off, she shoved the covers away and padded into the bathroom.

He sat up in bed, waiting for her to return. "Can't sleep?"

She started at his question, obviously not having realized that he was awake. "I'm sorry—I didn't mean to disturb you."

"You didn't," he told her. "I wasn't sleeping, either."

She hesitated for a second, then she came over and perched on the edge of his bed. She was facing him, with one knee bent on the mattress and the other leg hanging over the edge. She was close enough that he only had to lift a hand to touch her, but he didn't.

"I still can't believe you dropped everything to come to Atlanta," she said softly. "No one has ever done anything like that for me before."

"I didn't just drop everything," he said, hoping to score even more points. "I had to call Greg Roberts to cover my shift in the ER."

"Did he grumble?"

"A little, but he owed me for New Year's Eve."

"You weren't supposed to work that night?" she asked. He shook his head. "No."

"And if you hadn't taken that shift for him…"

"We wouldn't be where we are right now," he completed the thought. "I guess maybe I owe him."

She smiled at that. "I wanted you here," she admitted to him now. "I would never have asked you to come, but I really wanted you here."

"I want you to ask—if you ever need anything," he said.

"It's not easy for me."

"I know—you always want to do everything on your own. But you're not on your own anymore."

"Amy was right."

His brows lifted. "What was she right about?"

"There's a lot more to you than most people realize."

"She said that?"

"She did," Avery confirmed. "She also told me that she didn't believe you'd slept with Heather—despite the rumors."

"I always did like Amy," he said. "She's a smart woman."

"Did you and she ever…?" She trailed off, as if unable to put the question into words.

"No," he answered immediately. "I might have thought about making a move, but she's been in love with Ben for as long as I've known her—even when he was on the other side of the world."

She nodded. "She told me that he was gone for twelve years, and she never stopped loving him."

"Distance and time don't matter when you love someone."

"Do you really believe that?" she asked skeptically.

"I do," he confirmed.

"I guess that tells me everything I needed to know about why my fiancé fell in love with someone else only a few months after he went to Haiti."

"Are you still in love with him?" Even as the question spilled out of his mouth, Justin wanted to pull it back. Because if the answer was yes, he didn't want to hear it.

But she shook her head. "No. Definitely not."

"Then I'm inclined to think that neither of you was one hundred percent all the way in love," he suggested.

"Maybe not," she acknowledged. "But how do you know? It's not like your heart has one of those meter things with an arrow that shifts from 'casual affection' to 'all the way in love.'"

He smiled at the mental image. "You're right—it's not something you can see. It's something you feel." He slid his arms around her, drawing her into his embrace. "It's wanting to spend every possible minute with the other person and missing them every second that you're apart. It's knowing that your life is better, richer and fuller with that other person in it."

"It almost sounds like you know what you're talking about," she said lightly.

"I'm starting to." He brushed his lips against hers, a whisper-soft kiss. "I'm crazy about you, Avery."

"You make me crazy," she said. "Whenever I'm with you, I get all tangled up inside so that I don't know what I'm thinking or feeling."

"What are we going to do about that?"

She lifted her gaze to his. "You could take me to bed."

"You're already in my bed," he pointed out to her.

"So I am." She let her lips graze his jaw, his unshaven skin rasping beneath her soft mouth. "Can I stay?"

Forever, he wanted to say, but he suspected that kind of response would send her running. Instead, he said lightly, "I'd never kick a beautiful woman out of my bed."

"That's the rumor," she agreed. "But I'd rather not talk about all the other women now."

He tipped her chin up. "There's no one but you now. I don't want anyone but you."

"You do want me?"

It killed him that she even had to ask, that she had any doubts about his feelings for her. But he knew the question was rooted in deeper history. "More than you can imagine."

"I can imagine a lot," she said, lifting her arms to link them behind his head and draw his mouth close to hers again.

His arms tightened around her. "Then let me show you."

And finally he kissed her.

No—it was completely inadequate to describe the feel of his lips on hers as a kiss. It was a seduction of her mouth: patient, thorough, devastating. And Avery's mind was spinning around one single thought: *yes*. Her body was aching and straining toward one single goal: *more*.

And he gave her more. His tongue swept into her mouth, tasting and teasing. His hands slipped under her pajama top, touching and tempting. Her palms slid over his bare shoulders—those strong, solid shoulders, down his chest to his stomach—learning and loving all those hard, rippling muscles.

He lifted his mouth from hers only long enough to dispose of her pajama top, then he eased her down onto the mattress and stripped away the bottoms, too. He straddled her naked body, his knees bracketing her hips, holding her in position while he worshipped her body with his hands and his mouth. He seemed to instinctively know where to touch, where to linger.

No, it wasn't instinct—it was experience. The man had a wealth of experience in the bedroom, but she wasn't going to let that bother her now. She wasn't even going to think about that now. In fact, with his hands and his lips moving over her body, she could hardly think at all.

She reached down to stroke his hard length, and he jerked in her hand. "I don't know what it is about you that makes me respond like a horny seventeen-year-old."

"I wouldn't know—I didn't have sex until I was almost twenty."

"But I bet you drove all of the guys at your high school crazy, anyway."

"I doubt it. I was something of a nerd."

He nibbled on her lips. "I always thought smart girls were sexy."

"Prove it," she said, pushing his briefs over his hips.

"I will," he promised. Then, "I have condoms."

"What?"

"In my toiletry kit," he explained. "I haven't been with anyone else since you, and you've seen the test results so you know there's nothing to worry about, but if you don't believe me, I can go—"

"I believe you," she said, because it was true. Because—his reputation aside—he had never given her any reason not to trust him, and she no longer questioned that she did.

He kissed her again, long and slow and deep, while his

hands continued to touch and tease. It amazed her, how quickly and effortlessly he could make her body respond, make her yearn.

"You make me feel…so much."

"There's more," he promised, sliding farther down her body.

"Don't you want—"

He touched his fingertips to her lips, silencing her words. "I definitely want," he said. "And I will. But first, I want to show you some of the things we missed out on in the closet."

"I have no complaints about what happened in SC."

He smiled at her use of his code and slid his hands between her legs, urging them apart as he lowered himself between them. "Then you won't have any complaints tonight, either."

She felt his breath on her first—a whisper of warmth that made everything inside her tense and tighten. Then his fingers, parting the soft folds of flesh at her center. And then his tongue, just the barest flick of his tongue. Her hips bucked instinctively, a wordless plea for more. *Yes. More.*

He clamped onto her hips, holding her immobile while he took her with his mouth, licking and nibbling and sucking while she gasped and moaned. He took his time, drawing out her pleasure. And then, finally, her body flew apart, shattering into billions of shards of exquisite sensation, and he held her while all those sparkling pieces free-fell from the heavens.

"Open your eyes, Avery."

She managed to do so, though her gaze was still unfocused, the world still spinning. He rose up over her, then he slid into her—one slow, deep thrust that filled her deeply, completely.

This time, he moaned, a low sound of satisfaction. She tilted her hips, taking him just a little bit deeper, and though she would have sworn it wasn't possible, her body went from loose and languid to primed and ready again in a heartbeat.

He began to move in a slow and steady rhythm, stroking deep, deeper, causing the pressure to build inside her. Gradually he increased the pace. Faster. Harder. His skin was damp beneath her palms, his breath rasping out of his lungs in shallow pants.

She could tell he was close to his own release, but he was holding back, waiting for her. She'd never had a lover who was so completely unselfish, so single-mindedly focused on making her feel good. She wanted to reciprocate, to give back to him even a fraction of the pleasure that he'd given to her, but she was already caught up again in another maelstrom of desire, a myriad of sensations battering at her, overwhelming her.

Finally he stiffened, every muscle in his body going rigid, and then he emptied himself inside of her. When he could finally summon the energy, he shifted to lift his weight off her, but he didn't let her go. He tucked her head against his chest, where she could feel his heart beating in tandem with her own.

She should have been satisfied with what had happened in the closet, because being with him like this made her believe they could have more, made her want more…

But for now, at least, they had this. So for now, this would be enough.

Chapter Fifteen

Avery fell asleep naked in Justin's arms and awoke the same way. She wondered if she should feel embarrassed about her request to share his bed, and maybe she would have if he'd turned down her entreaty. But in the warmth of his embrace, she didn't feel anything but contented. Maybe even happy.

And while she suspected that she could easily get used to this, she knew she had to be careful. Whatever was happening between them now, she couldn't let herself hope that it would last. Justin had been great since he learned of her pregnancy and he seemed committed to being a father to their child. But his recent behavior didn't change the fact that he didn't do long-term relationships, and it would be foolish to expect that his commitment to their baby extended to encompass her.

But right now, she wasn't going to worry about any of that. Right now, he was with her, and she was going to enjoy the status quo for as long as it lasted.

His hand skimmed over her torso, from her thigh to her hip to her breast. He found her nipple and rubbed his thumb over the taut peak. She sighed softly.

He snuggled closer to her, so she could feel the rigid length of him pressed against her backside. "I love the sounds you make when I touch you."

"I love the way you touch me," she admitted.

"I love touching you," he said, nibbling on her earlobe as his hands continued their leisurely and sensual exploration of her body.

She turned in his arms so that she was facing him. "I want to touch you, too," she said, wrapping her fingers around the hard length of him and stroking gently.

His throaty groan signaled his appreciation and further stirred her own blood.

"I haven't had morning sex in a long time," she admitted. "Actually, I hadn't had any sex in a long time, prior to New Year's Eve."

"New Year's Day," he reminded her.

"So it was technically morning sex," she realized. "But not sleepy morning sex."

"Is that what we're having?" His mouth, warm and moist, closed over her breast, and waves of sensation flooded her body.

She gasped and arched. "I don't know," she said. "Suddenly I'm not feeling so sleepy."

"Me, neither," he admitted, parting her thighs with his knee.

She opened for him, embracing him fully and completely as he slid into her wet, welcoming heat.

Yes, she could definitely get used to this.

George Wallace lived with his second wife and her two daughters in a newer two-story brick home in North Fulton. Justin and Avery rented a car so that they'd be able to leave directly from there to the airport for their flight back to North Carolina.

Sharon met them at the door, her eyes lighting up with genuine pleasure as she hugged Avery close.

"It's so good to see you," she said. "George is upstairs on the phone. Just before you pulled up, he got a call from some cardiologist in England wanting to discuss a patient's treatment.

"I told him he could have ten minutes. If the call required more time than that, he had to call back later because he wasn't going to spend your entire visit on the phone." She turned to Justin. "I'm sorry—I've been rambling on and on without even introducing myself. I'm Sharon Wallace."

He offered his hand. "Justin Garrett."

"Come in," she invited. "I've got a pot of coffee on, or fresh juice if you prefer, and everything is ready to go on the table as soon as George comes down."

While Justin drank his coffee and Avery sipped her juice—because she was trying to cut back on her caffeine intake—Sharon set another place at the table to accommodate the unexpected guest.

"Where are Molly and Ruby?" Avery asked, referring to Sharon's daughters.

"They're with their dad this weekend." She moved the chairs around the table. "Another reason why the timing of your visit is so perfect—the house is far too quiet without them."

Avery knew what it was like to be shifted from the house of one parent to the next, but she'd never considered how it might feel from the other side, as a parent who only got to be with her child for half of the time—and she didn't like thinking about it now.

Footsteps sounded on the stairs and Sharon immediately started putting food on the table. There were scrambled eggs, bacon and sausages, home-fried potatoes and pancakes—and that was in addition to the fresh fruit, yogurt and pastries that were already on the table.

Avery introduced Justin to her father. She could tell George wanted to ask who Justin was—to inquire about his relationship to her—but didn't feel as if he had the right.

Over the past several years, their relationship had faded so there was little tying them together aside from biology.

"I hope you're hungry," George said instead. "Sharon's been cooking all morning in anticipation of your visit."

His wife waved a hand dismissively. "We don't get to see Avery very often—I just wanted to be sure she didn't go away hungry."

"The buffet breakfast at the conference didn't look this good," Avery said to Sharon. "Thank you."

Her stepmother smiled. "You're welcome—dig in."

"How was the conference?" George asked, latching on to a topic of conversation that seemed safe for both of them.

"No shoptalk at the table," Sharon interjected before Avery could respond.

Her husband sighed. "She doesn't have a lot of rules, but she's strict with that one."

Sharon offered a further explanation. "The difficulty with both of us being doctors is that we often get caught up in our work and forget that there's a whole world outside of the hospital."

"Some people would say that's only one of many difficulties," Justin noted, slanting a look at Avery.

A phone rang in the other room, prompting Sharon to push her chair away from the table. "Excuse me," she said.

They continued to eat more than talk while she was gone. The problem with Sharon's no-shoptalk rule was that Avery didn't have a lot of other things in common with her father—and she wasn't quite ready to share her big news just yet.

"I'm so sorry," Sharon said, returning to the dining room with her purse and keys in hand. "That was Molly on the phone. I need to go pick her up now."

"Davis is supposed to bring both of them back after dinner," George reminded her.

"Molly asked me to come now."

"But Avery's here and we were—"

"George," she said patiently. "I'm sure Avery understands that there are certain times in a preteen girl's life when she'd rather be with her mother."

"Oh," he said, his cheeks turning red as he finally clued in to what she wasn't saying.

"If you're gone before I get back, it was really good to see you, Avery. And to meet you, Justin."

"I'm sorry Sharon had to rush off," George said when his wife had gone. "She was really looking forward to spending some time with you."

"I'm sorry, too," Avery admitted. "But I'm glad Molly and Ruby can count on her to be there when they need her."

"She's a great mom," George agreed. "Certainly a much better parent than I ever was."

"Molly posted pictures on Facebook of her science fair," Avery noted.

"She won first prize," her father said proudly.

"It's nice that you were there with her."

He didn't have any trouble deciphering the subtext. "And I never was when you were growing up, was I?"

"Water under the bridge," Avery said.

"Is it?" her father challenged.

She shrugged.

George glanced at Justin. "Did she tell you what a lousy father I was?"

"No, sir," he said. "She told me that you were an excellent cardiac surgeon."

"Same sentiment, different words," her father acknowledged. "And I'll confess, I wasn't sure anyone could be a good doctor and a good parent until I met Sharon."

"She's a pediatric oncologist," Avery told Justin. "And she's never missed a school play or gymnastics competition."

George nodded, his attention shifting back to his daughter. "You can't know how many times I've wished I could go back and do things differently—be a better father to you and your brother."

"Maybe you'll be a better grandfather," Avery suggested.

Her father paused with his coffee cup in the air. "Am I going to be a grandfather?"

She nodded.

He took a moment to absorb the news. "Well, this is… unexpected," he finally said. "When?"

"September twenty-fourth."

"Are you planning to be there when the baby's born?" he asked Justin.

"Of course."

George sipped his coffee. "I was there when Avery made her grand—and loud—entrance into the world," he confided.

That was news to Avery. "You were?"

He nodded. "I hadn't planned on it and certainly wouldn't have rearranged my schedule to accommodate it, but afterward, I was so humbled and amazed and grateful that I'd had the opportunity to share the experience. Because there is absolutely nothing more incredible than seeing a child come into this world, especially when that child is your own."

"Why did you never tell me that before?" she said.

"It's not the type of thing that usually comes up in conversation," George replied.

"Maybe it should have," Justin suggested.

The older man nodded. "You're right. There are a lot of things that should have been said and done over the years and, as a result, I've had to live with the knowledge of everything that I missed out on."

"You know, Charisma isn't that far away," Avery told him.

George seemed surprised by her statement. "Are you inviting me to visit?"

She lifted a shoulder. "If you need an invitation. And if you can fit it into your schedule."

"I'll figure out a way," he promised, his eyes growing misty. "My baby girl's going to have a baby of her own, and that is something I definitely don't want to miss."

The whole weekend had been physically and emotionally exhausting, and as Avery settled into her seat on the plane beside Justin, she was grateful to finally be going home.

"I know I already said it, but thank you again, for everything."

He flipped up the armrest that separated their two seats so that he could take her hand. "It was my pleasure."

"You have an odd definition of pleasure."

He smiled. "Come on—it wasn't so bad, was it?"

"The second act was much better than the first," she told him.

"And the intermission?" he prompted.

Thinking about the night they'd spent together, she couldn't help but smile. "The best part of the show."

He smiled back. "I certainly thought so. And, as a bonus, your dad did acknowledge that he was a lousy father."

"Mostly because, I realize now, he didn't have the first clue about what he was doing."

"It does make you wonder," Justin mused. "They won't give anyone a driver's license until they've proved they can operate a motor vehicle, but there aren't any restrictions on who can be a parent."

"Pretty much any two people willing to get naked in a supply closet can make a baby," she agreed.

"I wasn't talking about us," he chided. "I happen to think we're going to make pretty good parents."

"I appreciate your optimism, though I'm not sure it has any foundation in fact."

"We both want this baby and are committed to doing what is best for our baby."

"Okay, that's true," she acknowledged.

"Plus we've got the whole sizzling sexual chemistry thing happening."

"I'm not sure that's going to help us be good parents."

"Maybe not, but at least you didn't deny the sizzling sexual chemistry. And since I don't have to work until two o'clock tomorrow, when we get back to Charisma there will still be a lot of hours that we could—"

"I *do* have to work in the morning," she interjected.

"Okay, so I won't keep you up *all* night," he said, his eyes and his voice filled with wicked promise.

She was more tempted than she wanted to admit, but she was wary of setting a precedent. Making love with him, even sleeping with him in Atlanta hadn't made her uneasy, because they were outside of their usual world. If she invited him to spend the night in her apartment, in her bed, that would be too much like letting him into her life. And then she'd be all the more aware of how empty her life was when he was gone.

She shook her head. "I've got some reading to do when I get home."

"Reading?" he echoed.

"All the materials I picked up at the conference."

He sighed regretfully. "I guess back to Charisma means back to normal again."

"I didn't think our normal was so bad."

"No," he admitted. "But last night was a hell of a lot better."

It was good to be home and in her own bed, but it was funny how the same mattress she'd been sleeping on for years suddenly seemed so big and empty. After only one night in Justin's arms, she felt as if she didn't ever want to sleep without him, and that was a very dangerous road to go down. Especially with a man like Justin Garrett.

He claimed that he'd never been with a woman that he wanted to be with long term—until her. And as much as she wanted to believe him, she wouldn't let herself fall into the trap of thinking that he could change. Despite his assertion that he wanted only her, she didn't know how long that would last.

But maybe she could just enjoy being with him for a while. Her body was certainly an enthusiastic supporter of that plan, but her brain—now that it was capable of functioning again—warned her of the danger to her heart.

She decided to heed the warning, knowing that she'd never been able to enjoy a purely physical relationship without wanting more. And it wasn't just her own heart she needed to worry about. In just over six months, they would have a baby, and she had to consider what was best for their child.

She was preoccupied with these thoughts so that when her phone rang Wednesday morning, she didn't even check the display before connecting the call. "Hello?"

"Avery, hi. It's Ellen Garrett calling."

"Hello, Mrs. Garrett."

"I thought we agreed you were going to call me Ellen."

"Right," she said. "Sorry, Ellen."

"I'll forgive you," the other woman said. "So long as you agree to have lunch with me."

"Lunch?"

"Is one o'clock good for you?"

"Oh, um." Her mind was a blank as to her schedule. "I guess one o'clock would work."

"That's wonderful," Ellen said. "What do you like to eat? Have you been craving any particular kinds of food?"

"Hamburgers," she admitted. "Big, thick, juicy hamburgers."

The other woman laughed. "How about the Grille?" Ellen suggested. "They have burgers on the menu but plenty of other choices, too, if you want something different when you get there."

"The Grille sounds good," she agreed.

Ellen Garrett was already seated in the restaurant waiting for her when Avery arrived.

"Am I late?" she asked, slipping into the chair across from Justin's mother.

"No, I was early. I was so eager to see you that I couldn't wait to get here."

"I was pleased you invited me," Avery said politely.

"And wondering why I did," Ellen guessed.

She nodded.

"My motives aren't complicated or nefarious," the other woman assured her. "I just wanted to spend some time getting to know the future mother of my grandchild and the woman my son hopes to marry."

Avery didn't know exactly what Justin had said to his mother, but she mentally cursed him for getting Ellen's hopes up—and making her be the one to deflate them again. "Justin only suggested that we get married because he thinks it's the right thing to do."

Ellen smiled. "You don't know my son nearly as well as you think you do if you believe he would be motivated by a sense of propriety."

"Actually, I don't know him very well at all," she acknowledged. "Which is one of the reasons that a marriage between us would be a mistake."

"One of the reasons?" his mother prompted curiously.

Avery looked away. "We're very different people—I'm not sure we'd be compatible."

Of course, Ellen was a very astute woman and she had no trouble reading between the lines.

"I can understand why you'd have concerns about marrying a man with Justin's reputation," she admitted. "He hasn't always been discriminating or discreet when it comes to his personal life, but he is unfailingly honest. He doesn't cheat and he doesn't lie and he has little tolerance for anyone who would."

"He has many wonderful qualities," Avery agreed, because she was talking to his mother and what else was she supposed to say?

"Have you met Nora Reardon?" Ellen asked. "Justin's half sister who works in PT at the hospital."

She nodded.

"Then you must have heard—or figured out—that John had an affair. It was more than twenty-five years ago and a tremendous betrayal of our vows and our family. It took me a long time to forgive him, to realize that I could."

Ellen unfolded her napkin and laid it across her lap, taking a moment to gather her composure. "When he told me about the affair, he didn't tell me—because he didn't know—that his mistress was pregnant. It was only last year that he found out he had a daughter, and though he immediately shared the news with me, the boys didn't learn about Nora until she showed up at our house on Father's Day."

"That must have been awkward," Avery said.

Ellen managed a smile. "Incredibly awkward and uncomfortable," she agreed. "And although Nora didn't stay long—and stayed out of touch for a long time afterward—it shook the whole family. But I think it affected Justin even more than either of his brothers.

"Because despite his faults and flaws—and I know he has them," his mother assured her, "he also has a very strong moral compass. And it took him a long time to forgive his father for breaking his vows and hurting me."

Ellen lifted her water glass to her lips and sipped. "My purpose in telling you this is to help you understand that Justin wouldn't have asked you to marry him if he wasn't prepared to commit himself to you, heart and soul. He would never make a promise he didn't believe he could keep."

"Maybe finding out about his half sister has something to do with his desire to marry me," Avery suggested. "To ensure that he doesn't miss out on his child's life the way John missed out on Nora's."

"If that was all he was concerned about, he would have hired himself a lawyer," Ellen said matter-of-factly. "Any decent attorney could protect his parental rights. If Justin asked you to marry him, it's because he *wants* to marry you.

"And, of course, you already know that I'd love for there to be a wedding before the baby is born, but for more reasons than the child you're carrying."

"What other reasons are there?"

Ellen smiled again. "That's something you need to figure out for yourself," she said gently. "But regardless of what happens between you and Justin, I want you to know that John and I are thrilled about becoming grandparents again, and we hope you'll let us help out in any way that we can. Whether that's watching the baby for a few hours so you can sleep after a long shift at the hospital or helping out with a few meals or just throwing in a couple of loads of laundry—whatever you need."

Her words were sincere and heartfelt, and Avery's eyes filled with tears.

Ellen rummaged in her pocketbook for a packet of tissues, which she passed across the table. "Justin's not going to be happy if he finds out that I made you cry."

Avery dabbed at her eyes. "It's not your fault—I think pregnancy hormones are running amok through my system, and you and John have both been so accepting and supportive. I guess I'm just feeling lucky and grateful and a little overwhelmed."

"Why would we be anything but accepting and support-ive?" Ellen asked her.

Avery could only shake her head. "I haven't begun to figure out my feelings for Justin," she confided. "But I can tell you that I've fallen in love with his family."

Now it was Ellen's turn to tear up. "That's a Garrett baby you're carrying," she said, "which means that we're your family now, too."

Chapter Sixteen

"I'm thinking of getting a name tag that says, Don't Hate Me—I'm His Sister," Nora said, wrapping her hands around her mug of coffee.

Justin finished the text message to a colleague and set aside his phone to give her his full attention, because clearly he'd missed something. "What are you talking about?"

She shook her head. "Do you really not see it?"

"See what?"

"The looks I get every time we come in here together."

He glanced around the atrium but didn't notice anything or anyone out of the ordinary. "What kind of looks?"

"Let's just say, if looks could kill, I would have been on my way to the morgue on my first day."

Nora had been working in the PT department for six weeks now and he tried—if their schedules allowed—to meet her for coffee at least every couple of weeks. The first time he'd invited her because he felt a strange sort of obligation, but the more time he spent with her, the more he found that he actually enjoyed his sister's company. "You have quite a flair for drama, don't you?"

"And you have blinders on," she countered. "The women here *all* want to be with you. Of course, if the rumors are to be believed, more than half of them already have been."

"The rumors are *not* to be believed," he told her firmly. "And you shouldn't pay attention to hospital gossip."

"So is there anything to the rumors about you and Dr. Wallace—or 'Wall-ice' as she's otherwise known?"

He winced at the unflattering nickname. "Don't call her that."

"I'm not the one who does," Nora told him.

Justin took a bite of his chocolate-glazed doughnut.

"And you sidestepped."

He chewed, swallowed. "What?"

"You sidestepped the rumors about you and Dr. Wallace," she explained. "If they were unfounded, you would have said so. The fact that you said nothing suggests otherwise."

"Did you ever think about becoming a lawyer instead of a physiotherapist?"

She shook her head. "My brother Connor is a lawyer—one in a family is enough. And you're sidestepping again."

"The rumors are unfounded," he told her. "I'm not having a torrid affair with Dr. Wallace. We are, however, going to have a baby together."

She gaped at him. "Seriously?"

He nodded.

"Why would you tell me that?" she demanded. "Don't you realize how quickly I could elevate my standing in the hospital community by sharing such a juicy tidbit of information?"

"I do," he confirmed. "But I know you won't."

She frowned. "You're right—but how do you know I won't?"

"Because you're my sister," he said simply. "And regardless of whatever differences we may have, family looks out for family."

"Not all families," she told him.

"Maybe not. But ours does."

"Ours, huh?" She smiled, just a little, as if pleased to be included but still uncertain.

"When you barged into our Father's Day family barbecue last year, you made a statement. Like it or not, you're one of us now."

"You guys take some getting used to," she said. "But I think I like being one of you."

"In that case, I'll tell you another secret. I'm not just the father of Avery's baby—I'm hoping to marry her."

Nora didn't seem nearly as surprised or impressed by that revelation. "Because she's pregnant?" she challenged. "Because Dr. Wallace doesn't strike me as the type of woman who would worry about having a baby without a ring on her finger."

"The baby's only part of the reason," he said. "The biggest reason is that I love her."

"The halls will be littered with broken hearts when that gets out," she warned him.

"Then it's a good thing I don't have to worry about it getting out, isn't it?"

After her lunch with Ellen, Avery was on her way home when she saw her brother's truck parked outside of the office of Renovations by Ryder. She pulled into the parking lot beside his vehicle and made her way into the building.

"Do you actually still work here?" she asked from the doorway of his office.

Ryder looked up from his computer and offered a quick smile. "Less and less all the time," he admitted.

She ventured into the room and gestured to a pile of envelopes on his desk. "What's all of that?"

"The network has decided to shift the show's focus next season. They're offering home renovations to three lucky viewers who write in to explain why they need *Ryder to the Rescue*."

"I heard something about that," she admitted. "How many entries have you got?"

"Over three hundred legitimate ones, so far."

She lifted a brow. "Are you getting illegitimate offers?"

He pulled an envelope from a smaller pile and passed it to her. "Check it out."

Curious, she opened the flap and pulled out a neatly clipped document. The front page was an official contest entry form, with the applicant requesting a makeover of the master bath. The next three pages were photos of the current bathroom—with the homeowner in each one. Naked. Lounging in the soaker tub; standing in the shower; sprawled on the granite counter.

"That's a gorgeous bathroom," she remarked. "I particularly love the glass-tiled shower enclosure with the body jets."

He nodded. "Absolutely no renovation required."

"So you just tossed the contest entry aside? Because I'm pretty sure that's a phone number beneath the lipstick kiss on the page."

"Not interested," he said bluntly.

"It must be tough being you," she teased. "A decently good-looking and moderately famous guy with women throwing themselves at you at every turn."

"It's tougher than you think," he acknowledged.

His obvious discomfort made her think about Justin and the way women were always throwing themselves at him. Because he handled the situation with such apparent ease, she hadn't considered that he might not want all the attention. Or maybe she was only considering the possibility now because she wanted to believe he was the man she needed him to be.

"Have you narrowed down your choices?" she asked Ryder.

"Not really. I've discarded some of the obviously unsuitable ones, but more and more are coming in each day. Thankfully, the contest closing date is Friday."

"I bet you put them all in a bag and draw out three at random."

He grinned. "You know me so well." Then his smile faded. "Except that the producers really want to push the local angle, so at least one of the chosen properties has to be in or near Charisma."

"So one bag for the local entries and another bag for the rest," she suggested.

"There's an idea." He turned away from his computer now to give her his full attention. "Tell me what's going on with you."

"Nothing too interesting. I saw the folks when I was in Atlanta."

"Did you tell them about the baby?"

She nodded. "Mom warned me that I didn't know what I was getting myself into. Dad was equally surprised—but surprisingly supportive. He actually sounded as if he was looking forward to becoming a grandfather."

"How are *you* feeling?" Ryder asked her.

"Actually, I feel great."

"How are things with the dad?"

She thought about the weekend she'd spent with Justin in Atlanta. She couldn't deny that her feelings for him were growing, but she was still afraid to risk her heart—and even more afraid to risk their baby's future. "Fine."

"You want to expand on that at all?"

"Nope."

"You might want to give him a break," her brother suggested. "He's not really a bad guy."

Her gaze narrowed. "How do you know he's not a bad guy?"

"I went to see him last week."

She shook her head. "This is exactly why I didn't want to

tell you who the father was, because I knew…" Her words trailed off and her gaze narrowed. "Wait a minute—I *didn't* tell you who the father was."

"No, you didn't," he confirmed.

"So how did you find out?" she demanded.

"Amy."

She frowned at that. "Where and when did you see Amy? And how did you get her to give up his name?"

"I ran into her in the paint department at the hardware store. She wanted to do the trim in her bedroom but she didn't know what kind of brush to use with the paint she'd picked, so I helped her out and we chatted for a bit." He shrugged. "In between our discussion about natural versus polyester bristles, I casually mentioned that you had some concerns about your baby's father sticking around and she immediately assured me that 'Justin' would never walk away from his child. In fact, 'the whole Garrett family' would support you and the baby."

"You think you're pretty clever, don't you?"

"I *am* clever," he reminded her. "And Amy left the hardware store with everything she needed."

"And you left there and decided to track down Justin." She shook her head again. "I can't believe he didn't tell me."

"It wasn't a big deal—we just had a couple of beers and pizza."

"You had beer and pizza with Justin?"

"And as we talked, I realized that Amy was right," Ryder told her. "There's no way that man is going to bail on you or your kid."

"Oh, well, what am I worried about, then?" she asked, her voice fairly dripping with sarcasm.

He slid an arm across her shoulders. "I know it's not easy for you to trust—especially after Wyatt and especially with this guy being a doctor, too. I'm just suggesting that you give him a chance—I think you'll be surprised."

"I don't want to be surprised," she insisted stubbornly. "I want him to be the irresponsible and unreliable Casanova I expected him to be."

Ryder kissed the top of her head. "I love you, sis, but you've got some serious issues to work out."

If Avery could face her father and tell him about the baby after what she'd been through with her mother, Justin knew that he had to talk to his brother. He made arrangements to meet him at the Bar Down, their favorite hangout, when they were both finished work.

"I haven't been here in a long time," Braden noted, sliding into the booth.

"You haven't been anywhere in a long time," Justin pointed out.

"Dana and I have been sticking pretty close to home," his brother admitted. "But it sounded like there was something important you wanted to talk about."

"There is." He nodded his thanks for the two glasses of beer that Chelsea set on their table.

Braden waited until the bartender was out of earshot before he guessed, "Avery's pregnant."

Justin frowned. "Where did *that* come from? You don't even know Avery."

"True," his brother admitted. "But I know that you took her home to meet Mom and Dad, and you haven't taken a woman home to meet Mom and Dad since...Darcy?" He waited for Justin's nod at the mention of his college girlfriend before continuing. "I figured you were either planning to marry her or she was pregnant."

Justin sipped his beer. "Or maybe I just wanted her to meet my family."

"So she's not pregnant?"

He sighed. "No, she is pregnant. But I was hoping to ease into sharing that news with you."

"No need," Braden said, lifting his glass to his lips.

"And I do want to marry her," Justin added.

"Wow. She must be something special."

"She's unlike any other woman I've ever known."

"Considering how many women you've known, that says a lot."

Justin growled his frustration. "I really haven't been with as many women as everyone seems to believe."

"No need to take offense. The rest of us mere mortals are simply awed and amazed by your legendary reputation."

"Avery isn't," he said, picking up his glass again.

"And yet she slept with you, anyway," Braden noted drily.

"It only took three years."

His brother chuckled. "She's really got you hooked, doesn't she?"

The choice of words reminded Justin of the feeling he'd had when Avery first told him about her pregnancy—of a hook lodging painfully in his gut. Maybe the hook was still there, but his feelings about the baby and for Avery were different now.

"I haven't thought of another woman—wanted another woman—since the first night we spent together," he confessed.

"So when's the wedding?"

"I'm still working on that."

"You asked her to marry you and she turned you down?" Braden's tone was incredulous.

He nodded.

His brother picked up his beer coaster, held it several inches above the table, then let it drop.

"What are you doing?" Justin asked him.

"Testing gravity, because apparently the laws of nature have been turned upside down."

"Ha-ha," he said. "And by the way, gravity isn't a law of nature but a principle of physics."

Braden waved a hand dismissively. "Whatever. I'm more interested in why she turned you down."

"She thinks I'm only trying to do the right thing, and she keeps insisting that it isn't necessary. She's promised that we can work out the details of a coparenting arrangement, if that's really what I want, but she has no desire for a legal union that's doomed to fail."

His brother winced. "She actually said that?"

He nodded.

"Ouch."

Justin nodded again.

"She'll come around," Braden assured him.

"I know," he said, attempting to project a confidence he didn't actually feel. "I just hope it doesn't take her another three years."

"My money's on you."

"So what's new in your life?" Justin asked.

"I'm trying to talk Dana into taking a vacation."

"Anywhere in particular?"

His brother stared into the bottom of his glass. "Wherever she wants to go," he said. "For the past few years, it seems that we haven't had a conversation about anything but babies. I just want to get away somewhere so that we can focus on us. I want my wife back."

"Have you told her that?"

Braden nodded. "She insists she hasn't changed, and I can tell she really believes that, which makes me wonder if the woman I fell in love with even exists anymore."

Justin found himself thinking about his conversation with his brother for a long time after Braden had gone. He knew marriage wasn't easy, but being surrounded by so many happy newlyweds at family events had allowed him to temporarily lose sight of the difficult realities.

His parents were a case in point. He'd always believed their marriage was solid. He never would have suspected that his father had cheated on his mother, because his father wasn't that kind of man. The ten-month affair he'd carried on with Fiona Reardon—regardless of the circumstances— wasn't just a betrayal of the vows he'd exchanged with his wife but their whole family.

Justin had been angry with Nora when she'd shown up, unexpected and unannounced, at their traditional Father's Day barbecue the previous year, demanding to see the father she'd never known. And then he'd been angry with his father for what he'd done to their family. But now he could also feel some regret and remorse for him.

John Garrett had missed out on the first twenty-four years of Nora's life because Fiona had chosen not to tell him about their daughter. He and Avery had fought their share of battles—and would inevitably fight many more— but she hadn't hidden her pregnancy from him and he was confident that she wouldn't ever try to cut him out of their child's life.

He was sincerely grateful for that, but it wasn't enough. He wanted more. He wanted to share all of the joys and responsibilities of parenthood with the mother of his child— the woman he loved.

Just when Avery was starting to feel confident that she'd successfully made it through the first trimester of her pregnancy, she went to the bathroom and discovered that she was bleeding. When she saw the bright red blood, panic rose up inside and her heart dropped into the pit of her stomach. She immediately called her doctor's office, only to learn that Richard Herschel was on holidays until the following week.

"If this is an emergency, please hang up and dial 9-1-1," the recorded voice advised.

Avery hung up and drove herself to Wellbrook instead.

"You're not on the schedule today," Amy said, when she walked in through the staff entrance at the back of the building.

"I know."

"So what are you doing here?"

"I'm—" She blinked back the tears that filled her eyes. "I'm afraid I might be having a miscarriage."

Chapter Seventeen

Amy immediately hustled Avery into an exam room and helped her up onto the table. "Why didn't you go to the hospital?"

"Because I haven't told anyone there that I'm pregnant and I didn't want them to find out this way."

"Did you call Dr. Herschel?"

She nodded. "He's on vacation until next week."

"Then I guess we're going to do an exam here," Amy agreed. "Tell me what's going on."

"I'm…I was bleeding."

"How much?"

"Not a lot," she admitted. "But more than what I would consider light."

"But it's stopped?" Amy prompted, picking up on her use of the past tense.

Avery nodded.

"How far along are you now?"

"Almost fifteen weeks."

"How do you feel?"

"Scared."

"I know," her friend said gently. "I meant physically. Any pain or cramping?"

"I don't think so," she admitted. "But maybe I'm blocking it out because I don't want to admit what either of those symptoms could mean."

"Okay. I'll get Monica to bring in the sonogram machine."

Avery nodded, because she wasn't sure she could say anything else through the tightness in her throat. While she waited for the nurse to come, she checked her cell phone for messages, but there were none.

She'd tried to reach Justin before she went to the clinic, but her call had immediately gone to voice mail. So she'd left a message, trying to keep her voice steady and calm as she explained that she was going to the clinic, and asking him to get in touch when he got her message. Obviously he hadn't received it yet.

After the ultrasound and a quick exam, Amy seemed much less concerned. "The bleeding has stopped and everything looks fine," she said. "Your placenta is in good position and your cervix is closed. The baby's heartbeat is strong and steady and he—or she—is very active, so there's no immediate cause for concern."

Avery exhaled a shaky sigh.

"But we don't know what caused the bleeding," Amy reminded her. "And although we have no reason to suspect it will happen again, if you want to do everything possible to ensure that it doesn't, you're going to have to focus on taking care of yourself for the next several days."

She understood what her friend was saying. It was the same advice she would give to any of her own patients, but those patients were the reason she felt compelled to protest. "But I have responsibilities—"

"No," Amy interjected firmly. "You're a fabulous doctor, but you're not indispensable. Your shifts at the hospital can be covered, your shifts here can be covered. But no one else can do what you need to do to take care of your baby."

She nodded. "Okay."

Amy's gaze narrowed. "Really okay? You're not just pretending to go along with what I'm saying?"

"I won't do anything to jeopardize my pregnancy," she assured her friend, laying a protective hand on the slight swell of her belly.

"Good. Then I only have one more thing to say."

"What's that?"

"You should call—"

Before she could finish, there was a brisk knock on the door. Frowning, Amy went to open it. Of course, Avery couldn't see who was on the other side, but she immediately recognized Justin's voice when he said, "The receptionist told me that Avery was in here."

"She is," Amy confirmed. "We just need another two minutes."

"I want to see her—"

"Two minutes," Amy said firmly again, closing the door with him on the other side.

Then she turned to face her friend, her expression contemplative. "I was going to suggest that you call Justin, but apparently you already did."

"Of course, I did," Avery said. "This is his baby, too."

"I know that," Amy acknowledged. "But you don't ask for help from anyone. Ever. You don't lean on anyone. Ever."

"Why are you making such a big deal out of a phone call?"

"Because it *is* a big deal. Because it proves that you're actually opening up to Justin, letting him into your life."

"It's not like he's really given me much choice."

Amy smiled at that. "Knowing Justin, I'm sure that's true. And I'm proud of you, anyway."

"It was just a phone call," Avery said again.

"And he came over here as soon as he got your message," Amy pointed out to her.

"So it would seem," she agreed.

"Because he's the type of person who will be there for you—whatever you need."

Before Avery could respond to that, Amy opened the door and gestured for Justin to come in. He immediately crossed the room to her and took both of her hands in his. "Are you okay?"

"I'm okay, and the baby's okay," she told him.

He turned to look at Amy, as if for confirmation.

She nodded. "The bleeding's stopped and the baby's vital signs are all good. But I want Avery to stay off her feet for a few days and to follow up with Dr. Herschel early next week when he gets back into the office."

"Has she agreed to stay off her feet?" he asked.

"She has, but I'd feel better if she had someone to stay with her and look after her."

"She doesn't appreciate being spoken about as if she's not in the room," Avery interjected. "And she's perfectly capable of looking after herself."

Justin shifted his attention back to her, and she could see the worry etched in his face. "I know you are," he admitted. "But I'd feel a lot better if you let me take care of you."

"Why?"

"Because it's the only thing I can do while our baby is growing inside of you."

"It's not necessary," Avery said again.

"Please."

She sighed, because she couldn't resist the plea that was in his eyes as much as the word. On the way to his condo, they made a brief stop at her apartment so that she could pack a few things in a bag.

"Are you hungry?" he asked, after settling her on his sofa.

"Starving," she admitted.

"I could heat up a can of chicken soup."

She made a face. "I'm not sick—I'm pregnant."

"So tell me what you want."

"A cheeseburger? From Eli's?" she said hopefully.

"I can get you a cheeseburger," he agreed. "Do you want fries, too?"

She shook her head. "Onion rings."

"Anything else?"

"Extra pickles on the burger but no onions."

He looked at her quizzically. "You want onion rings but no onions on the burger?"

"I don't like raw onions."

"Maybe I should write this down." He found a notepad in the kitchen and wrote down her order. "Anything else?"

She shook her head.

"Are you comfy there?" he asked her.

"Why?"

"Because I don't want you moving until I get back," he told her. "If the phone rings, ignore it. If someone comes to the door, ignore that, too."

She should have been annoyed by his bossiness but the truth was, she was touched that he was so determined to take care of her and their baby.

He was back within twenty minutes, with two cheeseburgers, two orders of onion rings and two chocolate shakes.

"This one meal probably contains more calories than I should be consuming in three days—especially since you won't even let me walk across the room," Avery said, unwrapping her burger.

"I'll make a salad for you for supper," he promised.

"The baby says thank-you, too," she told him. "Especially for the shake—apparently she has quite the sweet tooth."

"She?" he queried.

Avery shook her head as she chewed, then swallowed. "I don't know. I just don't want to refer to our baby as 'it' and most people automatically invoke the masculine pronoun, so I decided to go with 'she.'"

He smiled. "Why doesn't that surprise me?"

"Are you okay with 'she'?"

"Sure," he agreed, popping a crisp onion ring into his mouth. "The pronoun works just fine, and I think it would be fun to have a daughter."

"I thought most men wanted sons, as a testament to their masculinity."

"Doesn't the fact that I got you pregnant prove my masculinity?"

"I guess it does," she agreed, and took another bite of her burger.

"And truthfully, the sex of the baby doesn't matter to me. All that matters is that both you and 'she' are taken care of."

She smiled at his use of the feminine pronoun. "It's strange," she admitted. "I've known you for three and a half years but over the past couple of months, I've realized that I didn't really know you at all."

"Maybe because you didn't want to know me."

She nodded. "Because I was so sure I knew your type. And because I knew your type, I was sure you wouldn't want to have anything to do with a baby conceived in a reckless and impulsive moment of passion."

"I guess I can't really blame you for believing that. I've done everything possible to live up to my reputation."

"And people—myself included—often see what they expect to see. Until a couple of weeks ago, when I saw something at the hospital that made me revisit some of my assumptions." She picked up her cup and took a long sip of her milkshake.

"What was that?" he asked a little warily.

"You were with an elderly gentleman, sitting on those horrible plastic chairs outside of the ER, and he was crying."

"Mr. Ormond," Justin said. "He'd just lost his wife of sixty-eight years."

Anyone could pay lip service to those who were grieving, and often that was all doctors had time for or were capable of doing. Despite recent advances in medicine, doctors still weren't given much education or practical advice on how to deal with surviving family members after the death of a patient. They were taught the appropriate phrases, but compassion was something else entirely—and often lacking.

Avery had witnessed Justin offering sincere and heartfelt empathy to an old man who'd desperately needed it. The fact that, more than two weeks later, he remembered not just the man's name but the reason for his grieving showed her the capacity of his heart and unlocked something inside her own.

"She was with us for fourteen hours," Justin told her. "And he sat with her the whole time, holding her hand, brushing her hair, reading aloud to her from a favorite book. That kind of love and devotion, after sixty-eight years, is amazing. And humbling."

"Sixty-eight years," she echoed, amazed.

He nodded. "He had just turned twenty when they got married, and she was a year and a half younger."

"You listened to him."

"It was a slow night."

And maybe it had been, but she knew that wasn't the reason he'd taken the time. "You're an incredible man, Dr. Garrett."

He just shrugged, obviously uncomfortable with her praise, as he immediately proved by shifting the topic of conversation. "Does that mean I get to choose what we watch on TV tonight?"

She polished off her burger, then crumpled up the wrapper and tossed it into the take-out bag. "That depends on what your choice would be," she said.

Of course, they argued about what to watch. There was a classic Clint Eastwood Western that he wanted to see; she was more interested in a Sandra Bullock rom-com. In the end, she let him have his way and the movie did hold her attention—at least for a while.

She woke up when Justin carried her to the bedroom.

"I didn't get to see the end," she protested.

He sat her down on the bed and rummaged through the duffel bag she'd packed. "I TiVo'd it so that you can watch it tomorrow."

She looked around, as if trying to get her bearings. "This looks like it's your bedroom."

"Because it is."

"I can't sleep in your bed."

"It's the only one I've got," he told her. "Unless you want to sleep on the sofa—and I'm not letting you sleep on the sofa."

"You're going to sleep on the sofa?"

He shook his head. "It's a king-size, which is bigger than the bed we shared in Atlanta."

She wished that he hadn't mentioned Atlanta, because now they were both thinking about that bed—and the things they'd done in it. And suddenly the air was snapping and crackling with sexual tension.

He started to unbutton her shirt; she slapped his hand away. "What are you doing?"

"Helping you get ready for bed."

"I can manage."

"I think I can get you undressed without succumbing to my baser instincts." But his movements slowed when he pushed her shirt away, and he lowered his head to kiss her bare shoulder. Then his lips moved lower, trailing kisses down to the curve of her breast, above the scalloped edging of her bra.

"You said you wouldn't succumb to your baser instincts," she reminded him, a little breathlessly.

"Apparently I lied." He brushed his mouth over her nipple, through the lacy fabric, and she gasped as little darts of pleasure arrowed through her veins.

"We can't do this, Justin."

"I know." He drew in a long, deep breath, then released it.

When he reached for her again, his movements were brisk and efficient. He unhooked her bra, slid the straps down her arms and quickly tugged her pajama top over her head. The only signs that he wasn't as unaffected as he appeared were the ticking of a muscle in his jaw and the heat in his gaze when it met hers.

"Lie down so I can take off your pants."

"Usually a guy has to buy me dinner before he gets into my pants," she said, attempting to lighten the mood.

"I did buy you dinner," he reminded her. "And dessert."

"So you did." She leaned back on her elbows and lifted her hips off the mattress so he could slide her pants down her legs. Then he reversed the process with her pajama bottoms.

"Are you really going to hang out here for the next few days babysitting me?"

"Why not? I happen to like your company."

"Do you realize that you've spent every weekend that you haven't been working, for the past eight weeks, with me?"

"I wasn't actually keeping track," he told her. "Why— are you growing bored with me?"

"No, I just—" She changed her mind about what she was going to say and shook her head. "No."

"You figured I would be growing bored with you," he guessed.

She shrugged. "Even when I was younger—and not pregnant—I was never the life of the party."

"Well, despite your advanced age and cumbersome condition," he teased, "I happen to like the life we're building together."

"You don't want to build anything with me," she warned. "I can't hammer a nail in straight."

"That's okay—I can." And then, because he knew that wasn't really what she was worried about, Justin took both of her hands in his. "I'm not going to leave you. I'm not going to abandon you or our baby, not ever. I promise you that."

She shook her head. "You can't make that kind of promise."

"Yes, I can," he insisted. "Because I love you."

Avery shook her head, and the tears that filled her eyes slashed at his heart like shards of glass.

He forced himself to stay where he was, to let her see the truth of his feelings—even if it was a truth she wasn't ready to admit. He hadn't really expected that she would say the words back to him. Maybe he'd hoped, but he knew that it would take her time to process what he'd said, and longer still to believe he meant it.

He blamed her parents for that. From the little that she'd told him, and the little bit more he'd managed to glean through his conversation with her brother and meeting her father, not only had her parents been too preoccupied with their own lives to ensure their children knew they were loved, they'd also made them feel as if their love and attention had to be earned. If Avery got good marks at school, her father would take her out for ice cream. If she promised to be quiet while mommy was working in her office at home, she might be allowed to do her homework on the opposite side of the big desk.

Justin had never appreciated his own parents so much as he did after hearing Avery talk about her childhood. And while he knew there was no way to undo the damage that had been done by her parents' disinterest and neglect, he hoped he could heal it by loving her. Because he refused to give up on her or the family he wanted them to build together.

Except that Avery's response to his declaration proved that she wasn't ready to acknowledge or accept his feelings. He cupped her face gently between his hands and used his thumbs to brush away the tears that spilled onto her cheeks.

"I didn't expect a declaration of my feelings would make you cry," he said, trying to keep his tone light.

"It's been an emotional day."

"I know."

"I'm scared," she admitted. "I don't want to look too far ahead or make any specific plans when everything could change in the blink of an eye."

He knew that she was worried about their baby, and he was, too. So he let the subject drop—for the moment.

Chapter Eighteen

Tuesday morning, Avery had her appointment with Dr. Herschel. Justin went with her, and the doctor reassured both of them that everything was fine and there was no reason to suspect that she would have any further complications. He also reminded Avery to take her cues from her body—to eat when she was hungry, rest when she was tired—and to let the baby's father do as much for her as he was willing to do.

"You bribed him to say that, didn't you?" Avery asked, when she and Justin left the doctor's office.

"I didn't," he denied. "Although I might have if I'd thought of it."

She shook her head at that, but she was smiling.

"Are you going back to work tomorrow?"

"I am," she confirmed. "But I'm going to do fewer shifts at the hospital and shorter shifts at the clinic."

"I know you're more than capable of taking care of yourself," he acknowledged. "But maybe you could consider staying at my place for a while longer."

"Why?"

"Because knowing you're capable doesn't mean I won't worry about you," he admitted. "And because I want to watch your body change and grow along with our baby, and because I'd love to be there when you feel her move for the first time."

"A lot of first-time mothers don't feel their babies move until after twenty weeks," she told him.

"I'll try to be patient."

She shook her head. "That's not what I meant. I meant that I'm only in my sixteenth week right now—the novelty of having a pregnant roommate might wear off long before you can feel anything."

"I'll let you know if it does," he promised.

Still, she hesitated. Not because she didn't want to stay with him, but because she did. Over the past few weeks, she'd started to rely on him, his company and companionship more than she ever would have expected. And even though they hadn't had sex since they'd returned from Atlanta, she loved falling asleep beside him at night and waking up with him in the morning.

"I guess I could stay a little longer," she agreed.

It was three weeks later, after she woke up to go to the bathroom in the middle of the night, that she felt tiny flutters in her belly. When she realized it was their baby, she immediately nudged Justin awake to share the news. Of course, the movements were so subtle that he wasn't able to feel anything from the outside, but he seemed as happy as she was, anyway.

She continued to see Dr. Herschel on a weekly basis, and every week Justin was there with her. The baby continued to grow and thrive, and her belly continued to get bigger. Justin seemed to be fascinated by the changing shape of her body, but when he touched her—as he did frequently— it was with the cautious awe of an expectant father rather than the passionate desire of an ardent lover.

She knew that he was being considerate of her feelings and showing concern for their baby, but her body ached for him. So at her next appointment, four weeks after Dr. Herschel had given her permission to go back to work, she asked—without looking at Justin—if there were any restrictions on sexual activity.

The doctor seemed surprised by her question. No doubt he assumed that she, being an obstetrician, would understand that the danger had passed and there was no cause to worry that sex would jeopardize her pregnancy. Which she did know, of course, but she wanted Justin to hear from another professional.

He took the hint. That night, he made love to her passionately but tenderly. Afterward, he snuggled up behind her with his hand splayed on the curve of her belly, their baby nudged against his palm. He felt it that time, and when she saw the awe and wonder on his face, Avery acknowledged that all of her efforts to protect her heart had been for naught.

She wasn't just starting to fall in love with Justin—she was more than halfway there. All she could do now was brace herself and hope that her heart wouldn't shatter into a million pieces when reality hit.

Early in June, Avery and Amy were on opposite schedules but decided to meet at the Corner Deli for lunch.

"Things are slightly chaotic at the clinic," Amy warned, as she picked up her turkey club wrap. "Pam just broke up with her boyfriend."

Avery nibbled on a French fry that she'd stolen off her friend's plate. She'd ordered a salad for her own lunch because she'd already gained sixteen pounds and had promised herself that she would try to eat more healthy foods, but she figured one or two fries weren't really cheating. "They were together for a long time, weren't they?"

"Five years," Amy confirmed. "And because she moved

in with him last year, he's insisting that she be the one to move out. I suggested that she ask you about your place."

Avery shook her head. "There aren't any vacant units in my building."

"I didn't mean your building but your actual apartment."

She lifted her brows. "You mean the one that I live in?"

"I mean the one that you pay rent for," Amy clarified. "Which seems a waste of money when you're living with Justin."

"I'm not living with Justin," she denied.

"Really?" Amy's voice was tinged with amusement. "When was the last time you slept at home?"

The furrow in her brow deepened as she tried to remember and realized that she hadn't spent a night in her own bed since the miscarriage scare more than seven weeks earlier. She'd gone back to her own place periodically, to pick up a few things when she needed them, but Amy was right—she *was* living with Justin.

"Tonight," she declared. "I'm going back to my place tonight."

"But why?" Amy was clearly baffled by the decision.

"Because this wasn't supposed to happen." Avery said, referring not just to their current living situation but her feelings for Justin. "And I'm not even sure how it did. I agreed that we could figure out a way for us to work together for the sake of the baby, but I never agreed to live with him."

"Wouldn't living together make it a lot easier to work together—for the sake of the baby?"

"Sure," she admitted. "And if I continue to go along with this, the next thing I know, I'll end up married to him without ever planning for that to happen, either."

"There are worse things than being married to a sexy doctor," Amy pointed out.

"I don't want to get married, and I especially don't want to marry a doctor." Except that she did. In her heart, that was exactly what she wanted—a future with Justin and their baby. But the wanting scared her, so she buried it deep inside.

"We're not talking about any doctor," her friend pointed out. "We're talking about Justin—the father of your baby, the man who's wildly in love with you and wants to spend his life with you."

"Did he tell you that?"

Amy shook her head. "Sweetie, he didn't have to tell me. It's obvious in everything he says and does that he's head over heels. And I've known you long enough to know that you wouldn't be in such a panic about his feelings if you didn't feel the same way."

Her friend was right, of course.

But that knowledge did nothing to alleviate Avery's anxiety, because she believed that loving Dr. Romeo couldn't end in anything but heartbreak. And the longer she continued to pretend otherwise, the more devastating that heartbreak would be.

She was packing up the last of her clothes when Justin got home from the hospital later that night. As she folded and stacked, she realized that most of her wardrobe had found its way to his condo, along with her toiletries and cosmetics and all three of the suitcases she owned.

"Do you want to go out for dinner tonight?" he asked as he made his way toward the bedroom. "We haven't yet tried…" His words trailed off when he saw her bags lined up by the door.

Avery closed the closet.

"What are you doing?" Justin asked her.

"I didn't realize how much stuff I'd dragged over here," she said, her tone deliberately light. "I thought you'd appreciate me moving it out again so you could have your closet back."

"I don't want my closet back," he told her. "I want *you.*"

As she'd transferred her belongings to her suitcases, she'd reminded herself that this was inevitable, that Justin would be relieved by her decision to move out and grateful not to have to nudge her in that direction. She hadn't expected him to protest, and she definitely hadn't anticipated the hurt and confusion she could see in his eyes.

She tried to explain. "When you first invited me to stay here… I don't think either of us expected this to go on like this for as long as it has."

He was quiet for a minute, considering his response. Then he nodded. "You're right. I thought we would have moved to the next stage of our relationship before now, but I didn't think you were ready."

"The next stage?" she echoed.

He took her hand and led her over to the bed, sitting down on the edge of the mattress facing her. "I want to marry you, Avery. In fact, I planned to ask you tonight." He pulled a small jeweler's box out of the inside pocket of his jacket. "That's why I was late—I had to go pick this up."

She felt the sting of tears in her eyes. "We talked about this, Justin. When you first found out about the baby and suggested that we should get married, I said no."

"That was five months ago," he pointed out.

"Why would you expect my answer to be any different now?"

"Because of everything that's happened over the past five months," he said patiently.

She shook her head. "Nothing has changed."

"*Everything* has changed, Avery. Why can't you see that?"

"We had an agreement," she reminded him, refusing to let herself be swayed by the frustration in his tone. "This was supposed to be temporary."

"I tried to give you time, to accept how I feel—to believe that I want to be a husband to you and a father to our baby."

He hadn't told her how he felt—not in words—since

the first night she'd spent here at his condo, when they'd both been so worried about her health. As a result, she'd managed to convince herself that his feelings for her had changed—or maybe even that he'd been mistaken to ever think that he was in love with her.

But he said the words again now. "I love you, Avery. And I want to spend the rest of my life—every single day of it—proving that to you."

Every word he spoke made her heart soar a little higher, but she was determined to keep her feet firmly planted on the ground. "I think what's going on here is that our feelings for the baby are getting tangled up with our growing respect and affection for one another."

Justin shook his head sadly. "I watch you at work, and I'm continually amazed by how strong and fearless you are. But when it comes to your personal life—our life together—you're a complete coward."

"Maybe I'm overly cautious at times," she allowed. "But I'm thinking about our baby now and trying to do what's right for her."

"And you believe that leaving is the right thing for our baby? For us?"

"I believe it's inevitable." Deep in her heart, she knew that she was being unfair, that she was using the heartache from her past as a shield against him, but she couldn't help it. The scars of those ancient wounds were too deep—she couldn't risk her heart again.

"Okay," he finally said. "If that's what you really believe, I'm not going to try to convince you to stay."

"Thank you," she said, though the victory felt hollow.

This was what she wanted, so why wasn't she happy? Had she really been foolish enough to hope that he would fight for her?

He cupped her face in his hands. "I know what you're thinking," he said gently. "And you're wrong."

"What am I thinking?"

"You think I'm letting you go because I don't want you anymore."

"It doesn't matter," she said.

"It does," he insisted. "The only reason I'm not fighting you on this is that I need you to realize my feelings for you aren't about proximity or about the baby. They aren't about anything but you and me, and they're not going to change just because you're not living under the same roof with me.

"I know you've got scars," he continued. "I know it's hard for you to trust me when I tell you I love you, harder still to believe that those feelings are being offered without any strings or conditions. I thought five months was enough time—obviously I was wrong.

"But you need to understand that turning down my proposal and moving out aren't going to change anything. When I say that I love you, I mean that I love you forever."

She wanted—almost desperately—to believe him. But the strong and fearless woman he loved didn't exist in this world, and the weak and terrified one didn't belong.

He helped her load her suitcases in her car, because even when she was walking out on him, he was still determined to take care of her. Of course, when she got back to her own apartment, she'd be on her own with her luggage. Or so she believed until she saw her brother waiting for her.

"What are you doing here?" she asked.

"Your doctor called and asked me to come over here to give you a hand with some things."

"He's not *my* doctor," she said wearily.

"Is that why you moved out?"

It seemed ridiculous, when he was laden down with three suitcases, to deny that she'd ever moved in, so she said nothing as Ryder carried her bags into her apartment.

"Are you going to tell me what happened?"

"He asked me to marry him," she admitted.

Ryder sighed. "And you trampled all over his heart, didn't you?"

"He'll get over it."

"I don't know if he will—he loves you, sis."

"Do you really believe that?"

"I get that it's hard for you to recognize and accept his feelings," he said, dumping the luggage beside her bed. "We got screwed over pretty good in the parent department and I couldn't say for sure whether Mom and Dad loved us, or even if they're capable of those kinds of emotions. But that's on *them*—not *you*."

"I know," she said softly, but acknowledging the truth in her head was a lot easier than accepting it in her heart.

He tipped her chin up so that she had to look him in the eye. "Do you believe that I love you?" he asked.

She nodded.

"And do you love me, too?"

"Of course."

He wrapped his arms around her, offering the comfort he knew she would never ask for. "So why don't you believe that Justin could love you as much as you love him?"

Justin called her every day, just to see how she was doing. Even if he was working, he would find a couple of minutes to steal away to make a phone call. Sometimes they only chatted for a few minutes and other times they talked for much longer. Avery enjoyed talking to him and she found herself looking forward to their daily conversations, but she missed being with him.

Three and a half weeks after she moved back into her own apartment, she was on her way to the hospital cafeteria to grab a bite when she realized that many of her colleagues were looking at her differently. As if they were in on some kind of secret that she knew nothing about.

Then she walked into the cafeteria and saw it: an enormous banner stretched out across the back wall, over the seating area, proclaiming: Justin Garrett Loves Avery Wallace.

She closed her eyes for a second, but when she opened them again, it was still there. For not just her but everyone else who walked into the cafeteria to see. She wanted to turn around and walk out again, but she forced herself to ignore the stares and whispers and pick up a tray. She'd lost her appetite, but she moved toward the salad bar, anyway.

"The man sure knows how to make a statement, doesn't he?" Amy picked up the tongs to pile lettuce on her plate.

Avery had never been so grateful to see her friend, and her presence made her feel a little bit steadier as she added a few cucumber slices and cherry tomatoes to her own salad.

"Any idea what brought this about?" Amy asked.

"I'm guessing a severe head injury." She grabbed a bottle of water from a refrigerated display case and—because the salad was healthy enough to warrant dessert—a tub of cookies 'n' cream, then headed toward the cash.

Amy followed her to an empty table in the atrium, as far away from the banner as possible without actually leaving the dining room. "Do you believe it?"

"That he has a head injury?"

Amy rolled her eyes. "That he loves you?"

She picked up her fork and poked at her salad. "I believe he thinks he does."

"How do you feel about him?"

"I…miss him," she said.

"What do you miss?"

She missed seeing him every day, falling asleep in his arms at night and waking up beside him in the morning. She missed kissing him and touching him and making love with him. She missed their middle-of-the-night conversations, their playful disagreements and their spirited discussions. And she missed just being with him, even when they didn't have anything to say.

"Everything," she finally responded. "I miss everything about him, every minute of every day."

Amy nodded approvingly. "The question now is—what are you going to do about it?"

Apparently if a man decided to spell out his deepest feelings on a three-foot-by-ten-foot banner, he should expect a fair amount of ribbing and ridicule. None of it bothered Justin. What bothered him was that the banner had been up in the cafeteria for four days and, as far as he knew, Avery still hadn't seen it.

And how could a grand gesture be grand if the recipient was unaware?

The banner had been a last, desperate effort to help her realize the true depth of his feelings for her. And, so far, a futile one.

He was reviewing a patient's chart with a second-year resident when Avery showed up in the ER. He glanced at her briefly, and his heart hammered against his ribs as he refocused his attention on the resident to explain the next steps in the patient's treatment. She waited patiently until he turned to face her again.

Activity at the nurses' station had practically come to a standstill, with all eyes focused in their direction. She didn't seem to notice; he didn't care.

"Is there something I can help you with, Dr. Wallace?"

"I hope so," she said. "Do you have a few minutes to take a walk with me?"

He couldn't read much in her expression. She seemed a little nervous, but after studiously avoiding any personal contact over the past few weeks, that didn't surprise him.

He glanced at his watch. "I'm waiting on a report from radiology regarding a possible tibia fracture in Exam Six."

"Dr. Roberts is finished up in Two," Callie piped up

helpfully from the nurses' station. "I can see that he gets the report when it comes in."

"That would be great—thanks."

Avery didn't say anything as they made their way down the corridor toward the cafeteria, and he wasn't sure what to say to her. He knew how much she hated being the subject of gossip, and he considered that maybe the banner hadn't been such a great idea. Maybe he should warn her—

But before he could say anything, she walked directly through the food service area to the atrium. The strong, fearless woman, who could handle any medical emergency with a steady hand but who hated to be the center of attention and trembled when he touched her, didn't halt until she was standing directly beneath the banner he'd hung up four days earlier—and he'd never loved her more.

And that was before he realized a length of examination bed paper had been taped to the bottom of the banner. Her response, written with a Sharpie marker, read: She Loves You, Too.

He looked from the paper to Avery, who was watching him and chewing on her bottom lip, as if she wasn't quite sure of his response.

He put his arms around her and drew her close. "How did you finally figure it out?"

"I remembered something someone once said to me," she confided. "That love is wanting to spend every possible minute with someone, missing him every second that you're apart, and knowing that your life is better, richer and fuller with him in it. That's how I feel about you."

He lowered his mouth to hers, kissing her with all the pent-up emotion of the past few weeks and all the love in his heart. And she kissed him back exactly the same way.

"So where do we go from here?" he asked, when he finally eased his mouth from hers so they could each catch their breath.

"Well, I've offered to sublet my apartment to a colleague who needed a place, so I was hoping you might let me move back into your condo and share that king-size bed again."

"That sounds like a good start," he agreed.

"And my prenatal classes begin in a few weeks," she told him. "I could use a partner for those."

"Done."

"Then I'll want you there for the actual birth, too."

"I already told you that I'd be there for that," he reminded her.

She nodded. "And I was thinking it might be good for us to stick together after."

"How long after?"

"A long time," she decided.

"I like that plan."

"Okay, then." She nodded again. "That's good."

"It is good," he agreed, holding her close. "And it will only get better."

"I do love you, Justin. The feeling terrifies me, but it scares me even more to imagine my life without you in it."

"You don't have to imagine that," he promised. "Because I love you, too, and I'm not ever going to leave your side."

"I still want to take things slow."

"We can take them as slow as you want," he assured her.

"I'm not saying I don't *ever* want to get married, but I don't want to rush into it. I need to be sure."

"Then we'll wait until you're sure."

"Thank you," she said, and brushed a soft kiss across his lips. "In the meantime, will you do me a favor?"

"Anything," he promised.

"Will you please take down this banner that's hanging over our heads?"

He chuckled softly. "I'll take it down and put it up in our bedroom—to make sure you never forget how I feel about you."

Epilogue

Three months later

"I think I'm ready," Avery told him, zipping up the duffel bag she'd packed for the hospital.

"I hope so." Justin stood in the doorway with his keys in hand. "I've already called Dr. Herschel to meet us at the hospital."

Her labor had started several hours earlier, but her contractions were—she insisted—still mild and inconsistent. He wasn't sure how mild they could be when she sucked in a breath every time one started. She was gritting her teeth now and holding her belly as another pain hit. He immediately glanced at his watch, timing the contraction as she panted through it.

She nodded, indicating that it had passed.

"Thirty-eight seconds."

She nodded again as he picked up the duffel and slung it over his shoulder.

"I meant I'm ready to get married," she said.

He stared at her, not sure he understood what she was saying. "You're ready to get married?"

"Yes," she confirmed.

"When?"

She headed toward the door. "I was thinking that I'd like to do it before the baby's born."

"Wait a minute—are you honestly saying that you want to get married *now*?" he asked incredulously.

"I know the circumstances aren't ideal," she admitted, "but the more I think about it, the more I realize you're right. We should be married before we become parents."

"I love you, Avery, with all of my heart and soul," he said, punching the button to summon the elevator, "but there are times that I am completely baffled by your thought processes."

"I'm not asking for a church wedding with a hundred guests in attendance—more of a quick, informal ceremony, maybe performed by the hospital chaplain."

"What if *I* want the church wedding with a hundred guests in attendance?" he asked her.

"We can have a big reception at a later date, if it means that much to you," she promised.

He shook his head as the elevator dinged to signal its arrival. "You know the only thing that really matters to me is being with you."

"Is that a yes?"

"That's an 'I'll try to find the chaplain when we get to the hospital.'"

She smiled and brought his mouth down to hers for a quick kiss. "That's good enough."

But he did better than that.

He called his mother while they were on their way to the hospital, to tell her that Avery was in labor and that they were hoping to get married before the baby was born. He wasn't surprised that his parents arrived at the hospital only moments after they did. He *was* surprised to discover various other family members were already gathered in the hospital chapel—including his cousin Andrew and Andrew's wife, Rachel, who brought a hand-tied bouquet

of white roses for the bride and a matching boutonniere
for the groom.

But Avery's labor had progressed rapidly, and by the
time they were ready to begin, her contractions were much
more painful and intense and coming every five minutes.
The chaplain expedited the proceedings as much as he
could, but Justin could tell by the death grip Avery had on
his hand that she was struggling with the transition stage.

"Breathe," he said softly.

She nodded.

When it was time for his vows, he recited them as
quickly as he could. Then it was her turn.

"I, Avery Vanessa Wallace, take you, Justin Aaron Garrett, to be my—" She broke off on a gasp and squeezed his
hand so hard he worried that she was going to break a bone.

"We can finish this later," he reminded her.

She shook her head fiercely as she breathed through
the contraction, then picked up right where she'd left off.

"To be my husband. To have and to hold, from this day
forward, for better, for worse, for richer, for poorer, in sickness and in health—and in labor," she ad-libbed, squeezing
his hand again but much less painfully this time, "to love
and to cherish, till death do us part."

Moved beyond words, Justin leaned forward and touched
his lips to hers. "I love you."

"We haven't got to that part yet," the chaplain admonished.

"Sorry," Justin apologized automatically.

Avery smiled at him, because she knew he wasn't sorry
at all, then mouthed the words back to him. *I love you, too.*

"By the power vested in me by the state of North Carolina, I now pronounce you husband and wife." He closed
his book and peered over the rim of his glasses at Justin.
"*Now* you may kiss your bride."

He drew her as close as her belly would allow and

brushed his lips over hers again, just as another contraction started.

"Can we move you up to maternity now?" he asked her.

She nodded. "I think that's probably a good idea."

Amy immediately came forward with the wheelchair she'd kept at the ready. Justin helped his bride into it, then pushed her toward the door.

On her way out of the chapel, she seemed to realize that she was still holding her bouquet. She tossed it over her head—and it smacked straight into her brother's chest. But Avery didn't have time to wonder what that could mean— she had a baby to deliver.

Thirty-nine minutes later, at 8:52 p.m., Vanessa Erin Garrett was born. The baby girl weighed in at almost eight pounds and measured twenty inches. Her proud parents celebrated the birth—and their wedding—with family, friends and cookies 'n' cream ice cream from the hospital cafeteria.

* * * * *

DR. WHITE'S
BABY WISH

SUE MACKAY

CHAPTER ONE

'RESUSCITATED CARDIAC ARREST coming in from Court-ney Place,' the newest nurse in Wellington Central Hos-pital's emergency department called as he banged the wall phone back on its hook. 'Male, fifty-two, revived by bystander using CPR. ETA less than five minutes.'

'Thanks, Cody,' Dr Harper White replied. 'Resus Two when he gets here.'

Cody Brand added quietly so that only she heard, 'Apparently intoxicated as well.' The man was shaking his head. 'Seems a bit early in the day.'

Harper's gaze flicked to the wall clock. Eleven forty-five. Early? Hardly. Not in the world of accidents and incidents. 'Hopefully now a very subdued man.'

'You think he's thanking his lucky stars and swear-ing off the booze for good?' Cody grinned. 'Good luck with that.'

That grin could get the man anything—though not from her. But she'd have to concentrate on not giving in to the zingy feeling skimming her skin. 'I guess it is wishful thinking.' Harper watched as Cody strode into Resus Two and began checking equipment, despite it having been restocked and double-checked less than an hour ago after a middle-aged patient had been treated for a major allergic reaction to something she'd eaten for breakfast.

The new nurse left nothing to chance—something Harper appreciated but which also annoyed her at times. Other staff in the department did their jobs just as well. She gave a mental shrug. Maybe Nurse Brand was still settling in and she should leave him to it. No one else had complained, and it was far better than him being slack.

Turning away, she rubbed her temples with her fingertips, trying to relieve the tension building behind her eyes. She did not need a migraine. She had a fun weekend to look forward to, with a birthday party not to be missed. Reaching for the next patient file on the stack, she determined not to let a migraine or the nurse's well-muscled thighs and wide shoulders that blue scrubs did little to hide distract her.

'Why pick up a file when any moment now the ambulance's due to deliver? It's not like you've got time to treat someone else.' Karin, a registrar, grinned. 'Hottie's got to you, hasn't he?'

'I don't think so.' She hurriedly dropped the file back in place.

'You're made of stone?'

Harper tried not to smile but it was impossible not to. 'The man's built, no doubt about it.'

'I'd be worried if you hadn't noticed.' Karin picked up the file Harper had discarded.

'Like I'm looking for another man.' Harper glanced at her sidekick, who was also staring after Cody.

'Maybe not looking *for*, but you were definitely looking *at*.'

Yeah, she had been. 'You're single, so what's holding you back?' Harper retorted.

'Not my type. But you, on the other hand, need to get back in the saddle and—'

'Don't go there,' Harper interrupted, grateful for the shrill ring of the emergency phone yet again. For once the busy morning made her happy, if only because it would shut Karin up. No doubt only briefly, as the woman was known to talk far too much about things she should keep her mouth closed on.

Nurse Brand had picked up the phone instantly, and Harper couldn't help but take another appreciative glance. He'd been here five days and labelled 'Hottie' by the female staff within hours of starting. She couldn't argue with the name. No one could. He was made to be looked at—drooled over, even—but that was where it stopped as far as she was concerned.

For one, she worked with him, and this was her dream job, working with a dedicated group of highly skilled people all focused on helping their patients coping with difficult and often tragic situations. So far, what she'd seen of the latest nurse to join them had impressed her. He fitted right in. He might be easy going with those he worked with, but the moment someone suffering in any way at all came near him they had his undivided attention as he took care of them.

And, if she needed another reason to not be interested in him, it was that she'd had all the disappointment from men she ever needed. The ink was barely dry on the divorce papers from her last blunder.

Aren't you getting ahead of yourself? The guy treats you the same as every other person in the department with his charming disposition, his easy smile and relaxed wit. Why would you be special?

The phone was slammed back into its cradle. 'Suspected body packer coming in from the international airport,' Cody informed her. That deep, husky voice that reminded her of things she had no right to be thinking of sounded calm and focused on work, putting her in her place without even trying. 'Twenty-three-year-old male collapsed during an interview with Customs officers after nervous behaviour when a sniffer dog indicated on him.'

Harper groaned inwardly. She hated these cases. If the guy was carrying internally and had collapsed it suggested a balloon containing heroin or cocaine had burst. She'd lost a young female mule last year, and had seen another die years back when she'd been specialising in Auckland. It was a fast but very painful way to die. But she was getting ahead of herself. It was only supposition that the man was a mule, that a package had burst and that he'd die as a result. 'ETA?'

'Ten. Resus One?' Cody asked.

'Yes. I want you with me on this. Karin, you take the cardiac victim.'

'No problem,' Karin answered with a chuckle.

Harper scowled. She had not demanded Cody work with her because of his sex appeal. 'I need someone strong nearby in case the patient tries to fight us as we work on him. If he's absorbing cocaine or heroin he'll become aggressive as the pain gets worse.' No one else in the department came as big and, she presumed, as strong as Nurse Brand. 'I'm hoping the guy's suffering from dehydration after a long flight, or even the flu, but until I know for certain we have to be prepared for anything.'

Karin leaned close and said, so only Harper could hear, 'Hottie would make nice babies.'

'Shut it,' she hissed, now getting more than mildly annoyed. She couldn't have babies with any man no matter how hot he might be. It just wasn't possible when she didn't have a womb.

The bell rang, indicating a patient had arrived by ambulance. Unfortunately too soon to be hers, Harper thought. She needed a diversion about now. Karin didn't know how her comment hurt. It wasn't something she talked about, even when it should be old hat. Especially after what had happened with Darren. *Suck it up,* she growled at herself and followed Cody into Resus One.

Cody was already getting a fan out of the cupboard.

'You've dealt with a case like this before?' she asked him.

He shook his head. 'No, but I've read up on it. Soaring temps which have to be brought down fast if we want to save him, right?'

'Yes. Apart from that and the agitation, he'll also have high BP and could be fitting. *If* he's carrying and has absorbed a drug, which we don't know for sure yet,' she repeated aloud. Crossing her fingers wasn't very medical, but sometimes anything and everything helped.

'Do we soak him in cold water if he has a temperature?'

She nodded. 'Grab some bottles from the staff fridge.' While Cody did that she went to check the drug cabinet for something to help calm the patient and slow any seizures he might have. If… This was still all about *if* the guy had swallowed packages of drugs in the first place. Why anyone would do that was beyond her. In her book no amount of money was worth risking her life for.

Minutes later the shrill ring of the bell from the ambulance bay sliced through Harper's thoughts and had her moving fast. There'd be no time to waste if this was the worst-case scenario. No surprise that as she raced towards the bay she found Cody striding right alongside her. He never missed a cue. She called over her shoulder to the nurses waiting at the desk, 'Matilda, Jess—Resus One, now.'

A paramedic joined them as his off-sider began rolling the stretcher into the department. 'Mick Frew. Very agitated, making it difficult to get any obs.'

'What readings have you got?' Cody asked even before Harper had opened her mouth.

'BP one-seventy over eighty-nine and rising. He's been fitting for the last five minutes. It's been tricky enough to keep the face mask on him, let alone do much else for him. I couldn't take his temp but by the feel of him he's burning up.'

Harper studied their patient as they rushed him through to Resus One where the other nurses waited, ready to take obs and put an oxygen mask on. This was sounding and looking more like a package had burst internally. Definitely more than a dose of flu or dehydration, but she had to be one-hundred percent sure before she committed to treating him. Something else could be causing these symptoms. 'How certain were the Customs officers that he'd taken drugs? Do you know?' she asked the paramedic.

'Of course he has' was the cutting retort from behind her.

Harper spun around and came face-to-face with a dapper man who had the coldest eyes she'd encountered in a long time. 'Who are you?' Ambulance crews wore uniforms, not expensive, perfectly pressed suits worn by the man stepping towards her from the direction of the ambulance bay.

He shrugged. 'He's carrying. Cocaine. In balloons.'

Just one of those bursting would mean trouble, serious trouble, for Mick Frew. What if more than one had come apart? 'You seem very sure. I repeat, who are you?'

His eyes were glacial. 'Detective Strong to you.' He walked beside the stretcher, his eyes flicking between the young man and her.

He wasn't acting like any detective she'd dealt with. Not even the one she'd been married to. 'Well, Detective, I need to know how sure you are.'

'He's packing.'

'Right.' She'd still check Frew thoroughly but it was looking more and more likely that he had ingested drugs. 'Thank you for your help. Now, you'll have to leave. You know the rules. Only hospital staff and patients are allowed into Resus.'

The detective grunted, and she thought he said, 'We'll see about that,' but right then her patient began kicking and waving his arms in the air, the pain obviously becoming unbearable.

Cody caught an arm inches from slamming into Harper's stomach. 'Easy, Mick. We're all here to help you. We need to get you onto the bed, okay?'

She nodded thanks at Cody. That fist would've hurt if it'd reached her.

The transfer was fast and awkward as everyone tried to hold those flailing limbs without dropping their patient. The paramedic handed over the Patient Report Form and was gone with his stretcher, no doubt glad to have got shot of his aggressive pick-up.

'Check for a medic-alert disc on his arm,' Harper instructed Cody. She was running out of other options but could not afford to overlook anything, including an existing medical condition. Truth? She didn't want this young guy dealing with what was becoming apparent to all of them.

'Nothing,' Cody noted as he took a hit on his upper arm. 'Mick, steady, man. You're in hospital. We're the good guys.'

Harper leaned as close as she dared, one eye on those flailing arms. 'Mick, I'm Harper, a doctor, and I want to help you, but I need to know if you've swallowed any drugs.'

The young guy groaned, opening and closing his eyes rapidly.

'Yes or no?' she persisted.

A brief nod was his only reply.

'Balloons or capsules?'

Mick twisted his head to the side and stared briefly beyond her, fear and hatred blinking out of his stricken eyes. 'Balloons,' he croaked.

So the detective was right. The detective. She looked up, right into Cody's eyes, and saw her own uncertainty there which gave her the determination to get rid of the stranger. Turning around, she growled, 'I asked you to leave, Detective Strong.'

'So you did.' He sounded so smug a trickle of apprehension ran down her spine.

Cody said in a 'don't fool with me' tone, 'You will do as Dr White says.'

Nice as it was to have the nurse backing her, Harper had a definite feeling their visitor wasn't going to take any more notice of Cody than he had her. She glanced at Cody and nodded thanks again, appreciative of his attempt to help her with this horrid man. She didn't know why she thought him horrid, but she did. Probably something to do with those arctic-blue eyes that bored into her relentlessly. The complete opposite to the warmth she found in Cody's brief green gaze on the rare occasion he looked at her for an answer to some question.

Shivering, she glanced at the nurse now, not wanting to focus on that other man. But she still had to get rid of him. He was a hazard in the emergency room.

'Call security,' she mouthed at Cody.

Mick wheezed out some words.

'What did you say?' Leaning down to hear him better, Harper felt the heat radiating off his body. 'Jess, get the fan going as fast as possible.'

'Not cop. Supplier.'

'Mick? Really?'

He nodded. At least, that was what she thought his erratic head movement was.

Harper hoped against hope the man behind her hadn't heard or seen any of that. He wouldn't be pleased that she now knew for sure he wasn't a detective but a criminal. She thought fast. What to do? They had to work on saving Mick's life, get the so-called detective out of here and call in the real police, all at the same time. And she'd sent Cody out of the room. Squeezing the young man's hand, she whispered, 'Okay,' before straightening up.

Of course it was not okay. It was a minefield.

Cody was still there. Thank goodness. His presence and calm manner gave her strength. Catching her eye, he nodded once, tightly. Had he heard what their patient had said? Whatever message he was trying to send her, she wasn't understanding, and they were wasting time if Mick stood any chance at all of surviving the poison streaming through his body.

With a shaky breath she turned to the man causing her problems. 'This is an emergency department. Anything you want to ask my patient will have to wait until we've treated him.' *If he survives.* 'So please head out to the waiting area. Now.'

'Or what?' A rapid movement and a gun appeared between them.

'What are you doing?' she gasped as that trickle of apprehension became a torrent of fear. She was unable to stop staring at the weapon pointed directly at her chest, where her heart was beating the weirdest, sickest rhythm against her ribs. Definitely not a detective, then. Glancing out of the wide opening of Resus One, she could see only one person at the desk, and he was rapidly removing himself from sight. 'Call the police,' Harper begged silently.

'Hey, what do you think you're doing?' Cody moved around the bed fast, stepped up close to her so his arm touched hers and eyeballed her aggressor, anger darkening his face. 'Put that away.'

'You want to argue?' The man smirked as he waved the gun at Cody, taunting him to take a crack at him. 'I'm here to collect what's mine.'

That gun mesmerised Harper as it was moved between her and Cody in a very deliberate, menacing way. One little squeeze and someone could die. Just as simple, and horrific, as that.

She had to do something. Drawing what she hoped was a calming breath, but felt like an asthma attack, she said in a voice that didn't sound like hers, 'Stop this. Now. Our first priority's to save Mick's life. So get out of the way while we do all we can.' She glanced sideways to her patient. Damn. 'Cody, oxygen. Now. Jess, bring the fan closer. We need to get his temperature down fast.'

The girl was paralysed with fear. 'Sorry, yes, Harper.'

With Mick fighting him all the way, Cody struggled getting the mask on.

'Matilda, the water.' No reply. 'Matilda?' Harper glanced around but there was no sign of the junior nurse.

When had she snuck away? Now they were down to three. Not enough to help their patient, but fewer to be confronted with that gun. Hopefully it also meant they could expect help in the form of security or, better yet, armed police, shortly. Then what would *Detective* Strong do? Her skin lifted in goose bumps as she struggled to tamp down the fear threatening to rage through her and flatten her thought processes. Would they find themselves in the middle of a shooting match? She had a patient to care for; other staff to try and keep safe.

'The oxygen's flowing.' Cody's calm voice cut through her panic.

Her eyes met his and the fear backed off a few notches. Darn, but he was good. Cool as. She straightened her shoulders and dipped her chin to acknowledge she was on her game, however shakily.

Cody nodded back. 'I'll get the water.' He caught Mick's flying arm and tucked it down against the young man's body. 'Steady, mate. Think we'll strap you down for a bit, okay? Can't have you knocking out your doctor, can we? Jess, maybe you should get the water.'

Harper took the end of a strap he handed her. He had it all together—seemed completely unfazed about their unwanted spectator. She drew more strength from him. 'You and Jess do this while I go get some drugs.' She turned to come face-to-face with their interloper, and felt the cold, hard reality of a gun barrel poked into her stomach.

'I don't think so.' Those chilly eyes fixed on her. 'No one's going anywhere.'

'I am trying to save this man's life—a life that you mightn't care about—' she stabbed his chest without thinking '—but I do. *We* do. So get out of my way.'

'The only thing I care about are those packs in his

gut. They belong to me.' Cold steel jabbed deep into her stomach. 'Nothing, no one else, matters. Get it?'

She nodded. 'Sure. But I am going to do my absolute best to save Mick's life, whatever you think, so move out of my way.' She locked eyes with the man, fighting down the returning panic weaving through her tense muscles.

He waved the gun in her face, so close she tipped her head back. 'What are you going to do about it, doc? Eh? Wait until idiot here dies? Because he's going to. One way or the other. They all do.'

The firearm was menacing but even more so were the eyes locked on her as he continued. 'Save us all the trouble and cut him open so I get what I came for. Then I'll get out of your hair.' If he'd shouted or snarled, she'd have handled his statement better, but he'd spoken softly, clearly, and set her quivering with dread.

There was no getting rid of the man, nor was he going to let her get the midazolam Mick desperately needed. She wanted to call out for someone else to bring the drug but that meant putting another person in jeopardy.

'I'll go,' Cody intervened. He flicked her a quick look that seemed to say, *Hang in there, I'm on to this,* but she could be far off the mark. It had been a very fast glance.

The gunman snarled, 'No you don't.'

Cody shrugged exaggeratedly. 'We need more water and drugs and, if you think I'd do a bunk and leave Dr White alone with you, think again. The drugs cupboard is just on the other side of the doorway.'

Phew. Relief warmed Harper. As much as she'd like the nurse out of here and safe, she didn't want to be left without him watching her back as much as it was possible.

Her relief lasted nanoseconds. An arm slung around

her throat, cutting off anything she could've said to back up Cody. Her assailant hauled her backwards, hard up against his torso.

'Let her go.' Cody stood right in front of them, his hands loose at his sides, those impressive feet spread wide, looking for all the world like he regularly dealt with this sort of situation, this type of villain.

'Want to try and make me?' the man snarled, then tightened his hold around Harper's neck. Was he getting upset that things weren't quite going his way?

They weren't going her way either, but she could try to regain some control over the situation. Struggling to straighten up, she got hauled further off-balance for her efforts.

The grip tightened on Harper's throat, making her eyes water and feel as though they could pop out of their sockets any moment. Her windpipe hurt. But it was the latest wave of fear rolling up from her stomach that really threw her off-centre. She didn't have a chance of getting away from this man, or of saving Mick.

Mick. 'Let me go,' she tried to say, but nothing got past that arm pushing on her throat. Her fingers clawed at it, trying to loosen the throttling sensation. She couldn't swallow and breathing was a strain.

Her eyes fixed on Cody's. She hoped he couldn't see her fear. Looking deep into his steady gaze, she tried to draw strength from him, to calm down. She couldn't afford to let the assailant beat her. *Count to ten, think what to do.*

How in Hades did she count when even getting enough oxygen into her lungs was a mission?

Cody gulped. Strong was hurting Harper. But she was good. She might be terrified—he definitely was—but she wasn't taking any crap from the lowlife. *Go, girl.* No. *Be careful, stay safe.* Lowlife had the advantage and not once had he looked as though he'd be afraid to pull that trigger.

He guessed the guy had nothing to lose. No one would stop him walking out of here while he held that gun. Hopefully the armed-defenders unit would arrive soon and be able to work out a solution without anyone getting injured or worse. If someone in the department had dialled 111. If Matilda had stopped to tell anyone on her mad dash to freedom. He was afraid to look out into the department in case he alerted Lowlife to other staff or anyone that might be working towards taking him down.

In the meantime the three of them still stuck in here had to deal with the situation and keep out of harm's way. They weren't going to get the drug that might calm Mick down a little. The odds were stacking up against him as time ran out fast. And, while Cody abhorred drugs and the people who made a living out of them, this young man was paying a huge price, way too huge. He wouldn't be making the big bucks that people like Lowlife here would be. 'I'll run towels under the cold tap,' he told Harper. 'Then you outline what we do next.' He was trying to warn her to stay put, that they'd get this sorted.

But either she was playing dumb or was just being plain brave because she shook her head, and managed to speak, which indicated that the arm had loosened on her throat. 'We need icy-cold water, not tap water.'

Lowlife tightened his grip around Harper's neck again and heavily tapped the gun barrel against her skull. 'No one goes anywhere or the doc gets it.'

Harper's eyes widened and all the colour drained

from her cheeks. Her front teeth dug deep into her bottom lip.

'Let her go,' Cody growled. Fury was building inside him. 'Incapacitating her isn't going to change a thing.' It was obviously a painful hold. Her throat was going to hurt for days. He gritted his teeth. It was crazy to think anyone would have to deal with an assailant in a place where people came to get fixed up, but it happened.

Another man threatening a woman on his watch, though? No, it wasn't happening again.

'You think I won't use this? Huh? Want to see what happens when a bullet goes through brain matter?' Lowlife laughed, a hideous sound that must've been heard throughout the department and made Cody's skin crawl.

But it was the shock in Harper's eyes that really got to him. She probably hadn't encountered anything quite like this before, while he had. He had held his wife in his arms while she'd died of a knife wound to her heart. He'd been unable to halt the life draining out of her that day—had felt so useless, so helpless. Which was why the quiet evil about this man tightened his gut and had him fearing for Harper. That fear vied with anger. Nothing he said or did helped Harper while she was trying to help her patient. She did not deserve to be held to ransom. Or worse. Evil had no boundaries.

All the things he hated about bullies and nasty SOBs burst through him, and it took every ounce of self-control not to leap on the guy and take him down. That would really help the situation. Not. He'd probably get Harper killed in the process. He would not face that again. Once in a lifetime was once too often. He had to be careful; acting impulsively only led to disaster. 'Let's be sensible here. Dr White cannot save Mick's life while you're holding her.' Damn, but he hated grovelling.

'Who says we need to save the useless piece of garbage? I only want my drugs out.'

Jeez. Cody rammed his fingers through his hair. This guy didn't deserve to be breathing. 'Still need the doctor for that.' Though Lowlife probably had his own knife strapped somewhere on his body; Cody had no illusions about the man getting his merchandise back himself. Which only underlined the dire situation they were all in.

Harper blinked at him. Mouthed something he couldn't read. Her eyes tracked sideways towards the head of the bed.

The monitor? Reluctant to take his eyes off Lowlife while he held that gun to Harper, Cody quickly glanced sideways and saw the flat line on the screen. Mick Frew had gone into cardiac arrest. He hadn't even heard the changed electronic sound; he'd been so focused on the doctor and her captor.

Cody needed to act quickly before anyone else rushed in to help and found themselves in this dangerous situation. He immediately hit in the centre of Mick's sternum with his clenched hand, watching the screen intently. The flat line continued. Another thump and he said as calmly as possible, 'Paddles, Jess.' It wasn't Mick's condition churning his gut, but Harper's. Dealing with this cardiac arrest wasn't going to quieten Lowlife any, but no way could he ignore their patient either.

Thankfully Jess already had the paddles in her hands, even if she was staring at Harper.

As he shoved the paddles firmly onto Mick's exposed chest, he couldn't stop thinking about the doctor behind him. She was amazing, more concerned about their patient than her own life. She'd read the monitor, or heard it go into that monotone that went with lack of heartbeats, and had tried to let him know even when her windpipe was being squashed. She was some lady. *Careful, pal. Don't get too impressed. You'd hate to follow that up with something more caring.*

He held the paddles in place and said urgently, forcefully, 'Stand back.'

'Want to get closer, doc?' Lowlife chuckled.

Cody froze. Never before had he heard such an evil chuckle. It was a match for that hideous laugh. He tried for reasoned and calm. Tried very hard. Snarled, 'Stand back. If the doctor gets zapped, so will you.' Dumb idiot. Hadn't thought of that, had he?

Behind him Harper was hauled back so fast she lost her balance and fell into the man behind her, who also lost his balance.

The hand holding the gun wavered, the fingers tightening as Lowlife struggled to remain upright.

The air stuck in Cody's chest as he waited for the explosion as the trigger was inadvertently pulled. It didn't happen.

Instead, Harper dropped lower, fell to the floor. Deliberately? Lowlife no longer had her by the throat, or the gun at her head. Cody sprang forward, his shoulder aimed directly for the assailant's chest. They went down together, sprawling across the floor while the gun spun out of reach.

Harper crawled after the weapon as Cody worked at subduing Strong by flipping him on to his stomach and planting a knee in the small of his back. 'Don't even bother trying to get away.' Sometimes it was a bonus being a big man, Cody admitted as he looked around for Harper.

She was standing now, holding the gun as though it

was about to go off and shoot her. Her hands were shaking and her eyes were wide with shock.

Cody's heart squeezed for her.

Jess called from the bed in a terrified voice, 'Still no sign of cardiac function.'

Harper blinked, shook her head abruptly and shoved the gun into the waistband of her scrubs. Rushing across to pick up the paddles from where Cody had dropped them moments ago, she instructed, 'Stand back,' and delivered a jolt of electricity. And another, and another.

'Jess,' Cody called as the man under his knee squirmed and started swearing loudly. 'Go get help. Let everyone know we've got Strong under control, but as soon as the police arrive I'm more than happy to hand him over.'

Harper was zapping Mick like her life depended on it. 'Come on. Don't leave us now.' Tears ran down her cheeks and her bottom lip trembled.

'Harper. Stop.' Cody desperately wanted to go and wrap his arms around her, take away some of the shock presumably making her react like that. As if he'd get away with doing that. Even in the circumstances he knew Dr Harper White would not thank him for showing her concern—especially in front of the staff. Her reputation for being strong, solid and independent went before her, and in the week he'd been working here he hadn't seen anything to negate it.

Suddenly the room was full of gun-toting men dressed in the dark-blue overalls of the armed defenders squad and Cody relaxed for the first time in what seemed like hours but according to the wall clock was little more than ten minutes.

He couldn't help himself prodding the man beneath him as he stood up. 'You're history.' What he really wanted to do to the guy wasn't going to happen even though the creep deserved every moment of pain for what he'd done to Harper White. The fear in her eyes would stay with him for a long time. And then the anger. She was something else; she really was.

As cops grabbed their man, Cody crossed to Harper. 'It's over, doctor.'

Her hands were shaking as he took the paddles from her. 'Mick—he didn't stand a chance.'

As her fingers oh-so-gently closed Mick's eyes she said quietly, 'I'm sorry, Mick Frew. I am so sorry.' Then she slashed her sleeve across her face. 'Damn.'

Cody muttered around the road block in his throat, 'We weren't exactly given much of a chance.'

Watery eyes met his as her fingers went to her temples, rubbed hard. 'Unfortunately you're right.' Then she straightened up to her full height, bringing her head to somewhere about his shoulder.

A few unruly curls had escaped the wide band meant to keep them in place and were now stuck to her moist cheeks. Cody's fingers itched to be able to lift them away and tuck them behind her ears. But he didn't dare. He already loved this job, and wasn't going to spoil anything by getting offside with this particular doctor.

So why was he wrapping his arms around her and hauling her shaking body close to his? Because he needed to hold her against him. However briefly, whatever the outcome, he just did. Tucking her head against his chest, he dropped his chin on the top of her thick, soft hair and held her. Breathed in her scent of citrus and residual fear. Her being in his arms gave him strength, helped him settle his jittery muscles. He hoped he was giving the same back.

She's a perfect fit for my body. The realisation banged through him, made him tense.

Made Harper lift her head and look at him with puzzlement beaming out at him from watery eyes. She sniffed once and plastered a tight smile on her mouth. 'Let's go face the second round. There'll be questions from all directions.'

Slowly Cody unwound his arms from that warm body he shouldn't be noticing in any way. From somewhere deep he found a smile that was entirely for her. 'You did good, doctor. Really good.'

CHAPTER TWO

REALLY? I DID a good job? Of what? Harper asked herself as she stepped out of Resus One. Their patient was dead, the assailant had been taken down by Cody and she felt like a toddler who'd just had a huge sugar fix. The shaking had started in earnest now that she had nothing to focus on. That impending migraine had also become reality.

Turning to Cody, she saw his jaw tighten. His mouth flat-lined. Feeling out of sorts too? He'd been so calm in there, so reliable. Yet she'd felt a tremor in his body in that all too brief moment he'd held her close. His hug had been like a welcoming home, a comfort, a much-needed place of calm and care and warmth. Only during that hug had she known for sure how rattled he'd been by what had gone down. She liked that he'd shared the whole episode, including the fear. She stepped closer to him, still needing his strength, his deliberate calm.

Which was enough to make her step away again. She must not need anything about him, from him. Needing something from a man had got her into trouble before, had led to the wrong marriage for her.

'Hey, Harper, are you all right?' George stepped up to her. He was head of the department and her brother's friend—which meant Jason would already know about this, damn it all.

She swallowed, pain from where her throat had been flattened more apparent now she wasn't on high alert. 'I'm fine.' Her voice came out as a high-pitched squeak. Great. Now she was sounding like that sugar-overloaded toddler.

The department was in chaos with police going about their business while nurses and doctors hovered around the area, looking like they didn't know what to do or where to go, so they resorted to staring at Cody and her.

George took her arm. 'My office. Both of you. Jess, you too. Where's Matilda?'

Jess shook her head. 'I don't know. I haven't seen her. I'm on lunch break now, so can I go to the canteen? My boyfriend's there.'

'Of course you can, as soon as you've talked to the police. They'll want to ask you all a few things.' George looked around at his staff. 'Okay, everyone, we have a waiting room full of patients, and one in the ambulance bay. Let's try to get back to normal as quickly and quietly as possible. The police will be here for a while, and I expect you to be helpful and answer any of their questions.' He held a hand up. 'However, I do not want any one telling patients what has happened.'

Harper grimaced. Like he had any hope of every single person in the department keeping their mouth shut, but she supposed he had to put it out there. Texts would already be flying around the city, probably the whole country, and the moment Jess saw her boyfriend she'd be yabbering her head off. Not that Harper could blame the girl. Talking was a way of relieving the stress. Even she felt a desire to tell someone what had happened, but she wouldn't. That would be totally unlike her. But then how often did she have a gun held to her head? Her muscles tightened as renewed fear grabbed her.

'Cody, Harper, come with me. I'll get you coffee sent from the cafeteria shortly. And some food.' George's answer to everything was coffee followed by food. 'Come on. The sooner you talk to the police, the sooner I can send you home for the day.'

Harper shook her head. 'You said the waiting room's full. I can't just disappear.' At least, that was what she tried to say, but her voice was raspy and all broken up. Now that she was no longer dealing with the assailant and everything else, the pain in her throat seemed to be taking over. She needed something else to concentrate on so it would go on the back burner, at least until she got home.

Beside her, Cody growled, 'I'm sure the other doctors don't expect you back on the floor today.' Then his hands clenched at his sides. 'Gawd, what I don't want to do to that lowlife.'

'Not happening,' she croaked.

'Look what he's done to you, all because of his greed.'

It hadn't been only her. She spoke slowly and tried to ignore the pain. 'George, Jess is in shock. Someone needs to check her over.'

'On to it.'

She placed a hand on Cody's forearm. Since when had she done this 'touching colleagues' stuff? She guessed that gun had a lot to answer for. Working hard at getting her words out clearly, she said, 'Don't let him get to you. I'm all right. Truly.'

Cody covered her hand with his for a quick touch, sending his warmth through her. Again. She could get used to that. But she wouldn't.

'You're more than all right,' he muttered before glaring across the room to where the assailant was being hauled roughly out of the department by two cops.

He no longer looked quite so dapper or smug, but the eyes that locked on her momentarily were filled with hatred.

She shivered. 'Evil. Pure evil.' As Harper watched the man being taken away, she felt some relief seep into her body and loosen a little of the tension gripping her. Turning to Cody, she asked, 'How are you feeling?' She swallowed and kept going. 'You were right in the middle of it all. You hit the floor hard when you leapt on him.' She still couldn't get the sight of him doing that out of her head, probably wouldn't for days.

Eyes the colour of spring paddocks locked on her. 'Think my hip took a bit of a hammering but I didn't feel a thing at the time. I'll probably know about it tomorrow.' His wide mouth tipped upward into a beautiful smile that sent ripples of pleasure through her. He really was ridiculously good-looking.

'Ouch.' She didn't know if she was referring to his hip or her reaction to him.

His smile, like that hug, enveloped her in the sensation that they were in this together and that no one else had a part in it. Sort of like being in a cocoon with just Cody, which gave her a sense of it not being all bad. Not that she could find anything good about the last twenty or so minutes. She'd lost a patient. She hated that. No matter that the odds had been stacked against Mick from the moment he'd swallowed those drugs; she'd have done everything possible to turn the situation around—*if* she'd been given half a chance. *If* seemed to be the word of the day.

Someone tapped Harper's shoulder, and she nearly

jumped out of her skin. Spinning around, she half-expected to find the gunman standing there smirking at her. 'Don't touch— Oh. Sorry, George.' She'd totally overreacted. She rubbed her temples to calm herself down and try to ease the pounding that had cranked up harder than ever.

George gave her an understanding look. 'Take it easy. He's gone, Harper.'

'Yes.' He had, but how long before the sense of dread he'd caused left her? Going to sleep tonight might be a lot more difficult than usual.

'The police want statements from all four of you. Especially you and Cody. That's not happening in here with patients being treated. They'd overhear everything.' Despite the presence of the armed defenders and two detectives, the department head was in charge, and letting her know it even before she argued that she needed to be busy right now.

If—that damned word again—she was being honest, she knew she wasn't in any fit state to be dealing with emergencies or even the mundane illnesses presenting at the moment. But the idea of sitting in the office doing nothing but answering endless questions made her sick to the stomach. Glancing at Cody, she saw sympathy in his gaze. *I don't need sympathy. Especially not from you when you probably feel much the same way I do.* She had to admit he didn't look at all fazed by any of this, but he had been shaky in that hug. 'I suppose coffee would be good,' she conceded.

'I'm surprised you think you can swallow anything.' Cody watched Harper struggling to cope with the aftermath of the assault. She looked annoyed and a tad bewildered. No longer fearful, though, thank goodness.

What would she do if he hugged her again? She held her hands against her stomach with her fingers entwined and knuckles white. He suspected she was desperately hanging on to her self-control. The shock was catching up, and he wasn't immune either.

'I'll manage,' she snapped. Was getting feisty another way of covering up her feelings?

'Shouldn't one of our doctors take a look at your throat?' he asked. There could've been serious damage done.

'That's next on my agenda. You really shouldn't talk too much until everything's settled down.' George nodded at Harper. 'Want me to talk to Jason as well?'

'No.' Harper shook her head sharply at the boss, her eyes glittering angrily. 'No.' Then, 'I presumed you already had.'

'Been a bit busy. You do realise someone will have put it out there on the net? Jason probably already knows, and the rest of your family.' George gave her a pointed look.

If that throat had been in proper working order Cody had no doubt she'd have been telling George where to go, and it wouldn't be somewhere nice. She wasn't known for holding back on her thoughts, no matter who she was talking to. Who was Jason anyway? Her partner? She didn't wear a wedding ring. He had to be a significant person in her life for George to think he should be told about what had gone down. But, then again, why wouldn't Harper want this Jason character to know?

'I figured that since my vocal cords are in excellent working order I should be the one to phone him and say you're all right,' George continued as though Harper hadn't glared hard enough to poleaxe him.

Harper sighed as she lifted her hands in resignation. 'You're right. But no drama, okay?'

The man grunted. 'What are the chances?'

'None,' Harper muttered as Karin rushed up to engulf her in a hug.

'Hey, Harper, you poor thing. I couldn't believe my eyes when I came out of the treatment room and saw that man holding a gun to your head.' She raised watery eyes to Cody. 'I'm glad you saved her.'

Saved her was a stretch of the truth. But he was pleased he'd been able to take Lowlife down before he'd hurt their doctor any more than he already had. He really hated seeing people get hurt, and he particularly hadn't wanted to see anything happen to Harper. 'Thanks for the vote of confidence,' he drawled. 'But Harper saved herself. She started the ball rolling when she dropped to the floor.' His relief at Harper being safe was overwhelming. Today the outcome had been good. He wouldn't think back to the darkest day of his life—not now. Too disturbing.

They were still standing in the middle of the department while other doctors and nurses were ducking and diving around them now, bringing patients in from the waiting room. Cody had had about all he could take of people staring at him and clapping him on the back for doing a cracking job on the assailant. They meant well, but they had no idea what it had really been like in Resus One. 'Come on, Doc, let's get out of everyone's way. Go have that coffee George mentioned.'

'Doc?' Harper shivered. That annoyance with George transferred to him. 'That man called me "Doc".'

Comprehension slammed him. Of course, Lowlife had, and in a denigrating tone at that. 'I'm sorry, never thought about it.' He didn't want to rile her any more. Not after what they'd been through together.

Her shoulders drooped momentarily, then tightened again as she drew a long, slow breath. 'Thank you for knocking him down. I am grateful. You could've been shot.' Unbelievably her eyes teared up. Again. For him? Not likely.

He'd never have picked her for the weepy sort, but then today hadn't been exactly normal. Violence undermined the strongest of people. Even his gut had tightened painfully at the moment when that gun had appeared. 'Stop talking and give your throat a rest.' He reached to take her elbow, saw those watery eyes widen and dropped his hand. Of course he was out of line, even if he'd only wanted to help. Being overly friendly to a colleague at work, no matter how well intentioned, could be seen as overstepping the mark. Apparently that hug had been okay at the time but now any other move from him wouldn't be.

Harper muttered, 'I've seen violence in the ED heaps of times.'

'But never directed specifically at you, I bet.' The thought of that kind of personal, immediate threat brought back unpleasant memories. The looks on the faces of women in the pubs when their men came home from a dry six-week stint on the fishing trawlers. Some of the crew over-indulged in alcohol and drugs, then took the resultant mood swings out on their partners. He'd stopped going to the pub with the guys after a while, unable to cope with what he saw but never managing to prevent it. He'd tried talking them out of their rages, had taken some punches and given a few back in self-defence, but he'd never convinced those guys that what they were doing to their women was wrong.

Some men had a mind-set about using their fists that was impossible to change.

But that was then, and he'd moved on to a different world, or so he'd thought. 'Come on. George's office will be a lot quieter. Even with the police joining us.'

Her fingers worked her forehead, then her temples. 'You're right.'

'Are you okay? Apart from your neck and throat being squashed?' She looked paler than before. Shock would do that, though he thought something else might be going on.

'Of course I am,' she snapped and stormed towards the corridor that'd take them to the office affectionately known as George's cave. But at the door she stopped and graced him with a wobbly smile. 'Why wouldn't I be? It's not every day there's so much excitement in the department.'

'There's something we can be grateful for.' The fact that the man had held that gun to a doctor's head put today's example of crazy way up there on the scale of craziness. Apparently Harper hadn't seen as much of the rougher side of humanity in her working life as some medics in big city hospitals did.

'To think this is Wellington, not Los Angeles, where there are permanent armed guards on the doors.' For someone who shouldn't be talking too much, she was doing an awful lot of it. A reaction to everything that had gone down?

'You've worked in LA?' If she wasn't going to be quiet then a change of subject might be for the best about now. For both of them. Now that the showdown was over the adrenaline had backed off, leaving him feeling shaky, despite his previous experience with out-of-control thugs.

'No. Never. But I know people who have.' Then she turned the questions on him. 'I know nothing about you. Where were you working before starting here?'

'Invercargill. I did my training there and stayed on working in the emergency department for another year.'

'That suggests you're a late starter.'

Way past being wet behind the ears, for sure. Cody shrugged. 'I had a career change at twenty-seven.'

'From what?'

'Commercial fishing.'

'You're kidding me!' Surprise tainted her eyes.

He was used to that. Fisherman to nurse took a bit of getting around for most people. 'I've found my niche.'

Nudging her into the office, he closed the door to keep the noise of the department out and instantly wished he hadn't. The room wasn't much bigger than a shoebox and somehow this woman with all her questions seemed to fill it so that he couldn't put enough space between them. A scent of lemon or lime wafted in the air, reminding him of summer days in his grandfather's orchard. The days when he'd been young, carefree and a little hellion. A long time ago.

'Why Wellington?' She blushed. 'Sorry, none of my business, and not relative to the job.'

None of your questions are. But suddenly he couldn't shut up either. 'I'm originally from Kelburn.' *Yes, just along the road from the hospital.* 'My mum's still here and my brother has a home in Central Wellington, though he's currently working in Sydney at the General Hospital.'

'Medicine runs in the family then?'

He pulled out a chair for her and tamped down the jerk of annoyance at her surprise. He might be a big man but he had the manners of a gentleman. Except when it

came to dealing with thugs. 'My brother's an orthopaedic surgeon. Our father was a GP. Mother was a nurse.
And so am I.' And darned proud of it. It beat fishing
out in the middle of the wild ocean any day, or trying to
straighten out dumb jerks who thought the world owed
them. Though that had caught up with him here this
morning. Once again.

A brief knock on the door and two cops pushed into
the room, filling the remaining space, which brought
him closer to Harper.

'Statement time,' said the younger one as she gave
him the once-over—a slow, 'I like what I'm seeing'
once-over that stroked his ego but didn't have his brain
wanting to follow up. Nor his body.

Pulling out another chair, he copped a smirk from
Harper. So she'd seen the constable's appraisal. He
shrugged. Nothing he could do about it; he hadn't asked
for it. It just happened. He turned to the other police
officer. 'You want to ask more questions? Or just take
statements?'

The sooner this was done and that coffee arrived,
then the sooner he could go back to work and put the
morning behind him. That was if George let them go
back to work. He seemed pretty adamant that they were
going to have to go home for the rest of the day and rest
up. Matilda and Jess too. Harper wasn't going to like
that; he was sure of it.

When they were done with the police Harper pulled
out her phone and checked her messages. 'Who doesn't
know what happened?' she muttered and shut it off completely without answering any texts or emails.

Cody had texted his brother earlier to say he was
good and not to worry about him. They'd talk tonight.
Maybe. 'You're not putting it out there that you're fine?'

She seemed very reluctant to talk to her family or this Jason character.

'George did it.' Her mouth lifted slightly. 'He never does take any notice of what I want. No wonder he's friends with my brothers.'

Cody thought she was just as guilty of that after George examined Harper's throat and tried to make her take the rest of the shift off. Of course she refused, flouncing out to the department and picking up the next file on the way to the waiting room. George wasn't best pleased, but he relented in the end. They could stay to the end of the shift but were relegated to paperwork only.

'I'm fine, George,' Harper insisted with a scowl.

'You might think so, Harper, but you've had a huge shock. I'm not comfortable with you treating patients till you've had a full night's sleep. That's non-negotiable.'

Cody actually wouldn't have minded knocking off early for the day but he didn't want to leave Harper alone after what they'd been through. He felt weirdly protective of her after all the bravery she'd shown. She was quite a woman.

Careful, Cody. That way lies trouble.

'You feel like going for a drink?' Cody asked Harper at the end of their shift as they pushed through the swing doors and out into the corridor. 'We've certainly earned one today.' The rest of the shift was already at the pub just down the road, no doubt yacking about the event that had overtaken the department that morning, which kind of had him regretting his suggestion to Harper. He'd had enough of the talk. Already the truth had been expanded, the resultant stories getting way out of control.

'I don't think so.' She looked decidedly uncomfortable with the idea. Or was that about going with him?

His tongue got the better of him, as it was prone to do at the most inconvenient of times. 'You don't drink with your colleagues?' She wouldn't now, not if he was going to be there.

'I don't drink at all when I have a migraine.'

He swore. Now he knew why she kept rubbing her temples. 'How're you getting home?' he asked as he saw her blink furiously when they stepped out into the blinding summer sun.

'I have a car.' Her chin jutted out. 'How about you?'

'I have a motorbike.'

'Then you're not asking me for a ride home?'

'No, but I am offering to drive you home in your car. You are in no fit state to be behind the wheel.'

'Yes, nurse.' Her tone would've sounded sarcastic if there hadn't been resignation and tiredness lacing her words. It seemed as though now she'd stopped work she was unravelling completely. Her eyes were half-closed, and she dug around in her bag and dragged out sunglasses, which she slapped on her face before heading towards the staff car park.

He followed. 'You know I'm right. A migraine is hell, apparently. Do you get blackouts with yours?'

Her mouth tightened and she said nothing.

'Toss in that bruised and swollen throat, the shock of being held hostage, and you're in need of a little pampering.' Was he offering to pamper her? No, that had come out all wrong. But he was damned if he was going to retract his statement. He didn't do being caught on the back foot—not by attractive, sharp-tongued women, at any rate.

Harper ducked between vehicles, seemingly intent on the furthest row. When she reached a dazzling blue, high-performance car she pinged the locks and glared at him over the roof. 'Forgot where you parked your motorbike?'

Cody ignored her anger, believing it probably wasn't really directed at him but more at the situation she found herself in. He wanted to help her, be there for her, and knew better than to come out and say so. He tried another tack. Running his hand over the bonnet, he noted, 'Nice. Bet it goes like a cut cat.'

'Faster.' There was the smallest twist of her lips and a hint of laughter in the pained eyes she exposed when she removed her sunglasses to rub her temples again.

So heat did run along her veins. Not often, maybe, but obviously sometimes. Now, there was a challenge. She was into fast cars. But not today. He stared at her and held out his hand.

Harper stared straight back. At least, she tried to, but that migraine must've got the better of her because she blinked and her chin dropped. The keys sailed through the air and he snatched them before they landed on the paintwork. 'Careful.' Opening the passenger door, he waited patiently for her to come round and slide inside then, closing her door, he headed for the other side of the car, whistling under his breath.

Miss—was she a Miss, or a Mrs?—*Dr* White could be a pain in the backside. But she was also magnificent. He could appreciate the details without being tempted to learn more about her. If it hadn't been for the day's drama he wouldn't be regarding her twice. He wouldn't know that she had soft, muscle-tightening curves in all the right places. Or that she smelt delicious. She was clearly intelligent, and was a superb doctor. She was starting to sound too good. *Harper's nothing to me in any way other than as a colleague.*

Anyway, she had a Jason in her life.

* * *

Harper leaned her head back against the headrest and groaned. Talk about the day from hell. All she wanted was to crawl into bed in her blacked-out room and let the headache drugs that she would take now she'd finished work do their magic. Hopefully she'd sleep, and not have nightmares about that gun or the man wielding it.

'Address?' Cody asked.

Without opening her eyes, she rattled off the street and number, then sighed with relief when he said he knew where to go. Talking hurt, and if she didn't have to utter another word till next week she'd be happy. Not that she'd kept quiet earlier. It was like something had got hold of her tongue, had had her blathering away like she didn't know how to stop, even though her throat protested every syllable. Why had she asked Cody all those personal questions? It wasn't as though she had to have the answers to be able to work with him.

But after everything that had happened she'd felt a need to know more about the man who'd come to her rescue, who'd been there throughout the whole ordeal, who'd even understood her sorrow at losing her patient. He'd surprised her with how recently he'd qualified. She'd done the sums—he was in his early thirties. Fishermen had to be tough, physically and mentally, to cope with the conditions they worked in. She'd seen that in Cody today, and she'd also noticed the soft streak that made him so popular with patients.

Cody had stepped up, tried to talk the gunman into letting her go and hadn't hesitated to take him down when she'd deliberately dropped towards the floor. It had been a risk doing that but she'd felt Cody was a part of her, that he'd known what was going on in her head all the time. The way he'd reacted suggested he'd dealt with villains before. Intriguing. But nothing to do with her. Whatever Cody had done in the past, she did not need to know. That would be getting too personal, and there was no point in doing that when she had no intention of socialising with him outside work.

Cody interrupted her thoughts. 'You fixed for pills for that migraine?'

'Yes.' Like a doctor wouldn't be prepared when she had regular migraines. 'Of course.'

'Just checking. You want anything for home? Food, milk or bottled water? I can duck into the supermarket for you.'

'Got everything I need.' *Except a loving man.* She gasped. Where had that come from? Had that crack on her skull with the gun addled her brain? Not once since she'd packed her bags and walked out the front door of the house she'd shared with Darren had she believed she was ready for a relationship with another man. A quick fling, yes—anything deep and meaningful, no. If there was even a man out there who'd accept her infertility issue, she'd struggle to believe he wouldn't change his mind like Darren had done. She'd just have to wait until she was fifty and beyond wanting to be a mother before getting involved with someone.

Her gaze slid sideways to study the profile of the man next to her. He looked good behind the wheel in this big car. Strong, easy in his body, confident. Then there was his reliability—as far as she'd seen, anyway—and his friendly, caring side. There was that perfectionist element she'd noted before the morning had gone pear-shaped, but perfectionism could be a fault or a good trait. He could also get angry, as witnessed with their assailant. Controlled anger though, not a rant or rage.

'You're staring.'

She was. And liking what she saw more and more. A big enough reason to close her eyes again. Which she did, and sank further down the seat. Thank goodness for Fridays. The coming weekend would give her time to recover fully from the migraine. Whether she'd stop shaking from shock every time she thought about what had gone down in the ED by Monday was another story. What if the assailant *had* fired his gun? Had wounded someone—Jess, Cody or her? She shivered abruptly.

He placed one hand on her thigh, squeezed lightly and removed his hand fast. 'Don't think about him. It's over now.' He sounded so darned calm, as though nothing had affected him.

Yet his ability to constantly know what she was thinking riled her for no real reason. Again she pictured him taking that man down and her mood swiftly softened. He was very confident and for a large man he'd moved fast, light on his feet. The assailant hadn't known what had hit him. Which was just as well, or it might've been Cody feeling the hot end of that gun. She shivered. For some strange reason she took real comfort from his confidence and was inordinately grateful to him for how he'd dealt with the situation. Also for his tenderness in that hug. Confused. That was what she was.

Nausea swamped her senses. She was going to be sick. No, she wasn't. Not in front of Cody, nurse or not. That would be the final straw in a very bad day. Pressing the switch to lower her window, she leaned over and relished the air flowing across her face. It wasn't cold air, but at least cooler than what was inside the car. No doubt she'd look a right state by the time they reached home, but at this moment she couldn't care less.

'You need to stop?' Cody asked, already slowing the car and easing closer to the edge of the road.

'No. Keep going.' The sooner she got home, the better. The blinding pain behind her eyes was increasing in intensity, but at least the nausea was sort of under control. This was becoming the migraine to beat all migraines in her experience, no doubt exacerbated by the tension from earlier.

Her apartment was just around the corner. Soon she'd be shot of Cody Brand. Until Monday and work. With a bit of luck, by then they'd be back to being a doctor and a nurse working in the same department. Hopefully by then all the talk and texts would've died down too. She didn't fancy multiple reruns of today's event.

'There's a car in your driveway.' Cody's voice was deeper than most men's, yet it soothed her frayed nerves and battered mind. 'Want me to park on the road?'

'Great.' She'd forgotten about Gemma calling in after her shopping expedition so they could have a wine together. Not happening now; the mere thought of wine turned her stomach. 'That'd be fine. I'll shift the car later.' Tomorrow when she finally crawled out of bed.

Harper was hardly aware of Cody pulling up. He had her door open and was reaching for her elbow so quickly it came as a surprise. 'Come on. I'll see you to your door.'

'I can manage.' And she promptly proved herself wrong when her knees refused to hold her upright.

'Now, don't take this the wrong way,' Cody murmured as he swung her up in his arms and nudged the door shut with his hip. 'But falling flat on your face after everything else could really mess up your day.' He strode up the path towards her front door as though she was no heavier than a bag of spuds. A very small bag at that.

Harper didn't bother arguing. He wouldn't listen and she didn't have any energy left. Besides, it was lovely lying against that expansive chest and feeling strong arms around her. Arms she imagined holding her through the night. *Jeez, Harper, get a grip.*

'Harper? Jason said you were all right but you're not looking great.' Typical Gemma: go for the throat. *No, someone else already did that today.*

'Gemma,' she squeaked.

Her sister-in-law stood in the doorway, her eyes flicking between her and Cody, worry slowly turning to speculation as she studied Cody from head to foot. 'Or do I need to grab my bag and head away pronto? Leave you two alone?'

Harper cringed. She loved Gemma to bits but the woman had a mission in life to find her a man who'd accept all her problems without batting an eyelid— and from what she was reading on Gemma's face right this minute Cody was a prime target. No way in hell. Squirming out of Cody's arms, she stood shakily between him and Gemma. 'I've got a migraine.'

It seemed Gemma had become deaf overnight. She focused entirely on Cody and asked, 'Who are you?'

'I'm Cody. I work with Harper.'

Feeling Cody's hand on her elbow—again—Harper wanted to shrug him away but doubted she had the strength to walk unaided. 'I need to lie down. Going to take a rain check on that wine, Gem.'

'Your voice's all weird.' Gemma leaned closer. 'What's wrong with your neck? Jason told me about the gunman but you've been hurt. You're not all right, are you? That's why Cody's here.'

'Harper needs to get inside and lie down in a dark room.' Cody was firm, like he'd take no argument.

Gemma caught the message and led the way indoors. 'What really happened, Harper? Spill.'

'I— There—' Her throat closed over and tears filled her eyes. She raised her head, caught Cody's gaze and nodded at him.

'You want me to explain?'

Once again, Cody to the rescue. This was getting out of hand, but she dipped her head. Words were beyond her. Accepting help from any one didn't feature in her everyday life. Not even her overly protective brothers got a chance very often. But today, right now, she was all out of helping herself.

Cody told Gemma, 'Let's put Harper to bed first.' That was the most important thing to do. The whys and wherefores of the situation could wait a few more minutes. He smiled to himself with relief. At least this woman could help Harper out of her clothes while he hung out in the kitchen. He would not be disappointed at missing out on that treat.

Really? Really. Getting too close and personal with Harper was the last thing he needed. He had a feeling that getting to know her at all would undermine the defences he'd pulled around himself the day Sadie had died. The agony over his loss, the sense of failure and guilt, had taken many dark days and months to quieten enough for him to start moving forward, one tiny step at a time. He wasn't going to risk going back there again.

'I'm taking you home with me.' Gemma's hands were on her hips as she watched Harper gingerly sit down on her bed.

Harper shook her head but didn't open her eyes. She was probably beyond dealing with anything right now.

So Cody stepped into the gap. 'Harper's better off staying here, unless you live next door. She's not in good shape.' *There's absolutely nothing wrong with her shape.* Cody closed his eyes and dragged up some patience with himself. Then, looking at Gemma, he explained about the guy who'd caused all the trouble. 'Her throat's swollen and painful, and the whole event has been a huge shock. I don't know if the migraine had begun before that lowlife did his number on her, or it's a result of his actions, but it's a bad one.'

Gemma's face paled. 'You can't stay here after that. What would Jason say if I arrived home without you? I know it will be uncomfortable on the drive but you're coming home to the bay for the weekend.'

Harper's eyes flew open. 'But—'

'But nothing. I'll pack some clothes and we'll be on our way.' She spun around and stuck a hand out at Cody. 'No wonder she didn't introduce us properly. Gemma White, married to Harper's oldest brother, Jason. Thanks for taking care of her. One more thing, can you carry her out to my car when I've collected a few things?'

So that was who Jason was. Unexpected relief rolled through Cody. Not her husband or partner, but her brother. George must be pally with him if he'd wanted to tell him about what had happened to his sister. 'I hate to point this out but I don't think Harper's up to going anywhere.'

Harper lifted grateful eyes in his direction. She was definitely all out of energy. Exhaustion and pain filled her mesmerising gaze. Her body was slumped in a loose heap on the edge of the bed and he doubted her ability even to lift her legs up under the sheet. He couldn't take his eyes off her as she looked up at him.

But it was the sadness in that gaze that caused him to make a fool of himself. 'I'll stay here the night, keep an eye on you.' He nodded at Harper, who now stared at him, a mix of gratitude and horror further darkening those eyes.

Gemma nodded. 'That's a perfect solution. I take it you're a doctor, since you work with Harper?'

'Not a doctor. A nurse.'

Which was totally the wrong thing to tell this woman because she clapped her hands. 'Even better. A nurse is exactly what Harper needs. Right, I'll get you undressed and into bed, my girl, then leave you in the capable hands of Nurse Cody. He'll be able to sleep in the kids' room. Just as well I changed the sheets on the beds earlier while I was waiting for you to come home. That couch in the lounge may be big but not big enough for his bod.'

'Jeez, woman, do you ever come up for air?' Cody asked Gemma with a grin and was rewarded with a startled gasp of laughter from the bed where Harper had finally stopped staring at him. 'What?' he demanded. These ladies were full-on.

'I could get to like you,' Harper gasped in her new croaky voice.

That'd be good. No, it wouldn't. 'We'll see,' he answered airily, then made the mistake of glancing at Gemma and sucked in a sharp breath.

Her expression spelled mischief. Lots of it. 'This just gets better and better,' she murmured.

'Gemma.' Even with her swollen throat and feeling like hell it was obvious Harper was not pleased with her sister-in-law.

'Right, let's get you into bed so you can sleep off this migraine. Where are your tablets?' Gemma was already opening a drawer and pulling out some cotton night-dress thing that she held up with distaste. 'You don't listen to anything I tell you, do you, sis?'

Cody headed for the door. He wasn't hanging around while Harper removed her work clothes and slipped into that hideous yellow-and-pink-striped concoction. At least he agreed with Gemma on something. 'I'll get some water so you can take your tablets,' he called over his shoulder.

Ten minutes later, Gemma joined him in the kitchen. 'I hope you haven't got any plans for Sunday after-noon, because it's Jason's birthday, and Harper needs to be with us. The Whites are big on family stuff, you know? The brothers—' she wriggled her forefingers in the air between them '—will want to meet the man who looked out for her today. You must stay for lunch and the cricket.'

'Cricket?' he asked. What was this woman on about?

'You know—bat, ball and wickets. The kids can't get enough of it. Bet when you hit a ball it stays hit.'

'It's been a while since I swung a bat.' He shook his head. 'Thanks for the invitation, Gemma, but don't count me in. I've already got something on.'

'You sure? We have a lot of fun, there's always great food and—' she grinned '—ice-cold beer.'

Cody gave her a smile in return. 'Thanks, but no thanks.' Harper wouldn't be pleased if he accepted the invitation, however graciously it had been extended. They worked together; playing together wasn't part of the deal. He headed to the bedroom with Harper's water glass in his hand.

'Gemma giving you a hard time?' Harper asked as he handed her the glass.

Knowing Harper would back him all the way about not joining her family, he grunted, 'She insists I join you all for the birthday do on Sunday.'

'Oh.' She winced as she swallowed the pills. 'You'd have to stay all afternoon.'

What happened to her seeing things his way? 'I've got plans to spend the afternoon with my mother.' It was what he did in the weekends now that he was back in town. Her condition had lost her most of her friends and she was lonely.

'Bring her with you, with us.'

Yeah, right. 'Sorry, no can do. Mum's got dementia and needs watching all the time.' Not to mention how rattled she got when out of her usual haunts or was with people she'd never met.

'Well, you know best, of course. But there are plenty of us to keep an eye on her. She might have fun! The kids will be friendly. My parents and brothers and sister are quite nice most of the time. The brothers and sisters-in-law are housetrained on a good day.'

'I thought it hurt to talk.' He was over these bossy women. 'You sure you and Gemma aren't sisters, rather than related by marriage?' They had the same genes.

Harper grimaced. 'We'll talk some more tomorrow.'

That was it? She must be feeling even worse than he'd thought. 'Go to sleep,' he growled and strode out into the kitchen, where thankfully Gemma was waiting with keys in hand, ready to take flight.

'Thanks for doing this.' She grinned and stretched up on tiptoes to drop a sisterly kiss on his chin. 'I really appreciate it. Her brothers will be more than thankful.

Harper can be very stubborn at times and I know she'd never have come home with me tonight.'

'I must be stark, raving mad,' Cody muttered as the front door closed behind her. Outmanoeuvred was what he really was. It didn't sit comfortably. Not at all.

CHAPTER THREE

Now what was he supposed to do? Nearly five in the afternoon, a beautiful woman hopefully sound asleep in the room next door—which was not how he usually spent time with women in their homes—and he had absolutely nothing to do. He was not going to check up on Harper. What if she was awake? Or, worse, woke while he was in her room? She'd be calling him a pervert at the very least.

Staring around, he took in the multitude of framed photos hanging on the walls and standing on bookcases and the sideboard. They were mostly of kids, boys and girls—very young, middling and nearly teenaged, he guessed. Laughing, smiling, pulling faces, dressed in school uniforms, in shorts and shirts, ski outfits, swimming gear and playing cricket. Basically all about having fun. With Harper right amongst them—laughing and smiling. Cute, and nothing like the serious woman who kept everyone in the department on their toes as she worked alongside them.

The kids' room was where he was supposed to sleep tonight. So, Harper had children. Where were they? And where was their dad? He obviously wasn't Jason. Why hadn't Harper wanted her brother to know what had happened at work today? And where did George fit in?

Questions tumbled over and over in his brain, cranking up his agitation. It irked him he didn't know these things about Harper.

It really riled him that he wanted to find out.

Cody's chuckle was bitter. He'd loved Sadie deeply, and her death had made him wary of being so vulnerable again. Even nearly five years down the track he couldn't look back at those dark days without curling in on himself. Sure, he'd love a family, had bought a house suited for one, but to step up and take a chance? He was so not ready. The day might come when he was, but today wasn't it. He sighed. Nor was tomorrow.

Cody pushed the past aside and took another scan of the photos. No man seemed to be especially close with Harper, as in 'in a relationship' close. There were two men hugging her and some kids in many of the photos. Presumably one was Jason. The other could be another brother. Both guys were holding women with love written all over their faces, Gemma being one of them. So was Harper single or not? In any relationship? Divorced? There were those kids who apparently used the spare room, so there had to be a father out there, which meant a man in Harper's life in one way or another.

Harper's bedroom hadn't looked as though she shared it with anyone. It was too feminine, and not one item of clothing was male, there was no comb or shaver on the dresser, or the bits and pieces he'd expect on the bedside table on the opposite side of the bed to the one Harper had crawled into.

The mystery was no clearer in the second, tiny bedroom where two single beds with bright quilts, one with fire engines and the other with frogs printed all over them, took up most of the space. More photos were interspersed with pictures of everything from lions to

TV cartoon characters. Hell, he'd be having nightmares sleeping in here.

He *was* meant to be sleeping in here.

He might check out that couch. Except it was only a two-seater and he was six-five tall. Even these beds weren't going to be long enough but he'd be able to manoeuvre himself into a more comfortable position in one than on the couch.

On his hip his phone vibrated, giving him a much-needed diversion, though he didn't recognise the number on the screen. 'Yup?'

'Now I know you're definitely back in town.'

He recognised the voice of his old mate instantly, despite not having talked for years. 'Hey, Trent, been meaning to catch up, but got busy, you know?' Truth was he'd been reluctant to get in touch because he was uncertain of the welcome he'd get. At sixteen they'd been the closest of mates at school and into loads of mischief, but the day school had finished he'd headed out the gate without a backward glance, leaving everything and everyone behind.

Including Trent. Eager to get on with life, rebelling against settling into more study, this time at university, he'd put his surprisingly not-too-bad exam results aside and found a job down south on a fishing trawler. Despite only being seventeen, he'd already had the body of a rugby prop, so getting a job had been easy in an industry that required plenty of muscle.

'Police Inspector Trent Ballinger to you.' A deep laugh rumbled through the phone.

'Way to go, man. Well done, you.' Cody headed for the lounge and the garden on the other side of the sliding glass doors. He didn't want to wake Harper, and anyway he needed some fresh air after being holed up with her in the car and then here. Hell, even her home smelt of citrus, a scent he was rapidly accepting as Harper's scent.

'Saw your name on the report that was filed a few hours ago about Strong and his mule. It wasn't hard to track you down.'

His friend did have the New Zealand police resources on his side. 'That lowlife locked up good and tight?'

'You should've given him what for while you had the opportunity.' Trent sighed. 'I didn't say that. But, hell, the man hasn't stopped whinging since the boys brought him in. Anyone would think he'd been hard done by, losing those drugs.'

'It was tempting to give him a wee nudge.' He was not admitting to the knee slam in the lowlife's back, though. Trent might still be a friend but he was a cop first and foremost. 'How did Strong get in on the act in the first place? I presume he was waiting to pick up Frew outside the international terminal but he managed to slip into our department too easily. I wouldn't have thought the paramedics would've let him ride in with them.'

'He followed them, and strolled up to the ambulance bay as they were disembarking, waved a card that the paramedics believed was a police identity and walked on in.'

'Guess if you've got the balls you can get away with just about anything.' Cody was shocked at how simple it had been, and a tad angry.

'More like if you've got a loaded gun you can get away with most things.'

Cody swallowed. 'It *was* loaded?' After flipping out of Lowlife's hand, it'd spun across the floor to be picked up by Harper, who'd then stuck it under her waistband before attending to Frew. He shivered. Maybe luck had been on their side after all. 'I thought it might be but hoped I was wrong.'

'I think you'll find the hospital will be tightening security quick-fast,' Trent said.

'The old stable door trick.' It wasn't right that outsiders, detectives or not, could get in so easily. During the night no one got through, but it seemed daytime security was lax. 'From what I've seen of George Sampson so far, he'll already have someone looking into it.'

'How's the doc? She holding up?'

Cody chuckled. 'You always ask this many questions?'

'Occupational hazard,' Trent replied. 'You avoiding the question?'

No, he didn't want to talk about Harper, not even to a long lost, now found friend. Somehow talking about her felt like he was going behind her back, which made no sense whatsoever. He went with the medical. 'Her throat and neck are very sore but otherwise she's physically okay. Apart from a migraine that's knocked her to her knees,' he added in case Trent's lot wanted to question her some more today.

'Stress will do that.'

Cody got an image in his skull of that gun being held to Harper's head, and the rank fear pervading her sweet eyes. 'Not sure how she'll go with all the head stuff, though. It'll be tough trying to put aside the fact that someone threatened to shoot her brains out.'

'I hear she handled the situation well,' Trent said, then thankfully changed the subject. 'How long have you been back in town?'

He winced, regretting not phoning Trent sooner. 'Six weeks. Shifted Mother into a retirement home with hospital facilities and then packed up her house, sold off stuff, all of the usual.' It had been hard going through forty years of her possessions. She'd kept everything of his dad's since he'd died ten years back as well, including all his clothes, even his old pipes that he'd smoked in the evenings and the rods from trout-fishing excursions. The rods which were now in *his* shed in case one day he had a child he could take on similar forays. If he ever got brave enough to start over.

The trip down memory lane had at times made him laugh, and at others caused him to shed tears for the mum and dad he'd loved. Still loved. His mother mightn't be the same any more, with the dementia doing its number on her, but she was still Mother. Packing up everything and getting rid of most of the clutter had reminded him of fun family holidays to the beach when he'd been small, and of annoying the hell out of his older brother just because he could.

'So, you up for a pint?' Trent asked, reminding Cody he was in the middle of a conversation. 'I'm done for the day.'

He'd kill for one. 'I can't tonight. Got something on.'

'Found a hot female, huh?'

'Nah, haven't got time for that at the moment.' Stretching the truth wasn't a lie. Harper wasn't his type of woman; she was too focused on her career from what he'd seen, and obviously with family issues which she wouldn't want him getting involved in. *But she is hot. Sizzling.* He was seeing that more and more the longer he spent in her company.

'I heard about your wife.'

Who hadn't? It'd been headline news for days. 'It's history now.' Except the consequence was he didn't talk about personal things or want to put his heart on the line again. He knew the doctors had done everything they could to save her. It didn't make him feel any better.

'That when you took up nursing?' Trent had known he'd considered it, even at school.

'Yep. It was horrible not being able to help Sadie.' Huh? He didn't do talking, remember? It had to be the day that had screwed his brain.

'You back home for good?'

Cody managed a chuckle. 'I've bought myself a house that needs lots of work, a big sucker on the hill overlooking Oriental Bay. It's going to keep me out of mischief for years, so yes, I guess I'm here for the long haul.'

'You staying out of mischief? I must be talking to the wrong Cody Brand.'

If only he knew. Knowing he was stuck in this apartment tonight with a woman he'd only met five days ago, and who he was now babysitting, would bring Trent to his knees with laughter. As Cody stuffed his phone in his back pocket, he wondered just what was stopping him walking out and going to pick up his motorbike before heading down to the pub for that drink with Trent.

A promise that he'd stay the night.

A sense that Harper needed someone to keep an eye out for her. He always knew when someone wanted that—just didn't always do it right. But he kept on trying.

Cody *wanted* to be here, making sure Harper got through the night without any nightmares about what might've happened if everything had gone wrong.

And if that migraine got worse he wanted to take care of her.

It had to be the nurse in him coming out. He couldn't think of any other reason for letting his caring side get the better of him in this case. It wasn't as though Harper needed protecting from her would-be assailant. The guy was behind bars, for now at least.

But he couldn't help the memories creeping in as he twisted a cap off a lonely bottle of beer he found in the fridge. Looking out for Harper today had been instinctive, and easy. He'd have done whatever it took to get that man away from her. Now he'd do everything possible to keep on his guard with Dr White. Someone had to look out for his heart, and that someone was him.

Harper woke slowly. There was a vice around her head and drums behind her eyes. Her stomach ached, as did her throat.

But that was nothing compared to the film reeling through her mind, bringing into sharp focus the man with his gun and how he'd held it to her head.

At least she'd woken up before the pictures had got too violent. But now she didn't want to go back to sleep—not yet, anyway. She was shaking. How close had Strong come to killing her?

'Stop it,' she yelled at herself. Doing this wasn't helping at all. She had to be tough, put it all behind her.

Her mouth was dry. Reaching for the glass on the bedside table, she was disappointed to find it empty. She'd have to move.

Another tablet for her migraine wouldn't go amiss. What time had she taken the last one? Pushing up onto an elbow, she paused until the room steadied. Light streamed down the hall. Had she left the kitchen light on earlier? Or the one in the lounge? No recollection of being in those rooms came to her, but that didn't bother her. It wasn't unusual for her to drop into a deep sleep after taking the migraine meds.

Carefully sitting up and putting her feet on the floor,

she once again waited for her head to catch up with
the rest of her body. The headache had calmed down a
little. Or was it waiting to pounce when she went out
into the light?

Cody Brand. His name slammed into her head.

He was in her apartment somewhere. Sleeping in the
kids' room? Or sitting in the lounge watching television?

It all rushed in, setting her head spinning harder.
Gemma being bossy. Cody saying he'd stay the night
to keep an eye on her. He was why she'd fallen asleep
so quickly, all fear of being attacked again allayed by
his presence.

Most of all she recalled being held in strong arms
against a broad, warm chest and wanting to snuggle
even closer as he'd carried her up the drive. He'd made
her feel safe so often throughout the day. There were
a few other things he had made her feel too that she'd
prefer not to go into.

Oozing a stalled breath over her lips, she debated
crawling back under the sheet and pretending she hadn't
woken up. But the pounding in her head and the tightening of that band of pain wasn't going away if she didn't
have another tablet. And some water. She was so thirsty
her tongue was sticking to the roof of her mouth.

Standing on unsteady legs, she aimed for the kitchen,
hoping she wouldn't find Cody in there. The last thing
she wanted was for him to see her in her nightie, but
searching for the robe that she rarely used somewhere
at the back of her wardrobe would expend energy she
didn't have. She just wanted the tablet and water and to
climb back into bed.

The kitchen was empty, but the TV was on in the
lounge with the sound muted. Harper couldn't resist.
She peeked around the corner and gasped. That big body

was sprawled over her couch with the neighbour's cat curled on top of the chest she'd enjoyed so much. Her heart flipped. Cute. Who'd have thought it of such a large man? A gentle rumble erupted. Cody was sound asleep, snoring softly.

On the floor sat a takeout pizza box with two pieces left. Was she hungry? Stepping closer she bent down to steal a piece but got a whiff of cold melted cheese and something else unpleasant. Her stomach immediately protested. Fair enough. She didn't usually eat during a migraine episode.

Straightening up, she studied Cody. Stubble had appeared on his chin. What would that feel like against the palm of her hand?

She'd never know. Gripping her hands together in case she gave into the need crawling through her, she backed away.

Of course she didn't have eyes in the back of her head. Duh. Thump. The back of her leg banged into the coffee table and she sat down heavily on it. Of course the table shouldn't have been there in the first place. Who'd shifted it? Her eyes went straight to the man now waking up on her couch.

'Hey, you're up.' Cody stretched, carefully lifted the cat off and placed it on what little piece of couch he wasn't taking up. Then he sat up and Harper felt dwarfed. Not that she was tiny.

'I'm getting some water and going back to bed.'

'Want anything to eat?' He glanced at the pizza box and looked back to her. 'I can scramble an egg, if you like.'

Since shaking her head hurt worse than talking through her bruised throat, she said, 'No, thanks.' But she didn't move. Sitting here was easier than getting up.

'How are you feeling now?'

Spreading her fingers on her right hand she tipped her hand back and forth. 'So, so.'

'Going back to bed? Or staying up for a while? I'll change the TV channel. Cricket's over, anyway.'

'No. The flickering light would aggravate my migraine. What's the time?'

A glance at his watch. 'Ten-forty.' He stood up, stretching that long body no doubt to ease the kinks gained from lying on the couch. 'I'll get your water and tablets.'

She didn't need him running round after her. At the same time she couldn't find the strength to stand up and go get what she needed. 'Okay,' she muttered to his back as he strolled out to the kitchen, looking for all the world like he was used to being in her home.

Actually, he looked comfortable in here, like he belonged. He and the cat. Glancing sideways, she knew immediately how Puss had got inside. Cool air flowed in through the open glass doors and an empty beer bottle stood on the concrete by the barbecue table. He'd made himself at home, and Harper wasn't sure how she felt about that.

'Here you go.' A large hand with a glass and pill bottle appeared in front of her. 'Get those into you.' He sat down again. 'Some guy phoned about tennis tomorrow. Something about playing an inter-club match.'

She shook her head. 'You must've got it wrong. I can barely hit the ball over the net yet.'

'You're learning to play?'

'Uh-huh. I'm trying to learn to play. Who'd have thought it would be so hard to bang a ball across a net?' She'd joined the local club in spring and wouldn't be renewing her membership at the end of the season. In fact, she doubted she'd even go to club day again. 'What did you tell him?'

'It wasn't my place to say anything other than you'd phone tomorrow, though I sort of indicated you might be indisposed.'

'Define "sort of".' He'd surprised her. Most people wouldn't think twice about saying she was in bed with a migraine, or worse, describe the attack in the ED that morning.

'Said you had rehearsals for the Christmas ballet in town. He was a little surprised—apparently you're not very nimble on your feet.' Those spring-green eyes were twinkling at her.

'Look.' She lifted the edge of her nightie to reveal her scabby knees. 'Tennis is a blood sport.'

'You're meant to stay on your feet, not crawl after the ball.' His chuckle was deep and rumbly and did funny things to her insides, alternately tightening and softening her muscles. His gaze seemed fixed on her kneecaps, and the tip of his tongue appeared at the left corner of his mouth.

Tugging her nightie as far down her legs as possible, she studied him right back. Cody sitting on her couch was different to Cody attending an old man with a broken leg. She liked this version.

She liked the professional one too.

So what? She liked George at work and when he was hanging out with Jason. She enjoyed Karin in the department and when they sometimes had a meal in town on a Friday night.

But Cody? She liked...

'I'm going back to bed.' Pushing up to her feet, she swayed back and forth until the stars behind her eyeballs blinked off.

A hand took her upper arm gently. 'Take it easy.'

Pulling free of those fingers that felt like heat pads on her skin, she stumbled out of the room and down to her bedroom. Dropping onto the bed, she managed to swallow some pills and pour water down her throat— and down her chin and over the front of her nightie— before lying down and tugging the sheet over her head.

Playing ostrich in case her nurse decided to come and check on her.

'You all right under there?' Yes, the nurse had followed her. Or was that Cody the man?

Flicking the sheet off her face, she grimaced at him. It didn't work. He still leant in the doorway watching her, nothing but genuine concern in his expression. For her? No one else here, so it had to be. 'I had a dream.'

That gorgeous mouth flattened. 'A dream or a nightmare?'

'More like a movie where I had the lead role. You were in it, being as calm and useful as you were in the real deal, as was Strong—not being calm and helpful.' She licked her lips nervously. She didn't want to fall asleep and go through that again.

'At least I didn't change roles.' Cody moved, sat on the end of the bed and gave her another soft smile. She was getting to like those. 'Want a cup of tea? It might help you go to sleep. I'd tell you a story but I'm all out of them at the moment.'

Her mouth curved up in response to his smile. How could it not? Cody had a way about him that slipped through all her determination to remain aloof. A light, friendly way that did things to her insides, things that she'd thought long dead, things that weren't about friendship but about something more intense. *Not going to happen. It can't. He's bound to want children some day.* 'Tea would be lovely.'

Tea would be lovely, her brain mimicked.

What was it about this man that had her melting with just a glance? Could it be that strength of character she'd seen in play today? He hadn't faltered from the moment the so-called detective had stepped into Resus. *Be real. You were ogling him and salivating over his bod before the department's unwelcome visitor turned up.*

Whatever. Whichever way she looked at Cody, and not only at his physical attributes, he came up trumps. Fine. *Whatever,* she repeated under her breath. The fact remained she had failed at one marriage and the reasons behind that hadn't changed. She still couldn't have children, and her long hours at work hadn't lessened, not even when she'd changed jobs.

'Tea for the lady.' Cody spoke softly from somewhere above her.

Her eyes sprang open. That was quick. 'You move quietly.' But then she already knew how light he was on his feet. This morning's assailant hadn't seen him coming—at least, not as swiftly as he'd been taken down.

'If you were asleep, I didn't want to wake you.'

He only got better and better. Which was bad, bad, bad.

Cody rubbed it in some more. 'I'll listen out for you during the night in case you have another rerun of that movie.'

Her heart thudded against her ribs, while her stomach slowly melted into a pool of longing. Longing for a man who might really, really be as big-hearted and understanding of her as Cody appeared to be. *Stop these stupid dreams.* They were never for real and only came back to bite people on the backside. Hers especially.

'Thanks,' she muttered and sipped her tea. What else could she say?

It was still Friday. There were two days before she went back to work and needed to have put Cody into the slot he was meant to be in. Ah, but hadn't she kind of intimated he should go with her to Jason's birthday bash? Not with her, exactly, but she hadn't told him to stay away.

All this went to show that when a mad man put a gun to her head she couldn't be responsible for anything she did or said for some time afterwards.

Harper sank down into her pillows, pushed Cody away out of her thoughts and finished her tea, thinking about her family, all her nieces and nephews, and how much she adored them. Despite her day, she felt safe. Nothing to do with Cody. Nothing at all.

The next time she woke, daylight was lightening the edges of her not-so-good blackout curtains. Lifting her head slowly, she was relieved to find the pressure band around her skull had gone and the drummers behind her eyeballs had packed their bags and left. Yeah. Progress. She still felt wiped out and would take any movement slowly. Swallowing hurt like stink but the swelling at the front of her neck felt as though it might have lessened.

Climbing out of bed, she shoved into a tee-shirt and tugged on a pair of long gym pants—not a fashion statement, but at least she could saunter out to her kitchen and face up to Nurse Cody without blushing about her night attire.

His eyes widened and those full lips twitched when he saw her. 'You're not going to tennis, then?'

Okay, maybe a light blush. 'Has he phoned again?' Her head might be a load better but thumping around a court swinging a racket would not be the best idea she could have. It wasn't even on a good day, when all her faculties were in top working order.

'No. It's only a little after eight. Just thought that might be why you're up early. As in, early for someone who had the migraine from hell and had dealt with a mad man on her watch in the ED.'

'Eight is late for any morning of the week, no matter what's been going on.' She grinned. She couldn't help it. Cody did that to her, made her want to smile, grin, shout from the rooftop. Shout what? Um... No idea, but it probably wouldn't make a lot of sense.

'Want some breakfast? I popped out to the super-market early on.'

The mouth-watering smell of bacon cooking tempted her. A lot. But she knew better than to give into tempta-tion. 'Dry toast and herbal tea will do for now.' Though that bacon did smell delicious.

'No fatty food after a migraine?'

'I avoid it for a while.' Did he have to look so com-fortable at the stove too? Where didn't he fit in? Her ultra-modern kitchen had never looked so good, al-though a bit cramped for space. He could have been on the poster for the kitchen company; they wouldn't have been able to keep up with orders.

'So, no tennis today. But you've got that birthday party and a game of cricket tomorrow.'

'My cricket skills are no better than my tennis ones. I usually keep the score.' A sportswoman she was not. But there had to be something out there she could get into and enjoy, some hobby or game that would keep her busy and her brain engaged when she wasn't work-ing, or looking after one or other of 'the brat pack', as she called her brothers' broods. Glancing across at her dining table, she shrugged. The patchwork quilt she'd promised her mother hadn't progressed past the first few blocks.

'Nor are my sewing attempts. Though I can sew two pieces of fabric together, I get bored too soon. I must have the attention span of a gnat because the thought of making something Mum would be proud to have on her bed does my head in.'

Cody's gaze followed the direction she was staring in. 'I can't quite see you at a sewing machine. Seems too...'

'Dull? Simple?' She gave him a quick smile. 'Or complicated?'

He laughed, retrieved the pan off the hob, tipped the bacon onto a slice of toast, added pepper and slapped a second slice on top. 'You can stitch up people. I trust you to stitch fabric. Just didn't seem like your kind of hobby for some reason.'

'You might be right about that. Did you make it to the bedroom for a sleep last night, or stay on the couch?'

'I gave one of the beds a go. I slept on top. I've tidied up so the kids won't know I've even been in there.'

'To be honest they won't care who's been using their room.' Digging in the pantry, she found a packet of tea bags and a mug. 'As long as there's ice-cream in the freezer and chocolate in the cupboard, they're happy.'

'How many children have you got?'

The children question. It got to her every time even when she was used to it. Cody wasn't to know her history, so it was an innocuous question, or would be for most women.

'I haven't got any.' For a brief while there she'd felt totally at ease with this man in her apartment and forgotten the usual reasons why she didn't spend time with men who intrigued her. Now, though disappointment flared, she should be grateful to Cody once again—this time for reminding her that she was destined to remain single. Men wanted families as much as she did.

'Got that wrong, didn't I? Gemma mentioned kids yesterday, and that spare bedroom isn't decorated for any adults I've ever met.' He smiled softly.

And melted her heart just a weeny bit. 'Gemma was referring to my seven nieces and nephews, known as "the brat pack". There aren't many weekends I don't have some of them staying with me. This weekend is an exception, but then I'm going to be in Lowry Bay with them tomorrow. I might even head over tonight.'

'Seven, eh? That explains the people-mover Gemma was driving. How many of those seven are hers?'

'I'd say three. She'd say she's got four. She counts my brother as a big kid. She's right. He is.' When it came to sick or distressed children at the ED, she'd noticed Cody was a bit like Jason, with how he cheered them up by having fun. He too acted like a big kid at times. Except Cody appeared far more tidy and organised.

'Are you okay if I head away once I've cleaned up my cooking mess?' The subject of her and children was obviously done and dusted and she hadn't had to explain herself.

'I'll give you a ride to the hospital so you can collect your motorbike.' She was past the blackout phase and felt almost as good as new. Almost. A quiet day mucking about around here would do the trick. She gave another glance at her table. If she tackled that pile of fabric triangles she might bore herself into a stupor and forget Cody and migraines and assailants. Forget why she was alone and desperate to find something to occupy herself with so she didn't think about finding a man who'd love her regardless of her flaws.

CHAPTER FOUR

'HAPPY BIRTHDAY, BIG BROTHER.' Harper stretched onto her toes and kissed Jason's cheek, then handed him an envelope.

'What's this? Tickets to the one-day cricket match at the Cake Tin?' Jason was referring to the sports arena in central Wellington, so named for its resemblance to said tin.

'In your dreams, buster.' She knew their brother Noah was giving him tickets for that game. 'I've booked you into a spa for a leg wax and facial.'

'She's so funny this morning. That headache must've vamoosed completely.' He tore the envelope open with all the finesse of a one-year-old. As he read the voucher, his eyes widened with delight. 'Hey, Gemma, look at this. We're getting a break from our brats. A weekend for two in Blenheim for the wine festival. And guess who's brat-sitting?'

Harper poured herself a coffee from the pot bubbling on the gas ring and eyed up the crumpets on the bench. Not only had her head cleared but her throat had settled back to near normal and her stomach was ravenous. Spending last night here with her family had been just the cure she'd needed. She and Jason had talked about the incident in the ED which, along with knowing Cody would be there as well, helped her feel she could go back to work tomorrow morning without any qualms about the patients.

Last night Cody had texted to ask how she was. A simple message that had made her inordinately happy. But he hadn't said any more about if he'd come to the party today. He'd been reticent right from when Gemma had invited him, and she should be grateful, but that annoying devilish side to her nature was hoping he'd turn up.

'What time are we cranking up this shindig?' she asked Jason.

'First ball will be bowled at one-thirty, straight after lunch,' he replied.

'Your mum and dad will be here for lunch,' Gemma said.

'So any time soon,' Harper guessed. It was barely gone eight but no one in the White family stuck to times. They just arrived when they were ready, usually early, and everyone helped out with the food and the games and whatever else needed doing.

'I told Cody to be here in time for the cricket,' Gemma added with a wink.

Harper's mood wavered, hope warring with apprehension. Having Cody in the midst of her family was a little too close for comfort. They weren't best friends, or lovers, or anything other than work colleagues who'd been through a bit of drama together. But he did make her feel different, alive in a way she hadn't been for years. 'I have no idea what he'll do,' she admitted. In reality, Cody probably wasn't interested in attending her family celebrations. Why would he be?

'We need another fielder for the cricket.' Gemma grinned and dropped two crumpets into the toaster.

'While *you* need a big breakfast. You've hardly eaten a thing for two days.'

Darn, but the woman was bossy. Well, she wasn't getting the last word. 'I could do with losing some weight. The shorts I tried on the other day looked hideous.'

Jason laughed. 'The shorts or you in them?'

Brothers could be right pains in the backside. Harper swiped at Jason's forearm. 'Haven't you got a barbecue to haul out and clean?'

'The kids are doing that.' But he headed off to supervise, whistling tunelessly as he went.

By one o'clock all her family was sitting around the enormous outdoor table munching on sandwiches and the savouries Gemma had had everyone who'd dared step into the kitchen make. The sun was high in the clear blue sky, the temperature rising by the minute.

'It will be too hot to play cricket soon,' Harper commented.

'Never too hot,' one of the boys shouted.

'Sunscreen all round, brats.' Noah stood up and began stacking empty plates.

The roar of a motorbike blasted through the hot air, sending prickles of apprehension up Harper's spine. Cody had a motorbike.

The sound got closer, then a large bike turned into the drive. Moments later comparative silence settled. The kids raced across the lawn to gape at the fascinating machine. Harper stared at the rider pulling his helmet off. It seemed Cody Brand wasn't averse to joining her family after all.

Harper didn't know how to feel about this development. She hadn't prepared for it. She wasn't ready for the man now swinging a leg over the bike to join her family. Black leather suited him perfectly. Her heart fluttered roughly against her ribs. *Settle, girl. Settle.*

Cody looked around, locked eyes with her and nodded, a cheeky grin on his face.

Harper headed in his direction. Even if it turned out she didn't want him here, she wouldn't be rude enough to ignore him. 'Hey, this is a surprise.'

His grin didn't falter. 'You figured I'd be a no-show, huh?'

I hoped you would be. And I hoped you wouldn't. 'I forgot to factor in Gemma's powers of persuasion. No one ignores her.'

'I won't hang around for long, Harper. But as I was going past I thought I should at least stop by and say hello.'

No one went past Lowry Bay. Not unless they had something to do in Eastbourne, and she doubted Cody did. 'If you think you're…'

The rest of what she had to say was lost in shouts of glee from the children, gazing at the motorbike with excitement in their eyes.

'Wow. Does it go fast?'

'Can I have a ride?'

'I want a motorbike when I get bigger.'

Cody looked bemused for a moment, then he laughed. 'Yes, it goes fast. I'm Cody, Auntie Harper's friend.' Really? Yeah, maybe he was. 'Who are all of you?'

The eldest boy rushed in with, 'I'm Levi, he's Timothy, she's Mosey and that's Nosey.'

'Levi,' Harper warned. 'Alice and Greer,' she told Cody.

'And I'm Jason, one of Harper's brothers.' Jason held his hand out. 'Glad you dropped by. We owe you a beer or three for what you did on Friday.' The men shook hands before Jason said, 'Come and meet the rest of the clan. Hope you can bowl a straight line. Cricket starts shortly. We're just waiting for a couple of kids from down the road to turn up.'

Cody shrugged out of his heavy jacket.

Harper had to stop from reaching over and rubbing that leather. It would be warm from his body, soft where it had clung to his muscles. *Oh, for goodness' sake, stop it.* Maybe she needed a night with a gigolo. A laugh spluttered over her lips. *Yeah, right. Way to go, Harper.*

Cody glanced at her before telling Jason, 'I'm only stopping for a few minutes.'

Gemma might've been standing over on the deck but she had big ears. 'You're here now. There's no getting away from us until after dinner.'

Cody grinned and flicked his hand to his fore-head. 'Yes, mam. Thank you, mam.' Then he turned to Harper, and the grin faded. 'How's that head? The migraine gone?'

'Completely. The throat's not so raw any more either. How about you? No after-effects from dropping on that man?' Did his hip need checking over? She *was* a doctor.

'It must be fine. I mowed lawns and cleaned guttering yesterday.' There was a twinkle in his eyes, as though challenging her to ask more.

Did he want her to know about his life outside the department? 'Your place? Or someone else's?' Harper picked his jacket up off the bike seat. 'Don't leave this in the direct sun.' Any excuse to hold it against her chest and breathe in the maleness of its wearer.

'Mine. I bought a house when I got to town. It's a bit of a doer-upper. Not had a lot of TLC for years, I'd say.'

'A project, then.' He hadn't said where it was, and she wasn't asking, even when she wanted to know.

'I'm not much into sports either, except when it comes to playing with kids.' He shifted his gaze from her to scan the lawn where the guys had put in wickets and mowed a pitch. 'Looks like your family is really into it. How did you miss those genes?'

'You'll have to ask my parents.'

'They're here too?' Suddenly he looked very uncomfortable. 'There are a lot of you. Maybe I shouldn't have dropped in.'

'Hey, no one bites. Come and meet everyone, get it out of the way. Kids, leave that bike alone,' she told two of the boys. 'You don't want to be knocking it off its stand and getting hurt.'

'There are two helmets,' one of them noted. 'Does that mean we can have a ride?'

Cody grimaced. 'I thought Auntie Harper might go for one with me.' As an aside, he said, 'I didn't think about the kids when I brought it with me.'

Jason called across the lawn. 'Game's starting. Cody, you need to shed some clothes, man. It's too hot to be running after a ball in leathers.'

'I've got shorts and a tee. Where can I change?' he asked Harper.

Right here would work for her. 'I'll take you inside.'

'Come with me.' Levi grabbed his hand and began hauling him across to the shed. 'Only girls get changed in the house.'

'Glad to know I'm not girlie.' Cody raised his eyebrows at her.

'Levi's aiming for a ride on that bike,' she retorted with a smile. Definitely not girlie; no way. Not with those muscles, flat abs and that unquestionably male silhouette. Jerking her head around, she pulled her gaze away from him. Phew, it was getting hotter by the second around here.

'Here, you look like you could do with something cold.' Gemma handed her a glass beaded with condensation. 'Thought water was appropriate, given that you're already half tipsy just watching Cody.'

'Get away.' She snatched the glass and gulped half the contents down.

On her other side Megan, her other sister-in-law, waved a full wine glass at the man who had everyone's attention. 'He is rather yummy.'

'Quite different to Harper's last man. Think I prefer this one,' Gemma announced.

Harper scowled. 'Haven't you two got anything better to do?'

'What could be better than winding you up?' Megan grinned. 'If you couldn't care less, then nor would we.'

'Huh.' Harper couldn't think of anything to say to shut the two up and not get more stupid comments.

'Let's get comfortable under the trees and watch how he is with a ball and bat.' Megan grabbed her arm and dragged her over to where the kids had set up the outdoor chairs.

Without thinking, Harper said, 'If he hits the ball a neighbour will be complaining about a broken window. Those are serious muscles in his arms and shoulders.'

'Knew she'd noticed,' Gemma quipped. 'You should've seen her all snuggled up to the man's chest on Friday when he carried her into her apartment. Cute as, I'm telling you. He's yet to strip down to shorts and tee.'

'Hottie' didn't begin to describe the man. 'Stop it,' she spluttered. 'I'm telling you, I am not interested.'

'That's a shame, because I've invited him to Levi's birthday party in a couple of weeks.'

'You what?' Harper spun around in her seat so fast she flipped out onto the grass.

Amidst lots of laughter from her sisters-in-law, she was hauled to her feet and pushed back into the chair. 'Oh, boy, have you got it bad or what?'

'I have not got it any damned way. You're out of order inviting Cody again. Don't ever try pushing me into a relationship. You know the score.' Anger was replacing her lighter mood, the girls' idea of fun no longer remotely enjoyable.

Megan reached over with a hug. 'Just want you to be happy, Harper. You know we don't mean much by our teasing.'

She bit down on a sharp retort. She loved these girls as much as her own sister, Suzanne, but there were times she could happily bang their heads together. 'I am happy. A lot happier than when I was married. Okay?'

'Can't argue with that. Ready for a wine?'

'Not today. Want to be on my game at work tomorrow. Oh...' Harper's eyes fixed on those hands reaching up for a ball one of the kids had hit into the air as Cody strode onto the lawn. Big hands, strong, and yet she knew how gentle they could be... They snatched the ball out of the air.

Beside her the girls went into shrieks of laughter, but at least they refrained from making any more flippant comments. Suzanne joined them and pressed a glass of low-alcohol wine into her hand. 'You'll be fine with that.'

Then Cody glanced over and she felt her insides melt, or what was left of them after the previous meltdown. One look and she was gone. How would she manage to stay sane and sensible at work when he would be around all the time? She might have to talk to George about transferring to night shift. Except she preferred days; she hated the disruption to sleep patterns that working all night brought. Her contract was for days except in emergencies, and had been hard fought for, so to change it now would be a backwards step. To change it because of Cody would be dumb.

And if she did nights she wouldn't be seeing much of this rowdy lot, and that was not about to happen. Her family meant everything to her since she'd never have her own children. She wouldn't adopt or foster as a single parent. It wasn't fair on the child. When Darren had told her he'd changed his mind and did want a family, she'd reminded him he'd been agreeable to adopting a child, but somewhere along the way he'd become dead set against *that* idea. Just another of his promises he'd reneged on. What had she seen in him?

Again she found herself watching Cody. He was chasing down a ball. When he slid into the fence, the kids cheered. He clambered to his feet, a grin splitting his face. He was having fun. No one could fake that look of pure enjoyment.

He'd make a fabulous dad.

Harper's stomach lurched. No, no, no. She'd known it was wrong to have him join her family today, and yet she'd wanted him here. Now she had the proof of why he couldn't join them ever again.

'Where are you going?' Gemma asked as she stood up.

'Need my sun hat and some more sunscreen.' And to put distance between herself and that man turning her carefully organised world upside down, inside out.

Cody heaved the ball at the wickets and missed, which won him growls from the kids and applause from the women. All the women except Harper, who seemed intent on something on the grass she was crossing, going towards the house.

What was up? Moments ago she'd been yakking with her sisters and watching his every move. *Nearly every move. Don't get big-headed.*

'Catch it, Cody,' Jason yelled.

Hell, now he was day-dreaming. Not a good look, especially amongst this lot. Leaping high, he missed the ball. Again.

Levi sidled up to him. 'You said you could play.'

'Sorry, buddy. I wasn't concentrating. I'll do better from now on, okay?' He held his hand up to high-five the youngster.

The kid grinned and slapped his hand. 'You going to take some of us for a ride later?'

He should've parked around the corner and walked here. He'd known there were kids here—what boy didn't want to ride a motorbike sometimes? Not that he minded giving each one of the brat pack a short ride but there were a lot of parents, and even grandparents, who might object for safety reasons. 'We'll talk about it later.'

Of course, Levi wouldn't let him get away with that. 'As soon as the cricket's finished?'

'It might be too late. Isn't there going to be a barbecue then?'

'There'll be time. I'm first.'

Cody nudged him. 'Your turn to bat. And I haven't said I'm taking you or any of the others for a ride yet. I have to talk to your folks.'

No one objected as long as helmets were worn, trousers replaced shorts and Cody only drove them around the park at the end of the street.

'Only if I get a ride afterwards.' Jason nodded. 'I'm the birthday boy, after all.'

'You want to ride passenger or take the bike off on your own?' Cody asked, not knowing if the guy knew how to ride.

'I'll leave you in control, and promise not to hug you too tight,' he smirked. Then he turned to the women. 'Any of you want a turn too? Gemma?'

'Of course I do.'

Cody groaned. That barbecue was going to be hours away at this rate. 'We'd better get started.'

His new friend, Levi, called, 'Grandma, do you want a turn?'

'An enormous motorbike and a good-looking man going begging? Of course I do.'

Harper chuckled beside him. 'Relax, Cody. She hates sitting in a car when anyone else is driving. You're safe.'

Everyone laughed, and Cody shook his head. Then made a mistake. 'You going to give it a whirl, Harper?'

She was going to say no. He could see it in the set of her mouth, the slightly darker gleam in her eyes and the tightening of her body.

'Don't wuss out, Harper,' Jason called. 'You've always wanted to be a biker's girl.'

Annoyance flared on that beautiful face, but she locked her eyes with his and nodded. 'Take me to East-bourne and back.'

'I'll do better than that.' *Shut up, Cody.* 'I'll take you home at the end of the day.'

'I've got my car here.' She was looking stunned that she'd even agreed to go in the first place.

'I'll drop it off at the hospital tomorrow when I go for my scan,' Suzanne said.

'Scan?' Shock froze on Harper's face. Around them, everyone else was yelling and jumping up and down.

'You're pregnant? Yippee' was the general chorus.

'We were going to tell you all next weekend, since this is Jason's birthday, but it sort of slipped out.' A pink-faced Suzanne leaned into the man who'd just draped his arm over her shoulders. 'We've been waiting until the first twelve weeks were up before saying a word. It's been so hard to keep quiet.'

'Especially for you.' Noah was the first to give his sister a hug and shake his brother-in-law's hand.

Harper still appeared shell-shocked. Didn't she want any more nieces and nephews? No, Cody decided, there was more to her reaction than that. That'd be petty and, as far as he'd seen, Harper didn't do petty. He moved closer to her, not touching, but there for her.

Jason was watching Harper and nodded when he saw what Cody had done.

So what was her problem? When Harper took her turn to hug her sister, she struggled to let go and seemed to hold tighter, harder, longer than anyone else. Did she want a baby too? Was she jealous of her sister—when she didn't have a man in her life? But then he didn't know if there was or wasn't a partner somewhere. Just because she'd come alone to her brother's party didn't mean there wasn't a man out there who was Harper's other half. A very absent other half. Except she seemed taken with *him* at times. Now he was really confused.

'It's going to be fine.' Suzanne rubbed Harper's back and looked helplessly over her shoulder to her brothers.

Jason grabbed Noah as he made to take Harper's arm. 'Let's get the kids back playing cricket for a bit longer. Harper's going for a ride on that Harley.'

Cody got the message loud and clear, even if Harper

hadn't. When he turned her towards his bike she hesitated and glanced up at him, and then across to her
brother.

Jason nodded once. 'Go blow some cobwebs out of
your head, sis, and then Cody can be driven crazy by
giving all these kids a short spin around the park.'

Suzanne caught Harper's hand. 'Go on, get out of
here for a bit. I'm sorry how I blurted it out, but it's been
hard holding it back. It's so exciting, and—' She bit off
whatever else she'd been going to say.

Harper wrapped her arms around her sister. 'Don't
you dare be sorry. It's wonderful news. Really and truly.
I'm happy for you both.'

Cody brought the spare helmet across and handed it
to her. When she quickly placed it on her head and began
fumbling with the straps, he knew she was desperate to
get away for a while. 'Let me.' He took the straps and
did them up tight enough to keep the helmet in place,
but not so tight that her skin was scrunched, or made
that still-tender throat uncomfortable. Her warm, soft
skin was velvet against his fingers.

'Put these on.' Gemma handed over a jacket and some
track pants to Harper. 'You'll freeze otherwise.'

'Where shall we go?' she asked quietly, her mind obviously still absorbing her sister's news.

'Wait and see.' He shucked into his jacket, hauled
his leather trousers over his shorts, then straddled the
bike and waited for her to climb up behind him, before
roaring the engine into life.

'Hold on tight,' he said over his shoulder, and then
drew a sharp breath when she wound her arms around
him and laid her face against his back. He'd taken many
people for rides on his bike over the years, quite a few
of them women, but not once had he experienced the

heat and longing from a pair of arms around his upper body and a face lying tucked in against him as was pouring through him this minute. He mightn't want Harper White to be anyone special, but he sure as hell seemed to be having trouble keeping her on the same uninvolved level as any other woman he'd known since Sadie.

This was going to be a long ride, even if he only took her to the end of the road—all of three hundred metres. Suddenly he was afraid. Afraid that Harper was sneaking in under his radar, touching him in ways he'd never thought to know again. That couldn't happen.

'We going today?' The sharp question came near his ear and had him revving the engine louder and faster than he'd normally do.

'Sure thing, doctor,' he muttered, knowing she'd never hear him over the bike noise.

He took her through the township of Eastbourne and on toward Pencarrow Head, until they were alone apart from the seagulls and the wild shoreline, and then stopped the bike. 'Let's stroll along the water's edge,' he suggested as the roar of the engine died. He needed a break from those arms still encircling him before he did something they'd both regret. Kissing came to mind. Along with touching.

'I'd like that.'

She was talking about the walk, right? He turned on the seat and stared at her, sure his thoughts were easy to read and still unable to look away.

Harper sprang off the bike fast, as though she also wanted space between them. 'Do I leave the helmet with the bike? Or would it be best to carry it in case someone comes along?'

Cody shook his head. 'I doubt anyone with bad intentions will turn up in the next half hour.'

She slipped the helmet onto the handle bar. 'You can say that even after what happened on Friday? We never saw Strong coming.'

Of course she was still shaken by that. It'd have been more surprising if she wasn't. 'I'll take a chance on our helmets being here when we get back.'

Harper clambered over rocks to reach the sand, the breeze lifting her hair behind her. Long, shiny hair that made him ache to finger-comb it, made his manhood throb with need.

Damn it, he should never have visited the White family in the first place. Should've gone to visit his mother instead. But he'd taken his mother out to lunch yesterday and had learned she was unwell with a summer cold. The rest-home nurses thought she'd be better tucked up in bed today without visitors. He'd wanted to argue but had given in to the idea of joining Harper's family for the afternoon.

He ambled along behind Harper, drinking in the sight of her firm legs and gently swaying buttocks, wishing he'd followed through on that urge to kiss her, no matter the consequences.

He caught up with her when she paused to watch the inter-island ferry make its way between Pencarrow and Palmer Heads on its way to the South Island.

'I can't have children.' She continued staring across the water to the boat. 'But you probably already figured that out.'

He took her hand and began walking farther along the stony beach. 'No, I hadn't got to that answer yet.' He'd deliberately stopped thinking about her reaction to her sister's news the moment Jason had suggested he take her for a ride. He hadn't wanted to dwell on what he doubted he'd learn the answer to—not today, anyway. Who'd have thought Harper would just out and tell him? 'I can see why your sister's news upset you.'

'It shouldn't. I've had loads of experience of dealing with being told one of my family's having a baby, so I know how not to react.' Her fingers tightened around his as she spoke, and Cody wondered if she even realised they were holding hands.

He should let go. He'd only taken her hand as a comfort gesture and to move her on along the beach, yet he did not want to pull away. The warmth from her palm against his, the softness of those fingers interlaced with his, was the most wonderful sensation he'd known in a long time. So ordinary and yet so thrilling. Damn but he was turning into a softie.

Harper was still talking, as though getting something off her chest. 'I'm the godmother to every one of the brat pack.' She flicked him a quick look and he knew she hadn't finished.

But he also had something to say. 'No surprise there,' he told her before adding, 'They adore you, if what I've seen so far is anything to go by.'

'Chocolate and doing fun things will always get me that.' She smiled softly. Bending down, she picked up a handful of sand and let it dribble through her fingers as they walked, while her other hand still firmly held his. 'But being an aunt, even the best one out, doesn't take the place of raising my own children. Having my own babies.' Her sigh was so sad, Cody's heart clenched. 'I thought I had a chance to be a mum once, but the plans got changed.'

'I can't imagine what it must be like for you.' He couldn't. It was something he'd never considered, instead always believing that one day he'd have a family, teach his son to fish, or even his daughter, for that matter. But never to have his own child? Unimaginable. No wonder Harper had looked gutted when her sister had blurted out her news. No wonder Suzanne had been upset about how she'd spilled the beans. But then there'd have been no easy way to tell Harper.

'I guess no one thinks about it unless faced with the fact. I certainly didn't. Or maybe I was fooling myself, hiding from the truth. Coming from a largish family who all seem intent on doubling the world's population, the idea I couldn't contribute was implausible.'

He would've laughed at her attempt to lighten the mood but he was all out of laughs at the moment. This was something big, something that would've changed Harper's life. He had this inexplicable urge to make her feel better, but there was no way he could do that. This went deep, was very personal. It was surprising that she'd even shared it with him. What would she do if he gave her a hug? It wouldn't be quite like the hugs she got from her family. No way could he do platonic with this woman. Not any more, if he'd been able to at all. 'Can I ask why you can't have children?'

Her silence told him he'd gone too far. Fair enough. He'd known that the moment the words fell out, but she'd been so forthcoming up until now, he hadn't stopped to consider how much he could ask. Now she'd be wanting to head back to Lowry Bay and telling him to carry on to the city alone.

He resumed walking, back in the direction of his bike.

'I was born without a womb.'

Cody paused and turned slowly, so as not to make her suddenly change her mind about talking to him.

Harper sank to her haunches, scooped up more sand

and watched it dribble back to the ground. 'It wasn't picked up until my teens. I mean, why would it be?'

He dropped down beside her and took her hand again. 'Bloody hell, Harper. What were the odds, eh?' His heart was pounding at the thought of what it must've been like for her to find out.

'Higher than you'd think.' She sat down and wound her arms around her legs, resting her chin on top of her knees. 'I should remember that on days like today. I'm not the only one.'

'But as the years have gone by it's been harder to deal with?'

'Yeah, something like that.' She turned her head slightly so she could see his face.

His heart lurched at the sadness in her eyes. Hell, he'd seen almost every emotion in those beautiful eyes over the last couple of days. Even love, when she gazed at her nieces and nephews. This was one amazing woman, who gave of herself completely, even after all that had happened to her on Friday.

Without thinking, he reached for her, drew her close, wound his arms around her and lowered his mouth to hers. He kissed her slowly, as tenderly as possible, while his body was demanding, hard and hot. When she whimpered under his lips he deepened his kiss slowly. He wanted to dive right in, to taste her and hold her as close as possible, tight, but he held back, half-expecting a slap around the ears.

Until her hands began sliding up his chest to his head, her fingers pushing through his hair to massage his scalp. Then he knew this was right—for both of them. Come what may. Tomorrow they might regret it, today... Today he was living a dream, was kissing the woman who had him in turmoil all the time.

Her mouth opened under his and he slid his tongue across into her hot cavern and tasted her. His heart stuttered. Raw, hot need clawed through his gut and headed downward to where he expressed his need so effortlessly. *Easy, boy, easy.* Even in his fogged-up brain he knew acting on that impulse would be going too far. For now, he had to be happy with this sizzling kiss. And, hell, was Harper sizzling. What a woman. He melted in against her, held her tighter and kissed her until they both ran out of air.

Harper finally drew back, taking those lips just out of reach. Her breasts rose and fell too quickly. A delectable shade coloured her cheeks and her eyes were shining. 'Wow,' she whispered, running her finger over her top lip. 'Wow.'

That was one word for what had just passed between them. 'Hot' and 'intense' were two more. 'Unbelievable' would be another.

And downright disturbing.

Where did they go from here? 'Bed' was the first word to pop into his skull. But, despite everything, he still knew that wasn't happening today. There'd be repercussions, possibly insurmountable, if they stripped down naked and had their way with each other. He wanted Harper with every fibre of his body. He suspected she felt the same. But there was a wariness creeping into the stunned look in her eyes which told him to put the brakes on. His libido was going nowhere right now.

Pulling back so her eyes met his, she stared into him, deeply, right in. Looking for...? He had no idea; he only hoped he measured up to her expectations.

Then her mouth opened and the question tripped out,

low and filled with despair. 'Do you want children of your own one day?'

Now, there was a loaded question. If he said no, he'd be lying; if he said yes, whatever was unfolding between them would be gone in a flash.

He wouldn't lie. 'Yes. I do.' He pulled back and tossed a pebble down the beach to splash in the water. 'Not that it's likely to ever happen,' he added quietly.

To have a family, he'd have to risk his heart again. He'd have to believe he could protect her no matter what turned up. He wasn't ready to trust himself with someone yet.

CHAPTER FIVE

JASON SPRAWLED OVER the chair beside Harper, stretched out his legs in front, scratched his chest and yawned.

'Very attractive,' Harper drawled. 'No wonder Gemma calls you one of the brat pack.'

'She loves me as I am.' His mouth softened into a gentle smile as his eyes searched out his wife amongst all the kids hanging around the barbecue, where Cody was doing as he was told and cooking a mound of sausages and chops. Between Gemma and the kids, their new friend wasn't getting any free time to do as he pleased.

Harper pressed her lips—her well-kissed and still tender lips—together. Thank goodness. Somehow Cody voicing what had been no surprise about wanting a family was hard to swallow. There was no reason why she should care one way or the other, but his simple, 'Yes,' had provoked a tide of longing and sadness to overwhelm her. Coming after that bone-melting, knee-shaking kiss, she'd been lost, completely unable to compute everything and make sense of it all.

That kiss had blitzed her brain. Being held in those strong arms had given her a sense of belonging she didn't think she'd ever known before. She'd loved Darren with all her being, or so she'd thought. But not one kiss with him had given her the deep yearning for more that Cody's had. Or was that just because enough time had passed to forget things she and Darren had shared? But Cody's kiss had been unbelievable. Shattering. Life-changing. If she let it be. Which she couldn't. In the end, everything came back to her inability to have children. Even if Cody accepted that and went with whatever was unfolding between them she knew even the sincerest of promises could, and most likely would, be broken. She wasn't up to withstanding that a second time. Hell, she couldn't ask a man to give up his dreams for her. Not again. She'd learned it was too much to ask of any one.

There was no denying Cody's honesty. He must've known it would hurt her, and yet he'd still gone with the truth. She admired him for that. But in the end she'd demanded to be brought back here in the hope that being surrounded by her family could put some perspective on what had really only been a kiss. One hell of a kiss. It'd been hard not to ask him to drop her off and head away so she didn't have to see him and confront what was really getting her knickers in a knot—the fact she was becoming increasingly attracted to him. Unfortunately, the kids had had other ideas, namely their promised rides on the back of his motorbike, and he was still here after obliging them.

'He's got you in a right old twist,' Jason drawled.

Harper slapped her head. They'd been talking about Gemma. Nothing to do with Cody. Yet her very astute brother knew where she'd gone in her mind. To bring things back on track, and away from what felt like dangerous ground, she said, 'Gemma needs her head read, the way she puts up with you despite all your bad habits.'

What was it like to feel so safe with another person's love that you could act completely naturally all the time? To feel safe enough to be able to relax about everything? She'd thought she had that with Darren until he'd dropped his verbal grenade. Apparently he hadn't loved her more than anything or anyone, or enough to accept they wouldn't have children. He had accepted that. Only not in the way she'd believed. *They* wouldn't have children, but he would—with another woman.

One day as she'd strolled along Auckland's Mission Bay, trying yet again to make up her mind about what to do with her life now that she was separated from her husband, Harper had seen the dark-haired woman he'd left her for sitting and drinking coffee with girlfriends. At least, she'd presumed it was coffee. What she'd been absolutely certain about was the very mature baby bump that had said clearer than words that Darren had been with this woman before he'd left his wife. That scene had torn her apart, underscored the truth—there would be no reconciliation, no matter that she might forgive him if he came begging.

It had also added a final layer of protection around her heart. She would never, ever, put her heart on the line again. It would be her own fault if she fell for a man and then had to go through another break-up. She'd finally come to accept she had no right ask a man to give up his dreams of having a family.

'He's an all-right guy.' When Jason spoke so casually, he was usually hiding something.

He had a name. 'Define "all right".'

'I don't think I need to. You seem taken with him.'

Harper studied the man who'd been bugging the hell out of her head all weekend. Good-looking: tick. Kind: tick. Great with kids: tick. So what? Sexy, intriguing and annoying with his confidence: tick, tick, tick. 'I work with him. I like him. He was incredible in ED on Friday, so calm and constantly alert to the possibility of taking the creep down. Do I want to get to know him better?' *Yes. No.* 'I don't know.' She answered her own question honestly. 'But I do know I'm not going to.'

Just then Cody looked across the lawn directly at her and winked. Her mouth tipped up into a big smile. Warmth filled her. Yeah, she could get used to a man like Cody. And those kisses. But she wasn't going to, she repeated to herself. He wanted children.

'Sis, stop beating yourself up. It's wearing for you, and for all of us. Life threw you a hard ball, but we all get those.'

She gasped. Jason never talked to her like this. He was the fun brother, the easy sop who loved everyone and didn't want to stir up emotions. 'Says the man with three boys to adore.'

'You have seven nieces and nephews who love you as much as their parents and who spend a lot of time with you. You don't get the sleepless nights, or the arguments about what's for dinner, just the fun times. Yes, there's another on the way. Suzanne and Steve are ecstatic. You can't avoid that and, face it, you won't want to.'

Another black mark to erase. She didn't used to be so selfish, had always been thrilled every time one of her sisters-in-law had announced they were pregnant. But Suzanne's words had thrown her. Her baby sister was joining the parent club and she'd felt more left out than ever. 'I reacted badly.'

'You did.' Jason sipped his beer. 'Be grateful for what you've got and stop dwelling on what you can't have.'

'Easy for you to say,' she snapped as guilt and disappointment warred in her head. She hated that Jason thought her ungrateful, but he should try a little harder to understand.

'Remember that career I always wanted as a lawyer with our foreign service?' he said suddenly.

'The one you were determined to get even when you were still in nappies?'

'Yes, that one. I was offered a position with Foreign Affairs last year.' He stared across the lawn at his wife and children. 'I turned it down because my family mean too much to me. I couldn't bear to take them out of their home and schools and away from their friends for the sake of my own desires.'

'They'd have a wonderful life living in different countries.'

'They'd have had to make new friends every few years as we moved from country to country, probably have to go to boarding school for high-school education. I couldn't do that to Gemma. I couldn't live without my kids with me either.'

Harper looked sideways at her brother. 'You never told me.'

'You were working your butt off in Auckland, trying to get beyond Darren and his broken promises, trying to decide what to do next. You didn't need my disappointment as well.'

'But I'm your sister. We share everything.' But guilt came fast. She had been withdrawn and selfish during that time. Who knew what she might've said to Jason if she'd known what he'd been going through? Harper laid her hand over his. 'I'm sorry. I know how much you've always wanted a career with Foreign Affairs.' She sat quietly for a few minutes, absorbing this new information. 'How did Gemma feel about you taking the job?'

'She backed me either way—said it was important that I was happy. She was more than content to pack up house and shift to Toronto, our first posting, if that's what I wanted. But I knew it wasn't what she wanted, that she was afraid to move away from where she felt safe.'

Gemma had grown up in a welfare home. Her family and home were the most important things in her life—had made her feel grounded for the first time ever. Yet she was big-hearted enough to go anywhere with Jason no matter what the cost to her.

Harper sighed. 'You're a lucky man, Jason White. I understand you've missed your opportunity in a career you always dreamed about, but you've got a wonderful wife and family, and your current position as head legal advisor to the fishing industry is nothing to be sneezed at.' She was very proud of him. As she was of Noah and Suzanne.

'Exactly. I've lost one dream, but I've got so much more. As you have, if only you'd let go of the impossible dream and see what you've already got. Stop trying to change what you can't, and get on with finding the life you want, sis.' Jason stood up and looked down at her. 'You're smitten with Cody. We can all see it. Do something about it. Don't waste an opportunity for happiness.'

Harper stared at him as he headed towards the cheerful gathering around the barbecue. What did he know? That bit about not getting everything you wanted was all very well, but wanting a family was inherent in her. Growing up with loving parents who'd also doted on each other had taught her how important a strong, trusting relationship was. Not to mention having brothers and a sister, one of whom she could happily beat around the head right now. Jason didn't know what he was talking about.

And now her headache was back, banging inside her

skull, adding to her annoyance with the world. With her brother. With Cody.

But she had an apology to make. Where had Suzanne got to?

'Right, who's next?' At the ED counter Harper picked up the top patient file. Monday mornings weren't usually as frantic as this one had turned out to be. Probably a good thing, as it kept her mind off gun-toting strangers. And Hottie in scrubs. Scrubs would never be as bland and boring again. Cody certainly filled his out a treat. Flapping the file in front of her face, she tried not to grin when Karin laughed. 'It would be rude not to notice.'

'What did I tell you?'

'What's next?' the man himself asked as he approached the counter, moving those muscles like a panther. No wasted movement, all stealth and strength.

Patients. That was why she was here. Not because of a sexy man. *More's the pity.* A quick scan told her, 'A toddler with a button up his nose.'

Cody gave her a guarded smile. 'Small children and orifices—not always a good look.'

How had she got partnered with Cody today of all days? She'd tossed and turned most of the night because of him invading her brain matter, reliving that kiss so often she thought she could be ruined for any other man and his kisses. She might as well join the nunnery now. Spending the day working alongside him would only add to the tension tightening her own muscles, turning her stomach into a washing machine on spin.

She needed to be distant with him. How did she do that when she knew what it felt like to have those arms wound around her? And those lips on hers? But... Always a but. They wanted different— No, they hoped to obtain similar things out of life. But those things could never match up between them. So to avoid heartache she was determined to remain totally professional around him. Starting now. A couple of hours late, but at least she could begin as she meant to go on.

Except it was as though everyone else thought they should be together after what they'd shared here on Friday. The talk going around the department was still about the body packer and his boss, but at least no one was asking endless questions about how she or Cody felt any more. While meant kindly, those questions had become tiring, and had hindered her determination to put it all behind her. It hadn't been as easy as she'd thought to come to work today. She'd had to deliberately toughen her stance and put on a neutral face, but every time she walked past Resus One a cold shiver slid down her spine and she found herself looking over her shoulder, fully expecting to find a gun in her face.

She'd thought she was hiding it well until Cody had said quietly, 'Resus One's never going to be the same, is it?'

She'd looked at him, ready to snap that she was fine, but had met only empathy in those vivid green eyes. *Of course.* 'Not for a while, any rate.'

Those eyes, if not that voice, would be the undoing of all her good intentions. *Face it, Harper, those intentions are already unravelling.* She straightened her already straight back. She could lock gazes with the man and not feel her knees knock. Couldn't she? Better not try to find out now. There were patients waiting. Was it possible to fall in lust this quickly? *Quickly?* It had been over a week since Cody had started working here, days since he'd been her hero in Resus One. Falling in love only took an instant in some cases.

Love? Lust. *Love?* Crazy. Not when she'd vowed to avoid that particular emotion again. That didn't count family and friends, but Cody could never be just an every day kind of friend. She'd never be able to look at him without wondering what the follow up to his kisses would be like. Oh, she had her suspicions. But that was only the physical side of things. There was plenty more to Cody than his hot bod and those divine lips. Characteristics that were equally attractive as his body.

'Harper? Hello. Where have you gone this time?' Cody still stood in front of her.

'What do you mean, this time?'

'We were talking about Resus One and you went all blank on me.'

Not blank, but at least she could be grateful he hadn't known what was going on in her head. 'Resus One. That's what we talking about.' A glance at the innocuous room still had her shivering.

Cody shrugged. 'We could hold a party in there to banish the bad vibes.'

'A fancy dress one.' And just like that she relaxed, dropping the façade of being only a colleague who knew next to nothing about him. Not what she intended at all. But she couldn't seem to help it. There was a lot of talk doing the rounds about the hug she and Cody had shared after the police had taken the gunman away. Apparently it had looked seriously intense. The people talking about it didn't know the half of it. Harper's heartbeat went double-time every time she thought about it.

He said, 'You'd come as a pirate, brandishing a sword and slaying anything that moved.'

'Actually, I do a better parrot, all feathers and squawks.'

His eyes widened. 'A parrot?'

'Yes, with a very long beak, all the better to peck kids with, and claws that hold chocolate cake.' Her smile broadened as it came from deep inside. Yeah, it was good talking with Cody like this. It was good being with Cody full stop—therein lay the problem. But right now she couldn't be bothered with problems. She was tired, hungry and so ready for a strong coffee.

'This I have to see. Whose birthday is next in the brat pack?'

'Your biggest fan.'

'Of course. How could I forget when Levi mentioned it at least ten times? But he's getting too old for parrots. Or pirates.' Cody shook his head. 'Here I was, hoping to see you with your cake claws out.'

Harper rolled her eyes with amusement. Cody had been such a hit yesterday, he'd been invited to the next birthday party in her family. It was kind of cool, really. If she hadn't been trying to avoid him. Maybe she should toughen up and go with whatever came out of this liaison. Have some fun, enjoy the moment. *Eek*. Scary. Exciting.

Loud cries came from behind the curtains of Cubicle Three, thankfully interrupting her frightening train of thought. 'That's our cue.' Pushing the curtain aside, she went to meet their small patient. 'Hello, Jarrod. I'm Harper, the doctor who's going to make you better.'

The little boy yelled louder and the man sitting on the bed holding him, presumably his dad, looked uncomfortable. 'Sorry, but he's got himself into a bit of a state.'

'Hey, Jarrod, what's this?' Cody stepped up with his hand twisted into the shape of a...?

Harper had no idea, but Jarrod stopped yelling long enough to stare at the fingers that were now wiggling at him.

'It's Bobby the Bunny. Look what he can do.' Cody made hopping gestures across the bed, pulled faces and made ridiculous noises.

And had Jarrod completely entranced.

Harper sighed. No surprise there. Yesterday she'd learned how good he was with kids. Introducing herself to the man holding Jarrod, she confirmed he was his dad. 'Has Jarrod tried blowing his nose hard?'

'Lots of times at first, but then it hurt, so he stopped.'

'Any idea how big this button is?'

'Bigger than a shirt button, but not by too much, if I've got the right one.'

Harper moved closer. 'Jarrod, can I can look up your nose? Bobby Rabbit will be here watching you, okay?'

Jarrod screamed and turned his head into his father's shoulder.

Not okay, then. 'You're going to have to hold him firmly while I take a look,' she instructed the father. 'Nurse, can you turn Jarrod's head for me?'

After a fast and awkward exam, Harper shook her head. 'That's jammed at the top. I'm going to have to sedate him so that I can pull the button out with tweezers.'

'Wait a moment.' Cody disappeared before she had time to ask where he thought he was going.

Who's the doctor around here? Her bonhomie faded. Another reason why she had to keep that distance: Cody had no right to think he could take charge.

The curtain flicked open as Cody returned. He held his hand under Jarrod's nostrils. 'Big breath through your nose, buddy.'

'Pepper?' Harper shook her head sharply. 'I don't think a sneeze is going to fix this. That button's jammed tight.'

The first two sneezes proved her right. The third

one sent the offending round of plastic flying across the floor.

'Good boy, way to go.' Cody held his palm up in front of the bemused boy. 'High five, man.'

Jarrod's hand was ridiculously tiny against Cody's, but his smile was huge. 'High five, Bobby Rabbit.'

'Thank you, Nurse Brand,' she said, quietly enough he probably didn't hear. She wasn't sure she wanted him to. Reverting to calling him Nurse Brand underlined the fact he was bringing the worst out in her. He had her reacting to his charm as though it was something to be beaten into submission. *Afraid?* a niggly little voice in the back of her head taunted. Very. But she needed to remember that not every charmer was on a mission to hurt her as Darren had. They weren't getting the chance.

'Let's take a break while we can,' Cody said. 'We're late for lunch as it is.'

'You go ahead. I'm not hungry yet.'

'So that gurgling I've been hearing for the last thirty minutes is all in my imagination?' Cody shrugged casually, but his eyes were full of disappointment. 'It's not going to be easy for you to keep your distance from me in here. Staff take breaks as they can, regardless of who they're working with.'

'I just think—' What the blazes *did* she think? Before seeing Jarrod, she'd relaxed enough to be happy around Cody; now she wanted to avoid him. *Yep. Definitely afraid. So, toughen up and deal with it, with him.* First, he was right—staff went for a break with whoever else was going, regardless of their role in the department. Even George was happy to drink coffee with a porter or junior nurse, so what was her problem? 'Let's go. Canteen or the café over the road?'

Bewilderment shoved aside that disappointment

in Cody's eyes. Shaking his head at her, he managed, 'Café,' before heading for the staff room and his locker.

All too soon she was seated at a tiny table in a cosy corner of the café with Cody's knees knocking up against hers in the cramped space. Trying to move her legs to avoid him proved awkward and made her feel stupid, so she stayed put. Enjoyed the moment. Plates of food sat on the table between them; steam rose from mugs of black coffee. She forgot to remain aloof. 'You're good with children. Jarrod would've done anything you asked.'

'Kids don't look past what you're offering, just take you at face value. It's kind of refreshing.' As he bit into his pie, small flakes of pastry dropped onto his shirt.

It would be too easy to reach across and brush them off. One sandwich did not need two hands to hold it, but how else was she to keep them out of trouble? She bit into the bread and salad, chewing thoughtfully. When she'd swallowed the tasteless lump of what had been tomato and lettuce she told Cody, 'You're a lot like my brothers. Fun, and happy to act the clown if it gets you a laugh. You'll make a great dad to those kids you want one day.'

Cody took another bite of his pie, obviously not in a hurry to carry on that conversation.

Suddenly everything he'd said on the beach yesterday came back to her. Not just the bit about him wanting a family. 'You said having a family was unlikely for you. Why? Has someone hurt you so much you won't contemplate another relationship?'

The shutters dropped over his usually friendly gaze so fast she shivered. 'Eat your lunch, doctor. We've got a busy department awaiting us.'

She'd gone too far. All because Cody was getting to

her and her only defence to that was that, by getting to know more about him, she could find reasons for not wanting to have anything else to do with him other than at work. Her sandwich suddenly seemed dry in her mouth. She'd upset him, and that was the last thing she wanted. *Should've thought before putting her mouth into gear.*

It came from being out of practice at small talk, she supposed. Having been through a lot with Cody in the last few days was no excuse. 'I'm sorry. I expect people to mind their own business when it comes to my private life, and yet I've just overstepped the mark with you. I'm truly sorry,' she repeated.

Pushing his chair back, he stood, looming over her, though she thought that was unintentional, merely an occupational hazard stemming from being so tall. 'I've forgotten what you asked already. See you back at work. I've got a prescription to pick up for my mother.'

As he threaded his way through the lunchtime crowd, his broad shoulders tight, his head high, even through her irritation Harper felt her heart lurch.

See? This was why she had to stay clear of any involvement with Cody. The risk of being hurt frightened her. She'd heard Jason's warning yesterday, knew he might even be right, but that didn't make it any easier to take that first step off the tightrope she currently walked. Along with the fact she couldn't have children, she'd lost the dream of a happy marriage, which was even more important to her. She'd put heart and soul into the one she'd had with Darren. She'd loved him completely and utterly, would've done anything for him, given him everything. Yet in the end all he'd asked of her was his freedom.

The mug of coffee shook in her hands. She needed

something big to distract her from all this so that one morning she could wake up and say, 'Yes, I am truly happy with my lot.' Something that had nothing to do with Cody Brand. Because like it or not he seemed to have taken over her mind, her feelings, her body.

Patchwork and tennis hadn't worked. What should she try next? Abseiling? She shuddered. Not likely. Time to stop trying out all these different hobbies. She didn't need a hobby. She needed to make the most of what she already had. Which was a lot. Between doctoring and family there wasn't much spare time anyway. Even if she wanted to get bored and sew together all those pieces of fabric she'd painstakingly cut up in the first place there just wasn't enough time.

Which reminded her—she needed to cancel the order for a paddle-board. As if she was going to go out in the harbour with only a board and a paddle to get around…

Cody strode down the road, intent on reaching the pharmacy and putting distance between himself and Harper so as to clear his head of her, as a woman he had the hots for, before he had to go back and work alongside her as a doctor.

He could've used the hospital dispensary to get his mother's tablets but the air in there was stifling. Nothing to do with the hot summer's day either. This might be turning out to be the hottest summer on record but his discomfort came from being close to a fiery woman with a delicious mouth and beautiful eyes. A woman who kissed like an angel. And who asked far too many questions that probed places best left alone. The risk to his heart had increased tenfold since yesterday. Huh? Try since Friday, and that monster. Time to get some control back, tighten the hatches and keep her out.

Harper. Doctor. Adored aunt. Beloved sister and sister-in-law. Fun and amusing. Sad and unhappy.

For the life of him, he didn't fully understand her sadness. Sure, there was that baby thing. He got it. Really got it. If he couldn't have a family, he'd be gutted. But he'd swear there was more going on with her. He should just ask her outright. Like she asked him things he didn't want to answer? Have her stalking off in a huff? Exasperation trickled over his lips. He'd done wrong. Shouldn't have walked away from Harper's questions. He wasn't playing fair. Not with her. He was looking out for himself.

'Ten minutes,' the pharmacist's assistant told him as she read the script.

'Fine.' He headed outside to look at paint and wallpaper in the decorating shop next door.

'Can I help you?' asked a young, over-enthusiastic woman from behind the counter.

'Just looking,' he replied and suffered a flat smile in return, which made him feel bad. 'I'm still deciding what colours I want to use inside my house.' Now, there was a joke.

'Are you going to do every room the same? Or have different shades for bedrooms and the living areas?'

The problem with playing nice was it became difficult to get away without upsetting someone. As Harper had just found out. 'Maybe one colour, with different shades of it for different areas.'

He'd really upset Harper. There'd been annoyance on her face when he'd walked away at the café, which ramped up his guilt. They'd talked about her personal life quite a lot since he'd first taken her home to her apartment on Friday. Today's conversation was only a continuation of getting to know each other better. But he didn't do talking about his life, past or present. People read too much into things.

'Here're some paint charts to take home.' The girl shoved a small bundle at him and hurried off to talk to another man coming in the door.

'Thanks,' he called as he passed her on his way out. *Hope you have better luck with him than you did with me—on all counts.*

'What are you up to?' The voice of the person he'd been avoiding caught up with him as he reached the hospital entrance. 'Are those colour charts you've got there?'

Damn. 'Thinking of painting my bedroom,' he grunted, which was true. There was also the rest of the five-bedroomed house that was in serious need of fresh paint, amongst other things.

'You've got a lot of charts for one small room.' Harper's laugh was strained.

'It's a big decision.' He managed to smile back.

'How is your sense of colour?'

Crap. 'I'm colour-blind. Like, completely colour-blind.' He swore under his breath. That opened the door—wide.

Sure enough, Harper walked right in. 'Want some input? I managed to choose the colours for my apartment without making a botch-up.'

He'd already walked away from her questions once today. He really didn't feel up to doing it again, even if it meant disclosing more about himself than he was prepared to do. He tried for tactful. 'You're too busy. Anyway, it's only a room. The colour's not a major problem.' That wasn't really true. The whole house would look a disaster if he ended up painting it bright orange or another equally appalling colour. At least, he'd assumed from other people's reaction to his previous attempts at decorating that orange was a bad choice if he wanted soft and subtle.

'Of course.' Her tone was flat.

Didn't do so well, buddy. He huffed a sigh. 'I'm sorry. I mean, thank you, Harper, I'd appreciate your help. But you have to promise me one thing.'

She turned wary eyes on him. 'Yes?'

'That you won't set me up. Pick purple or magenta just because you can get away with it.'

Merriment flooded those beautiful eyes that he hadn't been able to forget for days. 'Tell me how you even know what magenta is. Or what purple might look like on your walls.'

'I don't.' He stood absolutely still, his gaze locked on those eyes that sucked him in and made him feel like he was drowning. Silently he willed her to keep laughing. He loved the sound of her laughter, the sight of it in her face and on her mouth; in the honest way she stood in front of him. She was a sexy package, but add laughter and she became something else. Adorable. Lovable. Lovable? *Gulp. Where were they? Colours. Right.* 'But it won't take long for someone to tell me I've screwed up.'

What was he doing here? Why was he inviting her into his home? He should be doing all in his power to walk away because she'd never want to take their friendship to the next level, even if he decided to take a risk. He should even be grateful that she wouldn't. But right this moment he wanted to enjoy the glow, feel her warmth, be with her.

Her smile widened with mischief. 'I guess you'll just have to wait for the verdict, then.'

'You're having fun at my expense.' He tried growling the words but his voice only came out light and happy.

'You bet.' Then she tugged a pager from her pocket and her smile faded. 'We're on. A stat one's coming through the door.'

As they rushed to the department Harper continued giving him the brief details. 'A multiple car pile-up on the Hutt Motorway. Five patients expected in the next ten minutes.'

'All hands on deck.' That would keep him busy and make the afternoon fly by. Fingers crossed there were no fatalities, before or during the patients' time in the ED.

'When's a good time to come look at your room and those paint charts?' Harper asked as they reached the staff room. 'Tonight?'

He shook his head. 'Not tonight.' Nor tomorrow, nor any time until he decided how far he was going with this—this need building up muscle by muscle inside him. 'I'll be out.' He'd agreed she could help because he'd felt bad about walking out on her in the café, but he couldn't have her in his home. That would be getting too cosy. 'I'll let you know when I've got a free night.'

'Your social life's that busy?' Her grin was a little sick looking, making him go from feeling bad to worse.

It just seemed he couldn't get it right with this woman. 'I'm always busy, not often socially.' That was a cryptic answer, and at the screwing up of her face he decided to put her out of her misery a little. 'I visit my mother often, and tonight I'm busy catching up with old mates from when I went to school here.' One, anyway. He was having dinner with Trent and his wife.

'Don't think you can get out of me choosing a shade of purple that'll knock your socks off.' Harper tapped him on the forearm. 'We have a date.' She blinked and gasped as what she'd just said must've sunk in. 'I mean, um, we'll sort out your decorating some time.'

'Let's go sort out accident victims first.' He held the door wide for her, and grinned at the tight back view she presented as she stalked down the corridor, obviously embarrassed with her choice of phrase.

If she hadn't touched a need within him he could've laughed. But she had, and he couldn't. 'Harper? What colour are your eyes?'

He knew when heat touched a face that the shade colouring the cheeks was pink. In this case, bright pink.

She told him in a low voice that sent shivers up his spine and tightened muscles that didn't need tightening right at that moment. 'Brown, with flecks of yellow and green.' She gave him a rueful smile. 'Just so you know.'

CHAPTER SIX

SO MUCH FOR keeping Cody at a safe distance. That question about her eyes was over the top, and warmed her right down to her toes. Her fingers tensed. *And* she'd gone and invited herself to his home—make that *demanded* an invitation—all because she'd been adamant about helping him decide on the colour for his bedroom. Bedroom. Not the bathroom, or kitchen, or dining room. The bedroom. Cody's bedroom.

Yeah, she got it. She'd made a monumental blunder and now had to work out how to backtrack without getting further into deep water. Though he had been reluctant to fix a day or time for her to visit, so that was in her favour if she was serious about changing her mind about helping.

What did it matter to her if he messed up and painted it orange or teal? Or purple? Her mood softened. So the man was colour-blind. He had a fault. A tiny, almost insignificant one, unless he'd wanted to be the captain on one of those fishing trawlers he'd worked on, but it was there. She liked him even more. Damn it.

This time a week ago she'd barely known Cody existed. Now all her spare time was taken up just thinking about him. He filled her skull with questions and nonsense and excitement. She'd even passed the donuts in the break room today without taking one, and she'd made a hair appointment for some highlights and to get the ends tidied. It was an appointment that was long overdue but which hadn't bothered her until—Cody. He was bringing out a side of her she hadn't seen in a very long time.

'You and Cody take Lisa Lang, thirty-one, compound fractures to right leg, possible fractured pelvis. Trauma injury to head. Unconscious.' George stood at the desk organising everyone. 'Resus Two.'

Phew. Not that she'd have time to relive Friday with the patient they were expecting, but so far today she and Cody had managed to avoid Resus One, thanks to George. 'How far out?'

'Next ambulance to arrive. Approximately five minutes.' George called out the names of other nurses to work with them. Then, 'Karin, you take the one after that. I'll be working with you.'

Harper blanked out the rest of George's instructions and concentrated on her patient's requirements. The first of which required a phone call to the on-duty orthopaedic surgeon.

As she did that the bell buzzed, announcing the arrival of their patient, and she saw Cody stride out to the ambulance bay in his fast but seemingly unhurried way.

Then Lisa Lang was wheeled into the room and that was the end of the brief quiet spell.

'GCS and BP?' Harper asked.

'Two and sixty over forty-five.'

'Way too low, even allowing for the fractures and head injury.' Harper issued instructions. 'Cody, IV lines and attach her to the heart monitor. Jess, ABCs. Cath, cut what's left of her clothes away from her chest and that leg for an X-ray. I'm going to intubate.'

Everyone worked fast and efficiently, but it took two attempts for Harper to get the endotracheal tube in place. Finally she was satisfied and straightened up. 'BP?'

'Still sixty over forty-five.'

No change was better than getting worse, but only just. She needed the BP to go up. 'IV?'

'Lines in place, open and running,' Cody told her.

'Right, I need X-rays of the right leg, pelvis and the neck. And a CT scan of that head injury.'

The orthopaedic surgeon walked in as the first image came up on the screen. He tapped the shattered fibula on the screen. 'Now, there's a mess. The tib's looking a little better.'

'BP's seventy over fifty-five,' someone called.

'It's coming up slowly.' Harper answered the surgeon's raised eyebrow and kept working with Lisa until she was taken to pre-op.

But there was no time to catch their breath, as Cody wheeled another patient in from the same vehicular accident. 'Janice Leigh, forty-one, soft head trauma, fractured ribs, possible punctured lung.'

'GCS and BP?' Harper asked. *Here we go again.*

Time flew by and the end of shift seemed to rush at them. By then the last of the victims had been brought in and four of them sent on to Theatre for surgery.

'You've got a chock-full waiting room to deal with.' Harper smiled tiredly at her replacement. 'I'm going home for a long shower, followed by dinner.' A lettuce leaf and tomato. Ah, to hell with it. If her hips were a little heavy, then today she didn't care. Her stomach was crying with need for food, and her energy levels required some input. This was only Monday.

'Some shift that turned out to be,' Cody muttered as he joined her on the walk out of the hospital.

How come he still looked so fresh? Fresh and fit and in very good shape.

Dash. Back to lettuce and tomato. Her determination got a much-needed boost as she observed Cody roaring out of the car park on his motorbike.

What a bod. What a man. What a dilemma.

She could never ask him to give up his need for a family. It wasn't fair. She had to learn to see him as a colleague and nothing more. Had to give up this unexpected need to get closer to him, to get to know him better.

She had to learn not to open her mouth and volunteer dumb things like helping with his home decorating.

Though it would be interesting to see where he lived, and what his taste in housing was. *It's none of your business, Harper!*

Maybe she should buy that board and paddle, head out to sea and never come back, because all she was doing right now was setting herself up for heartbreak. *Concentrate on your work, Harper; that's what's real.* The rest of the week flew by without any major incidents, which for Harper now meant someone holding a loaded gun to her head or the department being swarmed with armed police. The drama of an accident paled in significance, which didn't mean she felt any less concern or worry for her patients. No, they still got to her, had her heart aching for them, as they battled a cardiac arrest, a bleed out or broken bones.

But she felt able to take everything in her stride again—except for walking into Resus One, even when the room was empty; or a curtain being flicked open suddenly; or someone appearing behind her without having made any noise. Those things made her jittery, had her laughing loudly at inopportune moments or dropping a utensil unexpectedly. She'd noticed the same reactions in Jess and Matilda, and had talked to George about getting the young nurses counselling if they wanted it, while turning it down for herself.

The only time she felt completely safe was when Cody was working beside her, his calm demeanour soothing the stress tensing her body.

Now she turned from staring into Resus One to find Cody watching, and said, 'You seem to be coping with the aftermath. How do you do it?'

His smile was soft, contemplative. 'Who says I'm coping?'

'If you're not then you're putting on a good show.'

'That's a relief. I'd hate for everyone to see I'm really just a scaredy-cat.'

As if that would ever happen. The man was fierce in his gaze, in his determination not to be taken down, in his quiet but thorough way of dealing with anything that cropped up. 'Do you wake up during the night in a sweat with your heart pounding? Or leap out of your skin when someone comes into a cubicle far too quietly?'

She hadn't meant to reveal any of that, but around this man her mouth took on a life of its own. She hadn't decided if that was because he was so hot, or so caring, or helpful and understanding. All those attributes and more added to his sexiness, making him one hell of a package that had any cognizant female drooling and acting totally out of character. She was no more immune than any of them. It might be an idea to remember that and accept her feelings for Cody were probably being repeated everywhere.

He said, 'All of that, and other things, like looking

for short men with cold blue eyes in crowds.' It was unbelievable how much understanding filtered through
his voice.

Her head tipped back and she stared up at him. It
wasn't only in his voice, but it was darkening his eyes
and softening his expression. No, they had an affinity
for each other. She knew it—couldn't deny it any more.
What she did about it was up for speculation. She told
him, 'I haven't done that.'

'Good. Because once you start looking, there seems
to be more creeps out there than you'd ever imagined.'
Cody smiled softly, taking the sharpness away from his
words. 'But I think I'm getting over it a little. I'm not as
edgy as I was on Monday.' So why did his voice hold a
hint of tension? Why was it husky and low, goose-bump
lifting and spine-tingling raw?

Nothing to do with gangsters.

Harper coughed against her hand, trying to remove
the sudden dry tickle at the back of her throat. *Think
about the verbal conversation, not the hidden one.
Think practical stuff, not hot bodies and sublime release.* 'I'm hoping the weekend off will help, starting at
three o'clock this afternoon.' She glanced at her watch.
'In two hours and six minutes, but I'm not counting.'

'Something to be said for Friday nights and weekends,' he agreed in that voice that was still doing strange
things to her insides. Hell, and her outsides—her skin
was tightening at the thought of his hands touching her.
Huh? When was *that* likely to happen? Not at all, if she
had any common sense left, and that was debatable at
this moment.

Thank goodness for the two whole days and some
hours to do absolutely whatever she chose. Unfortunately she couldn't think of anything exciting or dis-

tracting that didn't involve Cody. 'What have you got planned for the weekend?' *Shut up.* Ridiculous, how disengaged her brain had become.

Cody's eyes widened slightly and he studied her as though looking for an answer to a question she had no idea about. Then he shrugged oh-so-nonchalantly and picked up a file. 'Not sure.'

'Not painting?' She still hadn't been to his place. Her impatience as she waited for the invitation she knew wouldn't come was getting to her.

'Probably not.' He deliberately glanced down at the paperwork in his hand. 'I'll go and get our next patient.'

Ouch. 'Cubicle Four,' she snapped, not happy at being put in her place. It seemed Cody wasn't having any problems keeping her at a distance after all. She must've imagined those intense looks, or misinterpreted them.

By the time he returned with a man holding a heavily bandaged hand against his chest, Harper had managed to pull on her professional face. 'I'm Dr White. What have you been doing to yourself?' she asked the patient as he settled onto the bed with help from Cody.

'I was replacing a pane of glass in my glasshouse and it slipped through my fingers.' The man winced as he held his hand towards Cody so he could unwrap metres of gauze. 'Silly old coot. My wife always tells me to be careful.'

A quick glance at the patient notes. Sixty-nine… nothing in his medical history to be concerned about. 'I'm sure you were careful, Henry, but accidents do happen. You weren't feeling lightheaded or dizzy when this occurred?'

'Not at all.' He was staring at his hand where all four fingers were sliced on the inside.

As his face turned pale, Cody gently pushed him onto

the pillows. 'Lie back and let Dr White take care of you.' Glancing across to her, he added, 'I'll get the suture kit.'

The curtain flicked behind him as he strode out. His face had been inscrutable, not an expression she was used to seeing when it came to Cody. Looking at her watch, she sighed. One hour and fifty-eight minutes of cold shoulder to get through. His sudden mood change annoyed her. What was so damn wrong with asking about his weekend plans?

'How bad is it?' Henry asked as she gently prised his fingers open again and studied the wounds.

'The cuts don't appear to have gone too deep but I'm going to put stitches in each finger. You won't be using this hand for a few days.'

Henry didn't look too unhappy. 'Will you give me something for the pain, doc?'

Her head shot up and she glared around the cubicle. Doc. He was here. The gunman had returned.

A large, gentle hand settled between her shoulder blades. 'Easy, *Doctor* White. Harper.'

Cody's calm tone instantly returned her to normal and brought her back into the cubicle with a man dressed in his gardening clothes, requiring sutures, waiting patiently on the bed, unaware of the shock he'd given her. Her breath sighed over her bottom lip. 'Thanks.'

Cody's mouth softened, and the corners lifted enough to show that everything was all right between them. His voice was low and husky as he told her, 'I've got your back, Harper.'

There really was no escaping the fact they were more than colleagues, not when he looked and spoke like that. Suddenly she let it all go, gave up trying to pretend she had to keep him at arm's length. Her heart lifted, expanded and warmth trickled throughout her body. Her eyes also got in on the act, getting a bit wet, and she hurriedly had to wipe her forearm over them. 'I know.' She did too. Even while feeling that resurging fear she'd known Cody would be there for her.

'Do I need antibiotics?' her patient asked, bringing her back to reality.

No, that wasn't true. She was already there. Whatever was going on between her and Cody, it was real. She found a smile for Henry. 'Yes, and a painkiller.'

She got on with stitching the injured fingers: the only sewing she found interesting and actually ever finished, she acknowledged with wry amusement. That pile on her table at home was destined for the bin, or to go to someone who'd actually enjoy working with the fabrics.

Cody returned to the cubicle after showing Henry out, flicking the curtain closed. 'At the risk of being turned down again, I'm going to extend the same invitation as I did last Friday. Want to go for a drink with all the crew when we're done here?'

'I'd love to.'

Surprise registered in those green eyes, lightening them to her favourite shade—spring grass. 'Good,' he muttered, his gaze firmly fixed on her.

So firmly she felt as though he was boring into her, seeing behind all the nonsense she put out there to try and keep him at a distance. The longer and harder he watched her, the softer and warmer she felt. Her mouth formed one word. 'Cody.'

One step and he was there, right in front of her, only inches separating them. 'Harper.' His hand lifted to her cheek, his finger tracing a delicate line down to her mouth, along her lips, then down over her chin, where he applied gentle pressure to tilt her head back. 'Harper,' he whispered close to her mouth, before his lips covered hers softly.

Her mouth opened under his, letting his tongue in to taste her, to allow her to taste him. She'd been reliving that first kiss all week, and it hadn't come close to the real thing. Soft went to possessive and demanding and their tongues danced around each other's; her heart rate shot through the roof while her body folded in against the hard wall of muscle that was Cody. His hands held her head. Her hands splayed over his forearms. His chest pressed against her breasts which ached where her nipples pushed against him.

'Oops, sorry. Warning—incoming patient.' Karin's voice slammed into the haze that Cody's kiss had brought over her. The curtain brackets slid noisily over the bar as Karin left them alone.

Harper stilled and pulled her mouth away from that kiss so slowly it took a while to notice she was no longer touching his lips. She sank onto the bed behind her, her legs no longer capable of doing what they were supposed to. Her eyes felt enormous, probably looking like headlights on a car.

Cody looked just as shocked. Or was that pleased with himself? His eyes had caught the same wide, staring bug hers had. That beautiful mouth that had devoured hers was curving up into a smile that had her heart beating even harder, more than she'd have thought possible. Could she be in danger of a cardiac malfunction?

She stared up at this man who turned her world upside down as easily as most men pulled on their pants in the morning. 'Wow.'

He grinned. Then a low laugh erupted from him.

'Yeah, wow.' His hand cupped her face, his thumb tracing her lips. 'Guess we'd better act like we're working.'

'There is a patient on the way.'

'There is.'

'He or she will need this bed.'

'And your doctoring skills and my nursing ones.' His smile widened.

'Did that really just happen? At work?' Where anyone could've burst in on them? Thank goodness it'd been Karin.

'Yep.'

Damn. Wow. Hell. What now? They'd stepped over the mark and there'd be no going back. Or if they tried to it wouldn't be easy to return to their former 'doctor and nurse' relationship. *Huh? You haven't strictly had that for a week now.*

Cody dropped his hand and stepped back. 'You're over-thinking it. Don't,' he warned before pushing the curtain open and looking out for their patient.

He was right. As always. 'That drink at the pub?'

He stilled, his hand gripping a bunch of curtain. He didn't say a word, merely waited.

'Think we can leave our vehicles here for the night and have more than one glass?' *And maybe get back to kissing at some point.* She'd sell her soul for another of those mind-blowing, knee-bending kisses.

His smile was slow, sexy and full of promise. At least, that was how she interpreted it. 'That's what taxis are for.'

'Right, in here.' Karin's voice was raised and there was a pause before she brought her patient in.

Harper tried not to look at her but it wasn't easy. Finally deciding to get it over with, she locked eyes with the registrar, as though to say, *So what? You caught us kissing. Big deal.* A massive deal, in fact. But Karin didn't need to know that.

'Well, well, well,' the registrar muttered so only she heard. 'What was it you said last week? "Not interested", I think. Hate to see you in action when you are.'

'Shut it, Karin,' Harper growled, or tried to, but only managed to splutter on a laugh.

'My lips are sealed. Unlike someone else's.' She winked and turned to the teenager she'd shown into the cubicle. 'Tell me about this abdominal pain. When did it start?'

Cody stayed with Karin as she diagnosed probable appendicitis when the girl admitted to pains in her right side. He drew some bloods for a CBC and CRP which would confirm if there was an inflammation of the appendix. He sat with the girl when she had a crying spell at the thought of 'going under the knife', as she put it.

All the while Harper cruised through his mind, never leaving, always reminding him of that kiss and how much he wanted to follow up on it. Just as he had on Sunday and all week since. Sheesh. A kiss was a kiss, but Harper's kisses were something else. Off the planet. Mind-shattering. Body-crunching. Full of promise. *I have to have her. As soon as possible.*

The thermometer he'd read after taking the girl's temperature hit the floor and shattered. His neck cricked at the sudden hard movement he made in response.

You what?

Have to take Harper to bed. Today, tonight.

This was not meant to happen. They were supposed to remain professional, with a little bit of friendship added in for good measure after all they'd been through together.

So why did I kiss her?

What choice did he have? As if he could've ignored that look in her eyes or dodged that welcoming, delicious mouth that had tormented him since their first kiss.

'Nurse Brand, you going to sweep up that glass today?' Karin was grinning from across the bed.

Dropping his head forward, he stared at the mess at his feet. Shoving a hand through his hair, he felt his gut tighten in disbelief. What an idiot. 'On my way to the cleaning cupboard.'

Karin poked her head out of the curtains to whisper after him as he left, 'I think Dr White is in Cubicle One, which is on the way to that cupboard.' Laughter laced the registrar's voice and grated on Cody's nerves.

'We'd prefer it if you could keep what you saw to yourself,' he ground out through clenched teeth.

'Relax, Cody. No one will learn anything from me. But you do realise everyone's already watching the pair of you? We might still be getting to know you, but the same can't be said for Harper.'

'Meaning?'

'That she's acting different these days. More out there and less control-freak mode.'

Really? Because of him? That'd be…wonderful. Cody swore under his breath. 'Has anyone considered she's still coming to terms with last Friday's incident and is having some major moments where it all comes back to her in full colour?'

Consternation flicked across Karin's face. 'I thought she was handling it amazingly well.' Then she lightened up again. 'I still think you're cheering her up immensely.'

'I need a broom.' He stomped off, not sure whether

he should be happy or annoyed about that last comment. Having Harper happy because of him—yes, he could go with that. Wanted to. He thought about her all the time. It seemed that, whether he was ready or not, he was stepping out into the risk pool because he more than liked her.

Which brought him right back to kissing Harper. *Amazing.* It definitely needed repeating. He paused at Cubicle One. The curtain was open and it would be rude to ignore the doctor standing beside the bed. Especially as she was looking straight out at him. 'Hey,' he said. 'You okay?'

'More than,' she responded in a hurry, and glanced at her watch. 'One hour and five.'

'That's for ever,' he muttered and headed away. If he'd thought working with Harper prior to that kiss had been hard, he hadn't had a clue. Kissing her outside of work was one thing, but now the department was no longer a no-go zone. Now... Now he wanted to haul her back into his arms and kiss her until she melted against him; kiss her senseless; kiss her until they were hauling off clothes and getting skin to skin. Hot, slick skin to hot, slick skin. Definitely not to be done in the department.

But there were other places.

CHAPTER SEVEN

THE PUB WAS CROWDED, even out in the garden bar. 'It's only just gone three-thirty,' Cody grumped as he placed a laden tray on the table, where eight of the day shift sat in various states of relaxation.

'It's twenty-six degrees outside, the drinks are cold and there's a one-day cricket game on the screen. Where else would anyone want to be?' Harper asked before sipping the Pinot Gris he'd bought her.

'You prefer your sport from a chair, don't you?'

'Safer that way. You've seen what happened to my knees at tennis. There's also a bruise on my thigh from a misdirected cricket ball last Sunday.'

'Not misdirected at all. You were supposed to catch it.'

Sitting on the bench seat beside her, he stretched his legs under the table, then shuffled his butt to move closer. Feeling her length against his leg, he sighed with pleasure. What could be better than this? *Taking her to bed.*

Jerking sideways, he shook the table, which sent waves of beer and wine slopping over the tops of the glasses and earned him a bunch of wisecracks from everyone. Everyone except Harper. She just stared at him with a half-smile on that mouth he wanted to claim, and a very knowing gleam in her eyes.

'I shouted the round. I'm allowed to knock things sideways. Okay, guys?' He grinned around at them all and picked up his beer. 'Cheers.' *And stop staring at me like I've grown another head, or as if I might've got too close to Harper.* He swallowed beer too fast, gasped and had to suffer the mortification of being slapped on the back by her.

'Harder, Harper. Give him what for. Cheeky so-and-so needs keeping in line.'

'Go, girl. Bang him between the shoulder blades. Yep, that's good.'

Bang him? Wrong phrase, Jess.

Harper must have picked up on the unintentional innuendo because she sat back in a hurry. 'Just trying to help a man in need.' She was rubbing her palms together, slowly, as if feeling something. Was she sensing his muscles under her hand?

In need? He certainly was. His glass slammed onto the table. *Wishful thinking, buddy.* He glanced at her face. *Or maybe not.* Looking around the table, he cringed as he met the steady and amused looks from each and every damned one of their colleagues. 'Who's up for a game of darts?' he asked and stood up abruptly.

The invitation is not extended to you, Harper.

Considering her lack of co-ordination when it came to anything sporty, he doubted she'd want to be throwing a sharp dart anywhere, so everyone was safe. Except him. He needed her to remain on that bench, drinking her wine and pretending he wasn't here. Then these knuckleheads might get on with their afternoon without stirring things up for Harper or him.

'I will.' Jess picked up her beer and followed him inside to the board. 'You any good at this?'

'Yeah, a little.' Champion of the local pub in Invercargill for three years running.

'Then we've got ourselves a game.' Jess laughed as she picked up the darts and handed him a set.

He'd go easy on her to start. He held a coin ready to toss. 'Heads or tails?'

Forty minutes later, he shook his head at Jess and said, 'My shout. You play a mean game.' She'd beaten his hide, well and truly. He saw Harper heading out from the bathroom. 'You want another wine?'

'Please. Outside again?' Harper asked. 'It's a little cooler out there. Though with the after-work crowd arriving it's getting crowded.'

'We could go find somewhere quieter,' he suggested hopefully after giving the order to the barman.

'Haven't you been trying to divert everyone's attention off us this past three-quarters of an hour?' Harper's smile twisted his gut.

'You're right. Okay, back into the fray.'

'I'm enjoying this.' She slipped her arm through his.

Instinctively he squeezed his arm to bring her hand hard against his ribs. Then gulped. 'Don't,' he said quietly.

Jerking her hand free she muttered, 'Sorry, don't know what I was thinking.'

'I think you do, but we are supposed to be acting like colleagues, nothing else.' Harper had to be the sensible one. He was beyond it.

A group of suits pushed past them, knocking Harper sideways. Catching her around the waist to prevent her falling, he growled, 'Watch where you're going, guys,' and got glared at for his trouble.

'Says who?' asked one smart-ass as he gave Cody the once-over and obviously found him wanting, probably because he wasn't togged up in a white shirt and business suit.

Harper slipped her hand into his and tugged him sideways. 'Leave them.' She took a long drink from her glass and placed it back on the counter, took his drink from him and put that beside hers. Then she headed for the main entrance, pulling him along with her.

'Where might we be going?'

'Your place or mine?' Harper grinned, though apprehension did cross her eyes briefly. 'I'm over pretending we want to be here, playing nice.'

What? 'Just like that?' Had he heard right? 'You're sure?'

Twisting her head to one side, she eyed him coolly. 'You have to ask?'

'Just checking.' He'd hate to get it wrong. 'Your apartment. It's closer.' Barely, but the sudden tightening making itself felt in his boxers needed dealing with—fast.

The sun blinded him when they staggered outside. A taxi was dropping off more punters and he waved furiously to get the driver's attention. Bundling Harper inside, he rattled off her address to the driver and sat back against her, draping his arm over her shoulders. What had just happened? One moment they were agreeing they had to be sensible around the others and then, wham, they were in a cab heading for Harper's apartment. *Can you drive this thing any faster, mate? I'm getting a little worked up back here.*

Harper laid her head on his shoulder, lifted it almost immediately and turned so she could place her mouth on his. 'It's not too late to tell me this is a crazy idea and that we should stop.'

It had been too late hours ago. From the moment he'd leaned in to steal a kiss in Cubicle Four, it'd been all over. They'd always been going to follow through after that. Not that in a million years he'd thought they'd be heading for Harper's apartment quite this soon.

When the taxi turned into her street, his heart rate shot through the stratosphere. Nearly there. Then the fun could really start.

Suddenly Harper sat up straight and cried out to the driver, 'Turn around. We need to go somewhere else. Cody, what's your address?'

Cody felt he'd been punched in the gut. 'What? Why? We're here.' *And I can't wait much longer to tear your clothes off and hold your naked body against mine, and...*

'Suzanne and Steve are in my apartment. We can't stop here.'

Too late. The taxi was slowing against the kerb right at the end of the path that led to Harper's open front door where Suzanne was turning to look their way.

Cody began hauling the brakes on his desire. It seemed they weren't about to get naked together. Not here, anyway.

Harper said, 'I totally forgot they'd be here. They're going to an awards dinner in the city and didn't want to drive home after.' Her look was imploring. 'Give the driver your address. Now.'

Cody pulled back from her a little. 'You can't drive away without stopping in. Suzanne's seen us pull up. She's going to be upset if you don't at least say hello.'

Harper pulled a face. 'Talk about throwing cold water on the moment. Please take me to your place.'

The driver was watching them through the rear-view mirror, the grin on his face suggesting he was completely up to date with the situation.

'Shortly.' He reached across Harper to open her door. 'Your sister is looking mighty puzzled at the moment.'

Harper's face shut down. 'Why didn't you just tell the driver where to go? I don't need to see my sister right now.' She didn't move at all.

'Are you ashamed to be seen with me?' Because, if she was, he was gone. Right now. To hell with how he felt about her or how much he wanted her.

'What?' Stunned didn't begin to describe her face. 'No.' Then louder. 'No.' Then a shout. 'No. Not at all.'

Relief poured through him. 'Then what's this about?'

'You know what they're like. They'll give me grief for days. The phone calls won't stop. The texts will get cheekier.'

'From what I've seen of your family, you all tease each other mercilessly over absolutely everything. You and I together for a night isn't something out of the ordinary.' Yes, it was, for a totally different reason. 'What I mean is, it's no different to them teasing you about that pathetic toss of the ball at the wickets last Sunday.'

Harper's mouth lifted a little from the flat line she'd been holding it in. 'I guess you're right.' Shoving the door wide, she slid out. 'Be right back.'

'What are you going to say?' he called after her. Beyond her, he saw Steve join his wife.

'I've come to get my toothbrush.'

Cody cursed. 'Keep the meter running,' he told the driver, grateful that his excitement had backed off enough not to be obvious to everyone. 'Be right back.'

'What are you doing?' Harper asked as he caught up to her.

'Getting the toothpaste.' He wasn't going sit in the car while she talked to her family. That would make him look gutless or rude, and he was neither. Nor was he ashamed of whatever he and Harper were going to get up to tonight.

Harper rewarded him with a grin before acknowledging her family. 'Hey, guys, thought you'd be downing cocktails at that swanky hotel already.'

'Obviously.' Suzanne smirked. 'Nothing gets underway for another hour, but if you'd like us to get out of your way then I'm sure we can find somewhere to fill in time. Hi, Cody. Good to see you again,' she purred with a mischievous glint in her eyes.

Jeez. Maybe he should've stayed in the taxi. 'Same back to you both.'

Harper slipped between them and headed down the hall, calling over her shoulder, 'Just grabbing a couple of things.'

Like what? Cody wondered, considering they'd headed this way to get undressed, not dressed up.

'Not staying for a drink, then?' Suzanne called after her.

Harper came straight back. 'You shouldn't be drinking. You're pregnant.'

'Strictly orange juice for me. But thought you might want to join Steve in a beer. If you've got time, that is.'

Cody felt laughter beginning to rise up his throat. These White girls knew how to wind each other up something awful and didn't care who else they caught in the web. He turned to Steve. 'Do they ever let up?'

'Better get used to it.' The guy nodded, then added, 'If you're hanging around, that is.'

'Jeez, you're no better.' He should've done as Harper

had demanded and told the taxi driver to turn around while he'd had the chance. Was he hanging around? Did he want to spend time with Harper? Time beyond today and what they were heading for at his house? Yes. Yes. Oh, hell, yes.

Steve chuckled. 'The White family is not for the faint-hearted.'

Right now Cody couldn't give a damn about his heart, faint or not. All he wanted was Harper in his arms so he could do things with her that no one else need know about. 'That meter's ticking over,' he called down the hall.

Suzanne added, 'He's impatient, Harper. Better get a move on.'

Steve just chuckled again and headed inside. 'I'm having my beer.'

Harper burst out the door, nothing more in her hand than the handbag she'd carried inside. 'Have a great night, you two.'

Get in, be seen to do the right thing and get out: Cody couldn't argue with that. He caught her elbow and started down the path. 'See you, Suzanne, Steve.'

'We'll see you at Levi's party,' Suzanne said.

'Maybe,' he muttered, and got a quizzical look from the woman he was hurrying towards the taxi. 'One thing at a time,' he told her.

Tonight was about Harper. And him. And that incredible need cranking up again with every step he took away from the nosey sister. Getting Harper into the cab made him hum. Giving the driver his address caused him to pause for a breath, then shrug. He'd already admitted to himself he was more than interested in furthering their relationship. Letting her into his home was another step in the right direction.

* * *

Cody's solid timber front door closed with a heavy thud behind them, and Harper gazed around at the wide entrance with massive painted pots filled with flowers placed strategically on either side. 'Those are beautiful.' The house was massive. She'd been wrong to think he'd bought a starter house. Unless he was aiming for a castle some time.

'Did I get the colours right, then?' Cody asked with a little hitch in his voice.

'Did you choose these?' Had he been winding her up about being colour-blind? She turned to look closely at him, wondering about that hitch, and saw nothing but pride in his expression.

'The pots are my mother's. She had them for years, since before they were fashionable. Dad gave them to her for their thirtieth wedding anniversary. Unfortunately there's nowhere for them in her room at the rest home. These need space to be appreciated. As for the flowers, I get the local florist to take care of those.' His chest lifted on a deep breath, drawing her gaze and reminding her why they were here.

As if she needed reminding, when her body was ramped up and in hot turmoil. Her heart hadn't stopped its heavy tattoo since they'd been in the pub. Not even seeing that smug, knowing look on Suzanne's face had quietened it down. There'd been a moment when they'd first pulled up outside her apartment when the heat in her belly had cooled a weeny bit. But one look at Cody, one word spoken in that husky voice, the slightest of touches from his hand and arm and, pow...where were the fans? She flapped her hand in front of her face. Her body needed relief. Relief of the kind that only a man could give, a man built like a sex god. Not any sex god either. Cody. The one and only. To hell with vases and flowers.

Harper reached for him.

He grasped her, those hands heavy and hot on her waist.

Pulling at his shirt, she pushed it up over that magnificent expanse of chest so she could see it, feel it, without the hindrance of clothing. His body was better than her imagination had conjured up.

Cody tugged at her blouse, pulling it free of her skirt, taking it up and over her head, his gaze fixed on her lace-covered breasts. Thank goodness she'd left her plain, sensible bras in the drawer that morning.

Leaning in, she kissed a trail over the warm skin tempting her. She started with one nipple and worked her way across to its opposite number, tasting, sipping, enjoying.

His fingers slid up under her bra, found her breasts and cupped them while his thumbs flicked back and forth over her taut nipples.

It wasn't enough. Her body craved Cody's. All of Cody's. Against her, inside her, with her. Her fingers worked the button of his chinos, then the fly that strained against the throbbing, hard heat pushing between them. Then he was filling her hands with all that hot length. Her fingers wound around his shaft, tightened, loosened, tightened.

Above her head, Cody gasped. His hands groped for her skirt, found the zip and jerked it down, shoving at it until it slid over her hips to pool at her feet. Then she was in his arms, being lifted and turned so her back was against the wall.

Winding her legs around his waist and her arms behind her head, Harper lifted her mouth to his. He was ready for her, his lips swollen and demanding. As she closed her eyes, Harper wondered if she'd fallen into a deep dream. This was beyond great, beyond anything she *could* dream of. The male scent of Cody's skin filled her nostrils. Those large, strong hands held her tight yet easy. They touched, teased, tweaked, caressed. They drove her to the edge in a very short time.

Pulling her mouth free, she managed a strangled, 'Cody…' before he claimed her again, giving more kisses, taking hers in return. Whatever she'd been about to say was whisked away in a haze of need.

She couldn't wait any longer. Her throbbing, moist sex was way past ready. 'Please,' she begged as her hands found him again, pushing his boxers aside.

'Wait.'

She couldn't.

'Condom,' he wheezed through gritted teeth. 'Pocket. Trousers.'

How was it that his chinos hadn't slid down to his ankles? Not enough movement could be the problem. She grinned under his mouth. Her fingers dug into his back pocket and thankfully it was the right one. She mightn't be able to last long enough to do a search of every pocket on those trousers.

'Hold on.' Cody tore open the packet with his teeth.

Wrapping her arms around his neck and tightening her grip with her legs, she obeyed. And then…then… He was filling her, with heat and movement, himself.

She'd been mad to think she could go without Cody even for the past week. She'd wasted days. Tipping her head back hard against the wall, she gave into the sensations tripping and ripping through her; gave in to the need clawing at her insides; gave in to Cody's hot demands and accepted his gift as he made love to her as she'd never been made love to before.

Cody scooped Harper up into his arms from where they'd finished up sprawled over the floor, precariously close to one of those massive pottery urns. 'Let's make ourselves comfortable,' he murmured near her ear and headed for the stairs that led to his bedroom.

'Mmm.' She barely moved, her eyelids stayed closed, but that delicious—yep, now he knew how delicious— mouth curved up into a beautiful smile that sent warmth spearing at his heart.

Whoa. His heart had nothing to do with what had just gone down between them. That would be plain dumb. No matter how great the sex was, how well they got on, what if he gave her his heart and he lost her? He couldn't guarantee he could survive that a second time. He'd believed after Sadie had been killed that nothing similar would happen to him again. Then along had come Strong and the body packer. Terrifying. Did violence follow him? What if something occurred he couldn't protect Harper from? He'd failed with Sadie. He wouldn't risk not getting it right for this surprise package in his arms. She didn't deserve his mistakes.

Harper's lips grazed his jaw, her tongue flicking over his lips, turning up his blood to race along his veins.

Now is not the time for this, his inner voice snapped. *Enjoy, have fun, forget consequences. Just go with the moment.*

Not a bad plan, he admitted. At the door of his bedroom, he paused. 'Now you get to tell me what colour to decorate in here.'

Her eyes slowly opened and she peered around. 'This is a bedroom? It's the size of my whole apartment.' Her head came up off his chest as she tried to take in more. 'Cripes. I don't believe what I'm seeing.' She snuggled down against him again, her eyes now shut and her mouth still smiling. 'I knew I was dreaming.'

Cody laughed as he gently laid Harper on the bed before crossing to open the windows and let some air in. The room pretty much got all-day sun, which on a day when the temperature had been high made it a furnace.

A light sea breeze obliged him, sending soft tendrils of cooler air over his skin. 'Feel that?' he asked as he lay down beside this woman who had him all shaken up. Or was that all melted down?

'It's wonderful. So is that finger you're trailing over my breast.' Totally uninterested in where she was, and only in what he was doing to her body, she stretched like a cat, her arms above her head, her feet reaching to the bottom of the bed. They were never going to find it, the bed being super-king-sized and Harper being about five-six.

But, now that he'd relaxed again and put other things out of his head, he loved watching those cute feet with their—blue?—nails moving back and forth across the cover. 'What colour's your nail polish?'

'Dark pink.'

'Not blue, then.'

Those eyes he'd grown very fond of twinkled with mirth. 'Nowhere near, buster.'

'For what it's worth, I like dark-pink-slash-blue.' He stretched out on his side beside Harper and draped an arm over her waist. 'It would look good on these walls.'

Her eyes widened and the twinkles just got brighter. 'Very masculine, I'm sure. You could have light pink curtains to match. Duvet in pink and white. Yes, I can see it now.' Her gaze roamed the room and her expression got a little serious. 'What an amazing space. You can do so much with this.'

'Starting with showcasing the view. I'm planning on bigger, lower windows so I can see out over the bay while lying in bed.' He still pinched himself that he'd been able to purchase this property. There'd been two other buyers trying to outbid him, but once he'd started he'd had to have it. He'd probably spent tens of thousands too many but as he intended staying put for the foreseeable future he knew it was money well spent. As long as he got the renovations right, as well as the colour scheme.

Harper was giggling. Giggling? What happened to serious? Now very immature and absolutely loveable. 'Don't make those windows too low or you won't be able to do anything interesting in this bed without an audience. Even if you are two storeys up.'

There was his cue, if he needed one. 'Then we'd better make the most of how things are at the moment.'

'I like the way you think.' She rolled into him, all soft, pliant and utterly desirable.

Would he ever be able to get enough of her? He hoped so or he was in trouble. 'Lie back and enjoy. This is your moment.'

'But I want to play too.'

'Oh, Harper, you're going to play, believe me.' And he proceeded to show her exactly what he meant.

Harper rolled over and put a forearm over her eyes to blot out the sunlight streaming in through the windows. Her body ached pleasurably everywhere, even in places she hadn't known existed until now. Not that she was complaining. Not at all. They were delicious aches. This had to be the best way ever invented to wake up. Shaking her head, she stifled a laugh. She'd got it bad. Got Cody bad. Crikey, but he'd delivered, more than once. More than twice. Even after taking time out for food, because they'd needed sustenance to carry on *playing*, he'd known how to keep her keen and willing. The man rocked.

She grinned and stretched, making herself as long as possible, reaching for each end of the bed and not quite making it. Maybe she'd finally found her hobby. One that didn't give her grazes or bruises, or bored her senseless.

'What's making you look so satisfied with yourself?'

'Oh, you know. It's Saturday and I'm not going to work. The sun's shining and the wind hasn't come up yet. I've got nothing I have to do by any specific time.'

'Zero to do with amazing sex, then. I get it.' Cody stood at the end of the bed, grinning down at her, that well-honed body just as mouth-watering now as it had been the first time she'd seen it. 'You won't be wanting your messages, then.' He held out her phone.

'Where did that get to?' She pushed up against the pillows and took it to scroll through the latest texts.

'Behind a flower pot and under these.' He held up her panties and swung them on one finger. 'Just as well we haven't reached the technological age where our phone screens automatically show the view.'

'Drat. I forgot to cancel that.'

'Cancel what?' The bed dipped as Cody sat down beside her.

'A paddle-board. I was going to give it a go but changed my mind.' She felt a little sheepish as his eyes widened and a laugh rumbled over his tongue.

'You what?'

'I figured if I fell off…make that *when* I fell off…I'd

have a soft landing and no scrapes or bruises.' She stared out at the sparkling blue-green harbour and shook her head. 'But why spend all that money when I know I'll only give up after the first attempt? I don't have a sports bone in my body.' She could give the board to the kids.

'I beg to differ. You can be very athletic when you find the right activity.'

When she caught his gaze, she saw amusement gleaming out at her and she blushed. 'Didn't even graze my knees.' Her eyes cruised over him and stopped at his scratched upper arms. *Gulp.* 'Did I do that?' She couldn't have.

'Yep.'

Contrition jarred her. 'I'm sorry,' she muttered. 'I don't... Haven't... Sorry,' she repeated lamely and stared at her fingernails. She must've been out of her mind with desire. Yeah, she had been. Cody had driven her over the edge easily, often, and she couldn't be held responsible for her actions.

'Hey.' A large hand covered both hers. 'What's a few light scratches in the heat of the moment? I didn't notice until I got under the shower and added soap to the mix.'

'Now, there's a thought. A shower.' Her muscles were in need of a warm soak—a long one, at that.

'Help yourself. There're towels on the heated rail. Want to stroll down to Oriental Parade after and find somewhere to have breakfast?'

'Sounds perfect.'

But as she stood under the jets of hot water she couldn't help wondering where this was going. One night of sex, the best sex ever, didn't change everything. She still had to work with Cody afterwards. She still couldn't give him children—which was getting way too far ahead of things. She still couldn't trust her heart to anyone either, not even Cody. Again, getting way too ahead of herself. Or was she? The feelings rolling through her at the moment were warm, soft, happy and…exciting.

Rinsing the knots out of her hair, she lathered Cody's shampoo through while her mind worked overtime. She was definitely getting way ahead of herself. She'd done that with Darren and had believed everything was working out perfectly. She needed to take a back step to protect herself, remind herself what the future held, because already it was apparent she couldn't have a few nights of sex with Cody and wave goodbye as she'd done with the two previous sexual encounters she'd indulged in since her marriage had caved.

A few nights? Who'd said anything about any more nights together? Neither of them had, but there hadn't been time. Easy enough to remedy. She'd started the ball rolling yesterday when she'd hauled him out of the pub. She could, and would, do something similar today if necessary, and somehow she didn't think Cody was finished with her yet.

She reached blindly for hair conditioner and opened her eyes. None. Damn. Her hair felt hard and icky with only shampoo through it. *Suck it up.* There wouldn't be a blow-dryer either. *Bad hair day coming up.*

Snapping off the water, she reached for a towel, soft, large and smelling of aloe vera. Rubbing her nose against the soft weave, she sighed with pleasure. So the man had taste in towels and soap powder. And she had it real bad. *Forget it, Harper. He's not for keeps.* He could be, if she'd had what he needed, but she didn't.

So, should she dry off, shuck back into yesterday's clothes and head out the front door with a casual wave and a *thanks for the great sex, see you on Monday* tossed over her shoulder?

Something like that made a lot of sense.

She always did sensible these days.

A little gremlin woke up fast. *So don't. Be different. Instigate more sex later today. Accept what you can't change and go for whatever you want anyway.*

That could end up with someone getting hurt. Cody. Or her. But the idea of having a relationship expanded as fast as she tried to push it away. After Darren, she'd believed she'd be single for the rest of her life unless she found a man over eighty who didn't want children interrupting his sleep, and she still thought that. But her conversation with Jason echoed somewhere in the back of her mind. Maybe she could have a different dream. What she could do, and it seemed really wanted to do, was have fun with a man. Not only in bed, or on the floor in the entranceway, but over breakfast on the Parade, going to the movies, playing cricket together with the brat pack, or spending time with her family and getting teased silly. Or choosing paint colours.

'You going to be all day?' Cody leaned against the doorframe, hands in his jeans pockets, for all appearances like he had the whole day to wait for her. 'You left the door open.'

She hadn't noticed. Warmth stole through her. Not rampaging heat that ended in an orgasm, but soft heat that touched her heart, her toes, her tummy and all places in between. He made her feel good about herself. Not something she'd experienced for a long time. For too long. 'I don't suppose you've got a drawer full of make-up anywhere?'

'I'm all out of it. You'll have to go completely natural, which is better than being plastered with goo anyway.'

That softness intensified. He paid the nicest compliments, even if not quite true. 'Then I'm nearly done.' She looked around the bathroom. 'You thinking about any changes in here?'

Cody nodded. 'There's not a room that doesn't need dealing with. I'll give you the grand tour before we head out.'

'The house appears huge.'

'It is.' He grinned. 'I visited when I was fourteen and in the rugby team. The coach owned it, and I've wanted something like it ever since.'

'You got the real deal.'

'Wanting this place is what started me on the property ladder. A fishing mate and I saved hard to go halves in a rundown shack that we could rent out. Soon we mortgaged it to the hilt and bought another, and then another, until...' his grin widened. '...here I am. Back in Wellington in the house of my teenaged dreams.'

'Go you.' She gazed out of the window at the harbour sparkling in the sun, absorbing how much he'd told her about himself. 'You'll never get tired of looking at that.'

'I agree. Even the windy days are wonderful. Then there are the ferries scooting back and forth, and the fishing fleet heading out to the Strait. It's great.' He was almost purring.

As they wandered along the Parade hand in hand Cody said, 'I'm thinking we should hire two paddleboards and give it a crack before you cancel that order. This could be the one sport you're great at.'

The sea was so calm she couldn't use that as an excuse. 'I haven't got any gear with me and I'm not immersing this skirt in salt water.'

'I'd have enjoyed watching as it got wet and figure-hugging.' He gave an exaggerated sigh. 'Not my lucky day. I could offer you one of my tee-shirts but that'd be all over the place on you, no figure-hugging going on at all. We'll have to drop by your place. You think those other two will still be there once we've had breakfast?'

'I have no idea.' She batted his arm lightly. 'You make it sound as though we're definitely following through on your idea of paddle-boarding.' Her problem being…? Didn't she want to have fun with him? Hadn't she been extolling the reasons she should let go and enjoy life?

'Relax. Your knees will be fine.'

They mightn't have got the skin scraped off them, but they were going to hurt like stink tomorrow, Harper decided as she stiffened into a slight turn three hours later. Breakfast had been long and leisurely, then there'd been coffee with Suzanne and Steve in her tiny back yard. Now finally they were on the water, and she was wobbling front, backwards and sideways, feeling like a drunk penguin. 'Keeping my balance is hard work,' she growled as Cody came close.

'Relax into the movement of the board, don't fight it.'

Easy for him to say. 'Go away. You're causing waves.' *Show off.* Just because he could do this without even trying. *So unfair.* She'd have to challenge him to a knitting contest next. Except she barely knew one end of a knitting needle from the other.

Damn, but he looked good wet. Those board shorts clung to his butt and thighs, making her mouth moist and her tummy tight. As for his chest… She'd never been a chest girl before but Cody was breaking all her norms.

Now he grinned at her. 'Waves are when water rises above the level.'

She didn't deign to supply him with a reply. Instead

she pushed the paddle deeper and pulled on the handle to move forward. Her arms were starting to complain about this added activity too. Paddling was definitely more strenuous than inserting IV lines or stitching wounds.

She snuck another sideways glance and had to stare. Cody standing on his board, looking for all the world as if he'd been born doing this, was a picture to remember. He had natural balance. 'How come you're so relaxed with this?' She could see his calf muscles adjusting as the board beneath his feet shifted. Unlike hers, which were tight and unyielding to any movement.

'Comes from years of staying upright on the deck of a heaving trawler.' Cody pushed the paddle through the water, his strokes effortless. Didn't she know it? Her face heated as memories of the previous night flooded her brain.

'Want to head back to shore?' Mr Oh-So-Good-at-This cruised close again. 'I'll shout you a cold drink.'

'And an ice-cream.' What had happened to the diet? *Tomorrow.* She began working the board around to face the shore—or make that she began *trying* to head home—but the current had changed and she wasn't going anywhere in the direction she needed to.

'Now I know where the brats get their love of ice-cream. They're copying Auntie Harper.'

A wave passed under her board and she froze, afraid to move in case she got it wrong and overbalanced. 'That's a proper wave,' she muttered through clenched teeth.

'Hey,' Cody was yelling. 'Back off. Can't you morons see what we're doing here?'

Harper risked twisting her head to the left to see who had caused his annoyance and her decidedly wobbly ride, and saw a speed boat about a hundred metres away going full throttle and sending out huge bow waves.

Slosh. Slosh. Water rushed at her, over her feet, and continued into shore. 'Do I paddle or freeze? Do I try to keep moving while balancing like a stork?'

The left side of the board lifted. Uh-oh. Her hands gripped the paddle handle. *Like that's going to help,* she thought as she leaned into the lift. The board dropped back flat while her momentum took her head-first into the tide.

Thunk. As she popped upwards, pain blasted into her skull. The board? It had to be. She kicked hard, hopefully away from it, and surfaced—to get a swipe on the chin from the paddle she'd let go as she'd fallen in. *Ow. Pick on me, why don't you?*

'Harper? You all right?' Cody straddled his board, reaching out to her, concern etching his face.

'My knees are fine.' She spluttered out a mouthful of salt water. 'Yuk. That's gross.'

'Those morons should've been driving their boat a lot slower. There are speed restrictions around here,' Cody muttered as he concentrated on getting her sorted. Catching her hand, he tugged her close to his board, hers following as the cord attached to both her ankle and the back of the board snapped tight. 'Hey, you're bleeding.'

'I got whacked, but not hard enough to do damage.' Or so she'd thought.

Strong fingers held her chin and tipped her head back gently. 'You're the doctor, but I'm thinking you're needing a couple of stitches on your chin.'

She began to feel a sharpness on the corner of her chin. 'Guess I'm going into work after all.' She didn't doubt he was right. He knew his medicine.

'I can take you to the weekend emergency surgery.

Though that will take longer, since you're not staff.'
Cody put his hands under her arms and hauled her up
to sprawl across his board. As easy as that. 'Stay still
and I'll paddle us back in.'

She shook her head. Was nothing too much trouble
for Cody Brand? He'd never used a board before yet he
was already turning them towards shore and calmly
pushing his paddle through the water despite that current. It would be too easy to get used to this, to come to
rely on him to look out for her.

Harper stiffened. No way. She watched her own back.
No one else did. Not even for a few weeks while they
had an affair. *Huh?* They were having an affair now?
Why not?

'You okay? You've gone quiet, and I don't like a quiet
Harper as much as the chatty one.' Above her, Cody was
smiling that heart-melting, 'I will take care of everything' smile that was his trademark.

'I'm thinking I like the sound of going to the surgery, wait or no wait.' There was less chance of people
from work knowing she and Cody had been spending
the day together.

'No problem. That cut hurting yet?'

'I'm trying to pretend it doesn't.' The sharp ache was
amplified with salt water sluicing over it as they bobbed
up and down. The daily summer sea breeze had arrived,
chopping the surface and adding to the pressure pushing them in a direction in which they didn't want to go.

But Cody had everything under control and within
a very short time he jumped off to push the board with
her still sprawled over it onto the beach. 'Here we go.'
He leaned down and lifted her up, placing her carefully
on her feet. 'Let me get that cord off your ankle.' He

looked across the beach to the van that the board-hire company operated from and waved. 'Give us a hand, will you, buddy?'

'Her sewing skills weren't too bad.' Cody dropped an arm lightly over Harper's shoulders as he led her out of the emergency surgery to a taxi he'd ordered.

She looked a little pale and those black threads weren't helping her appearance as she muttered, 'Two stitches, and the poor woman was terrified of making a mistake with you hovering over her. You're not a frustrated plastic surgeon, by any chance?'

'Me? Never. More into dress making,' he quipped.

'You have absolutely no problem laughing at yourself, do you?' There was wonder in her voice and those tired eyes.

'Don't see any problem with that. I know who I am and I'm totally comfortable with people having a laugh at me. Believe me, I'd never have survived nine years on the trawlers if I couldn't take the crap the guys threw at me. You're fair game with some of those rogues if you get too serious about just about anything.'

He felt her shudder under his arm. 'I've had a very sheltered life.'

'Huh? You can say that after our drug-runner incident? Or having dealt with Friday and Saturday night revellers and their drunken angst in the ED?'

'I guess.'

There'd been something else in her earlier comment. 'A previous partner didn't take kindly to being teased about his skills, or lack of?' Her history concerning partners was a complete mystery, and likely to stay that way, he acknowledged to himself.

But Harper did what she'd done last Sunday on the

beach. She blurted the truth quickly and emotionlessly. 'My husband had a great sense of humour except when it came to anything about himself.'

Husband? *Jeez*. Cody shoved his free hand through his hair. He did not do having sexual relations, sexual anything, with a married woman. 'I didn't know.'

'That I was married? I don't tend to make a big deal of it. It's an episode of my life I do not want to revisit.' She looked up at him and now there was emotion lining her voice. 'No point. What's done is finished.'

Phew. Was *married, not* is *married*. He could breathe easily again. 'How long have you been separated?' He should quit while he was ahead, but he liked learning little snippets of information about her. Marriage wasn't small, whether she'd separated or not. Okay, so he was nosey, or out to protect himself. He couldn't decide which.

'The divorce came through two months ago, right on the two-year anniversary of when we officially called it quits. I was in a hurry. If I wasn't going to be married in the full sense of the word then I wanted out.'

'I get that.' *I think*. But then he'd never been there; he would never have the chance to see his marriage through or leave it. That had been taken out of his hands by the man who'd killed Sadie.

'You ever been married? Or in a serious relationship?' Harper asked.

Don't want to go there. He could change the subject. But then he'd asked first. Which only went to show how much he lost the plot when he was around Harper. 'Yes. Years back. It lasted six months and then she died.'

'Cody.' Harper spun around to stand in front of him, her hands resting on his cheeks. 'I'm so sorry.'

His gut twisted at the sight of that genuine concern

for him. Her hands were soft and gentle on his cheeks. He placed a hand over one of hers and lifted it to kiss her palm. 'Me too.' Another kiss, then he stepped back.

'Don't want to talk about it?' There was no reproach in her eyes or her tone. Just a genuine concern that if he didn't want to carry on this conversation she'd be okay with that.

'Not really. It would spoil the day.' Wrapping his hand around her soft small one, he swung them high. 'I don't want to do that.'

'Then take me back to my place so I can change into something half-decent and we'll go out for a drink and dinner. My shout.'

'Yes to all of the above, except I'm shouting you.' When she began to argue he covered her mouth with his and kissed her, long and slowly, long enough for her hopefully to forget whatever she'd been going to say.

CHAPTER EIGHT

'WILL YOU LOOK at that?' Tim, one of the doctors clocking off from night shift, whistled as Harper took the notes he was handing her about a patient in Resus. 'Things get a little rough between you two over the weekend, did they?' He glanced from Harper to someone behind her.

Turning slightly, Harper saw Cody strolling in, looking totally ready for the start of the week and not at all as if he'd spent most of the weekend making love with her or doing other energetic activities.

Then, 'What did you say?' Cody snapped, that nonchalance gone in a flash.

'Joking, mate. Harper's chin looks like it's taken a nudge. What happened?' His question was directed at her.

But she didn't get a chance to answer.

Cody stepped up to Tim and growled, 'Nothing like what you're thinking.'

'Take it easy.' Tim stepped back. 'I said I was joking.'

'It's not a joke to suggest someone has been rough with a woman.'

Harper grabbed Cody's arm and pulled until he settled back down on the heels of his shoes. She shouldn't be touching him at work, but she had to get him to see sense. Quickly. 'Tim didn't mean anything. He certainly wasn't suggesting for one moment that you knocked me around.' Dropping her hand, she handed Cody a file. 'This patient's ours. Go and get her. Now.' She was talking to him as though he was a recalcitrant child, but he needed to get away from Tim and calm down.

'Yes, doctor,' Cody snapped, a flicker of hurt crossing his face before he all but snatched the file from her fingers. Tossing a glare at Tim, he turned to head for the waiting room.

Watching him stride away, his back über-straight, his head high, she said, 'I was paddle-boarding and fell off—took a hit on the chin.' What was bugging Cody, for him to go septic so fast? Had someone accused him of hitting a woman in the past? Surely not? He absolutely wouldn't do anything remotely violent—he was the proverbial gentle giant, except when confronted with a gunman in Resus. She'd swear her career on that, but that didn't mean someone hadn't accused him of some such action to get attention or make his life uncomfortable.

'Ambulance bringing in hit-and-run victim, male, twenty-four, cyclist. ETA fifteen—though it's the start of the rush hour, so that might go out further.' Karin had taken the call when Cody had headed for the waiting room on Harper's instructions.

'What's the damage?' Harper asked. Cyclists copped more than their share of shoulder injuries.

'Probable fractured clavicle, fractured humerus—otherwise nothing obvious,' Karin replied, unknowingly acknowledging Harper's thoughts.

'One for the orthopaedic crowd, then. You want to take him?'

Karin nodded. 'Absolutely. Thanks.'

'I'll be within calling distance.' She'd also look in on the situation regularly. Karin was a very competent registrar but it never hurt to make sure she didn't have any problems with a patient. Now, where had Cody got to?

There he was, escorting an elderly man and woman into Cubicle Two. His face was strained, though he spared a smile when the couple said something to him. 'Deep cut to thigh,' he told Harper in a less-than-friendly tone as she approached. 'Mr Gregory fell over the gardening fork and landed on some corrugated iron an hour ago.'

'He shouldn't have been digging the garden at all,' the woman Harper presumed was Mr Gregory's wife growled. 'He's been told to leave it to our boys.'

As Cody eased the man onto the bed, Mr Gregory retorted, 'I want to pick my veggies this summer, not next year. They never have time for a cup of tea, let alone to turn over the garden.'

'Maybe that's because you told them off last time they came to help.'

Okay, that was enough. Monday morning and crotchety patients—and nurses—was not how she wanted her week to start. 'Right, Mr Gregory. I'm Dr White. Nurse Brand says you've got a deep cut which we will probably have to sew back together. Let's take a look.'

While Cody removed the man's trousers, Harper turned to the woman. 'Mrs Gregory?' She nodded and Harper continued. 'Would you mind sitting over there? Thank you.' Right, everyone was in their place and she could get on with her day. Except she glanced at Cody and her heart softened. Whatever that altercation had been about, it had shaken him. There was a white line around his mouth, and his eyes were sending out spears to anyone who dared look at him, which was mostly her at the moment. *Well, I didn't do anything wrong.*

Cody looked up, those eyes wintry. 'I'll get the gear.' He nodded at the wound he'd exposed on the old man's thigh.

'Thanks.' She snapped on gloves and began to gently probe at the wound. 'When you do something you do it well, don't you, Mr Gregory? We're going to have a load of stitches in here by the time you go home.'

He winced when she touched the wound again. 'Yes, lass, I believe in doing a proper job, no matter what it is.'

'I bet you grow fabulous vegetables.' She chattered on to keep him occupied and hopefully not noticing too much pain. It also kept her mind off Cody and whatever his problem was.

'Do you grow a garden, doctor?'

'Can't say I've ever tried.' Could that be her next attempt to find something to do outside of work? No. She'd decided to give that up and focus on what she already had, hadn't she?

'Dr White is more attuned to sewing than digging.' That deep, husky voice came from behind her. The edgy tone had lightened a little.

It seemed she might almost be back in favour, though why she'd actually slipped out of it because of something Tim had said, she had yet to find out. 'And colour co-ordinating,' she risked. Looking directly at Cody, she was rewarded with a small smile, and knew everything was right between them again. Until she took him to task about his earlier reaction. That had not been good and, if the staff hadn't been aware they'd seen each other over the weekend, they certainly would be now.

'Mr Gregory.' Cody glanced at the older man. 'What

colour would you use for your bedroom if you were painting it?'

'Aw shucks, lad, ask the missus. She says I'm hopeless at that stuff, though I don't see anything wrong with a bit of strong colour myself.'

That set Mrs Gregory off on another tirade.

Harper hastened to finish suturing the wound, then left Cody to put a gauze cover over it while she went to print out a prescription for antibiotics and a mild analgesic for her patient.

'That chin looks sore,' Karin said. 'You must've hit the board hard.'

'It was the paddle that got me.' She signed the prescription. 'How was your weekend?'

'Quiet. Studied a lot, saw my sister for a bit, caught up on washing. Nothing exciting. No paddle-boarding with a hunk, for sure.'

Harper's teeth snapped tight. Then she forced herself to relax. This was no different from any other Monday morning except that she'd been with Cody over the weekend and didn't want everyone gossiping about them. 'I don't think I'll be doing it again.'

'What? Paddle-boarding or spending time with Hottie?'

Harper's brow tightened and she opened her mouth with a retort, only to be talked over by Karin.

'You shouldn't have left the pub looking like you were totally lost in each other if you didn't want people to know you'd get together.' The annoying woman nodded at her with a warning in her eyes. 'Stop letting everyone get to you and they'll soon find something or someone else to talk about.'

'But I haven't said anything.'

'Only yelled at Tim, stuck up for Cody and ignored

Jess when she asked you about your weekend.' Karin laughed lightly. 'So not like our well-mannered, polite and fun consultant at all.'

Harper pushed up from the chair. 'Thanks for the warning. I guess I did get a bit carried away.' But she'd been rocked by Cody's outburst. Would he tell her what it had been about? If they saw each other this week out of work, that was. 'Are you free to do dinner and a movie one night this week?'

'I am. Are you?' Karin winked and headed for the resus room.

I have no idea, Harper wondered as she headed back to Mr Gregory. *Yes, I will be. I can't cut off other friends because of one particular man.* She slipped into the cubicle and the breath caught in her throat at the sight of that man gently helping their patient back into his trousers while keeping the old man's dignity in place. 'Where have you been all my life, Cody Brand?'

'On a fishing trawler, getting on with *my* life,' he drawled as they watched the elderly couple walk towards the exit, Mrs Gregory giving her husband an earful about being more careful in the future.

Harper would've felt sorry for the old man if she hadn't noticed Mrs Gregory slip her hand into her husband's for a brief moment. Then she really heard Cody and her head shot up. 'Did I say that out loud?'

He nodded. 'You did. I'd ask what you meant by it but there's a waiting room full of patients, and a load of staff around here with ears bigger than their backsides.' He leaned over the counter for the patient files. 'Now, who's next?'

'My ears aren't that big.' Jess nudged him as she strolled past.

Harper took the file from Cody. 'I'll get this one.

You two continue your discussion on ears and butts.'
She was back to normal, feeling relaxed and happy to
be at work. The weekend had been one out of the box; it
might or might not be repeated, minus the chin whack,
and right now she was ready for anything.

As if to prove a point, the emergency phone screeched
as she walked past. Though it was Cody's job to answer
it, she automatically picked up the receiver. 'Wellington ED. Dr White.'

'Rescue helicopter service, doctor. Bee attack in the
Sounds. Patient male, sixty-five, no known prior allergies. ETA twenty-five.' The woman called out more
details.

'We'll be ready.' Harper put the phone down. 'We've
got a severe allergic reaction coming in.'

Cody knew he'd overreacted to Tim's comment, but hey.
He hated when someone went off half-cocked and didn't
bother to find out the real deal. That caused people distress or at the very least unhappiness. It had happened
with his mate, Jack: because of false accusations by his
girlfriend about hitting her, he'd nearly ended up in jail.

Cody's gut churned. Harper had been unhappy with
his reaction, and he couldn't blame her. There'd been
searching looks from her all morning that shamed him.
He should've shrugged Tim's comments away, as Harper
had.

Come lunchtime, he went for a walk in the blazing
sun and fierce wind to get some air to clear his head. He
was an idiot not to explain to Harper why he'd reacted
like that. It wasn't that big a deal, but he'd got used to
keeping quiet about what mattered most to him after
Sadie's passing. Was now the time to start opening up,
start letting Harper in a little?

Harper. She was getting to him. Sneaking under his skin, rattling his beliefs and worrying him stupid.

After just one weekend he was ready to spend more time with her. He'd even consider—no, he'd go with—having an affair for as long as it lasted. But that was as far as he'd go. His heart would cope with that, but no more.

So why did he feel as though he'd known her for ever? Why did the idea that they had a future together keep blindsiding him? Why the feelings of wanting to protect her, to be there for her all the time, to share everything with her? He enjoyed being with her; he wanted more and couldn't wait to get into bed with her again. All this after such a short time.

'You going to stand there all day looking like someone stole your coffee?' Harper reached past him to drop a completed patient file on the desk.

'Sorry. Having a rest on my feet.' He looked around the department and saw nothing untoward. 'Who's next?'

'A toddler with a dislocated thumb. You want to go and get him?'

'Sure.' He loved his job. Even on days like today. Yet right now it would be great to be able to head away and take his confusion out with a hammer as he put the boards back on the railing of his veranda. Or to slop some paint on a couple of walls. Except he had yet to decide on the colour and buy the paint. Harper's suggestion of deep cream didn't quite turn him on. Like he knew anything about it. Cream could be anything; what did it matter about the shade he painted the place when he couldn't tell what it was?

Except he was determined to make his house something special, to do it up and decorate it in the style it had been built in ninety-odd years ago.

He returned to Harper. 'Want dinner at my place tonight? I'd like to run some decorating ideas past you.'

Surprise filled her eyes, and the smile she found for him was a little lopsided as she nodded slowly. 'I'd like that.'

'Six o'clock suit you? I need to visit the supermarket and do a couple of jobs before you get there.'

Her smile widened and tied his gut in more knots than usual while giving his heart a nudge. The fireworks between them were unbelievably intense, like something he'd never experienced. Or had forgotten over the last few years.

He wanted more of Harper. Hadn't even begun to have enough of her. It could be that he'd never have enough. Damn it.

The day was a continuous stream of patients. Harper began to wonder if three o'clock would ever arrive, but finally it did. 'I'm exhausted. That's got to have been the busiest day in a long while.'

'You said that one day last week.' Cody had joined her in the staff room.

'Really? I must need a break. It would be cool to go lie on a beach somewhere for a few days.' A beach, sun, water: it sounded wonderful. Sunburn, paddle-boards knocking her head, mosquitos… It still didn't sound half-bad if she compared it to drug overdoses, broken bones and cut hands. She checked her phone for messages; she'd got the usual texts from the brats, and one from her sister reminding her about Levi's birthday. 'As if I'd forget that.' She had a present to pick up. She might as well go to town now and then it was done, box ticked.

'Forget what?' Cody asked as his locker banged shut.

'Levi's birthday. I'm going shopping.' Then she remembered Cody had been invited to the party. 'Will you be joining us on the day?'

His hesitation made her hold her breath until he finally asked, 'Would you like me to?'

'Yes.' Definitely. 'Can't think of any reason why not.'

'Except for your family giving us a hard time, but I guess we can handle them.' He could have sounded like he wanted that, not uncertain and wary.

'Glad you think so. They've been soft on you so far.'

'Really? Can hardly wait for the next instalment.' He nodded. 'You want help picking a present? Before I go to the supermarket?'

'I've already ordered it. He wanted a wicket-keeper's glove.'

'Any suggestions on what I can get him?' Cody looked hopeful.

She spoilt that straight away. 'Nope. You'll have to come up with something yourself. So, let's take my car and I'll drop you back here later.'

'Sounds good.'

Hopefully some time that afternoon or tonight they'd get to talk about what had caused his abrupt mood change that morning. Because she really wanted to know. From his swift reaction to Tim, it was obviously something ingrained in him, what made him the man he was, and she needed to know more about this man who'd caught her when she wasn't looking. So much so that she wondered if she might've fallen a little bit in love.

A little bit? Or a massive, heart-stopping lot? *He wants a family, remember?* She wasn't likely to forget. But it seemed that hadn't stopped her heart getting involved here. Which could become a problem.

'I'll come if you promise not to nag me about any-thing.' His words were light but his eyes told her he was serious.

'We're not going to talk about what happened with Tim, then?'

'No. We're not.'

That stung. It seemed personal stuff was taboo. She'd gleaned a few bits of information here and there, but nothing deep and revealing. Was she prepared to talk about Darren and his change of heart over her inabil-ity to have children? Possibly. But then it was early on in their—their what? It wasn't a relationship. Not yet. Probably never would be. A fling? As in, meet for sex and fun when there was nothing else going on in their lives? Or something more, that involved sharing meals and movies and her family parties? 'Whatever.' She shrugged, knowing she must sound like a petulant teen. There were a few of those around the place today.

Walking out to her car, they were both quiet. Harper was trying to move past her disappointment. She had no right to expect Cody to talk about private issues when she wasn't prepared to be totally open with him. That didn't mean she didn't want to push the buttons that would make him tell all.

'You're over-thinking everything.'

She pinged the locks on her car but instead of sit-ting inside in the heat that had built up over the day she leaned against the door, her arms folded on the roof, her chin on her wrist, and eyeballed Cody. 'I do that when I haven't got any clues to work with.'

He mimicked her stance from the other side, his gaze firmly on her, as though he was weighing up what to say. 'I'm sorry for the way I reacted this morning. It was a hangover from the past.'

Harper waited. That wasn't enough of an explanation.

His sigh was loud between them as he gave in. 'My close mate's girlfriend got drunk and fell off a balcony into a garden, collecting some massive bruises on the way. She used it against Jack, saying he hit her. Fortunately, her timing was out. We were still on board the trawler tied up at the wharf at the time. As it was, no one believed Jack until someone came forward to say they'd seen the woman fall.'

'That stinks.' How could anyone do that?

'It screwed Jack's life. Some people couldn't accept the truth and kept pointing the finger. He finally moved across the Tasman to settle in Perth.'

So he'd lost a close friend out of it all as well. 'I think I can understand your comments to Tim now.'

'But I should be toning them down? I get it. Sometimes I forget I'm not working amongst fishermen any more. He probably didn't mean anything by it.' He finally smiled. A tight, sad smile, but a smile.

Of course, that got him exactly what he wanted. 'Get in.'

As she drove towards the sports shop where she'd ordered Levi's present, her brain was busy thinking over the little that Cody had said. 'What made you decide to become a nurse?'

'Thought you were being too quiet,' Cody muttered. At least he was still smiling. 'You don't give up easily, do you?'

'I don't see what's wrong with asking that.'

His sigh hissed over his lips. 'Nothing, I guess.' He stretched his legs as far as possible, not far at all, considering how long they were. 'Okay, no. I always wanted to be a nurse right from when I was at school.' He stopped.

As she accelerated away from traffic lights, she asked, 'So?'

'I was a rebel, having too much fun with outdoor stuff to settle into more study. I was also intent on proving that the snide remarks suggesting I was a girl if I was going to be a nurse were wrong. What testosterone-laden teen isn't going to react by proving how masculine he is?' He grinned at her.

Harper chuckled. 'There's nothing girlie about you.' She knew intimately. Whipping into a vacant parking space right outside her destination, she stopped the engine. How lucky was that? 'Did you ever consider becoming a doctor?'

'Briefly, but nursing always held more interest for me. Anyway, by the time I was ready to change careers, I'd spent too long doing a very physical job. The extra years and the huge hours studying for a medical degree would've stifled me.'

'That makes sense.' Then, 'What happened to make you leaving fishing and go after your original dream?'

'Let's quit the questions, shall we?' There was a hint of anger in his voice. His door opened and he swung his legs out.

'I'm interested, that's all.' What was going on? The man was moody as all hell today. It didn't seem to matter what she said, she got it wrong.

He glared at her over his shoulder. 'Harper, drop it. I don't need this.' He stood up and closed the door with a little shove.

When she clambered out, she said, 'Sorry. But it was a simple question, nothing more. All part of getting to know you better.'

'You don't know when to quit, do you?' He blanched. Stepped back. Shook his head at her. 'We'll take a rain check on that dinner.' Then he walked away, leaving her wondering what had just happened.

She watched him charge through the crowds of shoppers and office workers, heading back the way they'd come, his shoulders tight, his head forward. *Did I really deserve that?*

Maybe. He disliked talking about himself, yet she'd kept pushing. But she wanted to know Cody, as in everything about him. They were getting close, had spent that amazing weekend together; of course she wanted to understand what made him tick, why he reacted to situations like he did.

So how dared he speak to her like that? She *didn't* deserve it; didn't need him to bite her head off.

He'd said 'a rain check' for dinner. Did he think she'd be hanging around waiting eagerly for his next invitation? He could go take a flying leap. She didn't do that for anyone.

CHAPTER NINE

HARPER PARKED AT work and shoved the door open, then grabbed it as a gust of wind blew through the car park. 'Whoa.' The image in her mind of her door bent back on its hinges was not pretty.

Not that there was a lot that looked good in there this morning. Cody had dominated her thoughts throughout the long night, and was still there now.

Her head throbbed with discontentment.

One weekend with Cody had not been enough. But she'd probably walk into the department and he'd be there with his smile, acting as though he hadn't walked away from her yesterday. *You wish.* Was he a man who forgave easily? But then, what was there to forgive? She'd done, said, nothing out of the ordinary as far as she could see.

During those long hours of the night, she'd begun wondering why he'd reacted so angrily, so quickly, to what she'd asked. Every answer she came up with had no substance—because she didn't know him well enough.

Out of the car, the wind caught at her hair, pulling strands loose from the band she'd wound round it earlier. Typical Wellington day—or so the rest of the country thought.

The roar of a motorbike told her that Cody had arrived. Should she wait for him and risk being snubbed? Or should she head inside and pull on her scrubs in readiness for another day?

Unwilling to be snubbed, she took the soft option. They had all day for her find out where she stood with him.

'Hey, Harper,' Cody said as she made her way to shift change-over.

'Morning,' she acknowledged, watching him walk to the changing room and wondering if that had been a friendly or not-so-friendly tone he'd used. Then thought, *this is plain childish. Of me and him*. She didn't do childish. She often growled at the brats for that. Thank goodness they weren't here to witness her slide from the rules. Right, she'd act as though yesterday hadn't happened when Cody joined the group.

She didn't get a chance to act in any way at all. An ambulance brought in two men from a truck that had gone over the edge of a bridge spanning the motorway. A serious spinal injury took all Harper's concentration for the next hour and a half.

Cody worked alongside her, friendly enough, but still with a glimmer of reproach in his attitude.

And that was how the week continued. The ease they'd known the previous week had gone, leaving them back to being two members of the day shift who got along fine as long as they stuck to work issues.

'You need some sleep,' Karin told her on Friday as they were winding up and handing over to the night shift. 'Hope you've got a quiet weekend ahead.'

'A birthday party with the brat pack.' Yikes, was Cody still going to join her family for that?

Apparently so. Sunday afternoon at Jason's again,

and Cody was playing cricket. Again. Harper was having a wine with her sister and sisters-in-law. Again.

She couldn't believe Cody had turned up after the week they'd had keeping their distance with each other. It didn't make any sense. As soon as the game stopped, she was going to bail him in a corner and demand to know what he thought he was doing.

Jason handed her a refilled glass. 'What's the lover's tiff about, then?'

'You want to wear this?' Harper held her glass up.

'That'd be a waste.'

'Then go play with the kids.'

Surprisingly, he did, and Harper started to relax a little.

Until Suzanne picked up where their brother had left off. 'Want to talk about it?'

Silly girl. She should've known better with her family. 'No.'

'So something's happened.'

The wine was chilled to perfection, but suddenly she wasn't enjoying it. 'Why does everyone think because Cody and I aren't falling all over each other there's something wrong? We work together, we're not soul mates.'

Gemma looked from her across to where Cody was bowling the ball and back again. 'Could've fooled me. You've both had the hots for each other right from that day the gunman held his weapon to your head. The way Cody carried you up the path to your apartment was so tender and loving, it made me all gooey inside.'

Harper could recall in a flash every detail, every sensation of those strong arms holding her against that wide chest. Now she knew his body better, she wanted more. Lots more. '"Loving" is a big word. We'd hardly talked until that day.'

'If it fits,' Gemma quipped. 'You two sure look like it does.'

'What's really the problem?' Suzanne asked.

Everything. Nothing. She wasn't telling them the nitty gritty of their argument when she hadn't figured it out herself, but she could raise what would eventually become the final devastating issue between her and Cody. 'He wants kids.'

'You've discussed this?'

'He told me the weekend we rode out to Pencarrow Head.' How could she have been so stupid as to think she could manage this? Could walk away from the best thing she'd ever known? Cody was…the man she'd fallen for. In a flash. Probably from the first time she'd taken notice of his hot bod in scrubs. He was everything she wanted in a man and a whole heap more.

Talk about setting herself up to get hurt. She couldn't blame anyone else. She also couldn't continue with the relationship—if it was still there.

'Writing this relationship off before you have a full and frank discussion with Cody is a bit like cutting your own throat when you're actually happy.'

Sisters could be so annoying and interfering. 'You think after Darren I'm going to put my heart on the line when I already know Cody has desires for a family of his own?'

'There are other options. Adoption. Surrogate mothers. It goes on all the time.'

'Why would Cody do that when he doesn't have to?'

'Because he loves you.'

Harper leapt to her feet, the wine flying through the air. 'Don't say that!' she yelled at Suzanne. *I can't cope with that.* 'What would you know? Next you'll be saying I love him.'

'Don't you?'

Yeah, she did. She'd finally admitted it to herself. But for her family to see it, that made it harder to pretend otherwise. 'Shut up.'

'There a problem here?' Cody had strolled across the lawn to stand a couple of metres away. He might have thought his expression was neutral but Harper would have sworn she could detect hurt lurking in his eyes and in the slight downturn of his mouth.

He'd overheard Suzanne. Or her. More likely her. She'd been the one yelling. 'Yes. Annoying sisters who don't know when to mind their own business.'

'Time for a bike ride, out where we went the other day.' Cody held out his hand. 'You need a jacket.'

'Excuse me?' She stared at him. Dropped her gaze to that extended hand. Extended in friendship? What else? But go with him on a ride so that he could quiz her about what he thought he'd overheard?

'Harper?' Cody asked. 'Jacket.'

So he wasn't taking no for an answer. Not that she'd given any response. She felt incapable of one. Had no damned idea what she should be doing. Going back to where they'd had their first kiss hummed with danger.

Behind her there was utter silence.

The easy option would be to go with him. At least as far as the gate. She had to get away from the girls. Needed time to think without their crazy input.

Harper grimaced as Cody revved the bike and headed for the main road. How much of that argument with her sisters had he heard? She cringed when she thought he might've overheard the 'love' word.

For the first time holding on to him was a nightmare.

Putting her arms around him made her want to cry for what they might've had. For that love she held for him but couldn't share. On an indrawn breath, she laid her face against his back. She felt his strength wherever she touched him; the strength that had drawn her to him in the first place.

It was as though she had to feel him, to smell him, be with him for one last day to store memories to take out in the middle of the night over the coming weeks and months.

The ride was torture. Time was running out. After today, they'd definitely be over. She would call it off. Falling in love with Cody had wrecked the hopeful fallacy that she could have fun with him without getting hurt.

At Pencarrow Cody helped Harper off the bike and walked beside her along the beach. He said nothing, but his head was spinning, his gut churning. She hadn't denied she loved him when Suzanne had pressed her. Gees. He jammed his fingers through his hair. Jeez. What was he supposed to do with that little gem of information?

Even as he wanted to lift her into his arms and spin them round in circles while grinning and kissing her, he fought not to run for his bike and take off as fast as it could go in an attempt to outrun the fear driving up through him. He couldn't do this, whatever 'this' was. He wanted to love Harper back, to have the whole family, home and Sundays playing cricket thing. He really, really did. But what if he lost Harper like he'd lost Sadie? What if someone like that lowlife with his gun happened again? What if…? A hundred questions exploded through his brain, none of them stopping for an answer.

They reached the end of the beach, both pausing to stare around as though they had no idea why they were there. *Well, hello, I don't. I dragged Harper here and now I don't know what to do, what to say.*

He certainly wasn't about to tell her he was frightened of what might be blooming between them. If it still was after the last hour.

Finally he asked, 'Why did your marriage break up?' *Why that question?* He'd no idea, but it seemed a good place to start.

'Darren left me because I couldn't have babies.' Her voice was quiet but determined. As though she wanted this over.

'You hadn't told him before you married?'

Now her voice rose and anger spat at him. 'Thanks a bunch. You honestly think that I'd hide something so important from the man I loved?' She dropped to sit on the damp sand. 'You believe I kept quiet in the hope he'd accept it once we were married?'

'That's not what I said. Not quite,' he admitted with a hint of guilt. 'I know you better than that.'

'I thought you did.' She shook her head. 'But really, I know very little about you, and the same could be said the other way round.'

He stared down at her, his heart beating hard and loud. 'So Darren just changed his mind?'

'Yes. After we'd been married for two years. After all his promises about finding other means to have our own family.'

Cody squatted down beside her. He wanted to take her hands in his, but even as he began to reach for her his old fear prevailed. Why touch her when he didn't want to continue a relationship with her? *As in, a marriage and happy-ever-after relationship? Who said you don't want it?* He did want it, badly, but he couldn't do it. Today, after hearing what she'd said to Suzanne, he knew he couldn't. Knew that he'd always live with the fear of something bad happening to her, of him losing her one way or another.

He picked up a small stone and hurled it at the sea. 'You got a raw deal.'

'Huh? You reckon?' Leaping to her feet, she stormed down to the water's edge, her small hands clenched into fists at her sides.

He followed, stood beside her and waited impatiently. For what, he didn't know, but there was more to come. It was there in her stance, in her face. Did he want to hear it? Yeah, he did. For whatever reason, he did.

I love him. Harper gulped, drew in a deep breath and squeezed her eyes shut. She loved Cody. End of. Yes, very much the end of.

Her anger intensified. How stupid could she get? Loving Cody was impossible. Not allowed. She'd never ask him to give up his dream of a family for her. Never. She kicked at the water, got splashed for her effort.

'What went wrong for your husband to change his mind?' Cody stood so close to her she could feel his heat, yet the gap between them felt as wide as the Cook Strait.

'What's the point of all this?' she snapped.

'Then I'd know.' He sounded so damned reasonable.

'Right. Then will you tell me why you never talk about your past? I doubt it.' The air from her lungs hissed over her lips. 'Take me back. Now. I'm done with this, with you.' They had to break up one day, so it might as well be today when they were already at loggerheads.

Cody looked away, went back to staring at that blasted stretch of water between the two heads.

'I loved Sadie very much.'

Harper waited, her temper not abating, but hovering, ready to explode. She wanted to hear him out, but he had to hurry. Her patience was at zero. Because she was hurting.

'When I said she'd died…' He paused and slowly met her gaze. 'She was murdered.'

Slam. Her anger evaporated. Instantly she reached for his hand. It was cold in hers. 'Oh, Cody, that's appalling.'

'She divorced her ex when he went to prison for fraud. We met around that time and fell head over heels in love, got married as soon as she was free, and life was sweet. Or so we thought.'

Harper continued holding his hand, shocked at what she was hearing.

'I came home from work one day to find her lying in the lounge, bleeding out. I couldn't save her. She never stood a chance once he stabbed her heart.'

Cody's voice broke. 'He planned it so I'd find her. He wanted me to pay for marrying his wife. He'd learned when I was home from a fishing trip, escaped from jail, headed straight for our house and waited until he heard me turn into the drive.' Tears streamed down his cheeks. 'I tried to save her. I did everything possible. It wasn't enough.'

'If her heart was stabbed it's doubtful anyone could've done any better.'

'That's what the doctors told me. Didn't help at all.'

That was when he'd changed careers; she'd bet on it. Wrapping her arms around him, she held him tight, feeling the ripples of anguish shaking his body.

It was a long time before Cody stepped away. He didn't say anything.

Harper told him, 'I'm sorry I made you relive that.' She couldn't not tell him now that he'd shared his horrific story. She owed him that much. 'Darren said he didn't care about not being able to have children with me. But he changed his mind and got another woman pregnant before he left me. Kind of like insurance, making sure the next woman in his life was fertile.' The past was sour in her mouth. 'I should be over this by now. I guess I am in some ways, but I'll never trust another man about this again.'

More hurt spilled into Cody's eyes.

She was sorry for that, but the truth needed to be put between them. 'Don't take it personally. It's just I couldn't stand to have my heart broken again.'

'You think I can?'

'I understand you can't.'

'So where does that leave us?' he asked.

She swore under her breath. She loved him. But... 'Even knowing each other's history, understanding the pain we've both been through, caring about each other...' She *thought* he cared for her. 'What you and I have had isn't going anywhere. It can't. There's a fundamental flaw in us having a long-term relationship. You would like a family. I can't have one.' She had to remind him, to put it out there again, just so that he didn't try to avoid it. 'End of.'

'Thanks for nothing, Harper.'

'Cody.' she sighed. She could go on explaining herself, but what was the point? He'd understand more than most how she didn't want to be hurt again. But would he understand she didn't want to hurt *him*? 'Can you take me back to my family?'

* * *

Cody wanted to race the bike down the motorway, break every speed restriction there was, go so fast he couldn't think.

But he didn't. Common sense prevailed. Just.

So Harper went home with him—in his head. Her words sliced him to shreds. They were finished. On her terms. *End of.*

'End of what, Harper?' he yelled as he flung the bike around the corner of his street. 'I go and fall in love with you and you say it's over.'

Not that he'd fessed up to his feelings. That old fear of getting hurt had raised its head the moment he'd opened his mouth to tell her he loved her back there on the beach. He'd wanted to, almost more than anything, but he hadn't been able to say the words.

This morning he'd left home excited to be seeing Harper, and determined to move past the chilly week they'd endured, to resume their affair and move forward. He'd also been looking forward to spending time with her family. They'd drawn him in, made him comfortable and relaxed, eager to share their lives.

But at Jason's place he'd heard the girls arguing, overheard Harper's sister saying she loved him and Harper not denying it. That had caused something deep inside his heart to crack wide open. Love had spilled out, blinding him into thinking it might be possible to banish his fears. Then she'd dropped her bomb. She wasn't having a relationship with him.

Which just went to prove he'd been right to remain uninvolved in the first place. Except he hadn't; he had got in so deep there was no way out.

He loved Harper. No ifs, buts or maybes. He loved her. And she'd tossed him. Easy as.

No. Be fair. Not so, if that anger and pain in her eyes was anything to go by. There'd be no going back on her statement, though. Her chin had jutted out in a 'don't argue' gesture. Her hands had become fists at his waist as they'd ridden back to her brother's house. And her abrupt nod goodbye had been like a knife to his heart.

At home he tore his helmet off and banged it down on the outdoor table by the garage.

Now what? He could open a load of beers and get blind drunk, or he could start on getting that railing fixed. Or he could grab one beer and sort the railing. *Good idea.*

He could also try and figure out where to from here with Harper. *Hell.* He slammed his fingers through his hair. He hadn't got over the shock of realising he loved her yet. Loved her so much he'd go to the end of the earth for her.

No, he wouldn't; he couldn't. That was terrifying. Pain had wedged in his heart today but it'd only get worse if he tried to follow through on his feelings. Harper had made his mind up for him about having children; she wasn't letting him decide if he wanted them more than her. Why did she of all people do that? He'd been making his own mind up about everything he did from the day he'd learned to talk, yet she'd just walked all over him.

Which might be why Harper had got under his skin and annoyed the hell out of him. She wasn't even giving him a chance to work out what he wanted, what was best for them both. She'd made a decision and that was that. He was not used to it.

From the day he'd walked out of those school gates he'd worked damned hard, had become wealthy by using his hands and brain and could hold his head high.

Cody drained the beer bottle in his hand and stared up at the building in front of him, waiting for the usual pride to suffuse his chest. This house stood as a testament to his success.

Though it might turn out to be a lonely dwelling if he couldn't have Harper with him. His heart was now hers. What he did about that was still up in the air. Telling her he loved her and asking her to share his life meant exposing his fears. Not tell her, and he'd be giving up his dreams of a loving woman and family at his side. Harper was that woman. As for the children, they'd work something out if they were serious about each other.

Yep, which was why he'd start on nailing up that railing. He always thought best when doing manual work. Hopefully by the end of the day he'd have some answers.

The next week crept past so slowly, Harper thought she must've slept through a weekend and worked two weeks in a row.

On Friday afternoon she handed over to the incoming shift and slunk away quietly, not looking in Cody's direction once. She couldn't bear to see that sad expression that had been in his eyes every day since Sunday. He'd managed to avoid working with her most of the time, and in the few cases they'd shared he'd been exemplary in his manner towards her.

She hit the supermarket, trying to dredge up enthusiasm for something to cook for dinner. Nothing appealed. Not even ice-cream or chocolate. Ironic, when the week before she'd been pretending to diet, and this week she was struggling to put anything in her mouth.

The meat chillers held nothing to interest her. The deli came up short too. Talk about being picky. Harper crossed to the fish cabinet. Last try before she went home to eat an apple.

'I do a mean baked salmon and salad.'

The shopping basket clattered to the floor as the voice that had been haunting her every night of the past week caught her attention. 'Cody.'

He picked up the basket and swung it between them. 'Do you like salmon?'

What if she did? They weren't sharing a meal, not when they'd barely shared a sentence all week. She tried for a shrug but didn't do so well. 'Sometimes.'

'Would tonight be one of those times? With a glass of Pinot Gris? On my veranda overlooking the harbour?' He didn't beg, but there was a lot of entreaty in the way he looked at her.

'Why?' She had to know if this was a 'let's make up and be friends' gesture, or something more intense and serious. Or had he come up with his own reasons why they couldn't be together?

'We need to talk. About a lot of things.' Lightly swinging the basket between them again, he locked those spring-green eyes on her. 'I've missed you.'

'You've seen me every day.' Her heart began to thump a little harder and faster than was normal.

'I've still missed you.'

Her next breath hitched in her throat. Damn the man. He had a way with words. Add in the longing in his eyes, and the softest smile now curving his lips upwards, and what could she say? How could she refuse him when she'd missed him every minute, every second, of the past week? She turned to the woman waiting on the other side of the cabinet. 'I'll take that whole salmon, thank you.'

Suddenly she was ravenous.

* * *

The small talk Cody and Harper managed for the next hour as they drove to his house and prepared dinner wasn't too bad. They discussed work and her family, and where Harper thought she might go for her summer break that she'd apparently put in for yesterday.

'Why Rarotonga?' he asked, genuinely puzzled. 'Now's the windy season, isn't it?'

'I want lots of beach and warm water, and no paddleboards.'

'Your chin looks okay now that the stitches are gone.' The tiny scar on the edge of her jawline was cute, and had him wanting to run his fingertip over it. He refrained from that mad idea. That could be pushing the boundaries. Yet some time tonight he'd have to. There were too many unsaid things lying between them that had to be confronted before he and Harper could move forward—together. He was determined they were heading into the future together.

With the salmon cooking slowly on the barbecue and the salad made, all that needed doing was to blanch the asparagus at the last minute. 'Let's take our wine outside.'

Harper followed and took a chair opposite him, which kind of suggested she wasn't quite as comfortable yet as he'd hoped.

Leaning across the table, he topped up her glass, then his, sat back and said, 'When Sadie died so did I.' He saw when she got it.

Her mouth softened and her eyes widened. She reached across the table to slip her hand into his. 'Go on.'

That was it, really. His chest rose as he drew in air. *Get this over with.* 'I'm afraid of losing someone I love again. That's why I let you push me away with no argument when you said we couldn't have a relationship because of your infertility. I want to change that. To prove I am better than that. To share your life—for ever, if you'll let me.'

She jerked her hand away, her eyes widening as she fixed him with a glare. 'You're feeling sorry for me?'

His fingers shot through his hair. Would they ever be able to have a conversation without misinterpreting everything? 'No, Harper. I don't. Well, I do, but my actions aren't based on sympathy.' *What actions? You haven't done anything yet except dig an even bigger hole to climb into.* 'I love you.'

She gaped at him.

He hadn't planned to say that yet; he'd thought he'd work up to it. But now some of the tension gripping him had starting easing, so he said it again. 'I love you. I knew it from the moment Lowlife held that gun to your head, and when after the initial shock you showed you cared as much for your patient as anything else that was happening. You're one gutsy lady.'

After a couple of beats, she said, 'I *was* scared witless when that gun banged against my skull.'

'Still a…'

'Let me finish.' She rubbed her temples in the way she had when she'd been getting a migraine. 'I'm scared way beyond that now. I love you too, Cody. Love you with every cell of my body. And that makes me afraid too.'

He didn't relax even as the thrill of hearing those words rolled through him. There was more to come. He saw it in her eyes. And he wasn't going to like it.

'Because of that, I am walking away from you, from us. I can never ask you to give up your chance of having a family. I can't and I won't. It would be selfish of me.'

'There are other ways to have children.'

Her head moved back and forth, back and forth, as though warding off his words. 'I heard that last time, but in the end it didn't happen.'

And she couldn't deal with the heartbreak again. He got it. In spades. He didn't have the words to persuade her to rethink her stance, so he stood and went to her, pulled her into his arms and held her tight, close to him, so they absorbed each other's warmth and tenderness. His chin rested on her head and he closed his eyes, absorbing every little movement she made, every place where her body touched his.

She pressed hard against him, her cheek against his chest, her hands around his waist, her breast moving up and down softly as she breathed.

He inhaled her citrus scent. Remembered that first kiss they'd shared. The kiss that had changed everything for him, had had him wondering if he could take a chance with her. Had had him doing it again at work, of all places.

They stood that way for a long time. Then Cody leaned back in her arms until he could see her face, saw when tears began to streak down her cheeks. Bending forward, he began to kiss her, murmuring, 'Don't cry, my love,' against her mouth. 'We're in this together.'

She stilled just as she'd begun nibbling his lip. Her mouth left his, making him feel chilled until he saw the warmth in her eyes.

'No one's ever said that to me before,' she whispered.

'It's true. I can't leave you. I won't, unless you push me away. All I ask is that you accept me as I am.' He had to trust that she would.

'Yes, of course I do.'

'Harper, will you marry me? Live with me for ever,

or at least until I'm old and grey and can't get it up any more to pleasure you?'

Harper's eyes widened in astonishment and a small, nervous laugh escaped her. 'That is a long way off, I'm sure. I've seen how easily you react to me when we're getting up close.' Then she sobered. 'What about children?'

'Sweetheart, there are ways. You know there are.' But he named a couple anyway. 'Surrogacy, for one. Adoption, for another. Or fostering, if you prefer. Quite frankly, it's more important that I'm with you. I love you so much, it's unbearable to even contemplate not being with you for the rest of my life. Children or no children.'

'I haven't told you, but I'd like a family too.' Her voice was soft and filled with a deep longing that broke his heart.

'Now who's trying to surprise who? I've seen you with the brat pack. I know how loving you are with each and every one of them. We'll do our damnedest to add to the pack one way or another.'

'Then, yes, darling Cody. I can't think of anything I want more than to marry you.'

He lifted her into his arms and swung her around. His heart beat rapidly, filled with love for this amazing woman who'd battered down all his resistance with very little effort just by being herself. 'I love you so much it hurts at times.'

'Then I'd better kiss you better.' Harper's mouth covered his in what turned out to be the longest, hottest kiss they'd experienced to date, and was only the beginning of greater things.

EPILOGUE

HARPER HELD THE precious little bundle wrapped in a woollen blanket cautiously in her arms and leaned her head against Cody's hip. Unbelievable. To be holding their daughter was beyond her wildest dreams. 'Isn't she beautiful?' she whispered.

'Very,' he croaked.

She looked up to see tears streaming down his cheeks and dripping off his chin. This man was full of emotion today. He had been since the moment the phone had rung at four in the morning to say Gemma had gone into labour. She loved that he showed his feelings. 'I think she looks like her dad.'

'I don't have a red scrunched-up face.' He dashed his forearm over his face.

'What do you think, Keely Tricia Gemma Brand? Does your dad look like you?'

'That's such a mouthful. Can't we drop two of the names, just call her Keely Brand? Think of her having to write that list down every time she fills in a document.'

'Absolutely not. I like using your mother's name as her second one and, as for Gemma, well, what can I say?' Tears welled up in her eyes and dripped down her face. Gemma was a star in her book.

She'd never forget the day, a month after their fabulous wedding, when Gemma and Jason had rocked up at the house looking so serious she'd feared for bad news. But, no; they'd come to suggest that Gemma be a surrogate mother for them. They'd stunned both her and Cody into silence for a long time. The idea had seemed wonderful, impossible, crazy, filled with so many problems that they should've said no.

Neither of them had been able to. Months of tests, counselling and talking to their families had followed before Gemma had finally been able to become pregnant for Cody and Harper through artificial insemination. Finally, Harper was a mum and Cody was a dad. A very proud one, by the look of wonder on his face.

'Here, your turn to hold her.' Harper didn't want to let Keely go but she held their daughter up to him, and smiled when he stepped back.

'Hell, no. I'll break her, or drop her or something.'

'You've held babies at work. You're going to be fine with your daughter.' Harper pressed Keely into his arms, watching the wonder grow as he gazed down at his beautiful bundle.

'Hello, sweetheart. Welcome to our world. I promise I'm going to try to be the best damned father ever.'

He would be. Harper already knew he was the best damned husband. Ever.

* * * * *

THEIR DOUBLE
BABY GIFT

LOUISA HEATON

For Becca xxx

CHAPTER ONE

SHE WAS RUNNING LATE. *Very* late. And as she stared at the clock on the car dashboard it seemed to be whizzing through minutes, as if a mischievous imp was maniacally pressing down hard on the fast-forward button.

Why was this happening *today?* Today of all days? Her first day back after maternity leave. Her first day as a single working mother, back in the A&E department she loved. A department that would now be all the quieter because Jen wasn't in it.

Dr Brooke Bailey had *so* wanted this day to start well. Because if it did—if she got through it—then that would be all the proof she needed that her decision to do this on her own was a good one.

It had seemed doable in the early months of her pregnancy, when bravado and optimism had got her through the days. She didn't need a man. She didn't need anyone. Only herself—which was just as well, seeing as there wasn't a whole lot of people she could turn to now. Millions of other single mothers held down a job and coped, didn't they? Why should it be any more difficult for *her?*

Only back then, with her rose-tinted spectacles on, she hadn't predicted that she'd be awake the night before going back to work, doing hourly feeds because Morgan wouldn't settle. She hadn't expected that the very second she'd decided to strap Morgan into the car for her com-mute to work Morgan would have an almighty nappy ex-plosion and would need to be taken back inside the house to be bathed and have everything changed.

Nor had she forecast that she would get caught in an endless traffic jam, tapping her fingers impatiently on the wheel as she glanced at the London Grace Hospital—so temptingly close, but unattainable—as she sat bumper to bumper between a four-wheel drive and a large white delivery van, listening to people sounding their horns. She was wincing with each one, hoping that the noise wouldn't wake her daughter, who was finally—thank-fully—asleep.

Beside her on the passenger seat her mobile phone trilled with a message, and as the traffic wasn't moving she decided to check her hands-free device.

It was Kelly.

Where are you? X

She couldn't respond. Not behind the wheel. Even if she *was* stuck in traffic. She'd seen enough evidence of what happened to people when they drove and texted. The cars might move at any moment. She could be texting and have someone rear-end her and give her whip-lash as well as a late mark for her first day.

Not only had she to find a space and park the car, she also had to get Morgan to the hospital crèche.

An event she'd been worrying about for weeks.

It had seemed such a simple thing when she'd first planned it—*I'll just put the baby in the crèche.* But what if her baby didn't like it? What if she screamed the place down? What if she clung to her mother and refused to let go?

She'd never left Morgan alone with a *friend*, let alone in a crèche for ten hours a day. Eric had seen to it that she'd lost touch with most of her friends. Had isolated her until no one was left. So that when she had walked away, when she had broken free, she'd felt so ashamed about what she'd allowed to happen she'd felt she couldn't call anyone.

It had just been her and Morgan. And that had been enough. Till now.

Snakes of anticipation coiled in her stomach at the thought of leaving her daughter, and she was just contemplating sounding her own horn when the traffic finally began to move and she could make the turning into the hospital car park. Free, she zoomed up to the barrier, wound down her window to let in the mixed aroma of exhaust fumes and recent rain, swiped her card over the scanner and watched the barrier slowly rise.

For the first time ever she could take advantage of the parent and child spaces on the ground floor near the lift, and she pulled into an empty space. 'Thank you, thank you, thank you…' she muttered to any car park god there might be, and got out of the car, opening up the boot to assemble the buggy.

She got Morgan into it in record time, and without tears, and headed on over to the lift.

As the lift slowly took her up to the floor she needed she contemplated what it would be like to work a shift without Jen.

Jen had been a recent friend. But an amazing one. An unexpected treasure Brooke had located when she'd first started working at the London Grace. At the time she had still been with Eric, but she'd been having serious doubts, starting to be sure that she would have to walk away from him, but struggling with her conscience about the best way to do it with her pride still intact.

Her mood had been low and pensive as she'd stood in the staff room one day, dunking a tea bag over and over. In had walked a woman with a bright streak of pink in her short blonde hair—a shade of pink that had matched the stethoscope draped around her neck.

She'd taken one look at Brooke, walked right up to her, put her arm around Brooke's shoulder and said, *'Whoever he is, dump him. No man should make you look like that!'*

It had been the beginning of a beautiful friendship, and when Brooke had dumped Eric, and then found out a few weeks later that she was pregnant and Eric wanted nothing to do with her or the baby, Jen had been the one who had picked her up, dusted her down and taken her to a show where there'd been masses of gyrating male strippers and lots and lots of hot, writhing, perfectly muscled flesh.

Brooke smiled as she recalled that night. Jen had been an absolute diamond. Rough-cut, maybe, but still one of a kind. And when Jen had discovered that she too was pregnant, and that they had due dates within days of each other that had just solidified their friendship all the more.

Jen's husband Matt had been in the army medical corps, and hardly ever at home, so she and Jen had grown their babies together, comparing bump sizes and ankle swellings and seeing who could hold their pee the longest before having to wobble off to the bathroom.

But I don't have Jen to pick me up any more. No one to pick me up if the day turns out to be the biggest mistake of my entire life.

As the lift pinged open and Brooke began striding down the long corridor that would take her to the hospital crèche she tried not to go over that phone call once again. When Kelly had called to let her know that Jen had died during the birth—complications from eclampsia.

At the time she herself had just delivered Morgan. Had been home for just three days and struggling to get her daughter to latch on. Frustration had been building and the sound of the phone had been a welcome distraction. A few moments to gather herself and calm down. Contact from the outside world.

And then...

She swallowed back tears. She could not cry today. It was stressful enough without going over Jen's death all the time. Life moved on. You couldn't stop its inexorable march. Jen was dead. Brooke was alone. *Again.* She was back at work. Late. She needed to get a move on or she'd have a cranky boss to deal with too.

She buzzed at the door and a staff member let her in.

'I've brought Morgan Bailey. It's her first day...' She tried to sound braver and more together than she really felt.

The crèche nurse wore a bright tabard decorated in a multitude of teddy bears, with a name badge that said *'Daisy'*. Like the flower, she seemed bright and sunny, as if her face had a permanent smile upon it.

Behind her, Brooke could see children playing in a small ball pit, others daubing painted handprints onto a long strip of what looked like wallpaper, others at a table drawing, another group listening to a story. Beyond was another door, labelled *'Baby Room'*, and as she looked the door opened and a tall man with a military demeanour stepped out.

But she had no time to concentrate on him—despite the fact that some tired, exhausted part of her sex-starved brain still worked and had registered how attractive he was. The bossier part of her brain—the exhausted, sleep-deprived, worried-about-being-late part—overrode all other messages.

She unbuckled Morgan from the buggy and lifted her out. 'She's been up most of the night, I'm afraid, so she might be a little grumpy. There are bottles in the bag…' she unhooked the baby bag from the handles of the buggy and handed it over '…with expressed milk. I've labelled them with her name, so you can give her the right ones. There's a teddy in the bag, that's her favourite—Mr Cuddles. She likes to sleep with it. You usually have to wind her twice before she'll go to sleep, and if you sing her *"Baa-Baa Black Sheep"* she'll cry, so please don't do that. And…and…'

She couldn't help it. The tears that had been stinging the backs of her eyes now readily began to fall. The moment of having to hand her daughter over was too much. Her little girl had been the one to keep her together these past few months. She was all she had, and now…

Morgan, sensing her mother's distress, began to cry, and now Brooke was feeling worse about leaving her baby. She stood there clutching her daughter, hiccupping her way through her own tears, as if giving her up to the crèche meant certain death.

I can't do this! I don't need to work, do I? I could wait a little longer, take some more time off. I—

Daisy reached forward to take the crying Morgan. 'We'll be fine—don't worry. Have you got the crèche app on your phone?'

The hospital crèche had developed its own app, so that parents could click in at any time during the day and receive updates about their child—whether they'd slept, when they'd eaten or had a bottle, what the child was playing with. There was even an option to access the crèche's webcam.

Grateful for the fact that Daisy was ignoring Brooke's embarrassing tears, she tried to breathe. Sucking in a breath and dragging a tissue from her pocket to wipe her nose, Brooke nodded. 'Yes.'

Daisy was still smiling and bobbing up and down as she gently swayed Morgan, trying to soothe her. 'You go off to work, then, Mummy. Don't worry about us.'

Morgan looked sickeningly distressed to be in a stranger's arms, which was disconcerting for her mother. 'I've never left her before. You'll call me if there's any problem?'

'Of course we will.'

'Anything at all?'

Daisy nodded, but as Brooke opened her mouth to ask another question she felt a firm hand upon her arm. The man she'd seen before looked down at her with intense blue eyes and said, 'It's best to just walk away. Don't look back.'

Brooke looked up at him hopefully, gratefully, with her ugly crying face still at full throttle, dabbing at her tears and trying to hold on to his words of wisdom. Had he done this, then? Did he know what he was talking about? He'd just come out of the Baby Room, so perhaps he'd just dropped off his own child?

'Really?'

'Really. Come on.'

He had a stern, no-nonsense tone to his voice. A voice that was used to issuing commands and having them obeyed without question. It was clear he expected the same from her. He gently draped his hands over hers, forcing her fingers to release the death grip she'd had on the buggy since letting go of her daughter, then took the buggy from her and parked it in the buggy bay. With a guiding hand in the small of her back, he purposefully escorted her to the exit.

Brooke was desperate to turn around and make sure Morgan was okay. She could still hear her baby wailing. Her daughter *needed* her. But the man blocked her view and ushered her out through the door and into the corridor like an expert collie dog herding a reluctant sheep.

'But I need to—'

He held up his hand for silence. 'No. You don't.'

Brooke stepped away and looked him up and down, irritated that he thought he knew what she needed. Sniffing desperately and wiping her nose with the tissue, she wondered just who this man was, anyway. She'd never seen him before at the hospital. But, then again, she'd never had reason to come to the crèche before and the hospital was a big place. He might work anywhere. He might be a new employee.

Wiping away the last of her tears, she stared up at him. He was a good head taller than she. With very short dark blond hair, longer on top. Piercing blue eyes. Trim. Oozing strength and quiet, confident dominance. That was something that usually rubbed her up the wrong way. Eric had been overbearing. Had tried to control her. It was the kind of thing to send up the warning flags.

'Look, I appreciate that you're trying to help me, but—'

'If they sense weakness it makes them more upset.'

She wiped her nose again for good measure, sure it was now probably as red as strawberry jelly. 'The babies?'

He gave one curt nod.

'She's five months old. The only thing she senses is hunger, tiredness and whether she's wet or not.'

'You'd be surprised.' He began to walk away.

Narrowing her eyes, Brooke followed after him. He was going in her direction anyway. She needed the lift again, to go down a couple of floors to A&E.

She pulled her mobile from her pocket to check the time.

Damn it!

The man got into the lift ahead of her. 'Which floor?'

'Ground level.' She noticed he'd pressed the 'G' button, but no other. Frowning, she realised that he must work on her floor. He might work anywhere, though— A&E, the Medical Assessment Unit, Nuclear Medicine, Radiology…

He was looking at her. Looking her up and down. And, sickeningly, she noticed his gaze appeared to be centred on her chest. *Men!* Feeling her cheeks heat, she stared back at him, trying to make him lift his gaze a good few inches upwards, towards her face.

'Is there a problem?'

'You…er…might want to get out of those clothes.'

'Excuse me?' He had some front! He'd only just met her!

What is it with men? They do you one tiny favour and suddenly expect you to drop your—

'You've got milk on your blouse, something questionable on your skirt, and you appear to be…' he smiled and looked away, as if he was preserving her modesty '…leaking.'

Leaking? Brooke looked down at herself and instantly felt her cheeks flame with heat. She was indeed in a state. Her boobs *had* leaked milk—no doubt due to Morgan's cries—she had a smear of what might possibly be poo at the top of her thigh from the earlier explosion, and there was indeed a smelly, sour milk stain, crusting away on her shoulder.

'Oh, God…'

She reached into her handbag for wipes, but she didn't have any. They were all in the nappy bag that she'd left with Daisy down in the crèche. She couldn't work looking like this! She'd have to put some scrubs on. Making her even more late!

The lift doors pinged open and both she and the military man stepped out and turned left towards A&E. Frowning, Brooke looked at him once again, noting his proud bearing, his *march* rather than stride, and the fact that they were both most definitely heading towards the same department.

'Do you work in A&E?' she asked, curious.

Had she embarrassed herself in front of a new work colleague? Staff did come and go frequently. It was a pressured environment—stressful. Some people couldn't hack it. But Brooke could. She loved it there.

'I do.'

'I work there, too.'

He stopped in his tracks immediately and looked at her, this time with a single raised eyebrow. 'This is your first day back after maternity leave?'

How did he know that? Unless her friends had mentioned it to him… 'Yes.'

His eyes widened. '*You're* Dr Bailey?'

She nodded, surprised that he knew her name. 'Yes. Who are *you*?'

He didn't answer right away, and it took him a moment before he held out his hand. 'Major Matt Galloway. Jen's husband.'

She was unaware that her mouth had dropped open. But she numbly reached forward and shook his hand anyway.

She'd meant to call. She'd *meant* to. Only… Life had

got in the way and she'd been struggling to cope herself. Life was harder and busier than she'd suspected it would be with a baby, and she was doing everything alone. Jen's death three days after she'd given birth to Morgan had made her postnatal blues a lot worse and she'd been grieving herself.

Trying to get herself together just to get dressed and out of the house had seemed an insurmountable task—and then there was the fact that she'd never met Jen's husband. She'd thought it might be awkward if she just turned up at their house on the other side of London. So she'd put it off and put it off, and when finally she'd thought that she really ought to go and offer her condolences and help so much time had passed she'd just felt that it wouldn't be right.

It had made her feel incredibly guilty, and now the last person she'd expected to run into at work was Jen's widower.

Had he just dropped off Lily?

She hadn't even been able to make it to Jen's funeral on time. She'd misjudged how long it would take her to get ready and out of the house, and when she'd got there the funeral had already started. She'd slipped into the back of the church and huddled in a pew at the back. Then—naturally—Morgan had begun crying and, not wishing to disturb the service, she'd crept back out. The only thing that would settle her daughter was being pushed in her pram, so she'd gone for a walk.

Returning to the church long after the service had finished she had stood looking down at Jen's grave, tears dripping down her cheeks. Feeling *so* alone.

She'd thought maybe that Jen would have forgiven her for being late. It was the kind of person she'd been. But Matt…? She had no idea how he'd feel. All she knew from Jen was that he was a stickler for rules and regulations.

'Erm…hello.' She managed a smile, aware now that he had seen her at her worst. 'I didn't expect to see you here.'

'I work here.'

He did?

'I've taken up Jen's post. I needed to be working after—' He stopped talking suddenly, his eyes darkening, and looked away.

'I'm so sorry for your loss. I did make it to the funeral. And I tried to stay, but…'

'But your baby started to cry and you took her outside.'

'You noticed?'

He nodded, looking at her strangely. 'I heard.'

'I tried to make it back, but by the time she'd settled you'd all gone.'

'That's okay. I imagine you had your hands full.'

'Well, I'm sure you did, too. How *are* things with the baby? It's Lily, isn't it?'

'Yes. They're difficult. She's teething. Not sleeping very well.'

Morgan had just started teething too, so Brooke knew the misery of that. 'It gets easier, they say. Let's hang on to that.'

He continued to look at her carefully. 'We should show our faces, seeing as we're both late.'

She nodded. 'Yes—yes, you're right. Don't want to anger the boss on the first day.'

'You haven't angered me.'

Brooke blinked. '*You're* my boss?'

'I'm Clinical Lead, yes.'

'Right…'

She wasn't sure what to say to that. The department had obviously gone through some changes she didn't know about. Why hadn't Kelly let her know? She'd mentioned they'd got some new eye candy in charge, but hadn't mentioned who he was. Why not?

'Well, I'm sorry I'm late.'

'Why don't you get changed and meet me in my office in ten minutes? There are a few new protocols you need to be aware of, and then I'll assign you your duties.'

'Sure.' She nodded and smiled as he marched off towards his office.

Her new boss.

Jen's *husband*.

She looked upwards, as if to heaven, and muttered, 'You had to throw me one last curveball, huh?'

She shook her head in disbelief and pictured Jen grinning down at her.

Her first patient was a guy in his forties. When she called his name in the waiting room he stood up, one hand supporting the other. His triage card said *'Query fracture left wrist'*.

Matt had assigned her to Minors. She'd gone to the changing room, got into a pair of dark blue scrubs. When she'd gone to put her own clothes into her locker she'd done a double-take, noticing that Jen's locker was just as she'd left it. No one had cleared it out yet. Seeing it there, with her friend's name still on it, plastered with pictures of Hollywood heartthrobs, had made her heart miss a beat. In a way she was glad that no one had rushed to empty it. It meant that Jen had been valued. Loved.

Brooke had scooped her long brown hair up into a messy bun and set off to see Matt.

He'd looked every inch an army officer, seated behind his desk with his straight back in his neat office, everything perfectly positioned and aligned. He'd clasped his hands on the desk in front of him and run her through the new burns protocols and triage assessments.

Sitting there, looking at him, she'd wondered if the reason he held himself so formally in check was because he might fall apart if he relaxed. He seemed very stiff and distant now he was working—nothing like his relaxed, friendly, affable wife, who'd thought nothing of draping her arms around the shoulders of friends, who'd positively warmed everyone with her wide smile and closeness.

And then he'd said, 'When you've dealt with each of your patients I'd like you to run your results past me before you discharge anyone.'

Run her results past him?

'Why?'

'Because I've asked you to.'

'You don't trust my judgement? I've been a doctor for many years. I know what I'm doing.'

'But I've never worked with you before, and though I'm sure you have a stellar reputation, Dr Bailey, I'd like to make sure that my department is operating at its optimum level.'

So…the sympathetic father persona had disappeared the second he'd clocked on. He was all business, and Brooke had felt slighted that she wasn't being trusted to treat a patient by herself, but would have to check in with Matt.

'Fine— Major.'

She escorted her first patient through to a vacant cubicle and got him to sit down whilst she pulled out a new file. 'So, do you want to tell me what happened?'

'Nothing happened. That's why I can't understand why my wrist hurts so much!'

Brooke frowned. 'Why don't you start at the beginning? When did the pain start?'

'I went to bed last night and my wrist was fine, but in the night I got woken suddenly by this intense pain in it—like lightning, it was. I sat up immediately and rubbed at it, and took some painkillers, but it was ages before I could get back to sleep. When I woke up it still hurt, and I noticed this bruising to the side of it.'

Brooke peered at his wrist. There was some bruising to it—like a dark cloud. Not much, though. 'Have you had a fall recently?'

'Not really. I was crouched down loading the washing machine the other day and I lost my balance slightly, put out my hands to stop myself from falling, but that's all. It wasn't a *fall*, as such.'

She examined his wrist and checked his range of motion. He could bend it and move it around without causing any extra pain. But he said he felt a constant burning sensation in the centre. She touched his fingers, asked if he could feel the sensation, if he had any numbness or tingling. He reported some tingling in his ring and little fingers. Capillary refill was good, and there didn't seem to be any occlusion of the blood vessels.

'I think, Mr Goodman, that you may have carpal tunnel syndrome. The pain waking you in the night is a classic symptom. But I'm going to send you for an X-ray just in case you've got a small fracture in one of the wrist bones, because carpal tunnel wouldn't cause this bruising.'

'Oh, right. Okay…'

'Do you need any more painkillers whilst you wait?'

'No, I can cope.'

She scribbled her findings onto his notes and then filled out a small slip of paper. 'Right, would you like to come with me?'

Brooke walked him to the main corridor and pointed out a red line on the floor.

'Follow that. It'll take you to a new waiting area in Radiology. Hand in the form, they'll take an X-ray or two, and then come back to the main waiting room. I'll call you in when we've got the result.'

'Thank you, Doctor.' Mr Goodman headed off.

Brooke headed over to the doctors' station to transfer her notes to the computer. Her friend Kelly was there too.

'Welcome back! Finally got here, then?'

'Yeah… Hey, why didn't you tell me that our new boss was Jen's husband?'

Kelly smiled. 'Because I knew how guilty you felt about not calling in on him, and I thought that if you knew he was going to be your boss then you would just fret for weeks about starting work and today was going to be hard enough for you! How is Morgan? Did she settle into the crèche okay?'

'She screamed her head off, which caused me to get upset, and that allowed our kind new Major to take great pleasure in letting me know I'd sprung a leak.' She patted her chest and raised an eyebrow at her friend.

Kelly laughed. 'Pads are in now, though, right?'

Brooke smiled. 'Pads are most definitely in. They might be the most unsexy thing a woman ever has to wear, but they don't half make your boobs look good.'

She pushed out her chest to emphasise their impressive size to her friend, unaware that at that moment Matt had come up right behind her.

He cleared his throat and Brooke instantly hunched over and spun in her chair to smile at him, cheeks flaming. 'Hi.'

There was a ghost of a smile on his face. 'How's everything going, Dr Bailey?'

'Erm…yeah…good, I think.'

She could hear Kelly sniggering behind her and made a mental note to kick her under the table later. How many more times would she get to embarrass herself in front of him? So far she'd cried, leaked milk everywhere, worn poo-stained clothes and thrust her breasts out on show like an amateur glamour model. What must he think of her?

'How are things with you?' she asked awkwardly, trying to fill the silence.

He smiled, and she briefly wondered why he didn't do that more often. It transformed his face completely. He was a good-looking guy, but holding that stern, stoic I-am-not-amused pose did nothing for him. But *smiling*? *Genuinely* smiling? He could compete with the best of those heartthrobs stuck on Jen's locker.

'I'm good, thank you.'

'That's great.' She smiled back, wondering what to say, what to do.

Why was this so awkward? She didn't normally have difficulty getting on with colleagues or superiors. Why was talking to him so different?

In her scrubs pocket, her phone trilled. Not wanting to check her phone with him standing there, she continued to grin at him, waiting for him to say or do something.

'Kelly, I'd like a quick word, if I may, when you're free?'

Kelly nodded. 'I'll be five minutes.'

'I'll be in my office.' And Matt turned on a dime and headed off.

Brooke let out a breath she hadn't been aware she was holding. Then she turned to Kelly. 'Wow. Way to go, Brooke. How come he calls you by your first name but calls *me* Dr Bailey?'

Kelly grinned. 'Probably because of my stellar good looks and beauty and because he wants to get in my pants.'

Brooke gaped. *'What?'*

Her friend laughed. 'I'm kidding! We've been working together for weeks now—he knows me more than you. This is your first day. He's just being polite. He hasn't met you properly over a packet of chocolate biscuits and a good mug of tea in the staff room yet.'

'And he has you?'

In her mind she could still see him striding away. Tall. Straight-backed. Determined. A man on a mission. He didn't seem the type to bond over a chocolate biscuit. Not with normal civilians, anyway. She wondered what he was like with his patients. Warm and fuzzy?

I don't think so.

'Absolutely. You don't know the man until you've shared your deep and darkest secrets over a good brew.'

She sighed. 'He doesn't seem the type to do that. He seems quite standoffish to me. At least on duty, anyway.'

'It's hard for him.'

Brooke looked at her friend sharply. 'It's hard for us all.'

'He's stepped into his wife's shoes. Taken her post. And he *knows* that we all knew her, that we all lost her, and most of all I think he's frightened of *you*.'

'Me? Why?'

'You were her best friend. Everyone here knows how close you two got. And when Jen *did* get a call from him, from the deepest darkest jungle that Costa Rica could offer, and got to tell him about her day…she talked about *you*.'

'She did?'

'Of course she did. Jen loved you very much. She

loved us all, but you the most. And he knows that of all the people in the world, you had a special place in his wife's heart. Apart from him, you were the one who comforted her, who gave her a soft place to fall when he could not. Who looked after her as she carried his child.' Kelly smiled. 'You're different to the rest of us mere mortals. He doesn't know how to be with you yet.'

'He doesn't have to be afraid of me. We both loved her.' All the sweet things Kelly had said had caused a lump to appear in her throat.

'He'll call you, Brooke. When he's ready.'

'He's keeping me at a distance on purpose?'

Kelly nodded, then grinned. 'Perhaps he needs to.'

Brooke gave her friend a questioning look. She was being ridiculous! She was no threat to anyone. Never had been, never would be. Men didn't need to worry about her. They never had. Not her father, not Eric, not anyone.

Major Matt Galloway was the least likely man she would want to get too close to. He was abrupt and controlling and…and…

And she'd sworn never to have another man control her ever again. Not after the way Eric had become. That had been bad.

'Do you need to wear make-up?'

'Why have you put on perfume?'

'I really don't think you should wear that *dress.'*

'Cover up more.'

'Were you flirting with that guy?'

She shuddered just thinking about him.

No. Brooke was never going to get involved with another man again. They were too much trouble. Look at Eric! Look at her father! Every man there had ever been in her life had let her down. Walked away when she needed them the most.

It had made her self-sufficient. Taught her that she could stand on her own two feet. Getting pregnant with Morgan and becoming a single mother had taught her that she could do anything, but most of all it had shown her that she didn't need anyone else.

And most definitely—most importantly—she knew that she did not need, or want, the approval or attention of her new boss Major Matt Galloway.

'Well, he has nothing to fear from me. My heart most definitely has a *"Do Not Enter"* sign.'

CHAPTER TWO

'DO YOU BELIEVE in broken hearts, Doc?'

Major Matt Galloway peered at his patient. She was seventy-nine, with fluffy white hair, and sat huddled in her wheelchair, as if life had beaten her down gradually, day after day. Pale, with dark circles under her eyes, she looked as if she needed a damned long sleep.

Yes, he *did* believe you could have a broken heart. Physically, there were lots of ways a heart could fail. But literally…? He saw people give up on life after the death of a loved one—die within days, hours or even minutes of a husband, wife or child. He'd thought it might happen to him once, but his body had stubbornly refused to give up. His logical mind had overpowered his heart and told it to suck it up, because he had a job to do. He had to be a *father*. And his principles had refused to let him leave someone behind who needed him.

'I do,' he said, but he was not keen to discuss his personal feelings with this patient. At work, he liked to remain professional. 'It says here on your chart that you have non-specific chest pain. Your ECG was normal, as was your BP. Why don't you tell me what you're feeling and when it started?'

His patient rubbed at her chest. 'I lost my Alfred three weeks ago. Cancer. After the funeral my chest began to hurt—up here.' She rubbed at a spot just above her sternum. 'It won't go away.'

'And if you had to rate the pain between zero and ten, ten being the worst pain you've ever felt, what would you score it at?'

'A good seven.'

'Does it hurt more when you breathe in? When you take deep breaths?'

'Sometimes. And when I twist in my chair, reach for something, sometimes it can be like someone is stabbing me with a hot pick.'

It sounded skeletal or muscular to Matt. But they'd taken bloods and he wanted to see what they said before he made a diagnosis. 'I'd like to examine you, if I may?'

She smiled at him good-naturedly. 'Normally I wouldn't mind if a good-looking man wanted to see more of me, but would you mind if you got a lady doctor to do it?'

He smiled back, not offended at all. 'I'll just get someone. Give me two minutes.'

He closed the curtain of the cubicle behind him and went looking for a spare doctor. They all looked incredibly busy, hurrying here and there. The only person he could see who was apparently doing nothing, standing by the triage board, checking her mobile phone, was Dr Bailey.

He'd known today was the day. That she would be returning after maternity leave. He'd known that today they would finally get to meet and his stomach had been a jumbled mess in anticipation. He'd heard so much about her—and not just from Jen. Apparently Dr Bailey was a wonderfully warm doctor—kind, caring, well-liked and respected in the department. But Jen had also said that Bailey was the loneliest person she had ever met. It was why she had befriended her. She'd said that this doctor gave so much of herself to others, including her patients, but always seemed somehow to be so alone. Afraid to reach out and depend on others.

He'd not known how to interpret that. Matt had never been alone. Raised in a large family of brothers, he had left them to study medicine, then enlisted. He'd had an army family. A whole platoon! And he'd had Jen, and then the news that there would be a little one coming along.

He'd never been alone until now. Oh, his brothers were always on the phone, and he sometimes heard from old comrades-in-arms, but Jen's death had isolated him. It was as if her death had quarantined him from others. As if he was contagious. There'd been plenty of visitors to bring him food, and to offer to help with Lily, but something was different. He felt tainted. As if people were afraid to get too close to him in case something happened to them too. Or maybe it was a vibe that *he* was giving off, making people feel that they *couldn't* get too close?

Jen had adored Dr Bailey. Loved her. He'd lost count of the amount of times his wife had laughed down the phone saying, 'Oh, you'll never guess what Brooke said today…'

He'd not expected the leaking, poo-stained, crying woman he'd met this morning to be *the* Dr Brooke Bailey. Nor for her to have awoken in him a protective streak when he'd heard her crying at the crèche. He'd empathised with her pain. Remembered how it had felt for *him* to leave Lily with a relative stranger.

The sound of her heartbroken sobs had tugged at his heartstrings and made his gut lurch. And that had been before he'd even known who she actually was! And that brief moment when she'd leaned against him, *into* him, enveloping him in her perfume as he'd guided her out through the crèche door, had made him yearn to wrap his arms around her.

And then he'd remembered she was a *stranger*. Someone he didn't even know. Whom he'd probably never meet again.

Until he'd found out who she was.

Now he would have to work with her, keeping her at a safe distance while knowing that the two of them shared a bond—their love for a woman now gone.

He knew Brooke Bailey had been the most important person in his wife's life—after him and Lily—and he'd been keen to meet this woman whom he'd felt sure would be intelligent, warm and sociable, just like his wife. A *together* person. Someone with whom he could also build a bond. No, he'd definitely not expected the woman he'd met this morning. Emotionally wrought and no doubt sleep-deprived too, if Lily's current behaviour was anything to go by.

'Dr Bailey?'

He saw her guiltily drop her mobile phone back into her scrubs pocket and look up, her cheeks colouring with a most beautiful shade of rose.

'Major! Sorry, I was just checking everything was okay at the crèche.'

He could understand that. The first few days he had left his daughter there he had done the same thing. Lily was the most precious thing in the world to him, and to hand her over to strangers had been difficult. It was easier for him now. He'd been doing it for over a month. Not so Dr Bailey. He had to make allowances.

'And is it?'

She nodded, seeming surprised that he had even asked.

'A patient has requested a female doctor for an examination. Are you free?'

'Yes. I was just looking for you, actually. You wanted me to report in before I discharged my patients.'

He could hear the reluctant tone in her voice but he dismissed it. It wasn't a personal thing he'd done, just because she'd been away from work for a while. He'd asked it of all his staff. He needed to know how the people who were on his team worked.

'Okay. I'll take a look at your findings once we've dealt with Mrs Merchant.'

He led her over to his patient's cubicle and, once inside, explained her symptoms and the results of her tests so far. Then he stepped back. 'I'll step outside.' And closed the curtain behind him, listening as Dr Bailey conducted her examination. He heard her ask to listen to the patient's chest, heard her check the range of movement and finally warning Mrs Merchant that she was about to press on the front of her chest...

'Ow! That hurts!' His patient cried out.

'Here?'

'Yes! Dear Lordy—what do you think is causing *that*?'

Dr Bailey let Mrs Merchant fasten her clothing again and invited Matt back in.

Matt nodded to let her know he'd heard what had happened and to deliver the diagnosis. 'I think you may have costochondritis.'

'What's that when it's at home?'

'It's an inflammation of the cartilage that joins your ribs to your breastbone. It's a very painful condition.'

'I know it is. I can feel it!'

'We'll just check your bloods first, but I think we can safely say we need to get you on some anti-inflammatories. I'll be back in a moment.'

They left Mrs Merchant and headed over to the doctors' station. Dr Bailey handed him her notes from the guy with carpal tunnel syndrome. He'd also got a non-displaced break in his scaphoid, the small bone at the base of his thumb, and she'd given him a splint to wear and prescribed painkillers in case it got worse. Simple enough. Direct, effective, and she hadn't wasted resources on tests that he hadn't needed. Exactly what he'd wanted to see.

'That's excellent. You can discharge him.' He handed back the file, expecting her to walk away from him and get on with her work, but she lingered, as if wanting to ask him something. 'Anything else?'

'Yes…' She looked around her, lowering her voice. 'Jen's locker.'

He straightened, felt his chin lifting. He was defensive because he hadn't got around to sorting it out yet. He'd felt that by doing so he would finally be wiping away the existence of his wife here. Seeing it still there each morning was reassuring. He could almost pretend that she was about to walk in through the door at any moment.

'Yes?'

'If you need someone to help sort it…when you feel ready…I'd like to offer to help.'

Jen's locker.

It was one last tiny island of his wife. Coming back home to the house from Costa Rica had been bad enough. There had been a whole houseful of her possessions to sort through. At first he'd not wanted to get rid of anything, thinking that Lily would want to know all about her mother when she got older. But seeing his wife's clothes draped over radiators and the shower rail in the bathroom had got too much, and he'd conducted a vast cleaning frenzy, taking bags of her stuff to local charity shops but keeping small things like jewellery, the odd knick-knack that Jen had loved, just in case Lily wanted them when she grew up.

Items that were precious—her wedding ring, her engagement ring, a clay pot she'd once tried to make at a pottery class. The pot had gone drastically wrong, and looked as if a four-year-old had tried to make it, but it didn't matter that it was ugly and misshapen. His wife's hands had made it—her fingers had deftly tried to mould the clay—and he'd been unable to throw it out. He knew that one day Lily would hold it in her hands and imagine her mother's fingers in the same places.

There were still photos of Jen at the house. He'd not made a clean sweep and erased her completely. She was still there. Her paint choices on the walls. Her silly magnets on the fridge. Her perfume in the bathroom.

Getting rid of her things had been painful, and when he'd come to work at the London Grace he'd forgotten that she would have a locker here. That was going to be very difficult. Touching the things she'd used and worn every day. Things that were as familiar to her as they would be new to him.

He knew he had to do it. At some point. It had been there too long already and everyone else had been too polite to mention it. Not that Dr Bailey was being impolite. Just concerned. And he understood that. She was right. It was maudlin to think that keeping a dead woman's locker undisturbed somehow kept her alive.

'Yes. I'll…get round to it later today.'

Her mouth dropped open. 'Oh! I didn't mean to force you to do it straight away. I—'

'It's fine. I should have done it a long time ago.'

'I'll help, if you need it.'

'I should be fine doing it myself. Thank you, Dr Bailey.'

He hadn't meant to be so dismissive of her. She was only offering to help him do a task he'd been shirking for too long now. But the tone in his voice had risen because she'd reminded him that he was afraid to tackle it on his own. Worried about what he might find in there. Something uniquely personal, perhaps. Some keepsake that would strike another blow to his heart when it was already so weakened.

She nodded, blushing at his tone, and though he liked the way the soft rosy colour in her cheeks somehow made her eyes sparkle that little bit more, he felt guilty as she walked away with that look of hurt in her eyes.

Had he meant to be so acerbic? Could he not have reined that in? After all, he'd become a master at doing that lately. Putting a tight leash on his emotions. It was easier, after all, to pretend that things didn't hurt. When you were on your own it was easier, anyway.

He briefly wondered who was there for Dr Bailey. Surely she wasn't as alone as his wife had made out? For a start, there had to be a father to her baby. Where was he? Jen had mentioned he was some low-life who had adhered to the adage *Treat them mean, keep them keen*. Though, thank the Lord, Dr Bailey had had enough self-respect to walk away from someone like that!

Matt sucked in a breath. Was he ready to do this? Was he prepared? There could be anything in that locker. Jen had been like a magpie at home, storing away anything that caught her eye, that she thought was cute. He might open the door and have tons of things fall out. She'd never been one for neatly folding stuff and putting it away properly.

Hopefully it wouldn't take too long.

* * *

He didn't know how long he'd been standing there, staring at the locker. It was just a bit of metal. Adorned with all the Hollywood heartthrobs that she'd liked to swoon over and gently tease him about. But it was her name on the door that seemed to be stopping him—*Dr Jennifer Galloway.*

It was like the entry to a forbidden land. A doorway to a world he wasn't ready to face. He kept trying to tell himself that he was being stupid. It was just a locker—it probably just held some clothes, or a pair of shoes and a hairbrush or something, but for some reason his brain and his heart were telling him that this was something he wasn't ready for—getting rid of the last vestiges of his wife at work.

'Can I help?'

He almost jumped at her voice. Turned to see Brooke standing in the doorway, watching him. And, though he'd been abrupt with her the last time they'd spoken, she appeared to be speaking to him with all the gentle patience of a mother to a child. No retribution. No blame. No hurt. Just a genuine desire to help him out.

Matt nodded and beckoned her in. 'I don't know what's stopping me.'

'What stops any of us but the fear of getting hurt?'

He gazed back at the locker. 'I'm a soldier.'

'You're a husband.' She leaned against the lockers and he glanced over at her. 'Being a soldier doesn't stop you from being human. From feeling.'

'I guess both of us have been confronted by things we didn't want to do today.'

She nodded. 'Have you a key?'

He pulled it from his pocket. So small. So insignificant. All he had to do was insert it into the lock.

A heavy sigh escaped him and he closed his eyes, trying to build up the courage to do what had to be done. But he just couldn't bring himself to do it. What if he opened her locker and it held her scent? Flowers and a summer's day? It would hit him like an avalanche, burying him and smothering him, away from all that was light. He wasn't ready. But he wanted to do it. Wanted to get it over with. Maybe if he just…

Fingers enveloped his and he opened his eyes to see Dr Bailey taking the key and inserting it into the lock. She turned it, and they both heard the clank of the metal lever.

Blue eyes peered into his soul. 'Open it.'

He didn't want to think about what he'd felt when her hand had wrapped around his. Didn't want to analyse the fact that his heart had begun to gallop, his pulse had soared and his mouth had gone as dry as centuries-old dust.

Instead, he stared at the locker. Hoping. Praying. And with an unsteady hand he reached forward to pull it open.

A pair of wind-up false teeth was the first thing that caught his eye and it made him laugh. *Relief!* He picked it up, turning it in his hands, looking at Dr Bailey in question.

'She used it sometimes with children.'

She smiled as she took it from him and he could see plainly on her face that she was reliving a memory. A memory of his wife that he didn't have.

He reached into the locker and pulled out a change of clothes—a tie-dye tee shirt and a pair of jeans. Beyond them were a couple of books that were extremely late going back to the library, a couple of pens, some soft-soled flat shoes and a notebook that said *Trust Me, I'm A Doctor*. And there, at the back, where only she would see it when she opened her locker for each shift to get ready, a picture of them both on their wedding day.

Gently, he released it from the tape holding it in place and looked at it.

'Your wedding day. How long ago did you get married?'

He glanced at Dr Bailey. 'Five short years ago.'

'You both look very happy.'

'We were.' It hurt to look at the picture, but not as much as it once had. He'd learned to accept it. Absorb it. Grief wasn't something you got over. Like an obstacle. It was something that you accepted, knowing it would stay with you for the rest of your days.

'I wish I'd known her for longer. You're lucky that way.'

He gazed intently at her and nodded, before putting the picture with the rest of the things. 'It's no use either of us living in the past. We've both got difficult futures ahead.'

'Being single parents, you mean? I think it's easier now than it was twenty years ago. At least it's accepted.'

He nodded. 'Who do you have helping you?'

She shook her head. 'No one. Not really.'

'There must be someone. Family?'

'I'm an only child. My mother died when I was very little and my dad… Well, he's never been the reliable sort. We talk on the phone. When he remembers.'

He could tell there was something she wasn't saying. Whatever it was, it was obviously hurtful.

'Any friends?'

'Jen was my friend. The only person who got close. So it's pretty much me and Morgan right now.'

'It's difficult, isn't it? Being alone.'

And then he realised he'd let his guard drop and he stiffened slightly, busying himself with Jen's things, lay-

ing them in the box he'd brought from his office, neatly
and in order.

He was surprised. He'd thought there'd be more. All
this time he'd spent fearing this job, and now that he'd
done it he realised there had been nothing to worry about.
He let out a breath and then he closed his wife's locker
reverently, slid her name tag from the front of it and
slowly started to remove her Hollywood heroes.

What to do with *them*? Throw them into the bin?

'I'll take them.'

Dr Bailey closed her hand around his and, surprised
again by how her brief touch made him feel, he released
the pictures and stared hard at her as she opened her
own locker and put them inside. It had been the weirdest thing. Not lightning, not fireworks. More a gentle
warmth. And he'd felt…*soothed.* As if a balm had been
applied to his soul.

'Thank you. For doing this with me.'

She turned to face him and smiled. 'It was my pleasure.'

No, he thought. *It was mine.*

By the end of the day Matt had already decided that Dr
Brooke Bailey was a very good member of his team. She
worked at a steady pace, and she didn't order extraneous
tests that would upset the department's budget. She got
on well with everyone, seemed very popular, and though
she might chat a little too much with her patients, rather
than discharge them quickly, he didn't think he had too
much to complain about.

Before she'd come back he'd heard from everyone that
she was a good doctor, but Matt lived by the axiom that
he'd make up his own mind about people. He took them
as *he* found them, and so far he liked what he'd found in

Dr Bailey. Now the drama of the morning crèche drop-off was long gone he could see the woman and the professional that his wife had become friends with.

As he headed towards the lift, so that he could get his daughter from the crèche, he saw that she was standing waiting for it to arrive, too. They'd spoken on numerous occasions throughout the day since emptying Jen's locker, and already he could sense that a tentative friendship was beginning.

'Enjoy your first day?'

She smiled at him. 'I did! Even though I was fretting about Morgan for most of it, it was nice to use my brain again and interact with adults. I think the most taxing thought I've had over the last few months has been whenever I've had to change a nappy, seen the contents and wondered, *What colour is that?*'

He smiled, having gone through the poo initiation tests that all babies presented to their parents. A sticky black tar to start, which looked like something that ought to be in a horror movie, oozing from a monster, then a khaki green that would hide any soldier in a jungle, and now they were into a kind of peanut butter effect. It had been an interesting journey, and one quite different from the Bristol Stool Chart that all doctors knew so well.

The lift doors pinged open and they both got inside.

'At least I didn't have to examine any grown-up's stools today.'

Matt smiled to himself. Life as an A&E doctor did have that unknown element to it. You never knew what kind of case was going to walk through those doors, from something as simple as a splinter in the finger right through to a dramatic cardiac arrest. That was why he liked it. There was so much variety.

It had been the same in the army. One minute he might

be dealing with a gunshot wound, the next dealing with an ingrowing toenail.

But he liked the adrenaline of working in A&E. The cases that needed to be worked on fast and efficiently, with each member of the team knowing their job, all of them working as a finely tuned machine to save someone's life. There was nothing quite like it.

'All jobs have their perks. Who knows? Perhaps tomorrow you might get your chance?'

She laughed, and the sound did strange things to his insides.

'I hope not!'

He glanced at her briefly, curious as to why this woman, above all others, somehow seemed to make him feel…*what?* Uneasy? No, that was wrong. It wasn't a *bad* feeling as such, it was…an awareness. Like the feeling you might get before a static storm. The air pregnant with expectation, holding a heat to it, a humidity.

Was it because of her connection to Jen? Was it simply because he'd been waiting for her return to work so that he could meet this woman his wife had loved?

That's it. It's because I know she was special to Jen.

He'd wanted to see just what it was about the enigmatic Dr Bailey that had made her so appealing to his wife. He could see that she liked to laugh, liked to enjoy herself and to make close connections with her patients. She liked others to feel listened to and cared for. But there was also a quiet assuredness about her. A silent strength that she didn't seem aware she had. It was her solitude, perhaps, that did that. That shielded her from her own possibilities.

'I'm sorry you caught me using my phone today. I don't normally. Not at work. In fact I don't normally carry my phone with me. But with it being Morgan's first day...'

He waved away her concerns with a swift movement of his hand, staring at the lift display, watching as they ascended to the floor they needed. 'It's fine. We all worry about our children—especially when we're new parents.'

She nodded. 'Thank you. I appreciate that. I really do.'

She was looking up at him, trying to convey her sincerity in her eyes. But it was hard for him to stand there, that close to her, and maintain eye contact, so he looked away. She had very pretty eyes. Bright and friendly. Welcoming. Open. Innocent.

He cleared his throat. 'It's not a problem.'

Was the lift much smaller today? There seemed to be less air. The walls seemed to be pressing them towards each other.

To his relief, the doors pinged open again and he walked behind her towards the crèche, feeling somewhat awkward. He wasn't sure what had caused it, or why thirty seconds in a lift with Dr Bailey had changed things when a whole ten hours with her in the same department had not.

So he walked slightly behind her, allowing her to go first and press the buzzer for the crèche.

Daisy let them in, beaming her ever-present smile at both of them, all white gleaming teeth and bright eyes, showing no signs of fatigue after spending an entire day with thirty-odd children under the age of five.

Matt wasn't sure he'd look as calm and collected as Daisy did if *he'd* spent that long with that many children. He loved kids, he really did, but he was finding it hard looking after even one baby on his own. There was no one to share the workload or the worries with and he missed that.

In the army there'd always been someone to talk to—colleagues, friends and, on the occasions when he had come home, there'd always been Jen. Now his home was conspicuously quiet.

'Lily's been an absolute treasure today! She did a handprint painting for you!'

Daisy unpegged a messy picture that was hanging from a string above their heads, like washing on a line. He looked at it, barely able to ascertain his daughter's handprint in the smudge of red, purple and brown. But her name *'Lily Galloway'* had been written in pencil at the bottom.

'Her first work of art…' He wasn't sure whether to act pleased or show that to him it was just a mash-up of paint on a page.

'Watch out, Michelangelo.'

Dr Bailey smiled at him, mildly amused.

'There's one for you, too, Dr Bailey.' Daisy unpegged another picture, this one in yellow and orange, and passed it over.

They both stood there awkwardly, trying to work out whether the pictures were upside down or not.

'I'll get Lily for you.'

'Thanks.' He collected Lily's buggy from the bay and folded his daughter's painting into the basket underneath.

Daisy came out of the Baby Room, carrying his daughter, who looked as if she'd just woken up, her blonde hair all mussed up and wafting around her head like a furry halo.

'Hello, Lily!' He reached out for her and, as always, was happy to see her reach for him, too. 'Hello, my darling, how are you today?' He kissed her on the cheek, inhaling that sweet baby scent and enjoying the soft squishiness of her little body against his.

Lily laid her head against his chest.

'Wow! She looks just like her mum. She's beautiful.'

He looked at Dr Bailey over his daughter's head, hearing the wistfulness in his colleague's voice. 'Thank you.'

'I mean it. She really does.'

Matt knew she was being sincere, but there was something else there, too. Loss. Grief. It reminded him that he wasn't the only one who had lost someone special. She had too. Her best friend.

As Daisy brought out Dr Bailey's daughter, he was struck by the similarity between the two. Morgan also had a thick head of brown hair that was slightly curling and wispy around her shoulders, and they both had the same eyes. Morgan peered at him, as if uncertain of this tall stranger who stood next to her mother.

He stooped over to put Lily into her buggy and then stood up again. 'Well, I'll see you in the morning. Goodnight, Dr Bailey.'

'Goodnight, Major.'

She smiled back and it so disarmed him, hitting him like a sucker punch to the gut, that he turned quickly and hurried away.

Five months.

It had been only five months since his wife had died. The wife he had loved and adored and had expected to be with right into old age. And yet he was already noticing another woman.

It's just loneliness. That's what it is. Missing someone to talk to, that's all. I don't have to read anything else into it.

He kept his head down as he headed back to his car. Trying to remain focused on his daughter's chubby little legs in white tights, the cute pink trainers his mother had bought for her. He tried to think about what his daughter had done that day, the painting she had done, the way she'd reached for him earlier. He was all Lily had now. She'd never known the love of a mother. Nor would she. He would have to provide everything for her. Be both parents, if he could. Provide the dreams for both of them.

Briefly, he cast his mind back in time to the day he and Jen had discussed moving to New Zealand. How amazing it would be. What a brilliant life it would provide for their future children. Jen had been in the back garden, swinging in the hammock, six months pregnant and eating an ice cream.

'I'd really like to go back there, Matt. My gap year there was the most amazing time in the world. The people were great—really friendly—and there'd be no problem with either of us getting work out there. There's a great little suburb in North Shore City, Auckland, that's perfect for kids. We should do it. Really consider it, I mean.'

At the time, he'd been busy planting some fruit trees in the back garden and Jen had been supervising.

'Move that one to the left a bit. Bit more. Bit more. That's it!'

He'd been home on a week's leave before he'd had to ship out to Costa Rica, and it had been one of the last times he'd seen her alive. He'd only been meant to be out there for ten weeks. He'd thought—they'd *both* thought—he would be home in time for the birth. But after he'd left, Jen had begun having problems with her blood pressure and they'd had to induce her early.

It had still been too late. Jen had had a massive fit from which she hadn't recovered. They'd put her on life support until he could get back from South America and then, holding his baby daughter in his arms, he had watched through a veil of tears as they had switched off the machines.

Just five months ago.

He'd had to adapt quickly, and he'd been thankful he had Lily to look after. His daughter had saved him from falling into a deep depression. She'd anchored him in the present when he'd been in danger of drowning in the past. He'd not had time to dwell on his loss the way he would have if she hadn't been around.

So, instead of never getting out of bed and living in the depths of despair under his duvet, he'd got out of bed. Got dressed. Taken his daughter out in her pram and walked. Sometimes for miles. Strangers had stopped him to admire his daughter, keeping his spirits lifted. They'd had no idea of the tragedy that had recently befallen him. They'd just seen a father out with his child. A beautiful baby girl. They'd wanted to admire her and cup her rosy cheeks and tell him how gorgeous she was, and each comment, each person, had unwittingly given him a reason to keep going.

'You're doing a good job.'

'Lily's okay.'

'She's thriving with just you.'

Jen would not have wanted him to wallow. That wasn't who she had been. She'd been a grab-hold-of-life person. A person who'd squeezed enjoyment into every second— as much as she could. And she'd told him once that when she died she didn't want a funeral full of people in black clothes, sobbing quietly into tissues. She'd wanted a celebration of her life.

Only that celebration had come too soon.

And now he was noticing another woman.

Guilt was a horrible sensation. He'd never really suffered from it before. Not like this. And, logically, he knew he shouldn't really feel guilty. Jen would have been *happy* that he was getting to know her new best friend.

And it wasn't as if he were cheating on his wife. No. He might no longer be married, but he was determined that Dr Bailey was just going to be his friend, the way she had been Jen's.

He stopped for moment and looked down at his wedding band. He hadn't removed it. It had never felt right. Its presence had somehow given him an extra layer of… protection.

But from what?

He decided he would wait to get home and then think about it some more. Right now he had to concentrate on his daughter. She was what was important.

But as he drove them home, as he sat waiting at traffic lights, humming to the music playing on the radio, his mind kept teasing him with glimpses of the beautiful and enigmatic Dr Brooke Bailey.

CHAPTER THREE

OVER THE NEXT week Brooke settled into a nice routine. She only had to work day shifts whilst Morgan was so little, and so each day she would drop her daughter off at the crèche, work ten hours, pick Morgan up, go home, get something to eat and then attempt to shoehorn Morgan into a night-time routine of bath, bottle, story and sleep.

It didn't always work.

Morgan seemed determined not to stick to anything as pre-planned as that. She was her own woman. Already! Sometimes she just wanted her mum to hold her and never put her down. Sometimes she wanted to be rocked. Other times she wanted to lie under her baby gym and bat at her toys, babbling away until the early hours of the morning. None of which helped Brooke get much sleep.

Morgan had no set sleep pattern that she could decipher, which meant that neither did her mother, and Brooke was beginning to notice on her drive into work that she was getting less and less accepting of delays and idiots on the road. Her temper was quick, her fuse almost non-existent. Thankfully at work her love for her job was somehow able to put her bad mood to one side. At least until the commute home again.

Then back at home her love for her daughter and her desire to spend quality time with her, after having left her at the crèche all day, ensured that she forgot about doing things for herself and instead concentrated on just being with Morgan, no matter how it happened. If it meant reading baby board books over and over again—fine. If it meant rocking her daughter in her arms all night—excellent. No problem.

She would do what her daughter needed because she was all Morgan had in this world. Morgan's dad, Eric, was not interested in her—thankfully—and Morgan's grandfather, Brooke's dad, was worse than useless and could not be depended upon. He'd met Morgan only once. In the hospital. He had not seen her since.

Brooke was used to such desertions. It didn't hurt her any more. Or at least she could pretend that it didn't. She just had to hope that when Morgan got older she didn't feel that she'd missed out on a grandfather. Or a dad.

Walking into work today, Brooke was mightily pleased with herself for not having to get changed into scrubs. She could wear her own clothes, having made it through breakfast without getting any baby food on her garments. It was a landmark day! Hopefully, she thought, the first of many.

So she was humming a little tune to herself as she picked up her next chart and headed to the waiting room to call in her next patient.

'Charlie Alcott?'

A young man stood up and made his way over to her.

'Hello, Charlie, I'm Dr Bailey. Follow me and I'll take you through.'

She led the way, still hearing a happy tune in her head, still feeling as if her whole body was smiling. It was good to be back at work and she was in her groove. As much as she adored and loved her daughter, she was happy to claim back her own body and use her brain to help people.

She closed the curtain behind Charlie and asked him to take a seat. 'So, what can I do for you today?'

'I think I've got Addison's disease.'

She frowned. Okay... This sounded more as if it ought to be something a GP dealt with, but who knew? You got all sorts of people coming into A&E, thinking it meant *Anything and Everything* rather than *Accident and Emergency*.

'Why do you think that?'

'I don't handle stress very well and I keep passing out. I looked online and a few websites mentioned Addison's, and as that can sometimes be fatal I thought I ought to come in and be checked immediately.'

Addison's disease was actually quite a rare condition of the adrenal glands that produced cortisol, the stress hormone, and aldosterone. It could affect anyone, but mainly affected women between the ages of thirty and fifty. Charlie was obviously male, and it said on his chart that he'd just turned twenty.

'You say you keep passing out?'

'Yeah. If I stand up too quick I get that head rush thing and dizziness and I have to sit back down again.'

She nodded. 'Okay. Well, first of all I usually advise people not to try and diagnose themselves over the internet. The online world is full of dramatic diseases and bad luck tales, and it doesn't have that real world advantage of examining a patient in person. Because everyone is different, Charlie—you know that, right?'

He nodded.

'Getting that head rush on standing might just mean you have low blood pressure, so let's check that first of all.'

She grabbed the BP cuff that was standard issue in each cubicle and wrapped it around Charlie's arm.

'Right—stay nice and still for me.' She inflated it and took his reading. It seemed normal. So was his heart-rate. 'I'm going to ask you to stand up and I'm going to check your BP and heart-rate again, okay?'

'Okay.'

'And stand.' When he stood, she inflated the cuff and watched him carefully. He grimaced slightly and went a little pale. 'Stay standing for me, if you can, I know it feels weird, but I'm here to catch you—don't worry.'

Charlie stood through it and she noticed on the machine that her patient's BP lowered only slightly, but his heart-rate soared.

She guided him back down into the chair. 'Do you experience any other symptoms?'

He thought for a moment. 'I've always been like this, I think. Sometimes I get palpitations. Like I can feel my heart missing a beat? And sometimes I feel sick and shaky when it happens.'

Brooke nodded, writing down his experiences. She was beginning to suspect something—but it wasn't Addison's and it wasn't something that usually showed in men. However, the one rule she could remember her first ever professor stating at university was: *Keep an open mind. There will always be someone who breaks the mould.*

She'd definitely begun to suspect that this was the situation here, but Charlie would need further tests to prove her theory of PoTS—postural tachycardia syndrome.

It was caused by an abnormal increase in heart-rate whenever the affected person stood up after sitting or lying down, and it mostly showed in Charlie's symptoms. His heart-rate had increased by just over thirty beats when he'd stood up, but that wasn't enough for a diagnosis. He needed an ECG and a tilt table test to confirm it properly. And they couldn't do that here in A&E.

'Okay, Charlie, I'm going to take some bloods from you to check your kidney, liver and thyroid function. And I want to check your blood count, calcium and glucose levels. I'm also going to perform an ECG, which will take a tracing of your heart.'

'There's something wrong with my *heart*?'

'From my initial investigation it seems unlikely, but we need to run some further tests to rule out other conditions. I think you have something called postural tachycardia syndrome, and I'm going to write to your GP and recommend that he refers you for a tilt test, which we can't do here. The ECG and the blood results will be through by then, to help with a diagnosis.'

'Is it dangerous?'

'Well, postural tachycardia syndrome isn't fatal, but sufferers are at risk of hurting themselves by falling or passing out. Whilst you're waiting for your appointment to come through be very careful getting up. Do it gradually, and if you feel faint try to sit or lie down and raise your legs. Drink plenty of fluids, keep active, but pace yourself. Don't overdo it and try to avoid long periods of standing. What do you do for a job?'

'I work in a call centre.'

'Okay—good. Try and stay away from too much caffeine, if you can. I'm going to write to your doctor now and see if we can get this sorted for you.'

'Thanks.'

He looked a little more relieved now that he'd talked over his worries. She was sure that he would be okay, but if he did have PoTS then they would need to rule out any other underlying conditions, such as diabetes or lupus, as soon as possible.

She drew some blood and stuck a small round plas-

ter in the crook of his elbow, and then went to find Matt
to report in.

It had niggled at first, when she'd found she had to
report in to Matt. Initially she'd thought he was doubt-
ing her abilities. But she'd found out that he'd checked
everyone's work and approved their tests during the first
week he'd started in the department. Apparently she'd
missed his starting speech to the staff about wanting to
ensure an *'efficient and highly capable department'*, but
she could appreciate that.

Now her first week was nearly over and this would
be the last day she checked in with him after each case.

I think I'll miss it.

The thought made her feel slightly perturbed.

After her initial annoyance, she'd grown to enjoy dis-
cussing her cases with Major Matt Galloway. He was
always pleased to see her, always listened intently, and
always gave great suggestions for further treatment if
she found herself torn between the right way forward.
He always told her she was doing a great job and when
she'd made a great catch.

Was it the feedback? Was it getting approval? She'd
never had that before, from anyone who mattered, and
receiving it felt strange. Oddly unsettling, but immensely
gratifying. She'd miss not going to him for advice. Miss
checking in with him all day long.

He was a nice guy, and she could see why Jen had
married him.

She'd struggled at first to match the severe, law-abid-
ing soldier husband to her fun-loving, spontaneous friend.
The couple seemed chalk and cheese. But as the days had
passed Matt had become more familiar to her, and she
to him. His guard had come down somewhat and he'd
smiled more, laughed more.

He'd even stood chatting to her one day in the staff room, over a mug of tea and a chocolate biscuit, and it had been just as Kelly had said. He was different when you got to know him and saw past his rules and regulations and the army officer bearing that he used as a shield.

He still wasn't calling her Brooke, though. It was always Dr Bailey and she, in turn, always called him Major. It had become a game. A tennis match. He would serve and she would volley.

She found him labelling a vial of blood and waited for him to finish before presenting her case, running through Charlie's symptoms, her diagnosis and referral.

'I agree, Dr Bailey. I imagine he'll also need an echocardiogram at some point, but we'll leave that to his specialist. That's excellent. I think I can happily sign you off now.'

He looked up at her and smiled and it totally disarmed her.

'Sign me off?'

'You don't need to check in with me any more. I feel totally assured that your practice as a doctor is just the type I need in this department. I trust you completely. You should be happy about that.'

'I am. It's just…' She floundered for words. Her brain had gone blank.

Why was she having such a hard time with this? She'd only been doing it for a week, and she hadn't liked it at the beginning, but that had been before she'd realised just how much she would get out of it. She didn't want to let that go. Realising how needy that made her feel, she frowned, angry at herself.

I am not a needy person!

She had promised herself, when she'd made the decision to carry on with her pregnancy and be a single mother, that she would do so with determination, authority and a belief in herself that she could do anything alone. Wasn't that what she had always done anyway? She was used to standing alone. Surviving without someone else's input. So why should a week of running to Matt have made her feel this way?

Brooke didn't like it. And all of those emotions must be running across her face, because suddenly Matt was standing up and had laid a concerned hand upon her upper arm.

'Are you okay?'

She snapped her head up, determined and bright. 'Of course. Why wouldn't I be?'

He looked at her carefully. As if he were assessing her. As he would a patient.

'I don't know.'

'I know I'm capable. I trust my own practice, I know what I'm doing and even though I've been away for seven months or so it doesn't mean that I lack any confidence in my own abilities!'

She was flustered. She could hear it in her own voice. That and a small note of hysteria. What the *hell* was happening to her? Was it still the effect of all those hormones that she'd had to suffer after she'd had her baby? The bloody things could linger for an age…torturing women with doubts and uncertainties.

You're not being a good enough mother…you don't know what you're doing!

And Matt…? Matt had been drip-feeding lovely words of encouragement into her empty soul and like a dry sponge she had sucked up every droplet of its goodness. Unaware that she had needed it so badly. It was like when she'd been at school, finishing her work before everyone else and taking it up to teacher to be marked and receiving words of praise and a gold star sticker. It had made her beam inside.

Matt frowned and made her sit in his chair. Then he knelt down in front of her, those eyes of his diving into her soul and having a good old rummage around.

Afraid of what he might see if she let him in, she pulled back.

'Go back to your patient. Discharge him.'

He glanced at his wristwatch. He was one of the few people she knew who still wore one.

'It's nearly eleven. We're owed a break. Find me and we'll go for a coffee. In the cafeteria,' he added, which was a special treat, instead of them hunkering down in the staff room.

The cafeteria at the London Grace had an excellent range of refreshments—including home-made cakes that were made on site and were full of calorie-laden deliciousness.

'Oh, I don't think we need to—'

He put his hands on both arms of the swivel chair. 'I insist.'

His voice had softened and that drop in tone went straight to her heart. He was not going to let her get away from this. Perhaps he knew something. That she needed this break?

Brooke stood up abruptly, breaking the prison of his arms, and went to discharge Charlie. She forced herself to focus, giving Charlie the best advice she could to keep himself safe until he got to see a specialist. Then she found herself walking back through the department as if on numb autopilot.

How had things changed so quickly? One moment she'd been humming tunes, sure of herself, and yet suddenly she was feeling lost at sea. Cast away on an ocean with no sign of land.

I'm exhausted!

Tiredness. That had to be it. She'd been so determined to come back to work and blaze a trail, making sure that everyone had missed her, needed her back with them. But Morgan's lack of any need for sleep had caused *her* to lose too many hours too, and she'd been running on optimistic adrenaline.

When had she last cooked herself a proper meal? She'd been going home and just grabbing whatever was in the fridge—usually a sandwich, or something on toast. Something quick that she could eat cold if Morgan demanded her attention.

It was impossible to work the way she'd been doing on hardly any sleep and without enough proper, nutritious food. Add to that the fact that she was breastfeeding, and she was totally drained. Seeing Matt throughout the day had kept her tank topped up. Had allowed her to keep going from one patient to the next because she'd known she would get to see him again. She'd become dependent upon him like…

Brooke swallowed hard and raised her chin. Perhaps she was like someone that she knew. And the idea of that sickened her—because she'd thought she was nothing like *him*.

Across the department, Matt caught her eye and beckoned with a tilt of his head. Pulled towards him like a magnet, she walked over to him and they headed out of the department to the cafeteria. Matt guided her to a table and told her to sit down, then went over to the self-service counter and came back with two cups of strong-smelling coffee, a bowl of fruit salad and a large apple turnover.

'Thanks.'

'They're both for you.'

'Both?'

'You look like you need it. When did you last eat?'

She searched her brain for any memory of a meal and vaguely remembered grabbing a yoghurt when she'd got home last night. 'A while ago.'

'You're breastfeeding, Dr Bailey. Keep going at this rate and you'll either make yourself unwell or run out of milk. Which would you prefer?'

She felt her cheeks colour at him asking her such a personal question, but then she remembered that first day when she'd leaked milk all over her new blouse. 'Neither.'

'I thought not. You've had that running-on-empty look for a while.'

Embarrassed that she hadn't been giving her all in looking after herself, or as a doctor, realising she really ought to know better, she shook her head. She'd kept herself going on fluids. 'I keep trying to be everything to everyone. My patients. Morgan. I guess I forget about myself sometimes.'

'Sometimes?' He poured milk and put two sugars into her coffee. 'For energy.' He smiled. 'It's hard trying to be both parents—I know how you feel.'

Of course he did. But *he* wasn't the one falling apart in the hospital cafeteria, was he? She pulled the cling film off the top of the fruit salad and forked a strawberry into her mouth. It tasted great, bursting with juice, flavour and sweetness. She hardly had to chew at all, and the next thing she knew she was spearing a piece of melon.

'I bet you make yourself a three-course meal every night, huh, Major?'

He smiled back at her and pinched a piece of kiwi fruit. 'Restaurant standard. I even do *petit fours* with my coffee afterwards.'

She looked at him with raised eyebrows, totally impressed, and then when he started to laugh realised he was joking. She took back the piece of kiwi fruit and popped it into her mouth. 'You don't need it, apparently.'

Matt smiled warmly at her, then glanced down and stirred his own coffee. 'Jen mentioned that you were on your own… You can tell me to mind my own business, but do you want to tell me what happened?'

She broke a piece of pastry off the turnover and ate it before speaking. 'Eric was…' She paused to think of the right expression. 'A learning experience.'

He nodded. 'What did he do for a living?'

'He was an actor—in more ways than one. We met at an after-show party. He'd just finished a run at the theatre, playing the part of the Bard, and I'd won VIP tickets to go backstage and meet the cast and crew. Theatre isn't really my thing—not unless it's got scalpels in it and an anaesthetist—but I went anyway and I met Eric. He was charming, handsome…a bit insecure but he hid it well. At first.'

'What happened?'

'He asked me out, I said yes, and we started dating. I thought he was great. Really nice, listened well, asked a lot of questions, seemed interested in me… But really he was gathering information…to make the best attack possible.'

Matt's brows furrowed. 'How do you mean?'

'It was nothing physical. It was mental. He started going out on his own, saying he was with friends when I suspected otherwise. And because I had no proof he made me feel like a crazy woman for even considering it. But then the comments started—questions that made me second-guess myself. Was I really going to wear that dress when it didn't suit me? Was I really not going to take any of the blame for the fact that he'd lost out on an audition? Was I really going to go out with friends from work when I should be spending time with him? He slowly and methodically tried to close me off from everyone I knew, and when he realised I wasn't going to put up with it he turned toxic. Getting hold of me at work to call me horrible names—that sort of thing. So I broke it off. Something I should have done earlier, but he'd made me doubt myself for a while—made me think that *I* was the one being unreasonable, that I didn't have the strength to leave him. He was wrong.'

'How did he react to you ending it?'

'Well, let's just say he has an amazing capability with swear words and derogatory terms.'

'I see.' Matt looked down at his coffee and took a small sip.

'He'd tried to make out he was a gentleman, but he couldn't carry off that role. Not full-time, anyway. I was glad to be out of it.'

'And when did you discover you were pregnant?'

'A couple of months afterwards. Usual thing—working so hard I wasn't paying attention to the calendar. It was only when I was educating a young girl about her own cycle that I realised the date and I just *knew*.' She munched on a piece of apple. 'Jen told me to forget him, and took me out on the town to show me that there was still fun in life.'

He smiled at the image. 'I can imagine her doing that.'

'She was great. She lifted my spirits. And when she discovered she was pregnant, too…' She laughed as she recalled it. 'She came over to me, bumped her belly against mine and said, *"The race is on!"*'

Matt carefully sipped at his coffee.

'I told Eric about the baby. He might not have deserved

it, but I thought he still had the right to know. Just because he was an awful boyfriend, it didn't mean he would be an awful father.'

'Is he?'

'A rubbish father? Yes!' She laughed again, wondering why she was laughing about it. Because was it truly funny? That Morgan didn't have a dad?

She'd never wanted the children she had to want for anything. She'd dreamed of having the perfect family. Two parents for her children. Children loved and adored from both sides. Enveloped in love and acceptance no matter what.

The smile died on her face. 'He didn't want to know. Said it was my *"mess"* to clear up. That he was with someone else now—as if I might want him back. I soon put him right on that score.'

'I'm glad you did.'

'I was so scared. About doing it alone. I wasn't sure whether I could continue on with the pregnancy.'

She felt awful about that now. Even admitting it was hard.

'I didn't know if I'd know what to do. I can't remember my own mother, what she was like and so I told myself it wasn't the right time to have a baby. I wasn't in a good situation, being on my own, and I had a demanding job, with long hours away. I didn't think I'd be able to do it—not without family to help. But...' She smiled again, lost in the past. 'I couldn't bear the idea of just ending the pregnancy. Jen convinced me I could do it alone. Told me that she would be there for me and that we'd raise our babies together.'

She tried to ignore the lump in her throat as she spoke. Jen had been unable to keep that promise, and Brooke had been so low when that call had come and she'd realised she would be on her own.

'You really have no family?'

She shook her head, determined not to let herself cry. 'As I said before, I have a father. Not that you'd know it.'

'He's not local?'

'Oh, he's local. He lives in Wandsworth. But he's not *present*. All my life my father has had an issue with alcohol—always looking for his next drink, thinking of nothing and no one else.'

'Addiction is hard.'

'You're telling me.'

She thought of how addicted *she* had become to seeing Matt after each patient. She hadn't been knocking back vodka at every opportunity, but she had become very quickly addicted to that uplifting note in her day. To that brief conversation in which she had been made to feel lifted. Better. Her cares gone away. Strangely soothed... her edges softened.

Just like an addict.

'The last time he saw Morgan she was hours old. Then he went out and got drunk to toast her arrival. Wet the baby's head.'

Matt reached across the table to lay his hand over hers. Then his features changed suddenly and he withdrew it again.

She was surprised, then reassured. The warmth and weight of his hand had been a reassuring presence that she'd needed. Needed. There was that word again. How quickly addiction could establish itself...

But why was she addicted to *him*? This was Jen's husband. He belonged to her dead friend. Was that it? Because he represented that friendship and the affection that she had lost? Was she trying to find it in him? Surely it had nothing to do with his dirty blond hair, his clear blue eyes and stubbled jaw. It couldn't have anything to do with the fact that he oozed masculinity from every pore whilst at the same time being kind, empathetic and respectful?

A gentleman.

Matt was everything Eric wasn't.

He cleared his throat. 'I was working on a patient who'd dislocated his knee when they told me that the General wanted to see me.'

She focused on his voice. The look in his eyes. Faraway and sad.

'I didn't think it was anything to worry about. I popped the knee into place and strapped up the leg before I headed over to his office. He told me to sit down, and the look on his face changed to one of such discomfort I honestly wondered if he was about to ask me to examine him privately.'

The ghost of a smile made its presence felt in the corners of her mouth as she imagined it.

'He told me that there'd been a telephone call from the Maternity Suite at the London Grace, and just for a brief second my heart soared at the thought that I'd become a father. That my wife had gone into labour early and already had Lily. But the General looked so sorry for me that I can remember my heart thudding in my chest as I waited for him to tell me that they were both okay.'

Matt stiffened in the cafeteria chair.

'He said that Lily was in the NICU. That it had been an emergency delivery and that Jen had not recovered from complications surrounding the birth. They'd put her on life support and I was to fly back to England immediately.'

He shook his head, as if he still couldn't believe the memory even now. After all this time.

'My brain couldn't compute that. All I could think of was the guy I'd just strapped up and sent on his way. The fact that I had other patients awaiting my attention, you know? It was as if to protect itself my brain had switched off from what the General had said.'

'It happens.'

'I got on the plane home in a daze. Looking at all of these people around me, busy with their lives—couples, families... And yet there I was, travelling back to switch off a machine that would end my own.'

Brooke saw his eyes darken as he recalled this painful memory, empathising with his grief, having felt the loss of Jen, too. Strange how grief could rip some people asunder but unite others. It was a powerful force. It did strange things. Caused people to behave oddly. Out of character.

'I can't imagine the strength you must have needed to find inside.'

He looked at her. 'None of us know the strengths we have until we're tested.'

He was absolutely right. Brooke felt that she'd spent her life digging deep for unknown lodes of strength.

'And none of us know the battles that others have faced or still face.' He leant forward again. 'There are lots of soldiers who come back home and look whole, but are broken inside.'

'You must know a lot of people like that?'

Matt nodded. 'Unfortunately. But we're here to talk about *you*. I don't want you pushing yourself to exhaustion, Dr Bailey. I value you as a doctor too much to lose you.'

He valued her.

As a *doctor*.

He hadn't said he valued her as a friend.

But she'd take it anyway. It had been a long time since anyone had valued her at all, and he was right. Perhaps she *had* been pushing the envelope a bit too much. If she didn't start looking after herself better then she wouldn't be able to help her patients or Morgan at all.

'Message received loud and clear, Major.'

He stood up and eased his way out from behind the table. 'I'm ordering you to stay here until you've consumed everything on both plates, and then at one o'clock you can meet me for lunch.'

'Lunch?'

'So I can make sure you refuel properly.' Matt smiled at her and gave her a mock salute before he marched away.

Brooke watched him go, a surprised smile on her face. Normally she didn't like men telling her what to do, and after Eric she had been determined never to let it happen again.

But there was something different about Matt. He wasn't overbearing. It hadn't been a demand, the way Eric would have delivered it. He hadn't said it to her as if she were stupid and he were trying to demean her.

He *cared*. Genuinely. About *her* welfare. And she wasn't used to someone doing that for her.

She'd always had to care for herself. Even when she was little…sitting at home, waiting for her dad to come back for hours, starving hungry. And when he had made it back the most he'd been able to manage to make for her had been something out of a can on toast.

With hindsight, it was probably the safest thing for him to have been in charge of. And although she'd yearned every day for him to ask her about her day at school he never had. And although she would get her paintings and her ten-out-of-ten spelling tests out of her bag to show him, her hard work had barely received a glance.

Her dad had physically been there, but it had been as if there was an invisible force field around him that she hadn't been able to penetrate. The fug of alcohol fumes had been a barrier she hadn't been able to break through. He hadn't connected to her at all.

She knew he'd turned to alcohol to get through the death of his wife—her mother. But by doing so he had caused Brooke to lose her father too. She'd been so young, just five years old, when it happened and all she had left were photographs of what they should have been. A happy, united family staring at the camera lens.

Coping on her own had become something so natural to her it was always a surprise when someone else looked out for her, no matter how small the occasion was.

Brooke sat there and ate the rest of her fruit salad and pastry, washing them down with the coffee and looking around at the other people in the cafeteria. Families. Mothers *and* fathers. Little toddlers being asked to sit still, to eat up, not to play with their food.

She smiled. It was all so normal for them.

Why had *she* not achieved that? Where had she gone wrong? Eric had been a mistake, but not Morgan. She adored her daughter, and would not be without her, but it didn't stop Brooke from feeling alone.

Had *she* caused it? Losing Jen just after the birth of her own daughter had made Brooke hibernate in the house. Not going out much...not being with people. Not letting anyone in. It had been easier to retreat into herself because that was familiar country. She knew the landscape. There were no surprises if she relied on just herself.

But wasn't life about overcoming obstacles? Facing

the challenges set before you? Fighting to be with those who would love you?

I need to let people in. Open up the borders.
Before I'm deserted altogether.

CHAPTER FOUR

MATT WAS STILL busy with a patient when Brooke had finished, ready for lunch. She sat at the doctors' desk and watched him carefully as he taught a young girl to use a pair of crutches. The girl, no more than eight years old, had a plaster cast around her foot and appeared to be struggling with her co-ordination. Matt kept adjusting the height of the crutches and knelt on the floor in front of his patient, smiling, encouraging her to move forward.

'Standing on your good leg, bring both crutches forward. That's it. Then swing your body forward, landing on your good leg. Excellent! Well done!'

She watched him stand and shake hands with the girl's father, and then he stooped one last time to say something to the little girl, who smiled shyly and nodded her head.

A warm smile appeared on Brooke's face as she watched, and she was still smiling when Matt came over to the desk to finish writing his notes.

'She looked sweet.'

Matt nodded, watching the father and daughter head out of the department, the little girl steady and determined on her new walking aids. 'She fell off a trampoline.'

Brooke raised an eyebrow. 'We ought to ban those

things. I'm sure we could cut down a good quarter of our workload if we did.'

'I agree.' He glanced at her and grinned. 'Though I'm sure our own daughters will want to spend time on trampolines at some point.'

'Yes, well, not if I can help it. I'll be keeping Morgan well away from anything like that.'

'Me too. But we can't wrap them in cotton wool. I know Jen would have *loved* the idea of Lily on a trampoline. And secondary schools often have trampolining in a physical education class. Are you going to ask for her to be withdrawn from those?'

She nodded firmly. 'Yes.'

'And what if all her friends start asking her why? What if she starts to feel embarrassed for being left out? You'll still be okay with that?'

She shifted in her chair. 'Yes.'

'Dr Bailey…I don't believe a single word.' He turned to face her, looking as if he was daring her to say otherwise.

'We all have to do things that sometimes go against the grain. I'm sure I can find other activities to occupy her and make up for the fact that I'm not risking her neck or her back or her ankles.'

'And what do *you* do that goes against the grain?'

She stopped to think. Unsure. 'How do you mean?'

'What do you do with Morgan that's different to anyone else?'

She opened her mouth as she struggled to find an answer, then closed it again when she realised, sharply that she didn't do *anything* with Morgan apart from feed, clothe and change her. They didn't really go out anywhere, except to the local park. But Morgan was too small to do anything. She hadn't even taken her to the local swimming pool for a splash-around, and Morgan *loved* being in water. Perhaps she wasn't the kind of radical, unique mother she'd thought she was.

'You know, there's something I need to tell you,' he said. He looked awkward. Uncomfortable. Whatever could it be?

'Such as?'

'Jen signed Lily up to this class months in advance, because it was oversubscribed. You know what things are like in London… Apparently it's very popular—great for babies' development…that kind of thing…and she kind of signed you and Morgan up to it, too.' He glanced quickly at her to see the effect of his revelation. 'I wasn't going to go, but…' He sighed. 'Perhaps we both ought to give it a try. Seeing as Jen wanted us to do it.'

She blinked. Remembered some vague conversation months back that she and Jen had had about baby development classes. They'd laughed about it. Chuckling about how silly they sounded, how pretentious. How it was more about the parents wanting to show off and have their offspring with a busier social calendar than they had themselves.

'A class?'

'Music Melody. I'm going to go—and you should too. It starts this Saturday morning at St David's Church Hall.'

Music Melody? A baby development class? In a draughty church hall? With a bunch of yummy mummies she wouldn't know, listening to babies banging away randomly on some clanging tin xylophones? It sounded like her worst nightmare.

'I…er…don't think so.' She laughed, as if it were the most ridiculous suggestion she'd ever heard.

'When did you last go out with Morgan to do something fun?'

'We have plenty of fun at home.'

He smiled. '*You* do, maybe. But what about Morgan? This kind of thing will get us out of our comfort zone and stop us from staying cooped up inside. Come on. I'm sure Morgan would love it.'

'But what about *me*?' she pleaded.

Going to a parent-and-baby group didn't sound like her idea of fun *at all*. She'd never been one for parties, or meeting up with friends outside of school. She never usually went to work bashes—not unless Jen had dragged her there.

Jen.

Jen had booked it for *them*! For *both* of them! She'd promised to be there for her, had said they would do things together. She'd *meant* it. Not knowing that she would never get the chance to fulfil that promise.

But Brooke could.

She sighed as she looked back at him, saw the twinkle of humour in his eyes and felt herself giving in. Perhaps it might be okay... And if it gave her a headache then she could take some painkillers afterwards.

'Fine. But why do you want me to go so badly?'

He let out a big sigh. 'Because I want to honour Jen's promise to you.'

She swallowed. 'Her promise?'

'To not let you do this alone. She told me about that.'

Oh. She felt oddly perturbed that he should want to do that. Honour an obligation made by his wife. He didn't have to. She'd managed all these months alone, and she and Morgan were doing okay. But it was sweet of him. Gentlemanly.

'You don't have to.'

'It's the right thing.'

'But we hardly know each other. I'm still a stranger...'

'As all the other parents will be. But I want to do right by my daughter and expose her to as much fun and joy as I can.'

She grimaced. 'Those places are germ factories. We'll probably all come down with bugs. Is *that* doing right by our children?'

'Building up their immune system! We put them in a crèche all day. It's the same thing.'

She supposed he was right. 'Okay.'

'Good. I've already told them you're coming.'

She stood up, grabbing her bag so they could go and get some lunch. 'How did you know I'd agree?'

He leant against the desk, his tall, lean frame effortlessly sexy. Even more so because he seemed totally unaware of it.

'Because you wouldn't let a good friend go to one of those terrible places alone.' He stepped away again. 'I'll probably be the only guy there. I'll get *the looks*.'

'Looks?'

'You know the ones… *Why has he come and not the mum? Where's his wife? Is he single?* You being there will protect me from all that.'

'You don't strike me as the type to need protection, Major. Don't you know how to kill people with just your thumbs?'

He smiled. 'Yes…but I think that's frowned upon at parent-and-baby groups, Dr Bailey.'

Brooke stared at him as he grabbed his jacket, checked his pocket for his wallet and wondered just what the hell she was letting herself in for…

As the days passed Brooke grew more and more nervous about meeting Matt at the Music Melody class. Sitting

with him at work for lunch was one thing—but socialising with him *outside* of work? What did *that* mean?

He knew it was just friendship, right? He knew it could
never go any further than that? Yes, she'd socialised with
Jen out of hours—but Jen had been a girl. She and Matt
were the opposite sex to each other, and it was a fine line
for them to walk.

She was already having difficulties with that smile
of his. Not only did it totally transform his face, but
every time he sent it her way she found herself wanting
more and more of it. She enjoyed making him smile. She
adored the camaraderie that was building between them.
And he had a wicked sense of humour when he let it out.
He made her laugh. Brightened her day.

But was that *all* that was developing? She couldn't
allow anything else to occur between them. That way
madness lay. Just the thought of it right now was turning her insides into all kinds of jumble. She could even
feel her mouth going dry. And to think she'd once complained about him keeping his distance by calling her Dr
Bailey and not Brooke…

Right now she was *ecstatic* that he was calling her
Dr Bailey.

*You stay over there, Major—that's right. Imagine I've
got a minefield around me.*

Brooke looked down at her next chart and frowned.
Two patients on one chart? She quickly scanned the notes
that the triage nurse had added: *Glued together.*

Smiling at the silliness of some people, she headed to
the waiting room. 'Rachel and Jake?'

A young teenage couple stood up, their hands locked
together, and following behind them, looking less
amused, two sets of parents.

Brooke raised her eyebrows at the teens and sent a look of sympathy towards the parents. 'Follow me.'

She took them to a cubicle and got them to sit on the small bed.

'You've glued yourselves together?'

They raised their clasped hands, looking quite pleased with themselves. 'We had to.'

'You *had* to?'

Rachel turned to look at her father and sneered. '*They* kept trying to split us up. Said Jake wasn't good enough for me—but they're wrong! We love each other and want to be together for ever, so we decided to prove it.'

'By gluing your hands together?'

Rachel nodded. 'That's right.'

'You couldn't just wait until you were old enough to get married?'

One of the parents bristled slightly. 'Don't give them ideas. As if *this* isn't bad enough! I've had to take time off work for this—and they're missing school. All because they're so childish they can't see what they're doing!'

Fair enough. She could understand the parents' point of view. 'Can I have a look at your hands?'

She examined Rachel and Jake's hands. They were stuck tight—glued around their palms and fingers. She'd have to be careful not to damage the skin in removing the glue.

She'd heard of other people coming across this in A&E, but this was a first for her. Rachel and Jake probably thought they were being unique and different, proving their devotion to each other, but all they had done was alienate everyone and give their parents even more reason to try and keep the two of them apart.

'Okay, I'll need to check which solution to use on this. Sit tight for a moment. I'll be back in a few minutes.'

She headed back to the doctors' desk and shared with Kelly the details of the case she'd got.

'Oh, I had a couple do that once.'

'Really? What? Here?'

'No, when I worked up in Birmingham. But they didn't glue their *hands*.'

She raised an eyebrow at her and Brooke grimaced.

'*Eurgh!* People do mad things when they think they're in love.'

'It's certainly an emotion that ought to come with a health warning.'

Brooke mused. 'Do you think anyone would pay attention to it, though?'

'I don't know. It would have to be a really clever TV advert. *'Warning! Falling in love can result in sleepless nights, stomach ache and heart pain. Use with caution.'*'

Brooke smiled. 'Let's not forget the terrible grief at its end. Look at what Major Galloway has had to go through.'

'Matt? He's survived it. He's in one piece, anyway.'

Was he? Or was he just very good at hiding his wounds? Brooke hadn't known Jen long. Less than a year. But they had become such great friends, so quickly, that she'd given her entire heart to their friendship. When she'd lost Jen it had hurt her terribly. And she still mourned the mother she'd never really known, too. Was she destined to always have a piece missing in her heart?

Was anyone totally whole?

Don't all of us have chipped, broken edges?

'I'm thinking of using warm, soapy water first.'

'On Matt?' Kelly raised an eyebrow. 'Could be interesting…'

Brooke smiled at her friend. 'On the two lovebirds in Cubicle Six.'

'Oh, right… Yeah, lots of soap and warm water. Slowly ease their hands apart—no tugging, no ripping. That should do it.'

Brooke stood up to get herself a basin, but then turned to ask Kelly one last question. 'How would *you* prove that you loved somebody?'

Kelly looked thoughtful for a moment. 'Without making them want to get a restraining order? Erm…I don't actually know. How would *you* do it?'

Brooke shook her head. 'I wouldn't. It's all a bit scary, if you ask me. Besides, I've got Morgan now. I don't need anyone else.'

Kelly returned a look that said *I don't believe you.*

She pondered, whilst she filled a container with warm, soapy water, whether someone like Matt, who had already been broken once by loving someone, would ever feel he could fall in love again. Probably not. He had his hands full, too. Both of them had a strenuous full-time job and both of them were single parents. Did either of them have time to fit in the needs and wants of another person who would control their hearts?

Not me. Definitely not me.

But as she headed back to the cubicle and began soaking the clasped hands of the two teenagers, who were still staring into each other's eyes, she couldn't help but think about Matt and how he managed to lift her spirits every moment she spent time with him…

There'd been a frost that morning. The first one of autumn, which was Brooke's favourite time of year. There was nothing she liked better than chilly weather, as long as it wasn't raining. Having to wrap up in woolly scarves, hats and gloves, her nose going red as she watched her own breath freeze in the air around you… And autumn brought Halloween and Bonfire Night, with hot potatoes wrapped in foil and everyone gazing heavenwards at the inky black sky, awaiting the fireworks show.

November the fifth was just a few short days away, and already she'd spent some of her nights listening to the occasional firework or banger going off in the local neighbourhood.

Last year she'd spent the evening with Eric, and as much as there had been fireworks in the sky there'd also been fireworks as he'd walked her home, arguing that she'd spent her entire evening staring at another man. She hadn't. But Eric had insisted that the man hadn't been able to take his eyes off her and Brooke had been encouraging him. One final nail in the coffin of their relationship.

This year she would go to an organised fireworks show with Morgan and delight in her daughter's pleasure at seeing fireworks for the first time. But in the meantime she had this Music Melody class to get through...

That morning she'd lain in bed, listening to Morgan babble away in the next room, wanting to stay under the duvet. It was the weekend, and she'd been looking forward to her customary lie-in of an extra hour. But the class started early, and she *had* promised she would go, and Matt was right. It would be good for her to get out of the house and it would be good for Morgan to socialise, even though she *did* spend the majority of her week in a crèche.

I do need to do something with my daughter other than drop her off and collect her each day.

And who knew? It might even be fun.

She dressed in some old jeans, threw on a tee shirt, a poncho and a beanie hat, slipped into her boots and got Morgan into her car seat.

'Okay. Now, I'm hoping we're going somewhere that will be melodic and harmonious, but as I'm guessing the majority of the orchestra is going to be under the age of one, I'm not holding out much hope for our ears. So if you could at least pretend to enjoy yourself—that would be great.'

Morgan responded by blowing a bubble with her saliva and smiling.

Brooke kissed her button nose and got into the driving seat. Part of her hoped that she would enjoy herself, but would she really find joy amongst a bunch of babies banging away on drums and tambourines? She'd forearmed herself by putting painkillers into her handbag, just in case the place gave her the mother of all headaches.

The GPS directed her through London to the required church hall, and she parked in its small car park, pulling into a space, noticing that Matt was already there, getting Lily's buggy out of the boot of his own vehicle.

'You made it.'

She got out of her car. 'You doubted me?'

He smiled. 'Not for one moment. Are you ready for this?'

'I've got earplugs, if that's what you mean?'

Matt laughed as he strapped Lily into her buggy.

Brooke scooped Morgan out of her own car seat and decided not to get the buggy out—she would carry her daughter inside.

She hefted her onto her left hip. 'What do you think? Are we about to discover this country's next great virtuoso?'

'You never know.'

Matt led the way into the hall and Brooke could feel nerves building in her stomach. She'd never wanted to come to one of these places. What if the other mothers wanted to talk? What if they asked questions? She'd have to tell them she was a single parent. That Eric had never seen his daughter and didn't care. What did *that* say about her, to have got involved with a man like that? It wasn't good, was it? It was hardly a letter of commendation regarding her assessment skills. Perhaps it would just be best to say she'd used a sperm donor?

But, then again, she was here to stop Matt getting *the looks.* Were they to pretend that they were going out? Were married? She'd noticed he still wore his wedding band. That would make Lily and Morgan twins, wouldn't it?

The church hall was warm and in the centre was a large carpet. Around the edges sat various parents holding their babies on their laps, or letting them crawl around on the floor. Everyone chatted happily, waiting for the class to begin.

Brooke sucked in a breath. *Here goes.* She stepped forward with Matt and they found a spot together on the edge of the circle and let Lily and Morgan say hello to each other in their own cute baby way. Mainly patting each other in the face with their hands.

A young woman wearing a bright yellow tee shirt with the words *Music Melody Maestro* on it clapped her hands together to get everyone's attention.

'Welcome, everyone! It's lovely to see so many of you here, today. My name is Melanie and I'm going to lead our group!'

Like Daisy at the crèche, Melanie appeared to be one of those people with a permanently sunny disposition. Brooke wondered if that was a requirement to work with children. Must always look as if you're having the *best* fun!

She smiled and sat Morgan up against her, holding onto her chubby little hands.

'Now, here at Music Melody classes we want children to grow up loving the language of music! And to do that we're going to start off with simple rhymes and songs that we can all do the actions to, so that our babies learn about rhyme and rhythm and melody. Music can touch the soul and bring happiness to all if we all just take the time to find the right song! So let's start with the simplest: *"Pat-a-cake, Pat-a-cake".'*

Brooke glanced worriedly at Matt. This wasn't an *instruments* class! This was *singing*! Why hadn't he warned her? Brooke was tone deaf and couldn't carry a note! Singing here, like this, out loud, where other people could *hear* her was not a very good idea at all!

But before she could say anything Melanie launched into the song, and so did everyone else around her.

Brooke opened her mouth and pretended to sing.

Matt seemed to be finding her discomfort terribly amusing. They'd gone from *'Pat-a-Cake, Pat-a-Cake'* to *'Twinkle, Twinkle Little Star'* and had just finished a rousing rendition of *'Old McDonald Had a Farm'.*

But that hadn't been the worst thing. Melanie, the alliterative Music Maestro, had said that each parent would have to suggest an animal, starting the verse off *by themselves.*

Brooke had felt horror creep into her bones, her skin crawling, and wished she could be anywhere but there. And as they'd gone round the circle, getting closer and closer to her, her mind had fixated on a goose, of all things, so she'd started her verse: *'And on that farm there was a goose, e-i-e-i-o. With a honk-honk here and a honk-honk there...'*

Her voice had sounded like a teenage boy's—squeaky one minute, deep the next—and the tune had been mangled beyond all recognition, but she'd got through it without her face melting from the shame, and when she'd glanced at Matt she'd been encouraged by his smile and the way he'd clapped Lily's hands together, as if in small applause.

He'd suggested Old McDonald had a turkey, and after he'd got all the other mothers laughing and singing along with him about gobbling the singing circle finally made it back to Melanie and the torture stopped for them all to get a cup of tea.

Brooke got to her feet thankfully, and headed over to the kitchen to stand in line.

'Enjoying yourself?' Matt caught up with her, his face full of humour and bonhomie.

'I'd rather be doing surgery on myself with a blunt spoon, but apart from that it's a thrill a minute.'

He laughed. 'I thought it was your kind of thing. Great singing, by the way, Dr Bailey. I've not heard notes achieved like that before.'

She pursed her lips. 'And you'll never hear them again! I think it's safe to say that I will never, *ever* come back here.'

'Why not?'

She turned to face him. 'Because this is not a class for babies. This is a class to humiliate parents and make them think that just because there are other adults in the room they're actually getting decent conversation.'

'You're not having a good time?' He tilted his head to one side and looked curiously at her.

'Sorry. I'm being a killjoy about your bright idea. Forget me. Go and talk to all the other mummies. They all seem very keen to try and get your attention.'

'How do you mean?'

She raised an eyebrow. 'You've not noticed? It's flirtation central here! I don't think I've seen more women flicking and playing with their hair whilst ogling the only person in the room whose testes have descended.'

He laughed. 'I hadn't noticed.'

But she could tell that he had. It had been a concern of his before he'd even got here, and he'd asked *her* along to ward off that sort of thing.

The queue moved forward and Brooke passed him a cup of tea, adding sugar to hers and grabbing a biscuit that felt slightly soft because it was so old. But it would do.

Had he really not noticed how all the other women had reacted when he'd walked in? Brooke had instantly seen them eye him, straightening their clothes, and a few less subtle mothers had even got out a compact mirror and checked they looked okay before beaming a smile in his direction.

Okay, perhaps they weren't being so obvious that a *guy* would notice, but she had. And she could see why they would be noticing. Major Galloway was a handsome guy with come-to-bed eyes and a rugged demeanour that oozed the fact that he worked hard and knew how to *use his hands*. Probably other body parts, too. Quite…erm… effectively.

But Brooke was immune to his charms. She felt sure of it. Besides, they were colleagues—that was all. They just happened to have two kids the same age.

Not being able to find a chair, she settled herself down on the carpet and lay Morgan on her back next to Lily.

'Jen would have found this place hilarious,' she said.

She noticed him stiffen at the mention of his wife's name. 'Probably.'

She dunked her biscuit in her tea and quickly pulled it out before it could break off in the drink, popping the whole thing into her mouth. As she munched on it she noticed that he was staring at her with a smile on his face.

'What?' she asked through a mouthful of crumbs.

'Nothing.' He looked away.

'No, go on. What did I do?'

He glanced back at her, finally capitulating. 'Jen used to do that. Eat the whole biscuit in one go, I mean.'

'Oh.' She hadn't realised. 'I'm sorry.'

He shook his head, smiling. 'You don't have to apologise. It's just a biscuit.'

'I just don't want to…'

'What?'

'Remind you. Make you sad.'

'A million things remind me every day. Especially Lily. It's good, though. Because why would I want to forget?'

She nodded slowly. 'Has it got a little easier? Since she passed? I know it's only five months since it happened…'

And now she felt awkward for having asked. For her, Jen was the first big loss that she'd ever had to face, since her mother's death. The grief was still difficult some days, but it was getting easier to bear. Sometimes something would happen at work, or with Morgan, and the first thing she'd think would be, *I must tell Jen.* And then she would realise, with a great thud in her heart and stomach, that Jen wasn't here any more. There was a gaping hole in her life and she didn't know how to fill it.

'I've accepted it. When I got back to England I was numb, and then I got angry. Wanted to rage against the world for taking her. But then I'd hold Lily in my arms and I could see Jen looking out at me, through her eyes, and I just knew that if Jen were there still she'd be telling me to stop being such a macho idiot, get a grip and move on.' He smiled. 'Did she ever say that to you?'

Brooke nodded. 'That I'm a macho idiot? Oh, absolutely.' She allowed a smile to play at her lips. 'She hated people being sad. She was always telling me to snap out of it whenever I was feeling low about my situation.'

'Did that ever work?'

'Sometimes. Every day is different, isn't it? Each dawn a new page on which your story can either have a high or a low.'

He nodded, as if he knew what she was saying exactly. 'Jen would want us both to have highs.'

'Not pharmaceutically!' She laughed, the sound escaping her almost like a cry, sudden and short.

She had to look away. Had to blink a few times to rid herself of the tears that were suddenly threatening. If Jen were here she'd be having a laugh a minute and Brooke knew it. Jen *should* be here. Singing with her baby. But she wasn't. And all because of a cruel twist in fate. Brooke was here instead, with Jen's husband, and suddenly it felt wrong. Very wrong, indeed. This was all just too cosy, too soon.

She put down her tea, scooped up Morgan and stood up. 'I think I need to go.'

Matt got to his feet. 'Go? It's not finished.'

'I just need to—'

He laid a hand on her arm. 'Dr Bailey.' He made her look at him. 'Take a breath. That's it. In for three and out for three. Nice and steady.'

He waited until he saw the panic leave her features.

'She would have wanted you here. With us. With Lily. She's not, but she would have wanted you here. To...' he smiled '...*endure* this. Come on...maybe in part two we can make a request. I think we ought to ask for *"Incy Wincy Spider"*. What do you think?'

She was trying not to be taken in by those eyes of his.

Perfectly blue, thickly lashed with dark hair. 'I hate spiders.' She could imagine him leaping to her rescue to rid her of an eight-legged arachnid.

'Then what would *you* ask for?'

She thought for a second. '*"Jack and Jill went up the hill"?*'

He seemed amused. 'Why that one?'

'Jack breaks his crown. I always liked the idea of fixing him afterwards.'

'And Jill? She came tumbling after.'

'Why not? In my version she breaks a bone or two.'

Matt settled her back on the carpet and handed her the cup of tea. 'We can get through anything together. You and I are strong.'

'You think so? I don't *feel* particularly strong sometimes.'

'Like Jack, it doesn't matter how many times we fall. As long as we always get up again. *Do* you keep getting up again, Dr Bailey?'

'I think I do.'

A smile lifted the corners of his mouth. 'I'm glad.'

Brooke made it through the next thirty minutes of singing. At first she just mouthed along, not feeling any of it, but as Morgan began to smile and squeal at all the actions, jiggling along, she soon got into her rhythm and started singing out loud, not giving one jot that she couldn't hold a note.

Who cared? Were the babies going to criticise her? Hardly. And the other mothers? Well, she was never going to see these people again. She could sound like a gurgling gutter and it wouldn't matter.

She was pleased she had come. And she was pleased to have come with Matt and seen him out of their work environment. He was a completely different person dressed in a long sleeved tee shirt and jeans. So strange, having only ever seen him in scrubs or a shirt and tie.

She was fastening Morgan into her car seat, clipping the buckles together and then closing the car door, when she became aware that Matt was waiting for her. She smiled at him and thanked him for asking her there.

'It was my pleasure.'

'Well, I guess I'll see you next week. Have a good weekend, Major.'

'You too, Dr Bailey.'

'Drive safely.'

'Always.' He began to walk away, but as he did so something inside her made her call out. 'Major Galloway…? There's a fireworks display in a couple of weeks in Hammersmith. It's meant to be really good…I've been looking forward to taking Morgan and I wondered if— you can say no…I won't mind…'

Spend more time with the lovely Matt Galloway? Was that wise? Was she being ridiculous to invite him? To offer to spend more of her free time with him?

How is that ridiculous? You're just being a friend.

'Er…'

'If *I* can get through the singing then it's only fair that you get through a few sparklers.'

She could see he was agonising over it. Had she pushed too hard? Was she reading too much into this friendship that he had promised to honour?

'Okay.'

She nodded. 'Great.'

'I'll see you on Monday, Dr Bailey.'

'Goodbye, Major.' And with a small wave she got into her car and started the engine.

Friendship was a strange thing indeed. It could develop at a lightning pace, go places you'd never imagined and hopefully tie you to someone you would trust your life to.

Whilst Jen had been alive Brooke had never really asked her too much about Matt, and Jen had hardly mentioned him. Acting the single parent to be in solidarity with Brooke's lonesome status? It had never occurred to her to ask more about the man that her best friend had loved.

But now she had the chance to know him.

And she was glad that she did.

CHAPTER FIVE

LILY WAS IN bed fast asleep and Matt was sitting on the couch, holding a cup of coffee and staring at the picture on the mantelpiece.

It was a picture that he and Jen had had taken on his last leave. He in his army uniform, Jen with her back to him, leaning against him as his hands embraced the gentle swell of her pregnant abdomen.

They were both smiling. Both of them imagining the brilliant future before them. His career in the army had been going strong, they'd been about to become parents for the first time and were at the start of their parenthood journey.

It was a trip that he had expected to take with his wife, yet now he was walking alone.

It was hard sometimes to look at that picture. Because how could they have known that everything was about to change for the worse? He hadn't known that that was one of the last times he would ever hold her. Hold them both. The only thing he could hold now was memories. And they were fleeting. Like trying to hold a cloud.

But he *could* hold Lily, and she was the burning image of her mother. Cute blonde hair, twinkling cheeky eyes. And that chuckle of hers… It didn't ever fail to make him laugh, too. It was such pure delight.

Jen would have loved to hear it. To be there for her daughter. Neither of them had suspected that she would succumb to eclampsia. Her pregnancy had been problem-free up to that point. Jen had been an extremely healthy person. She'd run half-marathons for charity every year. Had played in the hospital netball team when she could. The news from his General that Jen had been put on a life support machine had been like a tragic joke. Unbelievable. Surely they'd meant someone else?

Yet it had been horribly true, and each night when Lily was in bed Matt would sit in the heavy silence of the house and be thankful for having got through another day. It was all he requested from life now. Making it from sun-up to sunset. He had no more aspirations than that apart from ensuring that Lily was happy. She was his life now. His number one reason for putting one step in front of another.

It had been difficult in the early days. Caring for a newborn whilst in the grip of grief. People—family, friends—had helped as much as they could. But after a time their own lives, naturally, had pulled them away. And he'd emerged from the dark mire of his pain determined to provide the best life he could for his daughter. Not to flit from one posting to another but to take root, to stay in his new job at London Grace and be the best father he could for his little girl.

Meeting Dr Brooke Bailey had been a surprising bonus. When he'd been accepted by the hospital trust to take on his wife's post he'd known that at some point he would meet the woman who had recently been his wife's confidante. And she was every bit the wonderful person Jen had told him about.

And, though he'd only known her for such a short time—just a few weeks—he did feel as if they had a bond. Their mutual love of Jen, their work, and the fact that they were both single-handedly raising little girls. Since meeting Brooke he'd wondered if she sat in her own home at night, nursing a cup of cocoa, wondering what might have been if fate hadn't designated her to raise a child alone? How her life might be different with someone in it to help her?

Not that she needed someone. He wasn't implying that she couldn't do it alone. But Matt knew what having someone to love and lean on felt like, and he hoped for her that one day she would find that happiness.

The paramedics had wheeled in a little old lady, swaddled in a blanket, strapped to a chair. Ambling along behind them, struggling to keep pace, was an elderly gent whom Matt presumed was the husband.

Tina, the paramedic, handed over the details. 'This is Patricia Hodgson. She's ninety-one years young and a resident at Castle House. Normally fit and well, Patricia was found this morning by her husband, Arthur, with a droop to the left side of her face and aphasia. A FAST test was positive. BP was ninety over sixty and pulse eighty-four. SATS were normal at ninety-five per cent, but oxygen therapy was given anyway. Patricia was diagnosed with Alzheimer's two years ago and has a previous history of breast cancer during her seventieth year.'

Matt thanked the paramedics and organised his team, including Brooke, to transfer Patricia from the chair to a bed so the ambulance crew could leave and get to their next job.

Patricia looked tiny and frail upon the bed, and he noticed how gentle Brooke was with her as she covered the old lady's legs with a blanket and spoke gently to her, explaining what she was doing.

Patricia's husband, Arthur, stood off to one side, looking frightened and lost. 'Is she all right?' he asked in a frightened, gravelly voice.

Matt introduced himself to the husband. 'I'm Major Galloway and I'm going to be in charge of your wife's care, Mr Hodgson.'

'Arthur.'

'Arthur. It appears your wife has had a stroke and that the event has damaged the side of your wife's brain that deals with speech. I'm going to get her assessed quickly and then we'll get her off for a scan to see just what type of stroke she's had.'

'I just want her to be all right. She's frightened by strange places.'

Matt understood. For Alzheimer's patients, strange places that they did not know could cause undue stress. It was imperative that they keep everything as calm as they could.

'Perhaps you'd like to come and hold your wife's hand?' Brooke suggested.

'Won't I be getting in the way?'

'Not at all.'

Matt issued instructions to his team and watched as they all busied themselves around Mrs Hodgson, taking readings, assessments, and doing so in such a way that they did not upset their patient any more than she already was. The world was a confusing place for anyone with Alzheimer's, and not being able to communicate properly had to be an added upset. Not being able to find your memories was one thing. Not being able to find the right words for things must be torture.

When she was stable they took her to be scanned, to see if she'd had a bleed or whether there was a thrombus, or clot, that might need dissolving. A thrombolytic drug would do that, though there were dangers associated with its use.

'Is your wife on any medication that we should know about?' asked Brooke.

'Erm… I think she's on a statin, and something else, but she's not very good at taking them regularly. The nurses have a hard time getting her to swallow her medication. It's in this bag here.'

Arthur handed over to Brooke a small white paper bag that had various boxes in it. She passed it to Matt.

There weren't any drugs there to treat the Alzheimer's. There was no cure for the condition, although some drugs had been developed to try and slow down the progression of the disease. Matt noted the drugs that Arthur had brought in and wrote down his team's observations on Patricia's condition. It was all done within ten minutes of her arriving.

'Let's move her to Scanning, please,' Matt instructed.

They all walked together to the scanning room and watched as the images came down on the screens. A clot was noted in one of Patricia's smaller vessels and when they took her back to Majors department Matt discussed with Arthur the pros and cons of the thrombolytic.

'You do what you have to do, Doc.'

'Thank you. As your wife is unable to give me verbal consent, it's important that I get your permission. We'll give her the medication and then observe her closely.'

'And then she'll be able to talk to me again?'

Matt could hear the distress in the husband's voice. 'Hopefully.'

'She's all I've got. Me and her…we're the only ones left. She doesn't always remember me, but when she does she likes to talk. Words are all we have. And music.

Funny how she can remember song lyrics from the nine-teen-forties yet not remember me.'

'Alzheimer's is a difficult condition. It chips away at people. From one day to the next you don't know which piece has been taken until suddenly it's not there any more.'

Arthur nodded, his face grim. 'When memories are all she has, it's heartbreaking when she loses them. Not for her, so much. But for me. I need her to still be *with* me, you know?'

Matt did know, and nodded solemnly. He adminis-tered the drug that Patricia needed and went to update his notes. When he came back to check on her Arthur was sitting next to her, holding her hand as she dozed.

'Are you married, Doctor?' Arthur asked.

How was he to answer that? Yes? No?

'I was. Once.'

Arthur turned to look at him through rheumy eyes, hidden behind thick glasses. 'Was it happy?'

Now, *that* was easier to answer. 'It was.'

'I've had sixty-three years with my Patty. Sixty-three glorious years. There were moments, I'm sure, when she would've liked to have had me done in, but mostly we got on. She was a wonderful wife.'

'She still is.'

The old man nodded and looked back to his beloved in the bed. 'Yes. She is, but...' He shook his head, rub-bing at his brow with his free hand. 'I feel selfish some-times. And cruel.'

Matt tried to work out what he meant. 'Why cruel?'

'Since she was diagnosed with the Alzheimer's I've had to say goodbye to my wife. For the last two years I've watched her slowly vanish. There were times I wanted to shake her, to tell her it was *me*, her husband, to beg her for a moment when she might recognise me again. Then a few months back there came a day when she was lucid. She knew who she was, where she was, who I was—but the most horrible thing of all was that she knew what was wrong with her. What had happened to her and that soon she would be lost again. I've never seen my wife so terrified, Doctor. She grabbed my hands, begged me to stay with her until the end. Then, when the disease claimed her again, I was grateful. *Grateful!* And now all I want is for it to be over for her. So that it'll be over for me.'

Matt listened intently, understanding the man's pain. 'That's not selfishness. It's self-preservation. It's love. You don't want to see her suffer any more.'

Arthur met his gaze and nodded. 'I don't. I really don't. I've said goodbye so many times, thinking it was the end. Now, with the stroke, I wonder if it really is. Because I'm not sure I'm ready.'

'None of us are ever ready to say goodbye.'

He laid a reassuring hand on Arthur's shoulder and stood for a moment, watching Patricia's breathing. As he watched she opened her eyes a little and looked around the small bay in which she was situated, her gaze eventually falling on her husband.

'Arthur?'

Her husband grasped her hand. 'Oh! Patty!'

'Is it time for bed, yet, Arthur?'

'Oh, yes, my love! Yes, it is.'

Matt left them to have a moment alone and went to complete his notes. He sat at the desk, deep in thought.

Arthur had been saying goodbye for two years and it still wasn't enough time. And even though his situation was stressful Matt still felt that the man was lucky. He'd got to say goodbye. To hold his wife's hand. And no doubt when the time eventually came he would have the chance to be with her at the end.

Was he envious of Arthur?

As he considered this Brooke came into Majors with the results of Patty's blood tests.

'How is she?'

'Talking.'

'That's good. That's progress.'

'Yeah…'

He could feel her looking at him.

'Why so blue?'

'Because he gets to be with his wife as she nears the end. I never got that, and sometimes it just makes me feel like…'

'Like what?'

He laughed. 'Do you know what my wife's last words were?'

Brooke shook her head. 'I don't.'

'She was with her mum. Her mum had driven Jen to the hospital because of how unwell she was feeling. She was trying to be bright and optimistic, as she always was, and apparently the last conversation they had was about whether Jen should get her nose pierced.'

He looked at Brooke to see her reaction.

She smiled. 'That's good.'

'Good?'

'Yeah. Because she was talking about normal stuff. Everyday stuff. She didn't spend her last few minutes of consciousness terrified and crying. She was being herself. So…that's good.'

He looked back at the old couple, clutching each other's hands and staring into each other's eyes. 'I never thought about it like that before.'

Brooke glanced over at Arthur and Patty too. 'They seem very dedicated to each other.'

'He said they've been together for sixty-three years. I can't even imagine what that might feel like.'

'Sixty-three years of marriage?' Brooke sighed, supporting her chin on the back of her hand as she leant against the desk. 'I think that would be comfortable. Warm and snug, like a nest. All those years, all that *history*, surrounding you both like a safety net.'

'You're a romantic, Dr Bailey!'

She smiled at him, before her gaze returned to the couple in front of them. 'And a dreamer. But don't we all hope and dream for happiness in some way?'

Matt didn't answer. He stared at her profile—at the way her nose turned up slightly at the end, the fullness of her smiling lips, the gentle way one brown tress of her hair had escaped its messy bun and rested upon her shoulder. It looked soft and silky, and it seemed wrong to him that someone as sweet and lovely as her should be alone when clearly she had so much love to give.

He concentrated for a moment on his notes. *Blood pressure. Respirations. Pulse. Patient.* But his mind wouldn't stay focused. It was as if there was a small cyclone of thoughts whizzing around in there, picking up the leaves of his thoughts and tossing them into the mix—Jen, Brooke, Jen, Brooke.

Lily.

Yes. His daughter had to be his priority. Worrying about Brooke's love-life was not his responsibility. Nothing to do with him. She was his friend, but that was all she would ever be. He couldn't allow himself to think any more of her than that.

But if that was the case then why was the thought of her the only thing he could concentrate on?

* * *

Patricia recovered well, and after a few days spent in the hospital was returned to Castle House residential care, with Arthur still at her side.

Matt had watched them go, envious and yet also happy for Arthur and his wife. They still had precious days together, despite the Alzheimer's. Patricia was still there. Arthur could hear her voice. See her. Touch her.

It was a gift. And having met the two of them was giving him a new outlook on life. Yes, he still missed Jen. He always would—no doubt about it. But he had to be thankful for the short time they'd had together, and more than anything he had to be thankful for Lily and his friends and colleagues.

They were still here. They were here to talk to and spend time with. There was no point in locking himself away just because he felt alone. He had a duty to enjoy life. He'd promised Jen that he would. He'd promised to honour Jen's wish to help Brooke and Morgan. He was *still living.*

His wife, who had embraced life and fun and happiness, would not have wanted to think of him pining away for her. She would have wanted him to be out and about, showing their daughter the wonders of the world. Proving to her that the world was a beautiful place and that she was loved and cherished. Lily was the centre of his universe and he owed her that.

So he tried not to feel guilty each time he smiled, or laughed, or forgot about his grief. He tried not to dwell on it. Sometimes that was difficult. Especially late at night when he was alone and it would make him feel bad.

Keeping busy helped. When Lily was in bed, he'd start on his DIY projects. He'd finally got around to fixing that wonky kitchen cupboard, finally shaved a few millimetres off the bottom of the lounge door, replaced the broken tiles in the bathroom and repainted the main bedroom. He'd taught himself how to cook some recipes he'd never tried before, and given himself permission to relax and read all those books he'd never got around to.

At work he was trying to be more available for those people around him. He sat with them in the staffroom more, rather than returning to his office alone, he joined in with staff sweepstakes and signed up to do quiz nights and charity runs. He knew that everyone had noticed the change in him and it had made him smile inside.

After much thought, he'd finally removed his wedding ring. It now sat on his bedside table, where he could look at it each night and remember the day it had first been put on his finger.

And yet throughout it all he still sometimes felt a little lonely. Despite being surrounded by smiling faces, by people who knew him and cared for him. He still felt alone.

Brooke in particular, kept asking him if he was all right.

'I'm fine.'

'Really?'

'Absolutely.'

'Because usually when *I* say *I'm fine*, it means something else. Like, *Please leave me alone. I'm pretending to be okay.*'

He smiled at her. 'I really am okay. I'm…embracing all that life has to offer.'

'Are you?' She looked at him, assessing him, and he grew hot under her gaze.

'Yes.'

'You're still coming to the fireworks night this weekend?'

A pause. Then, 'Yes.'

'You don't sound that thrilled about it.'

'Dr Bailey, I am most definitely looking forward to coming with you and the lovely Morgan to the fireworks display. Lily will love it.'

She narrowed her eyes at him, her eyebrows wiggling, and it made him laugh.

Brooke smiled. 'That's better.'

'What is?'

'You laughing. You look better that way.'

'How do I look when I'm *not* laughing?'

She paused to consider her answer. 'Thoughtful. Brooding…'

He noticed her blush, which she quickly tried to cover up by taking a sip of tea from an oversized mug. What else had she been about to say?

It was probably best to spare her blushes and change the subject. 'How's Morgan getting on? Still teething?'

She nodded quickly, grateful for the change of topic. 'Yes, but she's not as grouchy about it now. The teething gel has been helping.'

'Lily got a tooth through just last night. She was so much happier when it was over. I got some sleep, anyway.'

Brooke smiled, but he realised it wasn't one of her usual smiles. It didn't light up her eyes the way it usually did. In fact she still looked a little perturbed by whatever she'd been thinking about when she'd mentioned how he was looking.

Odd…

Was she looking *guilty*? It was kind of reassuring to know he wasn't the only one who succumbed to guilt occasionally. But why would she feel guilty about *him*?

Unless…

Oh…

Eager to make her feel more comfortable, he got up. 'Well, I must get a move on. There are plenty of patients in the waiting room.'

She downed the rest of her tea and stood up, too. Just as eager, it seemed, to get past this little awkward moment as he was. 'Yes. My patient should be back from X-ray by now.'

'Anything interesting?'

'Just a query fracture of a metatarsal. He accidentally kicked a metal post.'

'Right. Okay. Well, I'll see you later, Dr Bailey.'

'Yes.'

She looked at him a little uncertainly and the only thing he could think of to do was give her a brief nod before he walked away. His heart was pounding, though, and his mouth was dry. But now he was away from her he could breathe.

Just what was that all about?

A simple conversation. Completely innocent. And then…*something.*

Determined to ignore it—perhaps he'd imagined something that hadn't actually been there?—he scooped up the next triage file and went to call his patient. Patients were good. Patients were intriguing. You could get lost in their problems as you diagnosed them.

And they'll damn well help stop me obsessing about Brooke!

Brooke stared at the X-ray on her computer screen, absently biting at her thumbnail. Her patient was lucky. There was no fracture anywhere to be seen. The kick had obviously just caused a soft tissue injury and that was responsible for the bruising and swelling. He'd just need rest, painkillers, and to put his foot up when he could.

If only she could diagnose herself as easily.

Something weird had just happened with Matt. Something odd. They'd been talking about whether they really felt fine, and she'd mentioned that he usually looked thoughtful, and brooding. And then…

She grimaced. *Sexy.* She thought he looked *sexy*! And as she'd realised that thought her body had leapt into overdrive. Her heart had begun to pound, she'd blushed like a teenager talking to her crush and her body had begun to tingle in all sorts of places! The kind of places that she hadn't used since giving birth to Morgan. And realising that, becoming aware of all that, had made her feel incredibly…what? Mad? Guilty? *Aroused?*

How could she be aroused by him? He was Jen's husband! He was totally off the market and not available, and quite frankly ought to have *Do Not Touch* signs draped around his neck, but…

Brooke groaned out loud.

'Something wrong?' Kelly peered at her from across the desktop.

Yes. She was wrong. She couldn't feel that way about him. Not *him*! What kind of friend did that make her?

'Everything,' she said.

'Oh, dear. Come on, spill—tell me all the grisly details.'

She looked at Kelly. She was another good friend. Married. Happily. Was Brooke going to end up fancying *her* husband, too?

'I hate myself.'

Kelly laughed. 'Oh, right. It's one of *those* days. I've got chocolate, if you need it. Whatever it is shall pass, don't you worry.'

'You promise?'

'Absolutely. Whatever it is will go away. Just like magic.'

Brooke wasn't too sure if that was true. Because now she'd admitted her thoughts to herself it was as if her mind was scrolling through all her previous interactions with Matt and she could see the subtle flirting that had been going on the whole time. Well, maybe not *flirting,* but she could sense in herself all those moments that she'd really *looked* at him and felt *something.*

So would it pass? Or was it something that had been inside her ever since she and Matt had met in the hospital crèche? Had it been bubbling away inside of her imperceptibly, the pressure slowly rising, until now she'd become aware of the heat?

Because it certainly felt as if she had a furnace inside her right now, and it was making her feel dreadful. Because what about Jen? Her memory? Lily? Morgan? She and Matt were *parents.* They both had their priorities, they both had excellent reasons for staying away from each other, and yet...

I've invited him out. To a fireworks night. I should never have done that! And he doesn't want to go. I can tell that he doesn't. He's just trying to be nice and...

Brooke knew what she had to do. Standing up abruptly, making her chair skid away from her slightly, she turned to Kelly. 'Where's Major Galloway?'

'Minors, I think.'

'Right.'

She went off to find him. Her chin jutting out with determination, her mind set on what she had to do to put this right. To end this nonsense here and now so that she and Matt could go back to being just colleagues.

As she passed the curtained cubicles she could hear his voice talking to a patient about what caused gout, and his dulcet tones, dark and soft, sent shivers down her spine. Good shivers. The kind that—

She opened the curtain slightly and popped her head in. 'Sorry to interrupt you, Major, but might I have a quick word with you when you're finished here?'

He turned to her, smiling. A smile that lit up her heart and confused her all the more.

'Sure.'

'Thanks.'

She closed the curtain and stood there, her eyes closed tightly, as she concentrated on her breathing. This was getting ridiculous. He was just a friend. *Just. A. Friend.*

She set off to see her patient with the damaged foot to give him the good news. He seemed mightily relieved not to have broken anything, but she sent him home with some crutches and instructions to stay off the foot for about a week. As she typed her patient notes into the computer she sensed rather than saw Matt arrive beside her.

'What's up?'

Her fingers froze over the keyboard as she sucked up a rallying breath. 'Bonfire Night.'

'Yes?'

'You don't want to go. I know you don't. So I'm letting you off the hook. You don't have to go with me. I'll be perfectly all right on my own with Morgan.'

He looked at her askance. 'Are you okay?'

She nodded quickly, smiling. 'I'm fine!'

Matt raised an eyebrow. 'Ah, yes—the *I'm fine* response.'

Then he laid a hand on her shoulder—supposedly in a friendly gesture, but to her it was something else. Something that was doing weird and wonderful tricks with her insides.

'I *want* to go with you. It'll be…good for me. Honestly. And I want Lily to enjoy it. Is that okay?'

He's touching me. His hand is just millimetres away from my skin…

She couldn't tear her eyes away from her paperwork. Afraid that if she looked into his eyes right now she'd be at risk of losing any last crumb of self-control she had. There were fireworks going off inside *her*, never mind at any display. Her skin felt as if it was sizzling. *Sizzling!* How had that happened? *Why* was it happening? And how the hell could she get herself out of this predicament?

I'm just going to have to keep my distance. Go with him to the display and make sure I keep a buggy's distance between us at all times. Oh, and not look at him. Because if he smiles at me then I'm done for.

'Okay,' she croaked.

He let go of her and returned to his patient, and she was finally able to breathe once more.

CHAPTER SIX

HE SHOULD NEVER have touched her like that. He'd suspected that maybe she was feeling a little attracted to him and he to her, but then it had gone out of his mind as he'd talked to his patient about uric acid and crystals and—

He'd reached for her to show her that it meant a lot to him that she should ask him to come to the fireworks display. Not just him, but Lily too. And yet the second he'd laid his hand on her he'd realised—too late—just what touching her was doing to him!

He'd let go as quickly as he could. Had turned away so he could gather himself and get his racing heart under control.

Bonfire Night for him wasn't just about sharing an evening with her. About watching a firework display in the sky. He was trying to get over something. To face up to his fears. To expose himself to something that he just knew was going to be difficult.

He didn't want to be afraid any more.

Bonfire Night was harmless. He kept trying to reason with himself. Nothing dangerous in it at all. Harmless rockets and cheap thrills, that was all. A few loud noises. Surely he could cope with that?

But now there was the other danger. Spending time with Brooke. Standing by her side, huddled close to her in the cold night, both of them staring up at the sky. She would be smiling and pointing things out to Morgan and he would be…

Matt sighed. He'd promised Jen's memory that he would show Lily the world. That he would not hide her from it. That they would continue to survive without her. That they would not pine, would not spend their life grieving. That they would join in, partake, engage. That he would be there for Brooke and Morgan the way Jen could not.

But there had to be a line. A line he would not cross no matter how she made him feel.

Lily was his world. He could not confuse her like that. Not that she understood, at this age, that she didn't have a mother.

But *he* did. He knew. And he wasn't looking for a replacement. He never would. It was just going to be Lily and him. And friends. Brooke would be a good friend, but nothing more.

He didn't want to admit that he felt disappointment at the thought. That he even felt a little sad. Brooke made his heart race. Her smile lit up his world and he felt good spending time with her. She made him feel safe and warm. She was easy to be with and he loved the way she laughed. It was infectious.

But it was scary how she made him question himself. His principles. His moral duty to uphold the memory of his wife and be respectful of how recently he'd lost her. Not even a year had passed yet!

Here he was, spending time with a wonderful woman, enjoying her company, feeling his heart racing madly, unable to pull his gaze away from her. And it was making him disturbed and afraid and guilty in equal measures.

Was it wrong? To be this close to her?

Whatever the answer was, it would have to wait. The fireworks display was tonight and he would be meeting Brooke there at six. The show started at six-thirty, which was perfect, because by the time it was over they wouldn't be too late putting the babies down for their bedtimes.

Lily's schedule was very important to him. She didn't have too many certainties in this world, but she did have a bedtime, and set naptimes and set feeds. Imposing a solid structure on her had helped him in those painful early days when he'd still been struggling with the loss of his wife. The hours of the day all checked off in a reassuring routine.

For now he was sitting on the floor with her, watching her play with soft, squishy bricks, babbling away as streams of saliva fell down her chin onto the bib that seemed permanently attached recently.

'We're going to see some fireworks tonight, Lily. Big, pretty lights and things that go bang. You'll like that. Yes, you will. Daddy won't, but you will. And you'll keep me strong, won't you? You always have.'

Lily looked up at him and smiled, a bubble forming at the corner of her mouth as she threw one block down on the floor. It bounced and rolled to him.

He picked it up and rolled it back, causing Lily to squeal with joy.

Such simple things. It didn't take much to make her happy. She was such an easy-going baby. Jen would have been so proud of her, their sweet little girl.

'I think I might put earplugs in—what do you think? Will that help?'

Lily offered him another brick.

'Too big, honey.' He smiled at her and took the brick

and, delighted, tried to clap her hands together, slightly missing.

He envied the easy joy of babies. They didn't seem to need much. They didn't seem to have cares or worries. They didn't know great pain or suffering. It was a pity that they all couldn't live in such simple terms.

He briefly wondered what Brooke was doing now. Was she sitting at home too, waiting for tonight? She was probably excited about it. She loved fireworks. He wished he had her enthusiasm.

It would seem that I am not content with my lot.

That bothered him. The fact that he felt something was missing but couldn't pinpoint it. He was healthy, he had a good job, a secure home, a beautiful baby girl. He should be happy. Satisfied.

But it was loneliness that impaired his wellbeing. He'd never been solitary before. He'd never imagined he would have to be. And yet here he was, counting down the hours until he could be with someone again. Someone who lifted his spirits and made him feel good.

Was that so wrong?

Or was he terrified in case it was right?

Brooke was counting down the hours. She'd been looking forward to this for a long time. Bonfire Night—one of the best nights of the year! It never lasted long, but there was nothing quite like forgetting all your worries and standing in the crisp, chilly evening, watching the amazing show up above.

It was carefree. There weren't many moments in life during which you could be carefree, but the night of November the fifth was one of them. And she had one particular fond memory of that night from childhood, when her dad had actually been sober enough to enjoy it with her.

She'd stood there, aged maybe seven or eight, and as the first fireworks had zoomed up into the sky, to explode in a mass of blue and green sparkles, she'd felt her dad slip his hand into hers and squeeze her fingers through her woollen mitten. Such a simple thing, but coming from a man who had been using alcohol to escape the grief he felt it had been an uplifting moment. Brooke had squeezed back and laid her head against his arm, her face turned up to the sky as she'd revelled in that singular moment in which her dad had seemed to say, *I'm here, sweetheart.*

They'd stood together holding hands for about half an hour, and then, when the display had been over, he'd walked her home, settled her into bed and then gone in search of his next drink. The loneliness of being at home without his wife's voice, his wife's presence, had been too much for him to bear.

She'd lived for those brief moments in which he reached out to her. But more often than not he hadn't. He'd told her once in a drunken rage that she looked too much like her mother and it was painful for him to look at her. That had broken her heart. But what could she do? She couldn't change her face, and though she'd tried dyeing her hair different colours she'd never liked the way she looked as a blonde, or a redhead, and had always reverted back to her long brown hair.

When she'd had Morgan she'd vowed to herself that no matter how much her daughter reminded her of Eric she would never blame her daughter for it. Even if every one of her features matched her father's and looked little to do with her mother she would love her child. She would treasure her always. She would never let her daughter feel that type of rejection from anyone.

But she did hope that her daughter would enjoy fireworks as much as she did. For a child they were magical and special, as long as they weren't afraid of the loud noises. She'd heard that tonight's display was going to be extra-special—the fireworks were going to be set in time to music. How amazing was *that* going to be?

Once again she checked she had everything ready. Warm clothes, tights and ear muffs for Morgan, fleece-lined boots, a thick cardigan and woolly hat, mittens for her. Perfect. She didn't want Morgan getting cold. There would probably be hot drinks available for adults, but not for babies!

And Matt would be coming.

Brooke let out a long, slow breath. She'd tried her hardest to let him off the hook, to tell him he didn't have to come with her, but he'd seemed determined. She liked it that he was sure he wanted to go, because at first she'd thought he wasn't. But now that she was experiencing these weird feelings about him she wasn't sure how she'd cope spending all that time with him. Away from work. Where people were relaxed and uninhibited.

She hoped and prayed she wouldn't do something stupid. Like gaze into his eyes for too long, or accidentally brush his hand, or—worse—*kiss him!* Because, heck, even though the *thought* of kissing Matt did spectacular, exciting things to her insides, she knew in the long run that it would be a mistake.

He was a widower. Still grieving. He was *off-limits*. It ought to be the law of the land that handsome, charming widowers should not be hit on for at least one year after their partner's passing, surely!

And she was going to be spending this special night

with him. Perhaps it wasn't all that special to him, though. Perhaps it was just her? Remembering the night that her father had finally seen her, reliving her childish excitement? Whereas for Matt perhaps it was just another night—a few bangs, a few lights, a waste of money going up in smoke. No doubt pretty, but he'd be happy for it to be over, so they could look forward to the *real* best night of the year—Christmas Eve.

Who knew? What she *did* know was that she couldn't let giddy excitement get the better of her. Carry her away on a frivolous impulse to do something stupid. Because— and she must make no mistake—doing *something stupid* with Matt would be appallingly embarrassing. They would have to work together afterwards, and she highly doubted that Matt would be receptive to her lips touching his.

No.

She would need to concentrate and keep her wits about her.

No forgetting his boundaries.

And no kissing Major Galloway!

The place was heaving with people waiting for the display to start. At first Brooke couldn't see Matt at all. Too many bodies…too many people bundled up in unfamiliar thick coats. She thought maybe he'd had a change of heart. Hadn't come after all. The disappointment that shot through her almost winded her. Until finally—suddenly—she spotted him. It was almost as if the crowd parted just for them.

Their eyes met and she sucked in a breath.

He's here.

The breath allowed her a moment to steady herself, get her heartbeat under control again. Back to its normal pace—or as near as she could make it. But his proximity, his singular presence, was having an effect on her. He looked particularly dark and dangerous in that black jacket, and his cobalt scarf brought out the sparkling blue of his eyes. Both his and Lily's cheeks already looked a little rosy in what was for her the perfect November evening. Crisp. Cold. With the promise of a frost tomorrow morning. He hadn't shaved either. She'd never seen him with stubble before and it added a certain delicious note to his appearance.

'You made it,' she said as he made his way through the throng towards her, using Lily's buggy like a plough.

Brooke saw various women notice him, just as they had at that awful Music Melody class, their eyes glinting in the darkness, hoping that he might notice them.

Only he didn't. He kept his gaze upon her, his face breaking into a smile as he got close. 'Just. I've been looking all over for you. I even considered putting up a flare.'

She smiled. 'No need for that.'

'No.'

She bent to say hello to Lily, who was sitting in her buggy kicking and swinging her feet as she batted hopelessly at the string of toys across the front of it. Like Morgan, she was wearing ear muffs. 'Hello, little one. Are you ready for all the pretty fireworks?'

'Bah-bah… Mmm… Pfft!'

Brooke smiled at her and looked up at Matt.

'I feel the same,' he added.

'Oh, really?' she stood up again and fought the urge to nudge his arm playfully. What was happening? One minute with the man and she was already feeling flirty.

Stop it, Brooke.

'How…erm…close do you want to get?' She meant to

the fireworks, but as soon as the words were out of her mouth she cringed.

'Er...not too close. You know—just in case the babies don't like it.'

He seemed apprehensive. Had he picked up on her feelings? Was he already at this minute regretting his decision to come out with her because she was starting to act like some crazy woman?

Because, looking at him right now, she saw he looked as if he wanted to run out of there. His gaze was flitting here, there and everywhere, as if checking for exit strategies. Only occasionally did his gaze fall upon her, as if to reassure her that, yes, of *course* he wanted to be here.

Everything about him—his face, his twitching jaw muscle, his body language—screamed that he wanted out. That this was the last place he wanted to be.

Brooke felt as if she was torturing the man by making him stay. Keen for him not to walk away and leave her standing there like an idiot, though, she sought to reassure him. 'It should start soon. Not long now.'

'That's great.' He stooped to pick Lily up out of her buggy and, thinking that was a good idea, she did the same thing with Morgan. At least holding her child she would have no spare hand to snuggle into his.

Both babies greeted each other by squealing and vaguely waving their arms in some approximation of saying hello, causing both parents to beam.

'I think they recognise each other!'

'I should think so. After all the time they spend together in the crèche. Daisy tells me they're quite the terrible twosome.'

Daisy was right. Brooke had seen them when she'd gone to the crèche to pick up her daughter after a long day. She'd often found Lily and Morgan playing side by side, or squealing with joy in the ball pit together. It was almost as if they were sisters.

'Should we get a drink or anything? Are you thirsty? I think they're selling hot chocolate somewhere.'

Matt shook his head. 'No spare hands for a hot drink. I'll survive, thanks.'

She nodded. He was right. They could hardly hold the girls *and* a steaming hot beverage. That would be a disaster.

All around them couples huddled together, and there was the aroma of hot chocolate, tea, coffee, and from somewhere jacket potatoes with beans was being served. It all reminded Brooke of Bonfire Nights from long ago, when her neighbours had cooked jacket potatoes in tin foil and served polystyrene cups filled with hot mushy peas and vinegar. There was something amazing about those familiar smells under the cloudless night sky.

From somewhere a PA system squealed into life and a man's voice welcomed them to the show. There was a little bit of housekeeping—they were told to stay behind the barrier at all times, given fire escape plans in case something dreadful happened, that kind of thing—and then his voice fell silent and a musical symphony began.

Brooke felt her heart accelerate. This was it! The moment they'd all been waiting for. She turned to look at Matt, to smile at him, and frowned slightly, noticing he looked rather hesitant and apprehensive.

But before she could say anything the fireworks began, screaming up into the night sky and pulling her attention away from Matt.

The colours lit up the night sky—pinks, purples, reds, greens, blues. There was a cacophony of explosions from rockets and sparkling glitter balls, whistling comets scattering light like flowers in bursts that split into smaller blasts—all of it to a background of music, the fireworks and the noise perfectly in time with the beat and rhythm.

Morgan was squealing with joy, clapping her little hands together, and Brooke was over the moon that her daughter loved it as much as she did! Her little face was lit up by the display above her.

'You love it! You *love it!*'

She turned to see if Lily loved it too, and was jolted from her bliss when she saw Matt standing there, frozen like a statue, his eyes tightly closed, his face screwed up as if he was in some sort of agony...

'Major? *Matt?* Are you all right?'

She grabbed at his arm to make him look at her, but he didn't open his eyes. He was muttering something to himself. Over and over. But she couldn't catch it. Couldn't make out what he was saying.

Hesitantly she reached up to lay a hand on his face. Standing close to him, almost face to face, she said loudly, '*Matt!* Open your eyes. Look at me. It's okay. Just look at me.'

She was scared. What was going on? Why did he look so terrified? He was an army doctor! He should be used to this kind of thing. He should—

And then realisation came to the fore and she knew what was wrong.

How could I have been so stupid?

Quickly she turned and put Morgan back into her buggy, strapping her in. She could still see the fireworks, but right now she needed to bring Matt back into the present. Because his mind was elsewhere. Stuck in a terrifying past event. She had to centre him. Ground him in reality.

Concerned for Lily, she raised her voice so he could

hear her. 'Matt? It's Brooke. Give me Lily. Let go of her. I've got her. That's it…'

She took the little girl and placed her in her own buggy. Strapped her in.

Then she turned back to Matt, placing a hand on either side of his face. 'Matt?' She waited a moment, torn with anguish at the look of pain on his face. *'Matt…'*

He opened his eyes, his gaze frantic until he tuned in to her voice and then it settled upon her.

As the fireworks continued above them, the bangs and cracks and whistling sound of gunpowder crackling all around them, people whooping and oohing at the sight, Brooke stood in front of Matt, her hands on his face, and made him look at her.

'Keep your eyes on me. You're okay. I've got you. They're just fireworks. They're not what you think they are. You're safe, Matt. Do you hear me? You're *safe*.'

His frightened gaze settled on her own and fixed upon her. 'I…I hear you. I'm s-s-safe.'

'Put your hands on Lily's buggy. That's it. Now, just listen to my voice and follow me. We're going to move away from here. But slowly! No need for us to rush. We're safe.'

She saw his hands were trembling, but he followed her orders.

Feeling sick, and guilty at what she'd put him through, she led the way out through the crowd, away from the field and onto the pathway, and then the road, over to where she had parked her car and beyond.

There was a small café lighting up the street, still decorated with spider's webs and pumpkins from Halloween a few nights earlier. They went in and settled down at a table.

Brooke ordered a couple of teas from the waitress and

gave Morgan a sippy cup of juice from her bag. Then she sat opposite Matt and took his freezing cold hands in her own and waited. Waited for him to be able to speak.

He looked a little worn out, but not embarrassed, which was good. For there was no shame in what had happened.

When the drinks arrived she added plenty of sugar to his and pushed the cup in front of him. 'Drink,' she ordered.

He reached for the cup and took a small sip, wincing at the sweetness. 'Thanks.'

'Is it okay if I give Lily a rusk?'

He nodded and took another sip before he looked up at her face and grimaced. 'I'm sorry I spoilt your night.'

Brooke shook her head. 'No. You didn't spoil it. It was *my* fault. I should have thought that you might have…I didn't know. I don't know where you were stationed, or what happened, but I should have considered the possibility.'

'The PTSD…it's…mild, actually. I hardly notice it until nights like these.' He glanced out of the window at the display that was still thrilling all the onlookers. 'I should have said something when you asked me to the fireworks, but I thought I could tough it out. For Lily.' He laughed ruefully. 'They're just fireworks, right?'

Post-traumatic stress disorder could be a crippling condition. It was an anxiety disorder brought on by a previous stressful, frightening or distressing event. Someone suffering from the condition would often relive that event through flashbacks brought on by triggers in the present day.

'Do you want to talk about it?'

She couldn't get his face out of her mind. The way he had looked as she had held his face in her hands. The way he had felt frozen, chilled by the night air and paralysed by fear. She didn't ever want to see him go through that again. And *she'd* caused it. By bringing him here.

If there was one thing her father had taught her it was that you avoided pain as much as you could. You evaded it, you did what you had to not to face it. The fact that Matt had chosen to come here anyway, knowing how the fireworks might affect him, made her feel proud of him. This wasn't a man who ran away from things that hurt. He was brave, and she wanted to be there for him because of that.

'I was pinned down by enemy fire in Afghanistan. We'd been ambushed. I was part of a medevac team. We weren't heavily armed—we'd been treating the locals, offering vaccinations and first aid, and then we were asked to relocate to help re-staff a field hospital. Twelve men and women were killed when the first trucks blew. Men and women I knew. Had worked alongside. People who just wanted to help, no matter who they were—English, American, locals. It didn't matter. People were people, you know?'

She nodded, listening.

'I dragged a soldier out of the road. He'd been hit in the leg and was bleeding heavily. He was screaming. We found shelter and we had to sit there. Waiting for hours. All around us there was the sound of gunfire and explosions. It just never stopped. I sat there, shivering in the freezing cold, not knowing whether I would live to see the sun rise. And all that time the shooting never stopped. I could hear bullets hitting the walls next to my head. Could hear people shouting. Yelling. Calling for help. But I was pinned down. I couldn't do anything to help them.'

She reached across the table to lay her hand upon his. 'I'm so sorry.'

'It was combat. It happened. It's just hard for me being outside at night, and then the sounds of all those fireworks going off...I...'

He didn't have to say any more. Didn't have to explain. She understood. Could see why tonight had affected him so. But still he had come to spend time with her. Honouring his wife's promise to her friend to be there for her despite the risk to himself.

That meant a lot to her. More than she could put into words. Because no one had ever been there for her like that. No one had ever put aside their own pain like that to be there for *her*. Not her father. No one.

He pulled his hand out from under hers and took hold of her hand, squeezing her fingers in thanks. 'You called me Matt.'

She blushed, nodded with a smile. 'I did.'

'Thank you.'

Unsure of how to respond, she sipped her own tea. 'I've put you through a lot tonight. I'd hate to think of you going home to your own place and being on your own after all of this. I have a spare bed at mine. And a travel cot that Lily could sleep in. Just so you're not alone tonight. If you want.'

She fully expected him to turn her down, but she really did hate the idea that he would have to go home alone after this. She knew what the nights were like once you'd put the baby to bed. Solitude could hit you like a brick. The house was empty. No sounds save for the ticking of a clock to remind you of your life passing with no one else in it.

Matt might be alone, but he had her as a friend and she wanted him to know that. It was an innocent invitation. One friend to another.

Please don't be alone tonight. I can be there for you like you were for me.

'Oh...that's really kind, but—'

'Please. I'd really like it if you came. Tomorrow is Sunday—neither of us have to work. We could spend the day doing something nice. Replace this memory with a good one. Lily can borrow Morgan's clothes if you don't have enough with you, and I have nappies and bottles and baby food. I even have a spare toothbrush.'

She was smiling, trying to think of all the reasons he might say he couldn't do it. She really wanted to spend this time with him. He'd done so much for her.

'You'd have to turn your underwear inside out, but...' She blushed, laughing. 'Come on—it'll be fun.'

He was smiling back at her. 'You've thought of everything.'

'I'm ambushing you again. But hopefully in a good way.'

Matt nodded. 'Okay. That'll be nice. A sleepover! I haven't done one of those since I was about eight years old.'

Brooke smiled back, pleased that he'd accepted. 'I don't think the concept has changed. You stay up late watching movies and eating popcorn. Or I can provide wine, if you need it.'

'I don't really touch alcohol, but I'll have cocoa if you have any?'

His cuteness broadened the grin on her face. 'Cocoa it is.'

Matt made her happy.

Very happy indeed.

And she was glad that she could make him smile. Especially after tonight. Outside, the fireworks were still raging in the sky, but not for much longer. They would leave when it was all over and the streets were filled with happy families.

For now she was content to sit in the café with him, nursing her tea with him still holding her hand.

It felt good. His touch. And even though earlier she'd been determined to keep her distance from him his contact now made her feel completely different.

They were people. People were tactile. They expressed care and affection through touch, didn't they? A hug to make people feel better. A hand on another to say, *I'm here for you. I care. You matter to me.*

And Major Matt Galloway mattered to her very much indeed.

CHAPTER SEVEN

'So this is home sweet home?' Matt carried Lily into Brooke's house and followed her through to the lounge. He hadn't known what to expect, but now that he was here he could see that it suited her perfectly.

It was just a two-bedroomed flat, in a tall tower of concrete and glass, but inside she had turned it into a perfect little retreat. He'd never had the eye of an interior designer, but he wished that he had. Dr Bailey had clearly known the kind of feeling she had wanted here.

There were comfy sofas covered in scatter cushions with cosy throws draped over the back. A bookcase in the corner was filled with well-thumbed books, and next to it was a lamp draped with a silk scarf, a recliner and a small cherry-red table piled high with more books. There was a small fireplace, filled with candles rather than coal, and protected by a screen so that Morgan couldn't get close. On the walls were soft watercolour paintings of animals, but instead of being portrayed in the normal colours of brown and grey they were pink and blue and rainbow-coloured.

It was a happy room. A cosy room. It oozed warmth and comfort.

'I like what you've done with the place. Love the artwork.'

'Thanks.'

He went over to a painting of a swan, created with brush strokes of green and blue, peering closer at it. Then he turned to look at her in surprise. '*You* painted these?'

'I'm just an amateur, but I like painting.'

'They're brilliant! If ever we run out of patients in A&E you've got another career you can fall back on.'

'Well, as I don't see A&E emptying soon, the art world has a lot to be grateful for.'

She went to put Morgan down, aware that both babies would need to go to bed soon. She opened the storage cupboard by the front door and pulled out the travel cot that she'd been given but never used yet. It would be perfect for Lily to sleep in.

Scrunching up her nose, she undid the straps and worked out how to open it. Thankfully it was easy. and she set it up in no time. 'I'll put this in the spare room. Morgan's cot is in my bedroom, so she shouldn't wake you.'

'I probably need to change Lily. Have you got a place I can do that?'

'There's a changing station in your room, or I've got a mat you can borrow if you don't have one.'

'Thanks. I'll give Lily her last bottle and then get her ready for bed.'

'Same.'

They both busied themselves settling their daughters. Brooke ran a bath, so that the two girls could have a bit of a splash, and once that was done they gave the babies their bottles and settled them to sleep.

Morgan settled quickly, as usual, so Brooke had a bit of a tidy-up whilst she waited for Matt to emerge from what would be his room for the night.

She felt strangely on edge. As if she'd had a shot of

adrenaline. She used it to clean the kitchen, being quite thorough, lifting things to wipe underneath, pulling out the toaster, making sure there were no crumbs left behind, wiping down the fridge handles—that kind of thing. It seemed easier to think about what needed doing than to think about how it would be to sit down with Matt in her *home*.

No man had ever made it back here since she'd left Eric. Even *he* had only seen the place a couple of times, preferring to spend time in his own place and make her come to him.

She liked it that it was her sanctuary. Her book nook. A warm, welcoming space that was just for her and Morgan. Their bolthole from the world.

To have Matt here felt…odd. But good.

Brooke rinsed out the sink and then filled the kettle to make them both a hot drink. Just as the kettle came to the boil Matt joined her in the kitchen.

'Finally! Thought she'd never settle.'

'She's in a strange place. Different bedroom, different bed—she was bound to be a little unsettled.'

He nodded. 'Thanks again for offering to put up with us for the entire weekend.'

She smiled at him. 'Not a problem. Kettle's boiled. Still up for that cocoa?'

'If you're having one.'

'Cocoa it is.'

'Thanks. I know I said it earlier, but this really is a great place you have here.'

She spooned cocoa powder into mugs. 'Thanks. It was important to me to get it right. It's the first space I've owned that's truly mine.'

'You've only lived with your father?'

'If *lived* is the right word for it, then, yeah. *Co-existed* might be more precise.' She added sugar and a splash of milk, then poured in the hot water.

'What was he like? Before, I mean...'

Brooke appreciated him not actually saying *before he became an alcoholic* out loud. She sighed, her back to him as she stirred the drinks. 'He was an artist. A good one.'

'Really? Watercolours like yours?'

'No. Acrylics, mostly.'

'What sort of thing did he paint?'

She turned to hand him his drink. 'I'll show you. Come with me.'

She led him through to the lounge area and settled onto one of the couches. She picked up the tablet that she'd left charging by the side of it. She typed the name Phillip Bailey into a search engine and various artwork soon showed up in the results.

A yellow buttercup sprouting through a solitary crack of cement; a rose growing in the middle of a desert; a vibrant tree with thick green foliage living in a wasteland desolated by war.

'He painted hope.'

'Hope?'

'He wanted to show that even in the darkest places life could grow. That beauty and joy could still be found in places you wouldn't expect.'

'They're amazing. Does he still paint?'

'He hasn't touched his palette since my mother died.'

Matt was silent for a moment, staring at the pictures, enlarging one that showed a flowering water lily in an oil slick. 'He lost his belief system?'

Brooke nodded. 'Yes.'

'When devastation struck him he couldn't see the flowers right before him? He couldn't see the light any more?'

'There wasn't any,' she said.

Matt turned to face her. 'But there was. There was *you*.'

Her? No. Matt was wrong. She'd never been her father's guiding light. His North Star. *Never*.

Her confusion must have shown on her face, because Matt went on.

'I've been where he has. We've both lost our wives and I know how that must have made him feel. Words can't describe it. To lose someone suddenly. Without warning. The one person who brightened your day inexplicably taken away. And suddenly there's this new person. This tiny newborn person who needs you the most, even as your heart is open, bleeding and raw, and you feel you can't dig yourself out of the mire.'

'But *you* did it. You didn't turn to drink.'

'No. But I wanted to turn to *something*. Anything that would take away the pain. In A&E we see all the different ways that people numb themselves. It's the human condition. We're not strong.'

'But you didn't do any of those things.'

'No. I saw Lily. Hours old. Wrinkly and squawky and crying. And I realised that what she needed to take away her pain was me. She'd not been held by her mother, so she needed her father. I was the only one who could help her. So I picked her up and promised her that I would protect her to the end of my days.'

He swallowed.

'I was still lost without my wife, my love. I was still bleeding with the pain of losing her. But Lily was my light. My guide through it all. I would have been nothing without her to keep me here. To keep me sane. Perhaps your father never saw that…that you could have been his rose in the desert.'

Brooke blinked back tears. 'He told me he couldn't look at me. That I reminded him too much of my mother.'

'I see Jen in Lily, too.'

'So why didn't my father hold on to *me*? Why did he not care? Why did he walk away from me when it mattered? If I was his light?'

Matt shook his head. 'I can't answer for him. I don't know.'

'He was weak. You're strong. That's the difference.'

'I'm not strong.'

'Yes, you are. All that you've been through and yet you're here. Lily's father. Dedicated, hard-working. *Sober*. A soldier who went to war and survived. You've got scars, but you've never weakened. Being a father is what drives you and I've never been enough to drive anyone.'

The words were out before she could stop them, and her cheeks coloured.

'Sorry—ignore that. I was just having a pity party. It's over now.' She gave a brief smile and sipped at her cocoa.

'You're entitled to be mad at him. He let you down. But I really don't think there's anything you could say to him that he hasn't already said to himself. He's still in hell, I'd say. The drink puts out some of the flames. For a while. But then when the pain comes back…the regret, the sorrow…'

'He goes back to the booze. To numb himself again.'

Could it be true? That her father hated himself for what he'd done to her? That he berated himself day after day after day for letting all these years pass, letting his baby grow into a woman and still not putting things right?

'Lily's lucky to have you. If my father had been *half* the man you are…' She glanced at him, not intending to hold his gaze, but she did.

The intensity in his eyes was shocking. It was as if he could see deep inside her soul and liked what he saw. As if he saw *her*. Not the public persona—not Dr Bailey, A&E consultant, a single mum—he saw *her*. The frightened, self-doubting version. But even seeing her vulnerable and exposed like that didn't make him turn away.

He was staying. Interested. Intrigued.

It was too much.

Brooke stood up, still holding her mug. 'Well, it's… er…been a long day. I ought to…turn in.' She vaguely waved her arm in the direction of her bedroom. 'Goodnight, Major.'

He stood up, facing her. 'Goodnight, Dr Bailey.'

She had to tear her gaze away. It was hard. As if he was a magnet, pulling her in, and it took every ounce of her nerve and strength to walk in the other direction.

Brooke lay in bed and stared at the ceiling.

Morgan was sleeping soundly in her cot, one little fist tucked up underneath her chin, her other arm cast over her head. She'd be good now, at least. The latest teething episode seemed to be over, which meant Brooke should be getting a full night of sleep.

But sleep remained elusive. Out of arm's reach. Ridiculously, she felt wide awake, and completely physically aware that Matt was just in the next room to hers. Literally feet away. Separated by a wall. A line of bricks. That was it.

He was in the next room!

She'd bet that he was asleep. He'd had a stressful evening, what with the panic attack at the display. The adrenaline of that must have made him tired. He was probably snoozing away in dreamland, completely unaware of where he was. Where *she* was.

Through a small slit in her curtains she could see the stars in the night sky. Twinkling points of light in the darkness.

Could it be true what Matt had said about her father? She'd always been angry with him for not being there for her, at the fact that he never wanted to talk about her mother or even spend any time with his daughter. She'd thought it was because she was worthless. Why else would he ignore her?

It had never occurred to her that it was too painful for him. That he'd loved her mother so much that the pain of her loss was too much. Because human beings didn't deal with pain very well. Self-medicating with whatever worked to take the pain away—pills, drugs, alcohol, cigarettes, food. When a child cried and wouldn't stop what did most parents do? They offered a biscuit or another indulgent treat, teaching children that to make the pain go away you filled yourself with something else instead.

Was her father still trying to make himself feel better? Could that be it? Perhaps it wasn't that *she* was worthless, not worth loving. It was just that he couldn't cope and had found the thing that worked for him, no matter how bad it was. He might once have made a living painting hope, but what if she who *should* have been his hope, his light in the darkness of his grief, had been too bright for him to look at?

Who wouldn't give anything to be numb when pain struck?

Yet Matt had pushed through *his* pain. Had been able to put his pain to one side so he could be there for his baby. He was solid. Dependable.

Attractive, gorgeous, a gentleman...

She let out a heavy breath and turned to her bedside table for her glass of water.

Damn! I didn't bring one in, did I? I was in such a hurry to escape that look in his eyes.

She needed a drink. She felt parched. And now she was aware of it she'd focus on it so much she'd never get any sleep!

Matt was bound to be asleep, right? If she crept out there, past his room, he'd never hear her go into the kitchen for a glass of water. It wasn't as if she was going to put the kettle on, or anything. She would be safe, right?

Perhaps I don't need a drink of water that badly?

Only she really did. And her legs felt restless. She needed to get up and walk, and he was in another room. It wasn't as if he was sleeping on the couch or anything.

Having persuaded herself that it would be safe to go and get her drink, Brooke threw back the covers and swung her legs out of bed. She wrapped her robe around her waist and carefully opened the door, aware that the bedroom door might make a sound at its widest point. She slipped through the gap and padded down the hallway, past his bedroom door and into the kitchen.

She breathed a sigh of relief and switched on the light. Blinking rapidly, she quietly opened the kitchen cupboard and grabbed a glass, filling it with water from the tap. Taking a long swallow of the refreshing fluid, she turned to go—and saw Matt standing in the doorway.

Instantly her heart began to pound. He was wearing only a tee shirt and boxers, and she couldn't help but notice his fine arms and long, muscled legs.

'I hope I didn't scare you—I needed a drink. I usually have one beside my bed, but being in a strange place I forgot all about it,' he explained.

'Same. About needing the drink, that is.' She gestured with her glass and smiled, noticing his hair looked a little ruffled, as if he'd been tossing and turning. 'Lily still asleep?'

'Out like a light.'

'Good.'

It was as if she couldn't take her eyes off him. He filled her vision.

'I'd best be getting back, then.' She went to move past him, through the doorway, and he did step to one side so that she could pass. But she made the mistake of looking up at him and smiling her thanks as she did so. Pausing. Ever so briefly.

His gaze locked with hers and she could read desire in his eyes—apprehension, fear, but most of all yearning.

She wanted to kiss him so badly, but she didn't want to overstep the mark in case he—

Matt stepped forward, his gaze going to her lips, then to her eyes, then her lips again.

Brooke's breathing changed and she stared back, taking in all the features of this beautiful man up close.

They weren't touching. Neither of them was overstepping their boundary, but both were fighting the urge to reach out and take what they wanted.

'Brooke, I...'

She looked directly into his soul. He'd said her name. 'You called me Brooke.'

'Yes.'

'Not Dr Bailey.'

'No.'

And he came ever closer, watching her intently, as if he expected her to place her hand on his chest at any moment to stop him. But she didn't stop him. She wanted him close to her—wanted to see what it would feel like. She wanted him to kiss her.

Brooke closed her eyes as his head dipped and his lips

touched hers—feather-light, brief. She stood there, her entire nervous system lit up like the national grid, waiting, anticipating more.

And he gave her what she wanted.

His hands came up to cradle each side of her face as he drew her to him and deepened the kiss.

Her whole body ached, desiring more of him as she kissed him back. He was all she could think of, and his lips, his kiss, fuelled a fire inside her that had long lain dormant.

All thoughts of caution, of whether this was right or wrong, went straight out of her head. All that seemed to matter to her at that moment was that he continued to kiss her.

Hesitantly, her arms embraced him, feeling the raw, hard muscles beneath his skin.

This man desired her. Wanted her. She had not expected this. She'd known—felt—that she was developing feelings of attraction for him, but she had told herself it was one-sided. That he would not feel the same. And yet here they were...

What did this mean? Was it just one kiss, or would it be more? She wanted more. Wanted to give in to what she was feeling right now and take all of him. Have everything he could offer right now and the future be damned!

But...they had to work together. They had their children to consider. They had to be responsible.

'Matt.' She broke the kiss and, breathing heavily, stared deeply into his eyes. 'We need to think about this.'

He stared back, then nodded, releasing her. And as he did so disappointment entered every cell in her body. She'd felt on fire, and instead of allowing herself to blaze she had doused the flames. She hated herself for doing so.

'You're right.' He stepped back, leaning his body against the doorframe.

She mirrored his movements opposite. 'We're work colleagues…we…' She couldn't think of what else to say. Her body, her mind was screaming at her to forget the doubts, just kiss him again!

'Have to be sensible?' He finished for her.

'Yes.'

No!

They stared at each other for a moment more, and then suddenly they were back in each other's arms, their lips pressed against each other's, the long lengths of their bodies pressed tight as his tongue found hers and she groaned.

She *needed* him. More than she had ever allowed herself to need a man. She didn't care about the consequences now. *Need* trumped everything else, and she cast her hesitations aside as quickly as he cast aside her robe.

She could feel him against her, his desire pressing into her, and then she was reaching for his tee shirt to pull it free over his head.

They staggered into the lounge and Matt reached under her long tee. She felt the wondrous heat of his hands upon her bare flesh, her breasts, and it was *everything*. His touch, his taste, his heat. It fed her. It was life.

How was it possible that he could make her feel this way? It had never felt this *urgent* with Eric and he was the father of her child. It hadn't felt this way *ever*. With any man. Not this intensity. Not this much.

Was it because there was already so much history between them? Even before they'd met they'd shared a history. A love for the same person. And that bond, that strength they shared, had pulled them together.

They were the same, Matt and her. Both traumatised,

both alone, both single parents facing the same struggles in the same work environment. Both of them hurt by previous encounters. There was a saying that misery liked company… Did hurt people naturally seek each other out?

No. It had to be more than that for them. They shared the same wound. They were two halves of the same scar. Perhaps that was why it felt so right to be in his arms. Because only together could they heal.

Brooke breathed his name as he moved into her. Felt the force of his need within her and sighed delightfully. This felt *right*. That was what counted. Even though she had tried to fight it, tried to keep her distance. Perhaps the reason they had failed at that was because they were meant to be?

No. She wouldn't allow herself to think that far ahead. Experience had taught her that people generally let her down. People she had thought she could rely on.

What mattered was the here and now. She would deal with today and not worry about tomorrow.

Not yet.

And it helped that the today—the *now*—felt so damned good!

He woke in Brooke's bed. It was still dark and the sun had not yet risen. He was used to waking early. A habit from his early army days, when he'd tried to cheat the agony of the drill sergeant crashing into his dorm, shouting and yelling.

He still liked to wake early. To lie there for a moment and mentally prepare himself for the day. It was a habit that had come in handy after Jen had died. He'd lie there for a few minutes, thinking of all he had to do to get through the day. Things that Lily would need. Things he would need to get done in the house. Whether they would need to go food shopping. The five-mile walk he would try to fit in, with Lily in her buggy, because it was important to get out of the house and not pine away in grief.

Grief, guilt, sorrow—they were all time-stealers and he could never allow them a place in his life. Not until he had control back. Not until the intensity of that grief had been absorbed and wasn't as sharp as it had been.

It took a moment or two for him to remind himself of where he was. Not his own home…not his own bed.

Brooke's bed. And she was in his arms as he spooned her. He inhaled her scent, her perfume, as she lay there and felt a pang in his heart.

She looked so beautiful. Her long dark hair over the pillow. Her naked shoulders so smooth and feminine. The feel of the length of her against his body.

His own body stirred in response and he closed his eyes to regain control of himself.

Last night had been…*amazing.* A gift that he hadn't expected at all. He'd been lying there, staring at the ceiling, unable to get his pillows right, tossing and turning, berating himself for his forbidden feelings for this woman who wasn't his wife.

His attraction for her had been growing steadily. He'd known that for a long time. But he'd told himself over and over that he would control it and do nothing about it—because it wasn't right.

But at the fireworks display he'd lost the present, had been thrown right back into the horror of Khost Province in Afghanistan. And as he'd heard the cracks and whistles of the fireworks he'd seen in his head the two trucks ahead of him being blown off their axles and thrown to one side. Felt the rush of adrenaline as he'd taken cover, aware that a bullet might rip through his heart at any second, but still going back for a fallen comrade.

He had no longer been standing in a field, watching fireworks with delight, he'd been back there, cowering under a hail of bullets, and she—Brooke—had brought him out of that.

He would not have thought it possible. But her touch, her voice, her insistence that he listen to her, had cut through the hell in his mind and pulled him out of his terror.

Her eyes... That look in her eyes had held him in the present and made him breathe, made him take root in reality again, and he'd been so thankful for that. When she'd said that she didn't want him to be alone he'd been grateful. The idea of returning home with Lily to put her to bed and be alone again with his torturous thoughts had been enough to make him accept.

He'd not said yes to get her into bed. He'd not said yes to see what would happen. He'd said yes because he'd genuinely wanted to be with her. To be wrapped in her protection and soothed by her presence, knowing she was just in the next room. Not to be alone again. Not again. Just for one night.

He'd got up for a drink not knowing that she was already up, and when he'd walked out of his room and seen that the kitchen light was on he'd almost faltered. Had almost gone back to his room. Only he hadn't. He'd wanted to see her. To say goodnight properly.

And then he'd kissed her.

Again, *she* had been the strong one—had tried to make them pause for a moment. Take a breather. Think things through. And he'd tried... But he'd still had the taste of her on his lips and he'd stamped down on all the doubt, on all the voices in his head telling him it was a

bad idea, because his body, his being, had been screaming that it needed her. That she was the other half of himself. The one who could save him.

And like a drowning man grabbing at a buoy, he'd
reached out and pulled her towards him, felt his soul
drowning in the pleasure of her touch, her kiss, her
heat—so much so that all logical thought had gone out
of his head.

But now the cold light of day was approaching. He
could feel it. Inching closer over the horizon accompa-
nied by his old friends guilt and doubt.

I buried my wife just months ago and already I'm in
another woman's bed.

Brooke thought he was strong. But he wasn't. He was
weak. And he'd proved that. Sleeping with Brooke, staying the night with her, had been everything he might have
dreamed of—but now he felt as if he was in a nightmare.
Racked by the intrusive thoughts in his head that told him
he'd taken things a step too far.

She'd asked him to stay over. To spend Sunday with
her too. And though he could imagine it would be de-
lightful, and the babies would have fun, he knew he had
to think practically. Right now they were in a bubble. A
lovely bubble. One he would struggle to leave. But it was
the right thing to do.

He couldn't live in a bubble. He had to return to reality. Strong people, the people to admire, were the ones
who survived in harsh reality.

He couldn't stay here, warm and cosy, pressed up
against her body. Because already he was wanting more
of her, could feel his body awakened by its need to have
her again, But it would be wrong. He'd be taking advantage. Brooke had tried to put the brakes on last night and

she'd been right to do so. He ought to be the strong man she kept telling him he was and do something about it.

Gently he rolled away from her and slipped out of bed. He stood there for a moment to see if she would wake, and already he could feel his reluctance to leave. But, no.

I have to do this.

He padded softly away, wincing slightly as the door creaked, and crept into the lounge, where their clothes had been discarded the night before. He got dressed and hung her robe and long tee shirt over the back of the couch, neatly folded. Then he went into the other bedroom and grabbed the rest of his clothes and checked on Lily. She was starting to stir. Snuffling and rubbing at her face with her hands.

Matt checked the time. Six-thirty a.m. Lily was right on cue. He had no idea what time Brooke and Morgan would wake, but if he had the nerve to wait and let Lily wake on her own then he would be able to get her out of here without her crying.

Back in the lounge, he found a notepad and pen by the phone and scribbled Brooke a note. He tried to make it sound friendly, and not as if he were rejecting her. Saying that he just needed to pop home, and as he'd woken early he'd decided to leave her to rest and sleep in on her day off before work tomorrow.

He read the note over and over, wondering if he'd pitched it right. It seemed okay to him, but he was very aware of the fact that Brooke felt men always rejected her, and he didn't want her to think the same of him.

They would be sensible. Sort this out. Work through it. Like adults.

They'd be able to do that, right?

He had to believe that they would.

CHAPTER EIGHT

HE'D SPENT SUNDAY trying to put the night he and Brooke had spent together out of his mind—but it had been impossible. All he'd been able to think of was the way she had felt, the way she had tasted, those little sounds she had made in the back of her throat as he had made love to her and how good it had made him feel to be wrapped in her arms.

It had been one hot night, and he knew it was a night that he would never forget.

He'd left his mobile phone at home and taken Lily out for their usual five-mile walk. He'd gone all touristy and caught the bus to Trafalgar Square. He and Lily had fed the pigeons, walked through Covent Garden and along the Embankment. They'd eaten out at a small family-friendly cafeteria, and then he'd taken her to a small park where there were baby swings and small slides for her to play on.

And all the time he had been looking at Lily, talking to her, laughing with her, he'd seen his wife looking at him out of her eyes and he'd felt terrible for moving on. Felt as if he was horribly leaving his wife behind.

They'd had so many dreams, he and Jen, for their future. And what had he done? Taken *her* old job, in *her* old department, in some kind of sad effort to be in the place where his wife had lived and worked so that somehow he could still stay connected to her. So that he could touch the things that she had touched, chat with the people who had become her work family, and so that he could meet the famous Dr Brooke Bailey, whom he'd heard so much about and who was owed a promise.

I think I might have taken that promise too far.

And now he was at work early, waiting for his shift to start and fanning through the pages of the most recent medical journal.

There were some cutting edge developments happening in the world of medicine. On every page was evidence of people moving forward. Doctors and professors looking to see how they could improve things for the future. They weren't sitting still, being static. They knew that to improve you had to change with the times. Take risks.

And when he came to the back of the journal, where all the job vacancies were, his eyes were drawn to one in particular.

Auckland City Hospital.

Auckland, New Zealand. The place where he and Jen had planned to go in the future. The city that had been their ultimate goal—a place to raise their daughter. A place where Jen had spent time during her gap year and had loved.

But would considering something like that now be a move forward or a move backwards? It was an old dream. A dream that he'd shared with his wife.

She wasn't here any more and he was. And although they'd spent many a time talking about how wonderful it would be for their daughter, would doing it now, applying for the post, be the best thing for Lily? Jen had promised

Brooke that she would be there to help her raise Morgan, but she'd also wanted to emigrate. To do what was best for *their* little family. Shouldn't that be his priority?

He'd taken this job to put down roots. He wanted the future to be stable for Lily. She'd already lost her mother—did she need to be moved from pillar to post? Never quite sure where her home was? It wasn't a simple case of packing up your things and jumping on a plane. It meant leaving people behind. Leaving behind a life he'd already started to create and never planning for the future.

He'd had that sort of childhood, following his father in his postings abroad. Sometimes he'd liked it—other times he'd hated it. But he had grown to love it. Had matured and chosen the same life for himself. Had enrolled as a doctor in the army and flitted around the globe whilst Jen had stayed rooted in one spot.

Was it the right thing to do?

'Looking for another job?' asked Kelly as she glanced over his shoulder, walking to her locker and removing her coat and scarf. 'Have we driven you crazy so soon?'

He stared at the advertisement and grimaced. 'Not sure…'

Kelly hung up her things and then grabbed her stethoscope, draping it around her neck, then her ID card to pin to the waistband of her skirt. She came over and sat beside him, glancing at the advert. 'New Zealand? Beautiful place.'

'You've been there?'

'No. But I've always wanted to.' She took the magazine from him and smiled. 'Perhaps I ought to apply? Give you some competition.'

He laughed. 'I don't know what to do. Jen and I always

said that that's where we'd end up working. We wanted to give Lily an amazing life in a brand-new beautiful country.'

Kelly nodded. 'And it would be. Do it now—whilst she's a baby—and she'll probably never even remember the UK.'

Hmm... He'd not thought about that part. She *wouldn't* remember, would she? But *he* would. And he'd never forget all the wonderful people he had met here. His friends and his family were all here. And he'd be leaving behind Brooke.

That would be hard. Reneging on a promise.

He tossed the journal onto the table. 'It was just a thought. Anyway, are you trying to get rid of me, Kelly?' he asked with a smile.

'Gawd, no! You're the only decent thing to look at around here. If you left I don't know what I'd do!' She got up to make herself a quick cup of tea, and as she stood by the kettle raised an empty mug. 'Want one?'

'Sure.'

At that moment Brooke walked in, her face stony, and headed straight to her locker.

Matt got up and went over to her. 'Hi.'

She didn't look at him. She yanked open her locker and shrugged off her coat, then got out all the accoutrements she'd need for the day. She closed her locker and walked out again, without saying a word.

He watched her go, feeling awful inside. Perhaps he hadn't pitched his note as well as he'd thought? And perhaps leaving his phone behind all day on Sunday had not been a good idea either, because when he'd got back he'd seen missed calls and texts from Brooke, clearly wanting to talk to him.

Which he'd never answered.

'What did you *do*?' asked Kelly. 'If looks could've killed you'd be lying on a mortuary slab right now.'

'Looks like I need to apologise.' He put his hands in his pockets as he thought about how best to do that.

Kelly handed him his mug of tea. 'Well, I sure as hell hope you're good at grovelling, because that girl looked like she meant business.'

He sipped his tea and was thoughtful.

There was a hell of a lot he needed to think through today.

Brooke couldn't believe it! That he'd just said *hi* to her as if everything was okay between them! As if he hadn't walked out on her like that and left a stupid note.

He'd said that he would spend the day with them on Sunday. She'd made plans in her head—a walk in the park, maybe a meal out, a good chat over some good comfort food, maybe taking some pictures of the babies together—something like that. Nothing special. Just things they could do together.

But then they'd made love—unexpectedly—and it had been the single most amazing thing that had ever happened to her. No man had ever made her feel that way. It had been as if…as if…

As if he loved me…

That *had* to be wrong, right?

But the way he'd made love to her… That couldn't have been just sex. It hadn't been just a quickie—wham, bam, thank you, ma'am. It had been *special*. Tender. Loving. She'd felt as if she'd found the lost part of herself, one she'd never known was missing.

Falling asleep in his arms, in her bed, had felt *so good*. To know that he was wrapped around her, the length of his strong body against hers, had made her feel safe and secure for the first time since *for ever*.

The scent of him, the feel of his hard body moulded around hers...

She'd woken with a smile upon her face. A silly, dreamy smile as she'd yawned and stretched—and suddenly realised that there was no one next to her.

Brooke had sat up, alert, feeling the sheets to see if they were warm, to see if maybe she had dreamed it all. The sheets had been cold and she'd been naked, and she never slept naked, and her body had felt pleasantly used. As if she were glowing.

She'd thought that maybe he was in the kitchen. Or perhaps he'd had to get up to check on Lily in the next room?

So she'd lain back in bed against the pillows, still with a smile upon her face, thinking that at any minute he would come through the door and say good morning, and maybe—just maybe—if the babies weren't yet awake, have a repeat of what had happened last night?

She'd felt glad that they had come together. She'd had no regrets. Not then. Because she'd felt sure that of all the men in the world Matt was not one of those who would walk away from her and leave her behind. And they'd moved forward in their relationship, hadn't they? You didn't have a night like that with someone and walk away.

But she'd waited, and she'd waited, and when she'd started to get that funny feeling in her stomach she'd got up and slipped on a tee shirt and knickers to go and look for him.

And discovered that the only thing left of Matt and Lily was a note.

Brooke,
I'm sorry, but I had to go. We crossed a line last night, and I should never have allowed it to happen.
　I didn't want to wake you. I know you offered for us to spend the day with you and Morgan, but I really think we should respect each other's boundaries, so I'll see you at work on Monday.
Many thanks once again,
Matt x

Many thanks? That was the response she got after what they had shared? *Many thanks?*

It was insulting. She'd tried to call him on his mobile, but it had just kept going to voicemail. She'd messaged him. Once. Then a second time. Then she'd worried that she might seem like some sort of obsessive stalker, so she'd stopped.

He would ring *her*, right? Surely it had *meant something* to him? Yes, they had crossed a line, but they had both wanted to. Hadn't they…?

But perhaps to him it hadn't meant anything at all? Perhaps she'd misread what was happening between them. And maybe she, so desperate for love and attention had mistaken his kindness for something more? To be left again like this was just so…painful.

When his silence had continued she'd got angrier and angrier that he'd apparently just dropped her like a hot potato after getting her into bed.

She was horrified that he could do that to her. Appalled. Aggrieved. Upset.

I've been used. He needed physical comfort and used me. Like I've always been used.

She wasn't sure she had anything to say to him. How

could he treat her like that after she'd told him how her dad had been with her? How Eric had been with her.

Brooke wasn't sure whether she wanted to rage at him, slap him across the face, or just never speak to him again. And his guilt had made her think of her own. Sleeping with Jen's husband, of all things! What had she been *thinking*?

But they had to work together. They had to be a team if the department was to run smoothly. So she'd thought the best way to be would be to say nothing at all. Not until the right moment presented itself. *Then* she would have something to say.

So she'd gone straight to work. Determined to fill her day with patient after patient after patient. With no more need to check in with Major Galloway she could get through her day without having to interact with him at all.

'Sarah Greenwood?' Brooke called for her first patient of the day.

A middle-aged woman stood up and followed her through to a cubicle.

'Hello, Miss Greenwood, my name's Dr Bailey. What can I do for you today?'

'I've been having these really bad abdominal pains. Like there's something trying to burst out of me. I feel… *full*. Bloated. It's horrible.'

'And how long have you been feeling like this?'

'A couple of weeks…I tried to call my GP to get an appointment, but I can't get in till near Christmas! I'm sorry, but I just had to come here—just to put my mind at rest if nothing else.'

'Okay. What type of pain is it? Is it a dull pain or a sharp one?'

Sarah shrugged. 'Both. It depends, sometimes, on what I'm doing.'

'And when was your last period?'

'Middle of October.'

'And is the pain all over, or just in one particular area?'

'It seems to be more on the left side.'

Knowing it could be any number of things, Brooke took Sarah's blood pressure, her temperature and her pulse. All seemed normal. 'Is there a chance that you could be pregnant?'

Sarah shook her head. 'No. I'm not with anybody right now.'

'No casual partners?'

'No.'

'When was the last time you had sex?'

Her patient blushed. 'Over a year ago.'

'Can I have a feel of your tummy?'

Sarah lay down on the bed and Brooke gave her a thorough examination of the abdomen. She thought she could feel a swelling on her patient's left side, possibly on her ovary, but she'd need an ultrasound to be sure.

'You can sit up now. Okay, Miss Greenwood, I'm not sure what this is, so I'll need to run a few more tests. Maybe get an ultrasound done—have you had one of those before?'

'No, but I know what they are. What do you think it is?'

'It could be several things at this stage. Let's do the ultrasound and see what happens. But don't worry—you're here now. I'll look after you.'

'I'm just worried that it's something serious. My mum had ovarian cancer, you see, and she started off the same way. I want to have children. I'm still young enough. And if it's something serious...'

The patient's family history was important, and it did not bode well. But that did not mean Sarah had ovarian cancer. It might be an ovarian cyst, which was often something simple to sort out.

'Do you have children, Doctor?'

Brooke nodded. 'I have a daughter.'

'You're lucky. I haven't found anyone yet who wants to stick around long enough to have children with me.'

Technically, neither had Brooke. Eric had been useless, and Matt… Well, she'd begun to think that he was the solid, dependable type, but she'd been wrong. Perhaps her radar was off? How had she managed to find men like that time after time? Did she have a big sign pointing at her head that read *'Needy and naïve'*?

'I worry I've left it too late, and now this…'

Brooke laid a reassuring hand on her patient's. 'Let's see what the tests say. It's way too early for you to be worrying before the results are in. I'm going to take a blood sample, too. Just to check and make sure there are no STDs.'

'Oh, I don't think I've got anything like that—'

'You'd be surprised, sometimes. Did you always use protection the last time you had a sexual partner?'

'Not every time, no.'

'And were you exclusive?'

She grimaced. '*I* was.'

Brooke smiled in sympathy. 'I'm sorry. So let's check that out anyway. I'll be back in a tick.'

'Thank you, Doctor.'

Brooke headed off to get a kit that would allow her to take blood, and also to ask one of the healthcare assistants to bring the portable ultrasound to her cubicle when it was next free.

'Dr Bailey?'

Hearing Matt's voice, she closed her eyes, telling herself silently to remain calm. She opened them again and turned around. 'Yes?'

'Could I have a moment of your time to talk to you?'

'I'm busy with a patient right now.'

'It's important.'

'My patient is important, Major Galloway. Now, if you'll excuse me?'

And she headed back, proud of herself for staying calm and polite and for not having looked at him. Because if she had she might have faltered. And she wanted to remain angry right now. It helped. Somehow…

She took Sarah's blood and then performed the ultrasound, moving the Doppler over her patient's abdomen and soon noting a large cyst on the left ovary. It looked benign, filled with fluid, but due to the patient's history it needed to be checked and tested to be on the safe side. It might burst on its own in time, or be reabsorbed, but it might have been there for a while. Sarah would need to see a specialist for further tests they just couldn't do in A&E at this time.

Brooke explained the situation and promised to write to her GP to arrange the referral. 'Try not to worry, Miss Greenwood.'

'Thank you, I'll try. But I can't promise. Not until I know for sure.'

'I understand. Take care.' And she waved her patient goodbye.

She went back to write up her notes. As she did so Matt came striding out of Majors, with Kelly following behind him.

'Dr Bailey, I need you to come with us for a major incident. There's been a large traffic collision just down the road and there are people trapped in vehicles. The paramedic on scene has requested doctors.'

'There are none on scene?'

'All mobile doctors and the HEMS crew are busy on other cases, and the advanced paramedics have been called to another incident ten miles away. We're the closest, and you and Kelly are the most experienced on my team.'

'Okay.' She'd been called out on a field team twice before. Once to the London bus bombings some years before, and a second time to a train crash. Both times had been horrendous.

She hurried to grab the jacket that would identify her as a doctor at the scene, grabbed the kit bags that were always ready and prepped for occasions such as this, and quickly hurried after Matt and Kelly.

They were taken to the RRV—rapid response vehicle—that would drive them to the scene.

Her thoughts were whizzing like mad as they negotiated their way through the thick traffic that had built up. It was agonising to sit there, inching forward like a snail. She almost felt as if it would be faster to get out and run, but then suddenly the cars parted and they could get through, and they arrived to find a refuse collection lorry had crashed through a car, up a pathway and into a café.

There was smashed glass everywhere, alarms were going off, and people were crying, looking horrified. Sickeningly, she spotted one or two people with their mobile phones out, filming it all or taking pictures.

But she had no time to worry about them. That was for the police to take care of. *She* was here for the casualties.

A fire engine was already there, and a fireman in a white helmet, indicating his high rank, was letting them in on who their casualties were.

'The driver of the lorry had a heart attack at the wheel. My guys have been giving CPR, but there's been no sign of life now for over twenty minutes. There were two other men in the truck, both have cuts and lacerations. The driver of the car that was smashed up is trapped within the vehicle and we're working to free her. There are also numerous casualties in the café, including a pregnant woman who has taken a blow to the abdomen. Multiple lacerations throughout, and we have victims in shock. One customer of the café was knocked down by the truck as it entered the building and appears to have broken his leg.'

Matt nodded. 'I'll take the guy in the truck. Dr Bailey, if you could handle the driver of the car and, Kelly, you check out the café customers. Triage only. Understood? I'll join you as soon as I can.'

They all nodded and headed off to deal with their patients.

Brooke made her way to the smashed up car, its bonnet crumpled and steaming, watching whilst firefighters tried to remove the roof. A fireman sat in the back seat, holding the driver's head still.

'What's the patient's name?'

'Vijaya.'

'Okay.' She removed a cervical collar from her kit, ready to attach it to the patient's neck. 'Vijaya? My name's Brooke and I'm a doctor from the London Grace. Are you in any pain?'

'My neck hurts—and my leg.'

'Okay... Well, you've got a handsome fireman holding your spine nice and straight for me, and I'm just going to have a quick feel of your neck before I put this collar on. I want you to tell me if anything hurts.'

With her fingers she probed Vijaya's neck, feeling along the vertebrae. 'Anything?'

'I don't know. It just hurts.'

'Were you stationary when the lorry hit you?'

'Yes. I'd just got in...was about to pull away. I'd just released the handbrake when the lorry hit me.'

'I'm going to check out the rest of you, if I can.' Brooke made a primary survey—checking for breaks, bleeds, anything obvious. 'Does your chest hurt?'

'A little.'

'Did you have your seatbelt on?'

'Yes.'

'And how does your breathing feel? Does it hurt to breathe in?'

'No.'

'Take a deep breath for me.'

Vijaya did so. 'It doesn't hurt.'

That was good. Brooke peered in as far as she could and saw that the engine block had been pushed in somewhat, and was pinning Vijaya's left leg. There was some bleeding.

'Can you wiggle your toes for me?'

'Yes.'

'You can feel both feet?'

'Yes. My leg hurts, though.'

'Your leg seems trapped, Vijaya. I don't know how badly you're injured—we won't know until we get you free. It shouldn't be long. Do you have any medical problems I need to know about?'

'I'm a Type Two diabetic.'

'Okay, anything else?'

'No. Well, I'm claustrophobic...'

Brooke could see the frantic look in Vijaya's eyes as the firemen put up a sheet to protect her from glass as they cut away the car's roof. Being trapped in the car with all these firemen about, and now the tarpaulin, must be very scary indeed.

She reached in and took Vijaya's hand in hers. 'I've

got you. Just a moment or two more. Do you have any family I can call?'

'My husband is probably wondering where I am.'

'What's his name?'

'Rav.'

'And his number?' With her free hand she pulled out her mobile and as Vijaya told them to her punched in the digits and listened to the phone ringing at the other end. 'He's not answering. I'll try again in a minute.'

The firemen suddenly lifted off the roof of the car and Brooke went round to the other side of the vehicle to try and get a better look at Vijaya's leg. She couldn't be sure, but she didn't think there was too much damage. It looked like a simple entrapment. The wound would need cleaning, an X-ray to check for any bone damage and possibly a few stitches. It was her patient's neck she was more worried about.

As the firemen worked to free her patient's leg, Brooke became aware of Matt at her side. 'Can you give me an update?'

Brooke gave details of her patient to Matt, being as robotic as she could, because right now, her anger and her upset had to wait. Matt nodded and then ran to check on Kelly. She watched him go, registering a look in his eyes that she had never seen before. But she guessed he must be used to scenes of such carnage. This sort of thing didn't faze him. He had a place in his head he could go to that allowed him to keep a professional distance and look past the screams, the yells, and see what needed to be done in the most efficient manner he could.

In moments he'd left Kelly and nipped into the café's interior, where she lost sight of him.

He was a good doctor. He really was. And she'd

thought he was a good man. One whom she could finally lean upon.

I should have known better.

The firemen freed Vijaya's leg quickly, and as a team they managed to get her onto a back board and lift her free of the vehicle. Brooke attended to the wound on her patient's leg, applying a dressing quickly to prevent further blood loss, knowing that she would get full treatment soon in an A&E.

She clutched Vijaya's hand one more time. 'You're going in an ambulance now. I've got to stay here to help more patients, but I'll come and check on you when I get back.'

'Which hospital am I going to?'

'The London Grace.'

'Oh. Right.'

'I'll see you there.'

She picked up her kit bag, disposed of her gloves and put on fresh ones, and then ran into the café to assist Matt.

She was like a bee. Flitting from patient to patient, assessing, dressing wounds, giving reassuring smiles and holding the hands of those who were wounded or frightened.

Matt watched her, glad that he had picked her for his field team, still hoping that she would give him the chance to explain himself.

He'd hurt her. He knew that. And that did not sit well with him. He was not the kind of guy to walk over someone else's feelings and it unsettled him.

He finished applying a splint to the patient with a broken leg and got him onto a spinal board for transport to an ambulance. He held the patient's hand as he walked alongside the trolley to the vehicle and he was smiling when he heard an almighty rumble and turned to see what the noise was.

The front of the café was obscured by a thick dust cloud and rubble lay all around. *Had the front of the café collapsed?* He saw, to his left, Kelly clambering out of the back of an ambulance. Was Brooke still inside?

He ran over to the front of the café, but a fireman held him back. 'You can't go in—it's not stable.'

'I've got a doctor inside!'

'We need to stabilise the area. Stand back.'

The firemen pushed him back, away from the frontage of the building. All he could think about were the people inside. The patients. *Brooke!* How close had she been to the front of the café? Was she under the rubble? Was she hurt?

Was he ever going to see her again and get the chance to say he was sorry?

I need to get in!

He made to dart forward, but the firemen had been watching him and placed a solid hand upon his chest. 'Stay right where you are.'

It took far too long for the firemen to put up joists and clear the rubble but finally, when the moment came and they allowed him in, he rushed forward, desperate to make sure that Brooke was okay.

He was met by a stream of walking wounded who were all clambering out into the light. He helped them all, his mind going crazy, before he was able to clamber over the debris to find Brooke—packing up her kit bag and hauling it over her shoulder.

The relief he felt was palpable. 'You're okay. Thank God.'

She looked at him, seemed slightly shocked, but nodded. 'I'm fine.'

'When the front of the café fell in I…' He swallowed. 'But you're okay. That's what matters.'

'I'm all right.'

'When we get back you and me are going to have that talk.'

'I'm tired, Matt, and I need a drink. Maybe a shower. I'm covered in dust.'

'Okay. But afterwards?'

She nodded. 'Afterwards.'

He pulled her kit bag from her shoulder and slung it over his, then took her hand, to her surprise, and led her safely out over the rubble.

Blinking again at the brightness, Brooke pulled her hand free of his and headed back to the RRV. Kelly got in beside her and he saw them exchange looks.

He got into the front and sat beside the driver. 'You did a great job—both of you.'

'Thanks.'

'There was just the one fatality. The lorry driver. I think he had a massive MI.'

The driver's myocardial infarction—heart attack—must have been instantaneous, and unfortunately, he'd been driving a large, powerful vehicle that had spun out of control.

You never knew when your time would come. Matt had once thought *his* time had come in Khost Province. Had been sure that at any moment he would be struck down. But he'd survived. Survived to become a father. To know his daughter. To know Brooke. And she was special. And he didn't want to waste all the good opportunities he had in life and make people miserable.

He'd lost his wife unexpectedly.

Did he really want to lose Brooke, too?

CHAPTER NINE

HIS MIND WAS in turmoil. Now that the adrenaline had gone—now that he was thinking rationally as he waited for Brooke to get out of the hospital's showers—he began seriously to analyse just how he'd felt when the frontage of that café had collapsed.

How had it come to be that he had allowed himself to develop feelings for another woman? And so deeply? Okay, so he'd never told himself that he wouldn't get involved again after Jen. He'd never said that. He'd known there might be the possibility at *some point* that someone might come along. He'd just never expected it this soon. And he'd certainly never expected it to be his wife's best friend.

He'd assumed it would be someone a long time in the future—when Lily was a teenager, maybe.

But for it to have happened this fast… That was what he was having trouble with.

Because when the front of that café had collapsed his heart had almost stopped. The horror, the dread that had filled him at the idea that Brooke was trapped, or hurt, or even dead under that rubble, had almost killed *him*, too. That another woman he cared for could be cruelly taken from him without warning… *Again*…

Matt looked down at the table and saw the journal

he'd been looking at earlier. It was still open at the page he'd left it. The tantalising possibility of a job at Auckland City Hospital.

It was an amazing opportunity. Fortuitous. Something he'd once dreamed of going for. Moving Lily to New Zealand would give her an amazing life, but no matter what he decided he would always put the welfare of his little girl first.

So what *was* best for her? The new life he and Jen had always wanted? Or staying here, where life was getting complicated? Could he have Brooke enter his life so deeply and be so integrated into it that Lily might call her *Mama?*

The thought of that made him feel terrible. Not because Brooke would be a bad role model as a mother. She was an excellent mum to her own daughter. But he wasn't sure he could cope with having his daughter call Brooke *Mum.* It felt treacherous.

He'd imagined raising his little girl and sitting her on his knee, getting out the photo albums and showing her pictures of her mummy and telling her all about Jen. About how like Jen she was. About how much they looked alike and how much her mother had loved her. He needed Lily to know that. And if Brooke was in their lives would that make things more complicated?

He picked up the journal and looked at it once again. Read through the job description, the requirements, the contact details...

Perhaps I need to keep my options open? I could just ring them for a quick chat. I could just see what it would all be about.

Yes, if he went to New Zealand he'd be leaving Brooke and everyone here behind, but perhaps that was what they needed? A fresh start. By staying he had enveloped himself in *Jen's* past, not his own. He had come here in an effort to know her better, to meet those who had loved her, in an attempt to keep her alive in his head. Getting involved with Brooke had been wrong. He'd lost his focus in a moment of lust and his feelings for his wife's best friend were strong now. He wasn't sure he should be feeling that way.

It was entirely possible that going to New Zealand would also be the wrong thing to do. He couldn't live Jen's life. He had to live his own. But his own life had also included the aspiration to move to New Zealand. To emigrate. To give his daughter a bright future in an amazing country. It was all so confusing.

Matt headed to his office and closed the door. He picked up the phone and called the number. He wasn't sure of the time difference, or even if anyone would answer, but he figured he could leave his details and ask them to email him.

But someone answered.

An actual person.

And so he began his enquiries about the vacancy.

The shower felt great. To just stand there motionless, letting the hot spray hit her body, her head, her shoulders, her back, feeling it washing away the dust and debris... pounding sore muscles that were still recovering from the adrenaline rush that had smothered her when the front wall of the café had collapsed.

For a moment she had thought she would die.

She'd been helping a patient, wrapping gauze around a penetrative leg injury, when she'd heard a strange creak and a groan. As if the world itself was about to crumble. And then it had felt as if the sky had fallen as the front of the café had come crashing down, filling her lungs with dust and grit as everything went dark.

She'd leaned over her patient, protecting her, covering her own head and hoping that somehow she would survive.

The only thought in her head had been *Morgan!*

Her little girl. In the hospital crèche, probably playing happily with something, or sitting in a puddle of paint, smiling, laughing. She could lose her mother at any minute. Morgan might have to grow without a mother as well as without a father.

Who would care for her?

Not her dad. Social services would never give a baby to a drunk. So that just left Eric, Morgan's father, and there was no way she would want that. And there was no way *he'd* want the intrusion of his child turning up in his sad little life.

And then she'd thought of poor Lily, who actually had no mother but did have a loving, kind father, and she'd begun to wonder, as she coughed dirt and dust from her lungs and wiped the grime from her face, whether she had misjudged Matt?

He wasn't a bad guy. She knew that. Deep down. He was a brilliant doctor. Kind and caring. Professional. He ran the A&E department beautifully. It had never been as efficient as it was now, under his leadership. And as a father, he was top notch. She saw it in his face whenever he collected his daughter at the end of the day. Just how much he'd missed her was in his eyes. In the way he would pull her towards him and breathe in the scent of her hair and kiss her. He was determined to be everything his little girl needed now that she was motherless.

And that night they'd spent together... Cads and users didn't make love to a woman like that. It had been more than sex, she was sure of it, so why had he walked away? And if he *was* a user of women—which she now doubted—he would never have left a note, would he? He would have just walked out. And, okay, he hadn't answered her text messages or phone calls, but she had no idea what had happened to him after he'd left her flat.

She owed him the opportunity—his chance to explain. Because life was too short to waste it on petty grievances. Matt was not her father. He wasn't Eric. And he deserved his chance to speak.

Switching off the shower, she got dressed and dried her hair, sweeping it up into a ponytail and then went to find him.

He was in his office, on the phone. His gaze met hers as she stood in the doorway and he held up his hand as if to say *two minutes.*

She nodded, happy to wait, and sat in the chair opposite, trying not to listen in but hearing words like *New Zealand* and *emigrating* and wondering who on earth he could be talking to.

Eventually he put down the phone and looked her over. Then he smiled, as if he was happy to see she had no cuts, no bruises, no injuries.

'You're okay?' he asked.

She nodded. 'I am. A little weary, but good.'

'I'm glad to hear it. When I saw what had happened I didn't know what to think.'

She gave him a polite smile, acknowledging his worry about her wellbeing. 'What happened, Matt?'

'The front of the café collap—'

'No. After our night together. You just left. You never answered my calls.'

He had the decency to look appalled with himself. 'I'm sorry. Did you see my note?'

Unfortunately. 'Yes.'

'I did want to stay with you. Spend the day with you, like we'd planned, but...'

'But?'

'I've not been with a woman since Jen died. I hadn't expected to be with a woman like that for a long time. And yet somehow there I was, in your bed, with you in my arms, and it felt *so right...* But I felt guilty. Terribly guilty. I don't know...it was a knee-jerk reaction, and I justified it to myself by thinking that I needed a shower and a change of clothes, and that I didn't want to monopolise your whole weekend...I'm sorry. It's not a good enough excuse. It was an instinctual thing. I just left. It was wrong of me.'

'And you didn't answer my messages.'

'I left my phone behind and went out for the whole day. I felt like I owed it to Lily—as if I'd betrayed her mother's memory and I owed it to her. It was no slight on you. What we had was...'

She waited to hear how he'd describe their night together. Hoping that he would confirm to her that he had felt the same way. That they'd discovered a deep connection between them...that it had been more than just sex. More than just a cheap night—something passionate and intimate and loving.

'Just magical.'

She allowed herself a small smile. So he *had* felt it too. That was good. She hadn't been imagining things. 'It meant something. Didn't it?'

'More than I suspected it would.'

Her smile broadened. 'What happened today at the café, when the roof came in. I thought that...I thought I might die. I'm not trying to be dramatic, but it made me think about life and how short it is. We've both lost Jen. I thought Morgan might lose me as well.'

'*I* would have lost you, too.'

She nodded. *Yes.* They'd both been hit by the events of today. 'I didn't want to waste any more time on being angry with you. That night showed me that we could have something special.'

'Brooke—'

'Let me finish. Please.' She leaned forward. 'You *mean* something to me. I never expected it. I never thought for a moment that I would feel this way about you. But I do, and I think if we're offered the chance of happiness in our lives we should take it.' She smiled. 'I don't often put myself out on the line like this. I don't declare my feelings. But I'd like to think that if you feel the same way about me as I do about you then we should embrace that.'

Her stomach was rolling as she spoke. Butterflies in their thousands were flitting around in her insides as she waited for his response. She hoped he would smile. Hoped he would come out from behind the desk and take her in his arms and hold her tight. Press her up against his body and whisper into her hair that he loved her.

But he remained seated behind his desk. His face was a mass of conflicting emotions. 'We *should* take chances—you're right. It's too easy to stay in our comfort zones, wrapping ourselves up in the familiar. We *should* take chances.'

She might be wrong, but she felt as if he was saying that to himself, rather than to her. Perhaps he was trying to persuade himself? He'd admitted to feeling guilty about what they'd shared, and she could understand that. It wasn't that long ago that his wife had died, and perhaps he was struggling with that more than she knew? Perhaps he needed a little extra time to get used to this change? To accept the fact that she had feelings for him and wanted to pursue a relationship with him.

Because she absolutely did. She might have been burned by men in the past, but the way she felt about Matt… She absolutely felt sure that he was worth it. That by putting her cards on the table she was making herself vulnerable, yes, but she was also being brave. She wasn't going to let her past dictate her future. She was going to take a chance on love *despite* that.

She'd thought she might die today. And she would have died without letting Matt know how she really felt. He needed to know. Anybody who loved needed to let the person they cherished understand just how they felt. It was an important thing to hear. Words had power. Magic. It wasn't just actions that proved how you felt.

Brooke decided to give him some time to digest what she'd said. 'I'm just going to go check on Morgan before I return to work, if that's okay?'

He looked up at her as if he'd been lost in his own thoughts. 'What? Oh, right. Yes. Sure…'

She headed to the door, and then a thought occurred to her. 'Earlier, when I first came in, you were talking on the phone about emigration… New Zealand. What was that about? Have we got a new doctor joining us?'

His face coloured. 'No. I…I was just chatting to a colleague who's thinking of going. Making a new life out there.'

'Oh. Sounds wonderful. I've heard it's beautiful out there. I think Jen mentioned it once.'

He nodded, his face stern.

'Well, I'll see you later, then?'

'Yes.'

She smiled a goodbye and left his office. He was clearly stunned by what she'd said. Surprised at the depth of her feelings for him. But it was important to her to be honest with him. Then there'd be no surprises, no disappointments. If he didn't feel the same way then she would hurt for a while, but she would get over it. In time. And she would know that she had been honest and open, and that was what was important. Honesty. Truth.

Because if you didn't have that then there was no point in having anything at all.

Morgan's face lit up at the sight of her mummy's unexpected visit. She raised her arms, asking to be picked up, and Brooke scooped her up and held her tight, kissing her cheeks and just breathing her in.

She stayed with her for a while, watching her play with pasta shapes, squealing and burbling, making all her happy sounds, picking up a particular piece she wanted to show her mummy and beaming when Brooke made a happy face.

Moments like these were precious. Watching her daughter made Brooke realise just how much she was missing out on. Morgan had long days here in the crèche. Ten hours every day. Monday to Friday. That was fifty hours a week that she didn't get to spend with her child. Morgan was growing quickly, developing at a breakneck pace, and she was missing it.

When she'd left Morgan at the crèche that morning it had been no big deal. She'd dropped her off, given her one last kiss and then walked away, sure that in ten hours she would see her again. No biggie.

Only she might have died today and she'd been so *nonchalant* about leaving her child. Had taken no time to breathe in her scent, to give her one last hug, to tell her that she loved her.

These early days were important and she was missing them—crossing off the days of her calendar at work instead of by her daughter's side.

Matt wasn't the only one who suffered from guilt. She did, too. It was something she would have to think about.

So she kissed her daughter goodbye, breathed in the scent of her daughter's hair and gave her one last hug before she returned to work. Maybe she could claim a week's holiday? Spend it at home with Morgan. Some of it with Matt, perhaps. Take some time out together to just *be*.

Entering A&E, she saw Kelly give her a wave, and as Kelly had been at the accident site this morning with her and Matt she went to give her friend a hug.

'Hey, what's that for?' Kelly asked, surprised.

'Just a hug to say I appreciate you. That I love you.'

'Aw, thanks. I love you, too.'

Brooke smiled. 'Crazy start to the day, huh?'

'You're telling me. But it was thrilling to get out into the field. We don't often get that opportunity. It was good to see the paramedics' side of it.'

Brooke nodded. That was true. The guys in green brought in the majority of their patients, and she was so used to them just turning up with people on stretchers or backboards it didn't occur to her to think about the sights they saw during the course of their working day.

'True.'

'I think it's good to have change, don't you? Keeps you fresh. Keeps you on your toes.'

'I think you're right.'

'I believe our Major is looking for change, too.'

Brooke frowned. 'What do you mean?'

'He was looking at a new job opportunity this morning. In New Zealand, of all places! You can't get more of a change than that.'

She felt her blood run cold as she began to understand. '*He* wants to go to New Zealand?'

'That's what he said. We'll miss him here, but I wouldn't blame him for going and giving it a try.'

Brooke's heart pounded fast and heavy in her chest as all sound around her seemed to grow fuzzy and indistinct. She became incredibly aware of each breath, her gaze dropping to the floor as she fought just to stay upright.

He lied to me!

She'd asked him outright! After all that had happened that morning—the collapse of the café, how close she had come to losing her life—the first thing he'd done was enquire about a job on the other side of the world?

Perhaps I don't mean anything to him at all!

'Brooke? You okay? You've gone very pale.'

'I…I don't feel very well.'

'Sit down for a minute.' Kelly pulled out a chair.

'No. I think I need to go home. It's nearly the end of my shift anyway. I'm going to go pick up Morgan. I need to be with her. Spend time with her. With the people who love me back.'

And she hurriedly began to walk away.

As each step took her further and further away from A&E her anger and despair rose inside her, and she fought back tears as she smacked the button to call for the lift. *Why?* Why had he outright *lied*? She'd laid herself bare before him and he'd lied. That he could do that to her, when she'd exposed herself like that…made herself open and vulnerable…

At the crèche, Daisy looked surprised to see her again so quickly. 'Dr Bailey! Everything okay?'

'I've come to collect Morgan. I… We need to go home.'

'Oh, okay. I've just put her down for a nap. Should I wake her?'

'Yes. Please. Hurry.'

'Of course.' Daisy scurried away.

Brooke stood there waiting, feeling humiliated beyond belief.

How many times would a man stamp all over her heart?

How many times would she allow that to happen?

Not any more.

Never, ever again!

Matt hammered on Brooke's front door. 'Brooke? Brooke, it's me. Please, would you just open the door and let me in? We need to talk.' He banged on the door again.

Behind him a door opened and the occupant came out. It was a young man wearing very loose jogging bottoms and a black vest, showing his perfectly honed gym body to perfection. 'Dude? What's with the noise? I'm trying to sleep in here.'

Matt looked at him, irritated. 'It's four o clock in the afternoon.'

'You never heard of night shifts? Brooke's at work. She works every day.'

'She came home. I know she's in there.'

'Well, she's not the type to ignore people, so you must have upset her big-time, dude.'

'Thank you for that observation.' Exasperated, Matt closed his eyes and turned back to hammer on Brooke's door.

Behind him, the man closed his door. Matt knelt down and opened Brooke's letterbox. 'Brooke? Please let me in! I'm disturbing the neighbours and I know you don't want me to—'

The door was yanked open and he almost fell forward. But he instantly got to his feet and stared at the woman he had too many feelings for.

'I'm sorry.'

'You say that a lot to me just recently. I'm not sure it means anything any more.'

'Can I please come in? Would you just give me a moment to explain?'

Brooke shook her head, tears glazing her eyes. 'No. You can't. I told you *everything*. Everything I felt. I laid myself bare to you. I gave you the opportunity to be truthful to me. But you lied. You want to go to New Zealand? Then you go, Matt. Don't you worry about me. I'll be fine.'

She went to close the door, but he blocked it with his foot.

'I wanted to tell you! I *did*! But I couldn't. Because if I had told you exactly how I feel then that would've made it real. If I'd told you that I love you then that would have been me closing the door on everything I had with Jen, and I couldn't do that. New Zealand was a dream. An escapist fantasy that I indulged in because I was afraid of what was happening between us! Don't you *see*?'

She stared down at his foot in disdain, then looked back up at him. 'No. You don't get to have the monopoly on being afraid! You think you're the only one? That because you've already lost one love you have the most to lose?'

She banged at his foot with the door.

'I lost her too! My best friend in the whole world! But you know what? I started to find another. I started to believe that this new friend was going to mean just as much. And I gave my heart willingly, only for it to be crushed— once again—by an unfeeling, inconsiderate coward who's afraid to admit how he feels! Now, you'd better remove that foot right now, or I'm going to go into my kitchen, find the sharpest knife I have and surgically remove it!'

She glared at him, tears and fury blurring her eyes, and he could do nothing but remove his foot and allow the door to be slammed in his face.

He stood there, momentarily stunned. Unsure of what to do. He didn't hear the door behind him open once again. Wasn't aware of the guy standing watching him, an amused smirk on his face, until he heard, 'Dude, you messed up.'

He closed his eyes, felt tears sting behind closed lids, and felt his heart break.

Brooke called in sick that first week. Then Personnel informed him that Brooke had taken some annual leave owed to her.

Matt sat in his office in between patients, feeling numb and broken. He'd made a big mess of everything. He had disrupted not only the department—because everyone wanted to know what was wrong with Brooke—but also his own life.

He was lost without her here. Not seeing her every day was torture, plain and simple.

He'd had fights with Jen, but nothing like this. Life seemed so bleak. He found it hard to smile. Found it hard to concentrate on what anyone was saying. Found himself drifting off into thoughts of that last argument as he sat in departmental meetings. He tried his hardest to find joy and smile and laugh when he was with Lily, but even she seemed subdued by his mood and cried a lot, constantly needing his hugs.

Hugging his daughter was the only thing that brought relief. He'd just sit and watch Lily playing on the carpet.

He *didn't* want to uproot them and take them to New Zealand. He'd panicked. Brooke was right on that score. He'd been scared. Scared of what his feelings for her meant. He'd lost control, just for a moment, and rung about that stupid job.

He should have told her about it from the beginning, but as he hadn't been definite about going he hadn't thought it was worth mentioning. It had been a blip. A small error in judgement as he'd frantically fought to regain control over his feelings. Because he'd felt as if they were running away from him. Like wild horses, their glorious manes flowing behind them as they ran across a grassy plain.

He'd tried to rein his feelings in, and he could see now that it had been the wrong thing to do. Because you couldn't rein in love. It was a wild thing. An uncontrollable animal that defied attempts to tame it. It would always be free. It demanded to be free. And accepting his feelings as truth was a big step for him.

He'd loved Jen. He would always love her. Every single day. But that love was not lessened by his love for Brooke. They were two separate things.

The fact that he still had the capacity to fall deeply in love had, at first been startling. But now it was painful. Because he'd screwed it up. He'd hurt the woman he loved and he didn't know how to fix it.

He'd tried apologising. He'd sent flowers. Had texted. Called. But she hadn't responded and he wasn't sure he could face the hurt of having her slam the door in his face yet again.

So he was giving her time. Because if he'd learned anything from Jen's death it was that time lessened the hurt. It didn't take it away. It didn't get rid of it completely. But you absorbed it better. It wasn't so raw and painful as it could be in the early days.

Time allowed you to take a deep breath and just *breathe*.

He was biding his time and hoping that maybe—just maybe—when she was ready to return to work she would let him tell her everything.

She had to return to work. Even if it was just to work out her notice.

So much had changed for her recently, and there'd been some startling revelations, but she knew she had to do what was right for her. And for Morgan. And...

Brooke closed her eyes and took a deep breath as she handed Morgan over to Daisy in the crèche. She wouldn't have to do this much longer. Not here, anyway.

Brooke had decided that what she and Morgan needed was a change and some rest. So she was taking a leaf out of Matt's book. She'd been rash before, hurrying back to work after her maternity leave, when she wasn't fully ready. And that rashness had caused her to do something silly. To fall in love with a man who was wholeheartedly unavailable.

She should have seen that—acknowledged that—but she'd been silly and allowed him into her heart. And, as in all the times before, in every single relationship she had ever had with a man, her feelings had been crushed.

But things were different now. She was taking back control. No longer a passive observer in her own life, letting things happen to her. *She* was going to be the one who made the changes. If Matt could consider going to New Zealand and leaving, then she could make huge changes too.

That meant putting in her notice, working it out, and

then she and Morgan were going to head to the south west coast for a while. Maybe Cornwall. She'd heard it was beautiful there. She was going to hire a mobile home and they'd pootle around the area for a few weeks whilst she waited to start the job that she'd accepted just yesterday.

She would be working at another A&E—far, far away from London and its great impersonal greyness. Its hustle and bustle. Its demand for you to hurry. For you to pay, pay, pay. It was a city in which you could lose yourself, and Brooke didn't want that. She wanted to relax more. To enjoy nature.

Her new job was in a town, yes, but the cottage that she'd seen was by the coast. It would be perfect to raise her children there. To live. To lie in bed and hear waves crashing against the beach. To hear the gulls. To take long walks along the coast, squeezing sand between her toes, watching her daughter and whoever was next to come sitting in the sand, making sandcastles…

Discovering she was carrying Matt's baby had come as a shock. They'd used protection, but she'd found herself one morning, peeing onto a stick and then watching the blue lines appear, bright as day.

How *could* she have got herself in the same mess she'd been in when she got pregnant with Morgan? Was she so naïve regarding her own feelings that she'd be one of those women with a brood of children, each of them with a different father?

She had no expectations of him. She could imagine his hurt, his pain at the prospect of a child who would become just another piece of evidence that he had somehow betrayed his wife.

I can't compete with a ghost.

She'd loved Jen so much! And she felt guilty to think that she was carrying her best friend's husband's child.

Even if a small part of her thought that Jen might be smiling at the development, up there in heaven. That Jen might even have plotted this herself!

Thrown you another curve ball, honey!

So Matt would receive two big pieces of news this morning.

She hoped he would be a big enough man to let her go. But another part of her hoped that somehow he might tell her everything she wanted to hear.

Miracles happened, didn't they? Wasn't she deserving of a turn at happiness? Hadn't she paid her dues? Finding out she was pregnant with Morgan had been a huge turning point in her life, and it was going to be the same with Matt's baby.

Now or never.

A new life was on its way. A new baby. Brooke had always wanted a family—a few kids, a husband. The perfect little unit.

So, okay, maybe life wanted to challenge her with this. Make her fight for what she needed. She'd never backed down from a fight. Had always stood her ground. Maybe she would get what she wanted some day, even if it wasn't now.

But she *would* get it.

She was determined.

CHAPTER TEN

MATT WAS IN his office. For a moment she watched him through the small window, saw the hunching of his shoulders, the lifeless look in his eyes as he stared numbly at a staffing rota.

She didn't normally like to see anyone hurting like that. But a tiny part of her was *glad* that it wasn't easy for him. Because she'd been feeling as if she was the only one suffering.

She rapped her knuckles on the door and he looked up, standing instantly, becoming alert when he saw who was standing there.

Brooke opened the door and went in. The envelope in her hand contained her notice. 'I've come to give you this.'

She passed it over and he took it from her with confusion, turning it over to see if the envelope gave any clue to its contents.

'What is it?'

'My notice.'

His face fell. 'Brooke, no…there's no need for that.'

'There's every need. I'll work my notice. I won't drop you in it by leaving you down a doctor.'

'Brooke—'

'I'm late. I need to get on.'

And she hurried out, her nerve failing her in delivering the extra bit of news that she knew would change everything. Handing in her notice and walking away was one thing. It showed courage and determination. Telling a man she was pregnant and having him want nothing to do with her turned the tables and would make her feel pathetic and alone. And she wasn't ready to face that just yet.

Maybe she could hold the news until her last day at work? She was in no hurry for him to reject her. She'd been there once before with Eric. She was in no rush to hear it a second time.

Even though she suspected Matt would probably want to do the right thing, him being the kind of person she knew him to be, a small part of her was worried that he would not. Lily was the most important thing in his world, and another baby, with another woman, was not ever going to be part of his life plan. It would throw him completely. And he would tear himself apart trying to do the honourable thing and yet also bear the weight of his betrayal to his wife.

She would wait. She still had time before there were any signs of her pregnancy.

Shoulders back, chin up, she grabbed the first patient's chart and headed back to work.

The letter was stark and to the point. She was leaving. Brooke was going to leave the London Grace!

Just the idea of that was...

He had no words for how it made him feel. His heart had jumped when he'd seen her at his office door. He'd been hoping that she had reconsidered. Was now willing to listen to his explanation. But she'd been brusque and kept their conversation short.

But she was here now. He had a month to get her to listen to him. And he didn't have to send her letter of notice up to Personnel just yet. He would hold on to it for a while.

Maybe he wouldn't be able to stop her from leaving, but he was determined that somehow he would get her to listen to him. Even if it changed nothing between them, he needed to tell her how he felt. How their relationship had blossomed into something that he'd never expected. How his feelings for her had grown into something he couldn't control and how that had made him feel.

Another knock on his door interrupted his thoughts and he stood up abruptly, hoping it might be Brooke. Only it wasn't. An old man stood there. A man who looked familiar.

'Arthur?'

It was Patricia's husband. The man who had brought in his wife after a stroke.

'You remember me?'

The old man shuffled in and Matt indicated that he should take a seat.

'Of course. How are you?'

Still reeling from Brooke's news, Matt forced himself to focus as he sank back into his chair.

'I wanted to come here to thank you, Doctor. You and your team.'

'Oh, well, there's no need—we were just doing our jobs. How is your wife?'

Arthur's eyes darkened slightly. 'She passed away a day or two after we returned her to the care home. It was peaceful. Her funeral was yesterday.'

'Oh. I'm so sorry for your loss.' He knew how Arthur must feel right now. He'd lost his wife. Had had to bury her. But *he'd* only had a few years with his wife. Arthur had had sixty-three years of marriage. He couldn't possibly imagine the level of loneliness the old man must be feeling.

'It was expected. The stroke took a lot out of her, I think.' Arthur cleared his throat and wiped his nose with the proper handkerchief he'd drawn from his jacket pocket. 'But I just wanted to say thank you for giving me a few extra days with her. They were important, all those minutes and hours we had, because she was sometimes lucid.'

'She was?'

Arthur nodded, smiling. 'Not for the entire time, but here and there—over the two days… You gave me back my wife. The stroke should have done her in, but you doctors—all your medicine, all your technology—gave her back to me. Just for a little while. I'd been afraid of her being lucid again. She'd been so upset the last time, discovering what was happening to her, but after the stroke it was like she came back to say goodbye. And that was precious to me, Dr Galloway.'

Matt gave a smile, but it was tinged with a resolute sadness.

'You never know how long you'll get with your loved ones on this planet, but when it comes to the end it's never enough, don't you think? We spend so much of life worrying about what other people think, what other people say, but when it comes to your final days is that what you worry about? Is that the most important thing? No, it's not. It's being with those you love. And if you're lucky enough to love, you embrace it. That's what Patty and I had in those final days. Love. And I needed to come here today to thank you for that.'

Arthur's words sank deep into Matt's soul.

He was right. The old guy was *right!* All the petty

day-to-day worries that he'd allowed to fester away in his skull meant nothing when he thought about it. If he was on his deathbed right now would he be worrying about what everyone thought of his feelings for Brooke? *No!* He'd want to be lying there holding her hand. Telling her how much he loved her! And knowing that she loved him!

Who were other people to judge when he should love again? Why was he allowing guilt to determine his feelings for her? Because, looking at himself right now, he saw that guilt was making him feel damned miserable! And who wanted to be miserable? When he was with Brooke he felt joy and contentment and happiness. Why couldn't he have that? Why couldn't *they?*

It didn't diminish the love he'd had for Jen. Not by one iota. And if other people thought that it did, then that was *their* issue.

Love—true love—was rare and beautiful, and if you were lucky enough to discover it you should embrace it, as Arthur had said. Not hide from it, nor feel guilty for having it. And there wasn't a clock or a timer on love. It could spring from anywhere. Unexpected and surprising. And didn't that make it all the more special?

'Thank you, Arthur. For coming here today. I really appreciate it.'

'Well, we appreciated *you*, Doc. That's it, really. I don't want to keep you. I know you're busy. Saving lives.'

Arthur was right. He had to save his *own* life. Because for the last few days he'd been drowning in guilt and grief and dying inside. *No more!*

He shook Arthur's outstretched hand and watched him go, and then he hurried off to find Brooke. He had to tell her everything. And if he hadn't messed it up too much he could be about to change both their lives.

* * *

It was hard to concentrate. Handing in her notice, knowing she was pregnant a second time and still not in a solid relationship, weighed heavily. But Brooke did her best. No matter what was going on in her personal life, she still had to put her patients first.

She was good at that. Putting other people before herself. It was something she'd had to do as a child and she'd chosen it as a profession. But though it usually brought her joy and satisfaction she felt no happiness today.

For her, contentment was a long way away, and she knew she would have to travel many a mile—both mentally and geographically—before she found her happy place.

Her current patient should not even be in A&E. He had only come here because he couldn't get an appointment at his GP for another three weeks and he was concerned about a pain that he kept getting in his knee.

She did her best. She examined the knee. Couldn't see or feel anything wrong with it. Her patient could put weight on it, and he had a full range of movement, but he kept getting 'a painful twinge' that would make him gasp out loud when it struck.

Brooke suspected he might possibly be developing arthritis. The man had it in his family history. So she wrote him a prescription for some painkillers and told him to see his GP if it got worse. There was nothing else she could do for him now.

Her patient left, grumbling under his breath about shoddy patient care, and though normally that would have angered her today she had no energy for it. She had no energy for anything. Since she'd fallen out with Matt it was as if the life had gone out of her. All her vim, all her pep, was gone.

'Brooke? I must speak with you!' Matt came barrelling down the small corridor like a man on a mission.

She turned away. 'I'm not retracting my notice, so please don't ask.'

It hurt that he wouldn't just let it be. Couldn't he accept the fact that she was walking away to save her heart? Her soul? It was painful to be here with him and not be able to wrap her arms around him freely and share his kisses. It hurt that he'd shown her what love between them could be like and then cruelly torn it away.

She tried to pick up her stride. To get back to the doctors' desk, write up her notes, and then see her next patient. Anything that would make him go away—because it hurt too much to have him here and not be allowed to love him.

'I'm not here about your notice. I'm here about you. And me.'

Brooke turned to look at him, despair written across her features. 'I really don't think there's anything left to say. You've made it clear how you feel about us.'

'*No!* I haven't!'

She almost flinched at his raised voice, and she looked about them and noticed that some people were listening in—Kelly from the cubicle she was in, applying a splint; Michael the senior nurse, who was restocking a trolley, and further away the healthcare assistant, Michelle, who was bringing in a pile of blankets.

Feeling her cheeks colour, and not used to being the centre of everyone's attention, she glared at him. 'Keep your voice down.'

He lifted his chin. 'I will not. I don't care who hears. In fact, they all need to hear it.'

'Hear what?'

'That I love you, Dr Brooke Bailey. I'm in love with you and I will *always* be in love with you.'

Brooke swallowed. 'What?'

'I made a mistake. I'm human. I'm fallible. I panicked when I realised just how much you were coming to mean to me.'

'Matt—'

'I know I hurt you. It was never my intention.' He made her lock eyes with his. 'That New Zealand job… It was a dream that Jen and I once had. For Lily. Since Jen died I've tried to do everything in my power to make sure that Lily will know who her mother was. I put her in the crèche that Jen would have taken her to. I took her to the classes she signed her up for, and I took her job, so that Lily would know the place and the people who shared her mother's life. I rock her to sleep at night, telling her stories about her mother. And then I met you.'

Brooke could see there were tears in his eyes, and it made her feel like crying too.

'You were like a cyclone in my ordered world. You were at the crèche. You were here at work, and even at home. When I was alone my thoughts were of you. And after that night we spent together—'

Brooke blushed.

'I didn't know what to think. I felt guilty, yes. Not for what we did. What we had was beautiful and magical and perfect, and I've never felt that way with anyone. But I felt guilty for the fact that I wanted to stay with you. Stay in your flat and never leave. Take every part of you that you might offer. I forgot Jen for a few hours. And that made me feel so…'

He couldn't find the word he wanted.

'I had to soak up my old life. Remind myself of what I thought was important. What other people would expect of me. To be the grieving widower. To show respect—to take years, not months, before I fell in love with another woman. But feeling like I've lost you has almost killed me. I've been miserable. Ask anyone—they'll tell you. Lily's kept me going, as she did before, but she shouldn't have to be my crutch. Like you were for your father. I want her to feel loved and celebrated and valued and cherished—the way that I…I feel for you. You kept telling me I was honourable and brave but I didn't believe it. I've only just begun to believe that I am, and I feel that way, because of *you*. I love you, Brooke, and I want us to be together. You and me. For ever.'

Tears trickled down her cheeks as she heard his words. They were *real*. Heartfelt. Honest. And all around them the staff were smiling. Waiting for her reaction. She looked down, saw his hands. His wedding band was gone.

'You let me down, Matt.'

'I know. But if you just let me love you I promise, on my life, that it will never happen again.'

'I want to believe you. I *do*.'

'Then take a chance on us.'

She took in a breath. Then another. Tried to steady her frazzled nerves. 'I want to, but I'm scared.'

He stepped forward and took her hands in his. 'So am I. But that's okay, because I think we're *meant* to be scared. Nothing worth having is ever risk-free, but I think if we're scared *together* then we can face anything that life throws at us.'

She looked down at their hands, stroked the pale stripe on his finger where his wedding band had used to sit. 'Life has thrown a lot at us, hasn't it?'

He squeezed her fingers in response. 'It has.'

She looked up into his eyes. Those beautiful blue eyes that she knew so well and saw in her dreams. Wasn't this what she wanted? His love? And he'd announced it to everyone! No hiding. No shame. He had admitted his feelings for her in front of them all. All she had to do was be brave enough to accept it.

He was speaking again. 'A wise man told me recently that all that matters in this world is love. That if you have it you should embrace it, tell the person who's your everything that you love them. Because at the end of the day—at the end of life—that's all any of us ever want to say. I want to tell you I love you every day, Brooke Bailey. Every *single* day.'

A hesitant smile lifted the corners of her mouth. Reached her eyes. It was as if lights were slowly being turned on inside her, and she could feel warmth filling her once again as she opened herself up to the possibility that everything was about to turn out all right.

'I love you, Major Matthew Galloway.'

He smiled, joy lighting his eyes. 'You do?'

She nodded.

'Then let's be together. For ever.'

He lifted her hands to his lips and kissed the backs of her fingers, one after the other, and then pulled her close and kissed her properly.

Brooke sank into his embrace, feeling as if all the missing pieces of her puzzle were found. She was complete. Whole. It was terrifying, yes, but they would face the fear of this journey together.

Being back in his arms felt wonderful. It was soothing to her frazzled and exhausted body, and just by pressing up against him she could feel her energy returning. As if he was recharging her spent batteries with the depth of his emotion. His embrace, his touch, was everything. And she would never have to be without it again.

'There's one more thing,' she said.

He pulled back, looked at her. 'What is it?'

She lowered her voice so that only he could hear it. 'I'm pregnant.'

His eyes widened in surprise and then, barely milliseconds later, he lifted her off her feet and began swinging her around in happiness.

Brooke squealed and laughed and begged him to put her down—which he did.

'You're pregnant? That's amazing!'

'It's still early days. Anything could happen.'

He nodded. 'But we'll face it together.' He linked his hand into hers. 'Have I told you today that I love you?'

She smiled. 'Once or twice.'

'Well, I do. I do, I do, I *do*.'

'Well, Major, that's a good thing. Because I love you, too.'

They fell back into each other's arms, and all around everyone who knew them smiled with happiness.

There was no judgement.

Just joy.

For them.

As there always would be.

* * * * *

MILLS & BOON

THE HEART OF ROMANCE

A ROMANCE FOR EVERY KIND OF READER

MODERN

Prepare to be swept off your feet by sophisticated, sexy and seductive heroes, in some of the world's most glamourous and romantic locations, where power and passion collide.
8 stories per month.

HISTORICAL

Escape with historical heroes from time gone by. Whether your passion is for wicked Regency Rakes, muscled Vikings or rugged Highlanders, awaken the romance of the past.
6 stories per month.

MEDICAL

Set your pulse racing with dedicated, delectable doctors in the high-pressure world of medicine, where emotions run high and passion, comfort and love are the best medicine.
6 stories per month.

True Love

Celebrate true love with tender stories of heartfelt romance, from the rush of falling in love to the joy a new baby can bring, and a focus on the emotional heart of a relationship.
8 stories per month.

Desire

Indulge in secrets and scandal, intense drama and plenty of sizzling hot action with powerful and passionate heroes who have it all: wealth, status, good looks…everything but the right woman.
6 stories per month.

HEROES

Experience all the excitement of a gripping thriller, with an intense romance at its heart. Resourceful, true-to-life women and strong, fearless men face danger and desire - a killer combination!
8 stories per month.

DARE

Sensual love stories featuring smart, sassy heroines you'd want as a best friend, and compelling intense heroes who are worthy of them.
4 stories per month.

To see which titles are coming soon, please visit

millsandboon.co.uk/nextmonth

JOIN US ON SOCIAL MEDIA!

Stay up to date with our latest releases, author
news and gossip, special offers and discounts, and
all the behind-the-scenes action
from Mills & Boon...

 millsandboon

 millsandboonuk

millsandboon

It might just be true love...

MILLS & BOON
True Love
Romance from the Heart

Celebrate true love with tender stories of
heartfelt romance, from the rush of falling
in love to the joy a new baby can bring,
and a focus on the emotional
heart of a relationship.

S